D0064276

The
DEAL

The
DEAL

Timothy J.
LAMBERT

Becky
COCHRANE

alyson books
los angeles

MANUFACTURED IN THE UNITED STATES OF AMERICA.

THIS TRADE PAPERBACK ORIGINAL IS PUBLISHED BY ALYSON PUBLICATIONS,
P.O. BOX 4371, LOS ANGELES, CALIFORNIA 90078-4371.
DISTRIBUTION IN THE UNITED KINGDOM BY TURNAROUND PUBLISHER SERVICES LTD.,
UNIT 3, OLYMPIA TRADING ESTATE, COBURG ROAD, WOOD GREEN,
LONDON N22 6TZ ENGLAND.

FIRST EDITION: JUNE 2004

04 05 06 07 08 a 10 9 8 7 6 5 4 3 2 1

ISBN 1-55583-844-8

LIBRARY OF CONGRESS CATALOGING-IN-PUBLICATION DATA
LAMBERT, TIMOTHY J.
    THE DEAL / TIMOTHY J. LAMBERT, BECKY COCHRANE.— 1ST ED.
        ISBN 1-55583-844-8
        1. GAY MEN—FICTION. 2. NEW YEAR—FICTION. 3. MALE FRIENDSHIP—
FICTION. I. COCHRANE, BECKY. II. TITLE.
    PS3612.A5465D43 2004
    813'.6—DC22   2003069635

CREDITS
COVER PHOTOGRAPHY BY COLIN HAWKINS.
COVER DESIGN BY MATT SAMS.

for
Jim Carter and Timothy Forry

Acknowledgments

With gratitude to Alison Picard, Nick Street, Tom Wocken, Timothy James Beck, Dorothy Cochrane, and Steve Code.

Additional thanks to the Cochrane, Lambert, and Wocken families, including companion animals for their unconditional love. And to all the usual suspects—you know who you are.

Prologue

New Year's Eve 1999 was proving to be a washout. We had been promised massive computer meltdowns, utility company failures, deranged flight controllers, a revelation that Pat Sajak was the anti-Christ, a shortage of batteries and bottled water, the regrouping of Menudo, carcinogenic tampons, and a marriage between Jennifer Lopez and Bill Gates. Instead, just before midnight in Texas at my "Come As You Were in College/Reform School Party"—nearly an hour after the ball had dropped in Times Square—we were still debating why we should be arguing about whether 2000 or 2001 marked the true beginning of the new millennium when most of us couldn't spell *millennium*.

Or at least those gathered around the keg in dear-old-school-days spirit were debating that. My friends Miranda and Alexander were huddled together on the neon-green beanbag chair—my big find on a shopping trip to a suburban Houston furniture store, purchased especially for the party—trying to top each other's unlucky-at-love stories.

My roommate Patrick was lying on the floor, eyes closed, feet on the sofa, wearing headphones and singing along to Prince's ode to the turn of the century, "1999." This was somewhat disturbing, since none of the rest of us could hear Prince. A drunk straight guy weighing no less than two hundred pounds who suddenly screamed

"So if I gotta die I'm gonna listen to my body tonight" in an off-key falsetto was disconcerting.

And Heath, who once did a stint as my future ex-boyfriend in a moment of senior madness circa 1992, was ignoring us all as he meandered through partying drunks to collect plastic cups, plates, and utensils to rinse off and put in the recycle bin. A real party animal, Heath was.

"Don't forget Donna," Miranda was saying to Alexander. Her voice pierced the din of the room like a lighthouse beacon cutting through fog on a cold, rainy night. "I walked in on her just as she was gettin' busy with my roommate."

"That's nothing," Alexander said. "Remember my boyfriend in college?"

"Which one?" Miranda asked. "You went through boyfriends like most people go through socks."

"Because they always screwed me over. And not in the good way. I meant Roger. Remember him?"

"Roger the Codger," I prompted Miranda. When it came to Alexander's exes, I felt like some kind of sexual sports encyclopedia—perhaps because every detail had been relayed to me complete with statistics, positions, and scoring plays.

"Oh, yeah! You were a freshman and he was a senior," Miranda remembered. She finished her cup of beer and held it out to Heath with eyes pleading for a refill. Heath took the cup and went into the kitchen where the kegs were, but I had a feeling the cup would get recycled and we wouldn't see him again for another hour. Or at least until after he cleaned the kitchen for the hundredth time.

"He said he'd teach me everything about being gay," Alexander continued. "How to dress. How to make everyone want me. How to fuck. Where to be seen. And who to be seen with. Instead, he taught me about crabs. How to get *rid* of them. And what it really means to date a slut."

"Sluts! You want a real slut? Sarah Cranwell, sophomore year," Miranda offered. "I was in love. She was in heat. Which I thought would be fine. Until I found out she was also sleeping with half the football team. Some lesbian she turned out to be. Although I think the Cougars did have a good season that year."

I nursed my beer while I listened to Alexander and Miranda. The three of us had been friends for nearly a dozen years, ever since we'd met as freshmen at the University of Houston. We'd seen one another through many academic and dating disasters.

Alexander Casey had barely squeaked through graduation with a degree in music. His parents' hopes that Alexander would become a productive member of society by performing with some symphony—hopefully in a city far beyond their bank account—or teaching music were dashed. Almost as soon as he removed his cap and gown, Alex began his career as the roving keyboard player and sometime-vocalist for a number of Houston bands. I had no idea how he supported himself, since he worked only when the mood struck him, but I suspected it had something to do with his indulgent grandmother who "understood" Alex's need to "sow his wild oats."

Miranda Morris, on the other hand, was an unapologetic trust-fund baby. Her family lived in Houston's upscale River Oaks neighborhood—her father was one of the people who survived the oil and gas fiasco of the '80s unscathed—but Miranda had little to do with them beyond using their contacts to place the jewelry she designed in a number of Galleria and Highland Village stores. At the prices she set for her jewelry, I was pretty sure she no longer needed the Morris money to support herself.

"Even after all the college bullshit years, I still can't find a real boyfriend," Alexander mused. "All the guys I meet want me to shut up, put out, zip up, and get out."

"And that's such a problem for you," Miranda said with a sneer. "Where the hell is Heath with my beer? I know what you mean, though. Women are the same way."

"Bullshit," Alexander said. "Everyone knows women are more into getting to know each other, expressing feelings, and working through problems. Especially lesbians."

"Hey, we're just as horny as any guy," Miranda countered. "We want to get laid like everybody else. I've been screwed over by women more times than I'd care to admit."

"For fuck's sake!" Patrick suddenly said, ripping the headphones off his head and tossing them onto the sofa. He sat up. "You guys sound like two old women comparing their bunions. This is a party. We're ringing in the new millennium."

"No. That's next year," Alexander said.

"Technically, it's 2001," I corrected.

"Whatever," Patrick growled. "Your 'Woe Is Me' contest is bringing me down, man. There's got to be at least fifty people here. There must be one dyke who can give you all the attention you need," he said, pointing at Miranda. Then he nodded at Alexander and said, "And this place is teeming with narcissistic, insecure pretty boys just like you. I'd say the odds of scoring are in your favor. Both of you. Just find someone and shut the hell up. I need a drink. Any takers?" Our hands all shot up, and Patrick left for the kitchen.

"I'm not insecure," Alexander muttered and ran his hand over his head. Gelled to messy perfection, his hair immediately snapped back into place when he moved his hand away.

"How can you live with that Neanderthal?" Miranda asked me.

Patrick Sullivan had become my roommate in college. Though everyone assumed he was a slacker on the fast track to nowhere, he'd actually graduated with a business major and a political science minor. Patrick's motto was, "Dude, like, whatever, man." Which was exactly what he'd said when I told him I was gay. I liked Patrick, because even though it often seemed like his mind was a million miles away, or on vacation, in an instant he'd offer a pearl of wisdom so lustrous and cultured that you couldn't begin to scratch its surface. Or he'd tell you to fuck off and turn his attention to his beer. What wasn't to like?

When we graduated, Patrick took a job with a high-profile corporate real estate firm in downtown Houston. The '90s marked a recovering economy in the city. Houston had learned its lesson and diversified. New businesses started snapping up office locations, and Patrick worked twelve- and fourteen-hour days, making an amazing amount of money. Then, without fanfare or explanation, he quit his job to invest in and manage Dinks, one of Montrose's few straight bars. His decision had been prescient, since Houston's gay ghetto was invaded by the group that had given Patrick's bar its name—double income, no kids—couples who bought townhomes as soon as they were built. They were more than happy to spend their money in Dinks, and I'd come to realize that Patrick's slacker-like personality concealed a shrewd businessman.

"Patrick tells it like it is," I answered Miranda. "As a gay man, I admire that."

"It's easy for him to criticize," Miranda observed. "He's got a girl-friend."

"Where is the illustrious Vivian?" Alexander asked.

"She's in Vail with her family for the holidays. Patrick refused to go because he doesn't ski and doesn't want to learn. His sport of choice is football."

"Watching it," Miranda added.

"Yes," I agreed, "from the safety of our sofa. Anyway, Vivian took two of her girlfriends with her instead."

"For Pete's sake! Not only does Vivian have the Missing Link as a boyfriend, but she has two girlfriends," Miranda whined.

"Maybe Patrick's right," Alexander said, shifting his weight on the beanbag chair, which almost caused Miranda to slide off. "We have a veritable smorgasbord of human morsels to choose from here. We have less than an hour until midnight and nobody to kiss. Let's turn our luck around and make a game of this."

"OK," Miranda agreed.

"Now you're talking," Patrick said, arriving back on our scene bearing a plate topped with Jell-O shots. "Winner gets laid. Loser gets screwed. Those are good odds."

"No. It has to be more than that," I disagreed. "You two were just saying that your dating life is a mess. Obviously you can get laid any time you want to."

"Right," Patrick snorted. "And I'm Bea Arthur."

"Thank you for that vote of confidence," Alexander said.

"In the right dress," Miranda coolly stated, "you could definitely pass, Patrick." She turned to me. "You apparently think you have some wisdom to offer."

"Him?" Patrick scoffed, looking at me. "Aaron's asexual."

"I am not," I protested. "I'm discerning."

"Is that a synonym for 'celibate'?" Miranda asked.

"I am *not* celibate. Anyway, I'm not the one complaining about my serial breakups. You two are a cliché, members of a group of people who constantly whine about seeking intimacy with some sympathetic someone. In reality, as soon as you're presented with a flaw or you've made a conquest, you start looking for the next notch on your bedpost. All while bemoaning your loveless fate."

"I don't even have a bedpost," Alexander muttered. "I sleep on a futon."

"Perfect illustration of your uncommitted lifestyle," I crowed. "A piece of furniture that can be folded up and easily moved to the next location. Just like your heart."

"Yeah, at least I have a waterbed," Miranda said. "Can't exactly heft one of those on your back and move out."

"Drain and run," I said. "Like a lesbian vampire."

She and Alexander scowled at Patrick as he laughed and said, "Aaron's right. Neither one of you has any interest in falling in love and making a commitment."

"Not that there's anything wrong with that," Heath said, sounding like a *Seinfeld* character, when he joined us with Miranda's beer. For a second he looked confused, since Miranda was hoarding the tray of Jell-O shots Patrick had brought us. Then he shrugged and began drinking her beer himself.

"There's not," I agreed. "Some of your best friends are happily single. The problem with you two is that you complain about it."

"Which comes full-circle to what I said," Patrick concluded. "Either find someone or shut the hell up."

"You make it sound so easy," Miranda said.

"Yeah, and anyway, I'm not going to settle just so I can say I'm in a relationship," Alexander said. "It's not my fault my boyfriends always turn out to be—"

"Wah, wah, wah," I interrupted, rubbing my eyes like a crying baby. "Like I said, you both tuck tail and run from every potential relationship."

"And not always because there's a problem," Heath agreed in his quiet voice. "In fact, you run faster when things are at their best."

I frowned at him, blocking out the heated protests and evidence Miranda and Alexander offered to dispute Heath's claim. Heath's words sounded vaguely familiar to me, and as I scanned my memory bank I thought of the night seven years before when he and I had broken up. We'd been arguing outside Rich's, a popular dance club, because Heath wanted to leave and study for his finals, and I was ready to party the night away.

"You're so fucking selfish!" Heath had shouted, ignoring the amused glances of people walking into the club. "In two more weeks finals will be behind us, and this will all be over."

"It's over now," I said, tired of hearing him bitch about my irresponsibility. I was going into finals with solid A averages in all my classes and felt entitled to celebrate and relax a little. "Why do you need me around if you're just going home to study? Go! Who's stopping you?"

"What do you mean, it's over now? School? Studying?"

"You and me," I'd snapped. "Jesus, Heath, don't we have enough to think about? Graduating? Starting careers? What do you want to do, pick out a china pattern and buy a house in the suburbs with track lighting and a golden retriever to sleep in the nursery? I just turned twenty-two. I'd like to have a little fun before I start living my parents' life."

I regretted the words as soon as they were out of my mouth. I knew that to Heath, my parents—my entire family—represented something he'd always wanted. His parents had never been married. In fact, he'd never even met his father, who took off as soon as he found out Heath's mother was pregnant. Laura Temple had struggled to pay for her education, and she'd always worked hard to give Heath a decent home. Heath put himself through college by winning scholarships, accepting financial aid, and working his ass off in whatever odd jobs came his way. I had the utmost respect for him, but I was tired of always feeling guilty about how hard he had it compared to me.

"You're breaking up with me?" Heath demanded. "Just like that?"

"Go home and study," I muttered. "We'll talk about it later."

"I don't think so," Heath said, his face flushed with anger. "I always told you we were too different to make this work. But the fact is, our relationship is like everything else in your life. It's too good for you to appreciate it. Run away from the best thing that's ever happened to you, Aaron. Run and find all the drama and upheaval you crave. In fact, I'll give you a little head start on drama right now."

I watched, speechless, as he strode away from me, reassuring myself that once he calmed down we'd kiss and make up.

I'd been wrong. Heath graduated and went to the University of Mississippi to get his Masters. I started teaching English at St. Gregory's, a private Episcopal high school. From time to time I heard about Heath from our friends, usually Miranda, who maintained a voluminous correspondence with him. After leaving Ole Miss, Heath took a position as a technical writer in the aerospace industry in Huntsville, Alabama. There were rumors about a couple of relationships, but by then I'd had a few of my own too, and Heath seemed like a distant memory.

Then, in 1997, Laura Temple had been diagnosed with lymphatic cancer. Houston had one of the best cancer hospitals in the country in M.D. Anderson, but there was little even they could do for Heath's mother. Heath came home to take care of her. I saw him for the first time in five years at her funeral. There had been no awkwardness in our embrace or our conversation. After he decided to stay in Houston, transferring to a division of his company that worked with Johnson Space Center in Clear Lake, we resumed our friendship with ease, with no hard feelings about our brief and doomed college romance.

As I looked at him now, I wondered if his comment about running was directed at me. But Heath appeared guileless as he laughed, listening to Miranda and Alex explain how their failed relationships were never their fault or their choice.

"One year," I pronounced, breaking into whatever Alex was saying.

"One year what?" Miranda asked.

"You've got one year to find a significant other, both of you. During that year, we'll all listen to your dating woes, in an effort to support you on your quest. If at the end of that year you're both still single, that's it. You'll be confirmed spinsters at thirty. Romance will be but a dream of the past. An unfound paradise."

"And you'll have to shut the hell up about it," Patrick said. "In fact, we've got to set limits on your bitching."

"Jeez," Miranda said, "you act like that's all we ever do."

"Yeah, what's your point?" Patrick asked.

"We're not that bad," Alexander muttered. "I hardly ever see you guys."

"And when you do, we always have the same four conversations. Funniest college memories, why Miranda's family is the most dysfunctional, why Alexander will never sell out with his music, and how unlucky at love you two are," Patrick said.

"We talk about Aaron's students!" Miranda protested.

"And Heath's secret novels," Alexander said.

"And if Vivian's around, how much more brutal law school is than anything any of the rest of us have ever done," Miranda said triumphantly. "In fact, if Vivian's around, who gets a word in edgewise?"

It was true that Vivian Taylor, who'd become the newest member of our little group when she'd started dating Patrick a couple of years before, tended to dominate any conversation that included her, but no one complained. And it wasn't just that most of us were intimidated by her brilliant mind. She could argue opponents down to a puddle of egoless pulp, after which she would gleefully switch sides and demonstrate how they could have verbally trounced her if only they would use their minds for something more than figuring out how to get laid.

Beyond that, we all enjoyed her because she was a fascinating study of contrasts. An avowed feminist who did what she damn well pleased, she doted on Patrick, baby-talking him and indulging his every whim. She would rant about the plight of Middle Eastern women while donning an organdy apron and cooking us a fabulous feast in her Donna Reed–perfect kitchen. Or tell hair-raising stories of injustice in our inner cities while cross-stitching samplers to give as Christmas presents.

I'd once had the privilege of helping her on a Habitat for Humanity project. As the day wore on, the rest of us started looking like illegal workers taken from the secret compartment of a truck to the fields in hundred-degree weather. Vivian actually emerged looking better than when she started, blond hair tousled, skin glowing, and not a single fingernail broken after a day of hammering. I didn't just like her, I wanted to *be* her.

"Well, Vivian's not around," Patrick was saying, "and if she was, you wouldn't dare say anything bad about her."

"Because she'd kick your ass," Heath agreed.

"My point is," Patrick went on, "I don't want to hear you two whine all year. I can't take it."

"Here's the deal," I said. "At least once a month, we'll meet as a group and get a full report on your progress. At that meeting, you are free to complain as much as you want. But at the end of the year, if you haven't found anyone, we're cutting you off. No more dating horror stories."

"You wouldn't really do that," Alexander said smugly. "You suffer vicariously through us. If you didn't hear our lousy heartbreak stories, you'd have to go find a boyfriend of your own."

"Or even a date," Miranda said.

"I do date," I protested. "I told you already. I'm not looking for a boyfriend."

"Then let's up the ante," Miranda said. "You get to spend Y2K avoiding a relationship, just like always. But next New Year's Eve, if Alexander and I have both found somebody, then you have to spend 2001 doing the same. That way, whichever year starts the damn millennium, we'll all be part of couples. Happy or otherwise."

"Hey, what about me?" Heath asked.

"Oh, you," Miranda said with disdain. "If we made the same deal with you, you'd have a husband by the end of the first day. Everybody wants to marry you."

"So you're saying I'm not husband material?" I asked, pretending to be injured.

"On the husband axis, you're Heath's polar opposite," Miranda said.

"Too bad Vivian's not here to draw up a contract," Patrick said. "There ought to be some kind of penalty if these two do their usual teeth gnashing and garment rending other than on the designated day."

"No, we made a deal. I'll live up to it," Miranda said. "Such talk will be confined to the Love Sucks monthly meetings."

We all turned to Alexander, who frowned and said, "If I can't talk about bad boyfriends, what will I talk about?"

"Maybe you could get a hobby," I suggested.

"Men are my hobby," Alex said with a sigh. "If I agree to this, and find a boyfriend by one year from tonight, then you'll have to find a boyfriend too, next year? You're agreeing to that?"

"Uh—"

"See? I knew he wouldn't."

"What duration constitutes a boyfriend?" I asked. "Like, if I found someone by April Fool's Day, but it was over before my birthday in June—"

"If we're with a significant other on New Year's Eve 2000, you have to be with someone on New Year's Eve 2001."

"Oh, no problem," I said. Knowing their attention spans, I figured the first part of the deal would be forgotten by summer. I sure didn't have to worry about a night that was two years away.

Excited screams from the kitchen and foyer alerted us that midnight was upon us. Miranda grabbed a Jell-O shot then passed the tray around, saying, "It's a done deal, then. To love."

"To new beginnings," Alexander added, holding up his shot.

"To clean starts," Heath said.

"To vodka," Patrick said with an air of finality.

We downed our shots, and I looked at my watch. "Five minutes," I announced.

"Who am I going to kiss?" Alexander wondered aloud.

"Don't look at me, man," Patrick said.

"This is hopeless," Miranda said and tossed her shot glass over her shoulder.

"Ow! Hey!"

A tall redhead in jeans and a midriff-baring top jumped sideways as the shot glass ricocheted off her hip. She slid on a discarded plastic cup and landed on Alexander's and Miranda's laps.

"Holy shit," the redhead said, untangling herself from Miranda's long blond hair.

"Are you OK?" Heath asked her.

"I think so," she answered and laughed, probably a little embarrassed. "I tripped. It's not every day I get assaulted by a shot glass."

"I'm sorry," Miranda apologized. "That was my fault."

The redhead rolled off of Miranda and Alexander and sat on the floor beside the beanbag chair. "My name is Jodi."

"I'm Miranda."

The two women smiled and stared knowingly into each other's eyes. Patrick rolled his eyes and laughed. Wearing a hopeful expression, Alexander tossed his shot glass into the crowd of people gathering in the living room.

A symphony of noisemakers, cheers, bells, and whistles announced the midnight hour. Miranda and Jodi kissed each other. I hugged Alexander and kissed his cheek. A laughing Patrick clasped his meaty hands on our shoulders and bellowed, "Happy New Year, boys! There. That's over. I'm gonna get a beer."

"Don't worry, Alex!" Heath shouted. "You'll be next."

Alexander looked at Miranda and Jodi, who were watching each other and laughing as confetti rained down around them. He sighed and started to say something, but I clamped my hand over his mouth.

"Sorry, Alex," I said. "You're not scheduled to whine until sometime later in January."

"Besides," Heath added, "you have 364 days to find a boyfriend."

Miranda rejoined our little circle and threw her arm around my waist, unsteady on her feet. "You'd better get moving, Alex," she taunted. "I'm winning."

"This isn't a competition," Heath reproached.

"Some of us are just lucky," Miranda said.

Heath smoothed Miranda's hair off her forehead and said, "Your girl is lovely, Miranda."

"She's not my girl. I just met her," Miranda protested, swatting Heath's hand away from her face.

"It didn't look that way from here," Alexander said.

"No whining!" Heath and I chorused.

"I wasn't whining! It was merely an observation," Alexander said.

"We're going out to dinner tomorrow night, so we can get to know each other," Miranda continued.

"See what happens when you stop yapping and take action?" Patrick asked, coming back.

"It's an auspicious beginning to a new year," I assured Miranda.

"A new century!" Heath agreed.

The kegs were empty and the Jell-O shots were gone, as was the food, so the revelers, most of whom had gone outside to watch the fireworks over downtown Houston, began moving on to other parties. Patrick gathered the stragglers for a big finish at Dinks. I opted to stay home and clean up the apartment. I was reading in bed when Patrick returned later with Heath, who'd planned to stay with us rather than drive the twenty miles back to Clear Lake. No one wanted to be on the freeways on New Year's Eve.

I pulled on flannel pajama bottoms and walked downstairs when I heard them come in. Patrick was just handing Heath some sheets to make a bed on our sofa.

"You know I've got a love seat in my bedroom that makes into a double bed," I yawned. "It'd be a lot more comfortable than the sofa."

Heath followed me upstairs and dropped the sheets on the love seat so he could start undressing. I watched without any awkwardness. The passion between us was so far in the past that I might as well have been watching my brother undress. If I'd had a brother.

"I just thought of something," I said. "Do you want to go with me to my folks' house later? My mother's doing her traditional New Year's Day black-eyed peas and greens for good luck and prosperity meal."

"I'm not averse to a little good luck and prosperity," Heath said. "Sure. I haven't seen your family in a long time."

"Don't make the love seat into a bed. Just come in with me," I said, moving the covers back. When Heath was down to his boxer briefs, he climbed in, now yawning as often as I was. He turned off the lamp next to the bed and we lay there, probably both a little drunk and too tired to sleep.

"Tell me the story of the Fisher family," Heath said drowsily.

I smiled, having forgotten how he used to do that to me in the old days when we couldn't sleep. I turned over and snuggled against his back. His hair tickled my face as I started the story with my parents' meeting.

"A long time ago, Jack Fisher was walking down a street in Fort Worth when he caught a glimpse of a girl about half a block ahead of him. He couldn't have said what she was wearing or told you a single thing about her except that she had the shiniest brown hair he'd ever seen."

"And it bounced when she walked."

"Right, it bounced, and Jack was enthralled. He followed the girl for three blocks until she stepped into a drugstore. Then he followed her in there too. She was buying cigars for her uncle."

"And a Dr. Pepper for herself."

"Her name was Rose of Sharon Kelly. She was named for a character in her mama's favorite book, *The Grapes of Wrath*. Everyone called her Rose, or Rosie. She was seventeen years old and already had more boyfriends than you could shake a stick at. But when Jack introduced himself to her, it was love at first sight. A year later, the two were married. They lived in a little house in Fort Worth until Jack got a job working construction in Houston, one of the fastest-growing cities in the country. They moved to the Bayou City in 1968, and in 1970 gave birth to their first child, Aaron. Three years later, they had Kelly. Then five years after that, just when Rosie felt it was safe to get rid of her maternity clothes, she had Anastasia."

"But no one calls her Anastasia," Heath reminded me.

"Right. Five-year-old Kelly couldn't get her tongue around the long name Anastasia, so she just called the baby Sister. After a few years, Jack started his own construction company. He and Rosie settled into their northwest suburban home and did all the things families do. Or they tried to. It wasn't long before they realized young Aaron was not exactly going to be a little league champion. He was a bookish, serious boy and secretly wrote poetry. He grew up and decided to teach English to rich kids who found Robert Frost 'cute,' William Blake 'way out there, dude,' and Bono and Alanis Morissette 'the most meaningful poets of our time.' Meanwhile, Kelly, who wanted all the Legos that Aaron shunned, grew up and became an engineer who loved to build bridges and design roads. Which is good, because Houston has lots of roads that are always under construction."

"Tell about Sister," Heath ordered me in a tone that showed he was fighting sleep.

I smiled. Even when Heath and I had been together, long before Anastasia had grown up, she was his favorite, as if he knew she was going to lead a charmed life. Miranda had told me that throughout the years of their correspondence, whenever Heath asked about me, it was more of an afterthought than anything else. He always wanted to know about my baby sister.

"Oh, Sister was a mess. Aaron and Kelly had their mother's dark hair and dark eyes, but Sister was a blue-eyed blonde like her father. She had the face of an angel and her mind could best be described as 'dizzy.' Sister saw fairies in the garden. She believed Farrah Fawcett and Mary Kay Ash were the greatest Texans of all time. The only activities that interested her were baton twirling and finding the perfect shoes."

I paused, certain that I'd heard Heath snore, but he growled, "Get to the good part."

"Jack was constructing an office building in the Willowbrook area and had been convinced by a guy on his crew, Sonny, to hire Sonny's troublesome nephew, eighteen-year-old Tad Parker. Tad wasn't a bad kid. He just had his head in the clouds all the time. They said he bent more nails than he hammered in. Concrete cracked around him and had to be repoured. Wallpaper slid off the wall when he walked by. The crew found Tad the most harmless jobs they could and kept a wary eye on him whenever he climbed scaffolding or got near power tools. One day, Sister visited the work site to get money from her father for a miracle bra or something. She and Tad got a look at each other and—bam!—just like her parents all over again, it was love at first sight. Of course, Jack was less than pleased, and with good reason. Before you could say, 'Watch out for that falling two-by-four,' Sister was a pregnant, sixteen-year-old bride."

Heath snickered, and I shifted guiltily, remembering how upset my parents had been. It certainly wasn't funny at the time.

"One of the reasons Tad couldn't keep his mind on his work was because he and his fellow computer geeks were heavily into gaming. He'd wanted to work construction to get ideas for a game they were creating. Sort of a fantasy game set in the distant future. Earth was nearly destroyed after a series of nuclear accidents, and the survivors were trying to rebuild it without being wiped out again by mutant rats or some such nonsense. Long and short of it, they found a company to market and distribute their game, 'Vision City.' They weren't as empty-headed as people thought and kept the rights to their game. When it took off, Hollywood came knocking and gave them an ungodly amount of money to option a movie based on 'Vision City.' Six years later, Tad and Sister have a five-year-old son, another baby on the way, a big house in The Woodlands, and are living happily ever after. That's the story of the Fishers."

Heath started snoring in earnest and I grinned, turning away from him and pulling the pillow over my head. His snoring didn't really bother me; it was kind of comfortable. It amazed me that someone hadn't snapped him up. Miranda was right; unlike me,

Heath was definitely husband material. I knew that he dated from time to time. There seemed to be no lack of available gay men working in the aerospace industry around Clear Lake.

But like the rest of us, Heath often fell victim to The One—the dream that there was someone in the world with whom we were destined to spend the rest of our lives. The One was a man who had no flaws. The One would never be late. The One would call out of the blue just because he was thinking of you. The One would serve you tea and toast when you were sick. The One would never channel-surf. The One knew what kind of salad dressing you liked and could order a meal at a restaurant for you with confidence if you were in the bathroom when the waiter came to the table.

I felt sorry for our prospective suitors, who had to compete with The One. It was like going ten rounds in the ring of love with an invisible opponent, knocked out by a competitor who didn't even exist. Every flaw in a suitor's character only made The One look better in our mind's eye, as my friends and I navigated our way through Houston's dating pool.

However, my dates had gradually diminished over the past few months. I went out with Alexander and Miranda, but I confined my attention to my friends instead of the men around us. I had finally accepted that nobody was perfect. Everyone was human and flawed in some way. That was fine. But it wasn't fair to them, or to me, to set standards and goals that nobody could possibly live up to. Instead, I listened to Alexander and Miranda whine about *their* dates, comfortable in the safety of the no-dating zone.

"The guy I went to dinner with last night not only chewed with his mouth open, he also talked with his mouth full," Alexander would complain. "Like I'm going to take someone like that home to meet the family."

"Wanda was cool," offered Miranda, "but she's an accountant. I know it sounds shallow, but I don't want to date an accountant. What would there be to talk about? Numbers? Please."

"That's like—oh, what was his name? The lawyer I met at the gym?"

"Mark," Miranda stated.

"Yeah, Mark," Alexander confirmed. "He was great. We had lots in common, had a great conversation, and he picked up the check at lunch. But he had thin lips. I can't date a guy with thin lips."

I would sit on the sidelines and feel sorry for the Marks, Wandas, and other unfortunate souls who probably sat by their phones after a date with any of us and wondered what they'd done wrong. Their real mistake was agreeing to go out with us and be judged.

I arranged my pillows so I could sit up in bed and watch Heath, still snoring, in the red glow of the alarm clock. I wondered what impossible standard of mine he hadn't lived up to. At the time, I'd thought it was because our backgrounds were too different. We had opposing needs and priorities, and contrasting views on responsibility and what was important. Maybe he had been right when he said that I wasn't ready to grow up.

I thought about the deal I'd made with Alexander and Miranda. I'd grown accustomed to my role as the single guy. The unattached teacher. I had almost convinced myself that I was meant to be alone, watching my friends in their relationships instead of being in one myself. I'd take notes and fill my journals with observations about romance in the safety of my home, with nobody to complain about my late-night writing habits or how grumpy I woke up in the mornings. There were no rules but my own.

"I don't have to be in love to write about it," I said aloud. I wasn't sure if I was stating a fact or trying to convince myself of something I didn't believe was true.

Heath stopped snoring and rolled over in his sleep. His hand slid over my leg and wrapped around my knee. "You've never been in love," he murmured, then resumed a steady snoring pattern.

"What?" I loudly whispered, unsure if he was awake. I prodded, "Heath, what did you say?"

But he kept snoring. I decided he'd been talking in his sleep, answering me from his dreams. I wondered if he would remember what he said when he woke up.

Even more to the point, I wondered if he was right. It didn't matter to me, though. I liked my role as the confirmed bachelor of our group. And I had little concern, considering Miranda's and Alexander's dating histories, that I'd have to make any changes on any New Year's Eve for the next decade.

National Hugging Day

Pop culturists offer different opinions on the day the music died. The night Buddy Holly's plane fell out of the sky. The month Elvis gained his first excess ten pounds and still asked for another fried peanut-butter-and-banana sandwich from the kitchen. The year the Beatles broke up. The decade that Barry Gibb turned to brothers Maurice and Robin and said, "Let's write something they can dance to." The December when fanaticism plunged to new depths and took John Lennon with it. When Sid may or may not have killed Nancy in the Chelsea Hotel. When Kurt Cobain proved that depression was more than a mood that went with flannel. When Mariah Carey hit notes that only dolphins found musical.

For me, the day the music died was clear. It was the day I got an issue of *Rolling Stone* with a bona fide musician on the cover, instead of the usual prepubescent actor or anorexic model—either would be barely clothed—and not only did I not know who he was or what his music sounded like, but *I didn't care.* I'd been warned that I'd one day find myself crossing that boundary between youth and middle age, but I'd expected it to happen somewhere around forty. Or, once all those sixties bands started making comeback tours, maybe fifty. But I wasn't even thirty.

Still, once I relaxed, I found that it made things a lot easier on me as a teacher. I stopped trying to listen to hip-hop or keep up with the teenage angst of *Beverly Hills 90210* and discovered that both my students and I were enormously relieved. Ignorance was bliss. I no longer attempted the mental leap it took to draw parallels between Brenda/Brandon and Electra/Orestes in my "Myths and Legends" classes. I no longer had to endure classroom discussions on the striking similarities between the residents of *Dawson's Creek* and Sparta.

I discovered that students who were teething while watching Sally Jesse Raphael and Geraldo Rivera had no trouble following the shenanigans of gods and goddesses, either Greek or Roman. And I was spared papers like one submitted to my Early American Lit colleague, in which a student explained, "One of the biggest influences on the main character in the book *Little Women* was when Winona Ryder moved to New York by herself." Outside of Xena and her gang, my students couldn't find much on television or at Blockbuster to help them dodge their reading assignments. So we got on rather well.

One of the features Houstonians bemoaned about the city was its tendency to tear down anything old and charming—buildings and houses—in favor of the new and tacky. Of course, this habit had benefited me as a Fisher, since my father was a builder. But St. Gregory's was a great example of another Texas quirk: the conviction that we could take anything good and make it bigger and better. St. Gregory's had been built to resemble what I imagined was some English prep school set among gently rolling hills, aging gracefully with ivy-covered stone walls, expansive lawns dotted with boys playing cricket, decaying halls reeking of centuries of hushed Anglican masses and good old British fortitude.

Our version, however, was set on the flat Texas prairie, its stone imported from who knew where and at what monstrous cost. Unlike the city's beautiful Rice University, which ushered in its visitors on quiet roads canopied by live oaks, you could throw a rock in any direction from St. Gregory's and hit a strip mall or congested highway. And our halls, freshly painted each year, echoed with unceasingly noisy, brash teenagers. I loved it.

I considered myself fortunate that I taught the lower grades at St. Gregory's. Though plenty of teachers swore that intimidated seventh graders turned into the spawn of hell a year later, I liked my eighth and ninth graders. I was spared the jealousy of teaching older students who drove cars I would never be able to afford. My little darlings were still being chauffeured to school by their soccer moms in minivans and SUVs. In fact, some were driven by actual chauffeurs.

Like Khalid Joseph, a fourth-period eighth grader who was my current problem child. Each morning Khalid was dropped at St. Gregory's door by a driver in full Arab dress. Khalid's father, one of Houston's preeminent neurosurgeons, had long ago assimilated himself into Western culture, as had his wife. However, their household staff was encouraged to do as they pleased regarding dress, religion, and social custom, and most remained loyal to their Middle Eastern traditions.

Khalid had spent his early years in London and spoke flawless, if somewhat formal, English. His reports and tests indicated a quick intelligence and wisdom beyond his years. His manners were impeccable, and he gave me no cause to discipline him.

What made him my problem child was his isolation from his fellow students. It wasn't their fault. I believed that each succeeding year of the MTV generation was more tolerant than the last. Also, most of their parents were affluent and moved among a diverse set of friends and acquaintances. One of Houston's claims to fame was its congenial multiculturalism.

Nor did Khalid, though undoubtedly descended from a variety of sheikhs and other rulers, consider himself superior to his classmates. What I had come to believe was that Khalid was possibly the most painfully shy fourteen-year-old I'd ever taught, and I was determined to bridge the gulf between him and his peers. I knew this was his last chance to learn to belong before hormones gave him a whole new set of problems to deal with.

My challenge was to mesh my role as a social facilitator–slash–amateur psychologist with some kind of classroom instruction so that no one caught on to me. A new semester was beginning; it was time to embark on the Trojan War. I did what any sensible person would do when seeking an answer. I invited myself to Vivian's for dinner and asked her.

"Hmm," she said, removing the skewers from my chicken cordon bleu before handing me my plate. "What's he good at?"

"I have no idea. Why?"

"You should give him a chance to shine in a way that will impress the other kids. So that whenever they need that particular skill or talent, their first instinct will be to say, 'Ask Khalid.' Especially if you can make an ally for him out of one of your popular kids. Preferably a boy. The class clown, the jock, someone all the kids like."

"Yes, I've seen that work," I said thoughtfully between bites of chicken. "But it's usually a more natural development. Not a setup."

"Whatever you do, don't make it look like a setup," Vivian advised. "And you can't just order some kid to take Khalid under his wing. Who's the most popular boy in your class?"

"That would be Justin Woodhill," I said.

"It's always a Justin," she said and sighed. "Take some more garlic mashed potatoes. What makes Justin special?"

"He's just one of those kids. You know the kind I mean. There's a glow around him. His walk is part strut, part glide. He'll always be a winner. A golden boy. Even at his age, he's never at a loss for a snappy comeback. The boys all want to be his friends, and the girls all have crushes on him."

"Yes, that's our guy," Vivian said. She chewed her green beans and thought it over. "Do you think Khalid is a good critical thinker? A big-picture kind of person?"

"He's pretty smart."

"You know how my mind works. Do a mock trial. Put Justin, as Paris, on trial for causing the Trojan War, and let Khalid be his attorney. You can get the whole class involved as witnesses, a jury, the judge. But mostly, you'll be giving Khalid and Justin a chance to know each other. If they have fun doing this, they might become friends."

"That could work," I said.

"Make sure your jury is loaded with girls," Vivian advised. "They'll love the mushy details of the love story between Helen and Paris."

"You know what might work even better? If Justin has to defend Khalid. After all, no jury would convict Justin of anything. And it would make Khalid the love interest of whoever plays Helen. With the love of the right woman, and the loyalty of the right man, Khalid will be our star."

"Well, there you go," Vivian said. "I'm happy I helped you work that out. Now you get to help me do the dishes."

Over the next few days, as we began reading the details of the Trojan War, my students became enthusiastic about the idea of a mock trial. I knew once I handed out the parts and set them loose, they'd have a blast. And having to present the details of the story as court evidence would help them retain it, so I could feel good about turning my own little crusade into a learning experience for everyone.

Especially Khalid, who blinked his large brown eyes warily at me when I assigned him the starring role of Paris. He was obviously nervous about being on the stand in front of a jury of his peers. However, he unsuccessfully tried to hide a shy smile when Justin, upon learning that he would be defending Paris, threw his fists in the air and yelled, "All right!" It was as if Justin was James Cameron learning that he'd won an Oscar. I knew he was happy because he would be able to stride about importantly in front of his classmates and spout such phrases as "Isn't it true that—" and "Wouldn't you agree that—" like the actors on *Ally McBeal*. After high-fiving his friends, he turned to Khalid and said, "We're gonna win, man!"

I was as excited about it as they were and immersed myself in my lesson plans, since I'd decided to use the trial idea for a couple of other classes too. Engrossed as I was, it surprised me to get a call from Miranda suggesting that it was time for our first monthly Love Sucks meeting.

"Friday is National Hugging Day," she said. "Seems like the perfect occasion to discuss the cruel and capricious nature of love."

"Does that mean you've struck out again?" I asked.

"I'm sorry, I'm not at liberty to discuss those details at this point in time," she said, sounding like a subpoenaed government official. "If you want to know, come to Café Adobe. Eight o'clock. Make sure Patrick and Vivian come too."

"It's kind of a busy bar night—"

"We can all go to Dinks later and make sure it's still standing after Patrick leaves it alone for a couple of hours. You have your instructions. Be there."

I had to admit that our agreement was working. Since Alexander and Miranda couldn't discuss their romances, or lack thereof, I found myself with a lot of free time. Their phone calls to me—usually hour-long diatribes about boring dates, lackluster sex, and morning-after escapes that would have stupefied David Copperfield—dwindled to fifteen-minute social calls that left me laughing when they couldn't think of other things to talk about.

Since our New Year's Eve party, I had hung out with Alexander twice. One time we went out for coffee and he acted like someone who'd just quit smoking. He'd nervously looked around the coffee-house, stirred his coffee incessantly, and seemed unsure what to do with his hands. I felt sympathetic; as a gay man, I knew that having something to bitch about and being forbidden to do it must be hard.

"You went out on a date last night, didn't you?" I asked.

Alexander, who'd been staring at a light on the ceiling, snapped his head in my direction. His eyes, at first as wide as spotlights, narrowed after a minute, and he studied me cautiously. It occurred to me that he thought I was trying to trip him up or goad him into complaining about his date so he'd violate the rules of the deal.

"You don't have to say anything. You can just nod 'yes' or shake your head 'no,'" I suggested.

He nodded.

"I thought so," I said. "This must be so hard for you. Not being able to talk about it. It's hard for me too, you know. I like to think I'm being a good friend by listening when you need to get things off your chest. This changes things for me too. I'm used to hearing about everything that goes on in your life. And Miranda's. Now that's stopped. It's like having your favorite soap opera canceled. Although I have been getting a lot done. But there are other things we can talk about besides your love life, right? Hell, we can even talk about me and what's going on in my life. I know my students aren't exactly riveting entertainment to you, but it's something. And this whole experience can only make our friendship stronger, because maybe we'll start talking about less superficial subjects. Right?"

Throughout my monologue, Alexander had been nodding, smiling, pouting, shrugging his shoulders, and making so many gestures that he looked like a mime on crack.

"Speak, Alex," I commanded. "You're not a mute. You can't talk about dating disasters, but you *can* speak, you know."

"Oh, yeah. I forgot," he said and laughed at himself. "This whole arrangement is driving me nuts, I guess. You're right, though. I'm used to spilling my guts to you and now that I can't, I don't know what to say."

"Whatever," I insisted. "We can talk about anything. What's going on with your music?"

Relieved, Alexander told me about how difficult it was trying to put together a new band. Since he couldn't complain about dating, he compensated by telling me about the untalented oafs who'd responded to his ad in the *Houston Press.* Apparently Alex had auditioned every tone-deaf, rhythmless, offbeat musician in the Bayou City and had finally found enough passable amateurs to put a group together.

"The drummer's a woman," he said with a grin. "There's nothing cooler than a chick on drums."

"Yeah," I agreed. "Remember the Bangles? Debbi Peterson rocked on 'Walk Like an Egyptian.'"

"Actually, that was a drum machine."

"Oh."

"This girl's more like Mary Stuart Masterson in *Some Kind of Wonderful,*" Alex explained. "She's got short bleached-blond hair and is really tough-looking. But hot."

"Just because you can't talk about the men you date, don't think the rules don't apply if you go back to dating women," I cautioned.

"Har har," was Alex's sarcastic response. "I don't think so. Besides, I don't date band members. Look at what Fleetwood Mac went through. That's why I don't even date guys that I'm friends with."

"Is that why we never slept together?"

"No. It's because you threw up on me at Hildy Weingard's party in college. Once someone throws up on you, it's difficult to imagine them giving you head."

"Thank God you've got your standards. All this time I thought it was because our signs were incompatible," I mused.

"Funny. Hey, I gotta get to practice. We're having our first jam session in an hour. Should be fun; wanna come?"

"No, thanks. I'll wait until you guys play in a bar so I can get caught up in the magic and rush the stage like a screaming, prepubescent girl. It'll be more festive for everyone that way."

"OK," Alex said and gave me a hug before leaving. "This was more fun than I thought it would be. I'm glad we can talk about other things besides my hellacious—"

"Don't do it!" I interjected.

Alexander was right; it was fun to talk about things other than dating. But the conversation had still been one-sided. I tried to convince myself that my life actually was interesting, but my fears were confirmed the next time Alexander and I got together. We went to a movie and afterward, Alexander begged out of going to dinner because he had rehearsal. I picked up a pizza and had dinner at home alone, as usual, since Patrick practically lived at Dinks, frequently slept at Vivian's, and used his room in our apartment as a glorified walk-in closet.

After dinner I turned on the television, but there was nothing interesting on. I muted the sound, leaving the picture on, and turned on the stereo. I danced around my living room but quickly got bored.

"Funny," I said aloud to myself, "Billy Idol always made this sound more fun."

Then I remembered that his song was actually about masturbation and, since I wasn't in the mood, I grabbed my jacket and left the apartment.

"Hey, man, what's up? Want a drink?" Patrick yelled at me from behind the bar at Dinks, where I ultimately ended up.

"No. I'm here pricing Bibles. Do you have the King James version in stock?" I asked sarcastically.

Patrick grinned and flipped up both middle fingers at me before mixing me a Stoli Madras. "What's up your ass tonight?" he asked. "Or is it what's not up there that's bugging you?"

Several of the people around us laughed, but we ignored them.

"Am I boring?" I asked.

"I would say that you're a very serious person," Patrick answered.

"But would you say that my life is interesting?"

"You're not James Bond, Aaron."

"I knew it. I am boring," I said and sighed.

"No," Patrick groaned. "No, no, no! There is no whining in my bar. Go find your other friends if you want a pity party. If you're Misery, you won't find any company here, Aaron. You know I don't play that way. Besides, Miranda left a message on the machine in my office. The bitch-and-moan session is Friday, not today. And never here. What's your problem?"

"Now that Miranda and Alexander can only complain one day a month, they have nothing to say to me. Even when we do talk, it's all about them. They never want to hear about my life. I'm starting to wonder about my friends. Do they want to talk about themselves because I'm boring? I have a life too, you know."

Patrick rolled his eyes and seemed about to say something but instead bit his bottom lip while drumming his fingers on top of the bar. After a moment filled by the sound of Chaka Kahn on the bar's sound system, he leaned into my face and said, "I wouldn't be living with you if you weren't, in any way, shape, or form, an interesting person. That's all I'm going to say on this subject. Now, make like Chaka and tell me something good."

I talked about my students and how excited they were about their impending trial. I told him about Khalid and Justin, how Vivian had dispensed flawless advice on handling the situation, and how the plan seemed to be working so far.

"I would've recommended a boxing match, but I guess there'll be less of a mess to clean up Vivian's way," Patrick said, thoughtfully rubbing his chin.

"A boxing match? What would my students learn from that?"

"I don't know. But it would be like Rocky versus Drago. The U.S. against Russia. The kids could represent different countries, and we'll see who wins and has the more powerful nation. You could pair up Khalid and Justin and—"

"Miranda's right. You are a Neanderthal."

"What about Miranda rights?" Vivian asked, sliding onto the stool next to me.

"I'm sorry, I can't answer you without my attorney present," I said. "Did Patrick tell you about Friday night? Eight o'clock at Café Adobe? Will you both be there?"

"It's what I'm living for," Patrick said before turning away to take a drink order.

"I'll be there. Speaking of attorneys," Vivian said, "how's your Trojan War crimes trial coming along?"

"Splendidly, thanks for asking."

As Vivian hammered me with questions, proving she would one day be great at cross-examination, I was able to do an occasional scan of the crowd. As always, I appreciated the mix of people the bar brought in. I couldn't think of anyone who wouldn't be comfortable at Dinks, with the possible exception of a religious fundamentalist. Which was OK; it was my understanding those types did their drinking on the sly.

Since it was a school night for me, I left after Vivian and I played a couple games of backgammon. She won, of course.

Thursday was devoted to testing, and Friday the kids weren't at school. I ditched an afternoon in-service meeting, going home to catch up on my laundry before the weekend started. Just as I was congratulating myself on my efficient use of time—I still had a few hours to go to the gym and get cleaned up before the get-together at Café Adobe—my phone tolled the end of my control over my day and destiny.

"Hi," my baby sister chirped. "What are you doing?"

"Leaving for the gym," I said, immediately suspicious of her cheerful tone.

"Oh. The gym, huh? I'm really in a bind, but that's OK. Don't worry about it. I'll try to call Kelly again."

"Cut to the chase, Stasi," I said, using her *Stah-zee* nickname instead of the more affectionate *Sister* we usually called her. "I'm sure Mom and Dad told you that Kelly's at some conference in Dallas."

"That's why she hasn't answered," Stasi said. "Damn. No, really, it's OK. I'll call you later."

I sighed, knowing this was a ritual we had to go through. It was her way of charming someone to get what she wanted, so that by the time she was finished you felt like she was doing you a favor by letting you do something for her.

"Even if I am going to the gym," I played along, "maybe I can offer some solution for your problem."

"It's just that Tad didn't realize when he scheduled a meeting with some marketing people tonight that I was already committed to my friend Lexie's bridal shower. I mean, I'm one of the hostesses! I have to be there. But TP's sitter has mono and I couldn't—"

TP was her five-year-old son, Tyler Paul, and before I could rudely assure her that there was no way in hell I was going to babysit him, I heard my call waiting beep.

"Hold on, Stasi, I've got another call," I hurried to interrupt her. I clicked over. "Hello?"

"Hey," Heath said. "I left work early and thought I could hang out there until we meet everyone else at Café Adobe."

"Sounds great," I said. "Hold on; Stasi's on the other line."

"Sister?" Heath asked in a happy tone. "Did she call you, or did you call her?"

"What difference—she called me," I said. "It'll only take me a second to get rid of her."

"No, disconnect me and call me back on my cell phone. I want to be conferenced in with you two."

"Uh, you and my sister are not my idea of the lucky daily double," I said.

"It'd be a trifecta," Heath said.

"The trouble with writers is, they belabor a metaphor."

"Hang up and call me back!" Heath ordered.

I clicked back to my sister and said, "Hold on. Heath wants me to connect us in a three-way call."

"Oh, yay," Stasi said. "I love talking to Heath."

When I had them both on the line, I sat and listened to them coo at each other like two sickening lovebirds.

"I guess you and Aaron must be doing something tonight, huh?" Stasi asked, apparently finally remembering that I was on the line too.

Before I could assure her that we were, Heath said, "We're meeting some friends for dinner. But not until eight. We're just hanging out until then."

"Really?" Stasi asked. "I thought you were going to the gym, Aaron."

"I was, but then Heath called, and I changed my plans."

"The shower will probably be over by the time you have to leave for dinner," Stasi said.

"What are you talking about?" Heath asked. After Stasi explained, he said, "We'd be happy to keep TP. And if we leave before you get back you can just pick him up at Café Adobe."

"Thanks, you're a lifesaver," Stasi trilled. "He'd have disrupted the shower."

"But won't disrupt our dinner at all," I muttered.

"I've hit traffic. I'm hanging up," Heath said. "See you later, Sister." He clicked off without another word to me.

"I'll be there in about twenty minutes," Stasi said before she too hung up.

"I hate cell phones," I grumbled.

By the time Heath and Stasi simultaneously arrived at my door, I had the apartment as child-proofed as possible, remembering past incidents with TP. True to form, he charged through the door and immediately pulled a cushion off the sofa, finding an empty Frito bag and a sock.

"You really should get a housekeeper," Heath said, taking these items from my nephew.

Stasi giggled and said, "One night we had some friends over, and somehow we ended up blowing up condoms like balloons and batting them around the room. Have you ever seen one of those things pop? They go to pieces. A week later, Tad's parents were over, and TP pulled a broken condom from behind a chair cushion and handed it to his grammy."

Heath laughed and said, "What did she do?"

"She looked at my pregnant belly and suggested that we learn the proper use for such things," Stasi said. "TP, be good and mind your uncles. Thanks, Aaron." After a quick hug for TP, she was gone, which was his cue to start wailing.

"Great," I moaned, desperately looking around the room for something to distract him.

Heath dug in the bag Stasi had left and took out a juice box. TP showed him how to do the straw then plopped down in front of the TV with an expectant look.

"I don't suppose you have a video?" Heath asked.

"Do you think he'd rather see *Plow Boys* or *GI Jocks*?" I asked.

Heath rolled his eyes and dug through the videos until he found a copy of *The Little Mermaid,* which I hadn't even realized we owned. When I said as much, Heath replied, "Apparently you don't. Unless Blockbuster sells their videos in rental boxes now."

"No wonder Patrick doesn't go there anymore," I said. "I wonder what the late fees are for that."

In any case, it did the trick. Twenty minutes into the movie, his face stained with juice, TP was snoozing on the floor. Heath seemed to enjoy the movie, though, and by the time we left for dinner they were both in mellow moods.

"Oh, look, Tyler has two daddies," Miranda said when we found their table. Judging by the look of things, at least two rounds of margaritas had already been consumed.

I barely had time to take my chair facing the patio before Vivian managed to order margaritas for Heath and me, strap TP into the appropriate child's seat with a cup of crayons and some brown paper in front of him, and move the chips and salsa closer to Patrick.

"Good grief, Donna Reed, take a load off," Miranda said. "You're making me dizzy."

I was exhausted from the battle of washing TP's face and figuring out how to strap his child seat into my car. Although at five he could legally ride with just a seatbelt, he was small like my sister, so she still insisted on his kid's seat. Even Heath admitted that astronauts had less complex restraint systems.

As the others chattered around me, I gazed wearily toward the patio, unmoved by the array of handsome men. I was definitely not built for the rigors of parenthood. After a few minutes I realized that two guys sitting at one of the outside tables were exhibiting strange behavior and the people around them kept leaning away from their table.

"What in the hell are they doing?" I asked.

Only Miranda seemed to hear me, and she stared through the window, trying to interpret what appeared to be some kind of complicated chair dance. "Good grief," she said.

"What am I missing?"

"Look at the empty chair at their table."

After a second, I saw what she'd seen. What we Texans euphemistically called a "palmetto bug"—giant tree roaches that rarely ventured inside but could not be eradicated from our abundant foliage—was doing a run up and down the empty chair. Every time it went out of sight below the table, the two men leaned back to see where it had gone. Then it would dash back up the chair, and all the nearby patrons would angle themselves as far from the bug as possible. Miranda sighed as she realized that most of them were craning their heads in search of a waiter. Within seconds she was on the patio, brushing the bug to the floor with a napkin she'd grabbed on the way and promptly squashing it under her Doc Marten. The sound of applause followed her as she came inside.

"What a bunch of sissies," she said, plopping back down at our table.

"You're a hero," Alexander said. "But are you a single hero?"

"Not yet," Patrick groaned. "Can we at least order first?"

At that moment the waiter arrived, and we ordered. As soon as he left, Stasi joined us with hugs for everyone.

"Was he good?" she asked me as she looked approvingly at TP's drawing. Before I could answer, she said to TP, "Honey, I recognize your giant brown bug, but what's that little thing it's eating?"

"Uncle Aaron," TP said.

"He's totally out of my will," I said.

"You were going to leave him your video collection?" Heath asked.

"I have a few items of value," I insisted.

"I don't think he'd have as much fun with your sex toys as you do," Patrick said.

"Too bad I can't stay for this enlightening discussion," Stasi said, helping TP out of his chair. "Say thank you to Uncle Aaron and Uncle Heath for taking care of you."

"Thank you for taking care of me," TP said, looking absolutely cherubic.

"What a precious boy," Vivian cooed.

I walked Stasi and TP outside, watching enviously as she shaved nine-tenths off the time it had taken Heath and me to strap in the child seat and my nephew.

"Thanks so much for watching him," she said again, hugging me goodbye.

"He was fine," I said.

"I know. You don't fool me with your gruff act. You can tell me it's none of my business, but are you and Heath back together?"

"We're just friends."

"I thought since he came with you for New Year's dinner, and then seeing you together tonight..."

"Nope. Friends."

"Oh, well," she said, sounding regretful. "He's a great guy."

"He is," I agreed. "But we're—"

"Just friends. I got it."

When I went back inside, Miranda had already started her tirade. "Is it too much to ask that there be one single full-fledged lesbian in this city of four million people? Did someone forget to tell me that bisexuality is the hot new trend?"

"Jodi?" I surmised.

"She was great. Fun. Funny. She loved my jewelry. She's the only chef I know who doesn't change jobs every other month. She even works out at the same gym as me. She comes from a reasonably sane family. Why, why, why must she also worship at the shrine of the penis?"

"How narrow of you," Patrick said.

"I'm not narrow. I'm experienced in the ways of bisexual women. Just when you're ready to rent a U-Haul and move into paradise, some idiotic trouser snake slithers up and tempts her away. I am *not* going through that again."

"It doesn't have to be that way," Vivian argued. "If she's worth it, and the relationship is strong—"

"That's my rule, and I'm sticking to it," Miranda said. "No bisexuals need apply."

Patrick sighed and turned to Alexander to ask, "What's your tale of woe?"

"Moi? I have nothing to bring to the group this month."

I frowned, wondering why he looked so guileless, and said, "I thought you'd had some dates."

"So? Nobody special. Nothing that might develop into a relationship. I've been too busy with Tragic White Men."

"Right, so tell us about them," Miranda said. "That's what we're here for."

"No, it's the name of my new band. Tragic White Men. It's like a parody of all those privileged guys who sing whining songs about how tough their lives are."

"But you *are* one of those—oh, never mind," Patrick said, digging into his nachos.

I chewed my spinach enchilada and continued to stare suspiciously at Alex, certain he was keeping something from us.

"What?" he asked, catching sight of my expression.

"The two times I've seen you, you definitely led me to believe you had stories to tell. What are you hiding?"

"Me? I'm not hiding anything."

"Hey, Aaron, don't force him to make something up. So far, this is the best Love Sucks meeting ever," Patrick said.

"It's the first one," Heath pointed out.

"Which means they're all bound to be downhill from here," Patrick said. "Can we just enjoy the lull? Maybe we could even talk about something besides their miserable love lives. What a concept!"

"Oh, all right," Alex huffed. "I met this guy named Shane. He auditioned to be our lead singer. He definitely had the hair for it. All tousled and streaked. He's a very pretty boy. But the problem was, his *voice* was too pretty. We're going for this kind of gravelly, rough effect, and he didn't work out for the band. But I thought he might work out for me. We actually had a date. A real date. Does anyone remember those? We went to the Ambassador for dinner, then to see *The Sixth Sense*."

"Again?" Vivian asked.

"He hadn't seen it," Alex said.

"I see culturally challenged people," Miranda hissed.

"And therein was the problem," Alex said. "He didn't get it! How can you not get it? The blond streaks must have peroxided his brains right out of his head."

"I resent that remark," Heath commented.

"Yeah, yeah, tell it to his hairdresser," Alex said. "Of course, we still had sex. But there's no way I could ever have a relationship with him. All hair. No substance."

"Maybe we should stop pursuing the pretty ones," Miranda said.

"Why?" Alex asked. "There must be some men who are handsome and intelligent."

Without planning it, Heath and I both raised our hands, and everyone laughed.

It was, however, an apt description of Heath. His blond hair was cut short and cute. He wore little round glasses that hid his green eyes and gave him a scholarly look. He was clean-shaven, and his clothes always looked tidy and fit his body well. He was a couple of inches taller than me at six-foot, long-legged, and could be described as lanky, though he had a certain grace I'd admired from the first time I met him, when we were sophomores. He'd been, for a short while, one of Alexander's roommates. The boys in Alex's rundown bungalow close to UH were too rowdy, though, with revolving bedroom doors that meant the house was very seldom peaceful.

Heath had finally ended up in the apartment over Miranda's parents' garage, an arrangement that suited everyone. He looked after the Morrises' home when they traveled, so they charged him no rent, and he was able to buy a little pickup truck that was his proudest possession. These days he drove a BMW, one of the few symbols of his success that he had allowed himself. I was sure it had never given him the same satisfaction his tiny truck had.

I remembered how surprised I'd been the first time I undressed him. Because he was always working or studying, he never joined the rest of us when we played hooky to frolic on the beaches in Galveston or went to Splash in Austin. So I'd never seen his body until we ended up in bed together. Heath was one of those men who looked even better nude. A soft blond down covered his arms and legs. The hair that lightly covered his chest, or went from his bellybutton down his abdomen, was a little darker, and his skin had a perpetually creamy look even without benefit of tanning.

His appearance alone should have clued me in that we were not meant to be a couple. Couples were people who would end up looking more like each other over the years, and Heath was my opposite. Though I was nearly as tall as him, he was all legs, whereas most of my height came from the waist up. When I was a kid everyone had called me stocky, which I interpreted as a warning that I was going to turn into John Belushi, a look I knew I wasn't funny enough to carry off. As a result I was overzealous about exercise, especially running, ending up with a slender adult body that looked boring unless I forced myself into the gym every spring. I had dark brown hair, thicker than Heath's fine blond hair, and brown eyes. The only things we'd had in common were that we were both English majors and we shared a voracious sexual appetite for each other.

Those days were over. The sex was behind us. Heath wrote technical documents for NASA while I taught spoiled kids. What we had in common present-day was that we'd survived our failed romance to become comfortable friends; we knew each other's literary tastes and could recommend authors to each other; and we clucked like mother hens over the antics of our two little chickens, Miranda and Alexander.

"OK, business is taken care of. Love sucks," Patrick said. "What's new with you, Heath?"

"Funny you should ask," Heath said.

"You're seeing someone?" Miranda asked, turning big eyes on Heath.

"No. Well, occasionally, but that's not what's new. I'm changing jobs. There are always rumors about layoffs in aerospace, so I've decided to do something else."

"You sold another novel, didn't you?" Vivian asked.

"Who ever said I sold *one*?" Heath asked.

No matter how we goaded him, Heath never talked about his writing. Alex was sure he wrote bodice rippers. I voted for mysteries. Miranda figured they must be boring, technical books. Vivian believed they were children's books. Only Patrick never bugged Heath about his secret life as a writer.

"What are you going to be doing?" I asked.

"Do you remember Dr. Voss?" Heath asked. "He was one of my mother's doctors." I nodded, and he said, "He and a couple of his colleagues do a lot of publishing. I'll be helping them research, write, and edit their articles, conference papers, and speeches. Whatever they need."

"That's a real shift," Vivian said. "From aerospace to medicine."

"I like the challenge," Heath said. "It's time for a change."

"So you'll be working in the medical center?" Miranda asked. When Heath nodded, she continued, "Does that mean you'll be moving closer?"

"I've already found a new place. A little house in the museum district."

"That's huge news," I said. "Congratulations!"

"Thanks. I'm looking forward to living closer to everyone."

"I'm so excited!" Miranda said. "When are you moving?"

"The end of this month."

While we finished eating, he told us about the little bungalow that would be his new home. Afterward, when we all drove to Dinks, I was disappointed that he rode with Miranda instead of me. I'd wanted to ask him more questions about the new job. Then I remembered that his car was parked at my place, so I'd get my chance to interrogate him later.

Unfortunately, by the time we closed the bar, even though Patrick went home with Vivian, which meant Heath and I would be alone at my place, we were both too tired to talk much. We stood next to his car, commenting on how warm it was for January.

"I wonder if I'll ever live in a place where it gets really cold," Heath mused. "I'll bet I couldn't handle it."

"I went to Minnesota with a friend one time in March and thought I'd freeze to death," I agreed. "Do you want to come in? Or you can stay, if you don't want to drive to Clear Lake."

"It's going to be great when I'm living inside the Loop," Heath said. "I don't know. I've got so much to do this weekend, getting ready for the move."

"My weekend's clear. If you stay here tonight, I can go with you tomorrow, if there's anything I can do to help you."

We stared at each other. I felt like the air between us was suddenly charged with something tentative and fragile. I realized that I wanted to kiss him, but I wasn't sure what that meant, and it scared me a little.

"Sure," he agreed. "I'll stay."

When Heath and I were alone, it was easy to feel like nothing had ever changed between us and we were still a couple. He knew what music to play on the stereo and got a bowl of ice cream for me, knowing that ice cream before bedtime was one of my vices. As he entered the living room, he turned on the lamps and knowingly avoided the switches for the lights on the ceiling. We shared a look of amusement because of the fight we'd once had when I first told him that overhead lighting gave me headaches. Like two children, we kept antagonizing each other by flipping the light switches on and off while we fought, making the bedroom look like a nightclub with strobe lights.

Eventually the switch broke, an electrician was called, and Heath decided it was more cost-effective to let me have my way.

"What did you think of the first Love Sucks meeting?" he asked.

"Fine, I guess," I answered, still thinking about my unexpected attraction to Heath and wondering what it all meant. I watched as he put a spoonful of chocolate ice cream in his mouth and slowly slid the spoon from his lips. "I have to admit, I wonder how long this will last."

"You don't think Alex and Miranda will keep up their end of the deal? Or you don't think they'll find anyone?"

"I wonder if it's wise to force love on someone. A deadline for love doesn't really ring true. Does it?"

"I don't think love was in the rules, Aaron. The only stipulations were that they had to turn a date into a relationship and not bitch and moan about it so much. Are you worried that they might succeed, and you'll have to give up your precious bachelor life next year?"

"No," I said emphatically, resisting the urge to fling a spoonful of mint chocolate chip in his direction. "That's not it at all. I just don't want anyone to get hurt. Not only Alex and Miranda, but the poor fools who get involved with them."

"I get it," Heath said.

"Plus, now that they can't complain," I continued, "I hardly talk to them anymore. This whole thing is making me insecure. I'm questioning the significance of our friendship if all Alex, Miranda, and I ever had to talk about was their misery."

"Aaron, that's insane," Heath said, and I began licking my bowl clean, which I knew annoyed him. "Stop that. Give me your bowl."

As I surrendered the bowl, his annoyance at my regression was belied by his mouth, which twitched at the corners as if he was try-ing to suppress laughter. He took our bowls to the kitchen while say-ing, "You never were one to accept change."

"What?" I called after him. "What do you mean?"

"The deal you guys made has changed your friendship," Heath answered, returning to the sofa. "There are guidelines now. Most friendships don't have rules, but now yours do. That's going to change things, obviously. And don't second-guess Alex and

Miranda, because they still care about you. They're dealing with the changes too. It may be awkward for everyone at first."

"You're right," I said, thinking it over. "I hadn't looked at it that way. Thank you."

"You're welcome," Heath said, placing his hand over mine and giving it a gentle squeeze. "Any time you need a little perspective, give me a call."

"At least you'll be closer to home now," I said, brightening.

Heath looked into my eyes and smiled. For a moment we sat frozen in place. I imagined that my mind was a Polaroid camera and took a mental snapshot of the two of us together to analyze later. I wished that I had longer to try to read his eyes and decode the message he might be trying to send. But he let go of my hand, stood up, and said, "I'm going to bed. I have a big day tomorrow."

Hours later, after I'd stayed up to record the day's events in my journal while Heath snored, I turned out the light and climbed into bed beside him. He'd bypassed the usual martyr routine of offering to sleep on the sofa bed so as not to disturb me. Instead, he'd simply undressed and climbed into my bed without a word on the subject, instantly falling asleep in that annoying way of his. While some of us had to unwind and mentally talk ourselves down in order to fall asleep, Heath went out as soon as he closed his eyes. It was as if he had an OFF switch.

"If only you came with a MUTE button as well," I mused aloud, arranging my pillow behind my head.

However, I wouldn't have wanted to mute the advice he'd given me earlier. Heath had a way of opening my eyes to what should have been obvious. I'd been thinking only of myself instead of my friends. The friendships that Alexander, Miranda, and I shared were changing. I only hoped the changes would be for the better.

Heath turned over in his sleep, and his arm smacked me in the face.

"Ow!" I exclaimed and threw his arm off me.

"David, stop," Heath mumbled, then laughed sleepily.

David? I rolled over, away from him, and angrily began counting sheep.

Susan B. Anthony's Birthday

I'd hoped helping Heath as he sorted and boxed his possessions might give me evidence as to the identity of the mysterious Dream David, but I was sorely disappointed. Having lived with Patrick for a decade, I was used to straight-guy messiness. But Heath's apartment might just as well have been a monk's cell, devoid of clues as it was.

It wasn't that he didn't have expensive things. Leather furniture, beautifully crafted Cambridge lamps, and his antique bedroom set and restored secretary were only a few of the subtle indications that Heath had done well for himself over the years. They were also the reason his friends believed he had some means of supplementing his income.

It was the spartan order in which he kept everything that thwarted me. There were no stacks of papers or mail, no journals or coffee-stained manuscripts, not even pictures to give me any information about his private life. A single photograph of his mother rested on his marble fireplace mantle. Even the boxes he'd already packed were marked by room rather than contents.

He also assigned me to pack the one room that would be least likely to offer any insight into his life: the kitchen. He had full sets of antique Fiesta dinnerware and flatware, and six-set groups of

Fostoria stemware and glasses. His pots and pans were obviously used, and he had lots of spices, so he definitely cooked. But did he cook for one or two?

I couldn't even use our time alone together to try to worm information out of him with subtle, well-timed questions, as he'd loaded the CD player and turned up the volume while I started on the kitchen. Then he disappeared into the deep recesses of his walk-in closet to begin packing clothes. I would have sworn he was deliberately toying with me, except he had no reason to know that my curiosity was driving me crazy.

All in all, it was a totally unproductive day for sleuthing. It worked out well for him, however, since he drove me like a pack mule. I was still too sore a couple of nights later to find any enthusiasm for the gym. Instead, I dropped in on my friend Ramon. His incessant chatter and flirtatious ways could almost always coax me out of a disgruntled mood.

"Oh, no, Aaron is grumpy," Ramon said in heavily accented English when he opened the door and saw my face. Which was ridiculous, because he couldn't speak a word of Spanish. Even his parents, first-generation citizens as they were, barely had accents. Ramon only used his accent as an accessory when he thought it made him appear cuter.

"Stop it," I said. "You sound like the Taco Bell dog."

"Everybody loves the Taco Bell dog!"

"I hate the Taco Bell dog."

"You'd hate a glass of ice water on a hot day if you thought it quenched your smoldering charm," Ramon said, dragging me into his bedroom.

"Cut it out," I said. "I don't want to be seduced."

"I want you to see my new disco outfit, lamb-pie," he said. "Should I try it on so you can compliment me on how it accentuates my perfect little bubble butt?"

I dropped on the bed and watched as he whirled around the room, throwing various ensembles together as if we were backstage at a showing of Isaac Mizrahi's spring collection. When he took off his jeans and stood in his boxer-briefs, trying to decide which outfit to model for me, I growled, "All right. Come here."

It was never earth-shattering, mind-blowing sex that we shared. He liked to call himself my favorite little fuck friend, and it was true. I was comfortable with him. We understood each other's preferences and knew there was no danger of falling in love.

Afterward, he rolled over on his stomach and propped his face on his hands to watch me.

"What?" I asked.

"Tell Papa all about it," he said.

"You're three years younger than I am," I reminded him.

"Not tonight. Tonight I am the old Huichol wise man."

"Don't use words if you don't know what they mean," I said.

He laughed and said, "The Huicholes are a tribe of Mexican Indians. Speak to me, young one, and tell me what troubles you."

I rolled my eyes and said, "I think Heath has a lover."

Ramon sat up and shrieked, "Heath? Your long-lost love? So you *do* still have feelings for him! I knew it. Tell me every sordid detail. Leave out nothing. Only in this way can I help you, my lust-muffin."

"I do not have feelings for him," I said. "I simply hate mysteries. He always knows everything about everyone, but on the subject of himself he's a fucking sphinx. Is that fair?"

"Details, what are the details?"

"A group of us went out last week—"

"Love sucks."

"Well, yes, it does, but that's not—"

"The meetings," Ramon said impatiently. "You told me about your plans for monthly meetings."

"Oh. Right. Yes, it was our Love Sucks meeting. It was late, and he decided to stay in town."

"In town? Don't speak to me in euphemisms. He stayed where?"

"At my place. In my bed."

"Ah," Ramon sighed. "In bed with the tasty, golden Heath bar. Tell me!"

"I'm trying, but you won't shut up."

"I'm like Helen Keller," he promised, doing some kind of *Miracle Worker* routine which involved his hands "accidentally" exploring me under the sheets.

"You're certifiable," I said. "It wasn't like that. He just slept in my bed. I didn't, because he snores so loudly. At one point, he rolled over, and his arm hit my face. When I pushed it off, he said, 'Stop, David.' So I'm wondering, who the hell is David?"

"David," Ramon breathed. "Beloved of God. The little boy with the pebble who brought down the giant. I suppose that would make you the giant."

He let out a cackle and I jumped him, pinning him to the bed. "It's not good to taunt the giant," I warned him.

"Ho, ho, ho," he said.

"Takes one to know one," I answered.

But I'd been right. By the time Ramon left to dance the night away and I went home, I was in a much better mood. It endured over the remaining time until moving day, when all of us had promised we'd help Heath. I, of course, had an agenda. Those boxes had to be unpacked sometime.

Heath was scheduled to move during the first weekend in February. Dressed in our oldest clothes and armed with bottles of water, Miranda, Alexander, and I drove to Clear Lake to help him load up the moving truck he'd rented. When we arrived, Heath and Vivian were sitting on the sidewalk, waiting for us.

"Look who decided to join us," Heath said, gesturing to Vivian.

"Where's Patrick?" I asked her, since he'd presumably spent the night with her after working at the bar.

"He's at my place. Mouth hanging open and drooling," she said, her eyes flickering toward the sky with feigned disdain. Then she added, for clarification, "He worked really late. He's still sleeping."

"It's a good thing you cleared that up," Miranda said, "since that description applies to Patrick at any time of the day."

"OK, people," Heath said, spreading his arms and motioning us toward him. "Let's get in a huddle."

Alexander, not exactly a morning person, looked stricken. It was as if Heath had suddenly asked him to eat live earthworms.

"Who does Heath think he is?" he asked. "Andre Agassi?"

"Somehow, I doubt there's much call for a huddle during a tennis match," I said.

"He's the only sports figure I know," Alexander said somewhat sheepishly. I laughed and moved into the huddle next to him.

"OK, men—"

"And women," Vivian said, interrupting Heath.

"And wimmin," Miranda added.

"OK, team," Heath said, trying a different tactic. "We're here for one reason and one reason only. Move those boxes. I won't lie to you. It's not going to be easy. There'll be lifting. There'll be carrying. There'll be sweating. There'll be stairs."

"Why couldn't you live someplace with an elevator?" moaned Alexander.

"And there'll be bitching, whining fags trying to break your spirit," Heath continued. "But we've got a job to do. I know you can do it, team! We will get that truck loaded! We will unload it into my new house! And we will get it done before 10 P.M. so I won't have to pay an extra fifty dollars! Now get moving! Those boxes won't move themselves, you know!"

Heath played his coach role to the hilt, slapping my ass as we all cheered and ran upstairs to his apartment to start moving his things onto the truck. From then on, however, he morphed into Julie the cruise director from *The Love Boat,* guiding us through the correct order in which boxes should be loaded into the truck. Then he'd mark them off on an inventory that he carried around on a clipboard.

When we began moving Heath's possessions out of his apartment, we were full of vim and vigor, happy to do our friend a favor. But after working like ants for a couple of hours, carrying his possessions down to the truck and trudging back for more, our spirit began to wane.

"Aren't we done yet? My arms are starting to ache," Miranda complained.

Vivian entered the apartment and hefted another carton onto her shoulder. "This is a great workout," she said to nobody in particular and went downstairs.

"Here, Miranda," Heath said, studying his clipboard and pointing to a stack of boxes by the bathroom. "Take one of those down. They're mostly linens and are liable to be lighter."

"I'm fine," Miranda snapped and lunged for a box marked BOOKS. She grunted audibly as she carried it out of the apartment, muttering and swearing under her breath.

Alexander lumbered back into the apartment, stopped in place to wipe sweat from his face, and whined, "Why couldn't you live in an apartment building with an elevator? Huh? Why?"

When we arrived at Heath's new house in the museum district, Patrick was waiting for us on the front porch. "I come bearing lunch," he said, rising from the porch swing and offering bags of sandwiches.

"My hero," Vivian said, wrapping herself around Patrick and kissing him.

"Thank God," Alex said, taking a bag and following Heath into the house. "I'm starving."

"Gimme that," Miranda ordered and grabbed a bag with bottles of fruit juice from Patrick's other hand. "I can't believe how thirsty I am. I could drink Lake Conroe."

After Heath gave us a tour of the bungalow, we sprawled on the bare floor of the living room and ate our lunch. Miranda enlivened the conversation with her version of ghost stories—scary tales about the perils of buying an old house with pipes that groaned, floors that warped, and windows that had to be propped open with books, lava lamps, or whatever was handy to keep them from crashing down and shattering.

"Thanks for bringing the food, Patrick," Heath said, refusing to be daunted. "It was so thoughtful of you."

"Yeah," Miranda agreed. "And so out of character."

"All right, I'll confess. Vivian called me on her cell phone and asked me to pick up lunch," Patrick admitted.

"I figured it was the least he could do, since he slept through phase one of moving day," Vivian explained. Patrick knelt behind her and began rubbing her shoulders and arms.

"Ew," Alex said, shielding his eyes and pretending to be disgusted. "Straight people touching."

With Patrick's help, we had the truck unloaded and returned to the rental agency well within Heath's designated time frame. Alexander left for rehearsal, since Tragic White Men's debut performance was only two weeks away. Miranda lingered, helping to free Heath's kitchen appliances from their boxes. But once Patrick left for Dinks and Vivian went home to study for an exam, Miranda begged out of unpacking.

"I'd like to stay and help," she said, "but I have several jewelry orders to fill."

"And then there were two," Heath said, once Miranda had left. "It's been a long day, Aaron. You don't have to stay."

"I know," I said.

"Really," Heath insisted. "I can take it from here."

"Are you trying to get rid of me?" I asked. Though I was joking, I wondered if his mysterious David was coming over to help him move in. I'd been hoping to find revealing evidence while helping him unpack, but if David was going to make an appearance I was definitely sticking around.

"No, not at all," Heath said. "I just figured you must be tired. And unpacking can be so boring. But if you're willing to stay, who am I to talk you out of it? Can you help me with the stuff in the living room?"

We set to work arranging the furniture in the living room to Heath's specifications. It was easy, since he'd already sketched out a rough map of the house and drawn in where he wanted everything placed. As we unwrapped books, candles, and other knickknacks, I wondered if Heath would let me help him unpack his bedroom. I was certain the clues I was hoping to discover regarding David would be sealed in the cartons and bags in there.

Then I unwrapped an oil painting. I sat down, turning it against the light, and examined the image. I ran my fingers over its bumpy surface; the multitude of brushstrokes that made up a single sun-flower in a field of wheat. The painting made me want to laugh and cry at the same time. It wasn't the picture of a sunflower that tapped into my emotions, but the memories attached to it.

Heath and I had purchased the painting together during our stint as a couple. On a day off from classes, we drove aimlessly around Montrose, darting in and out of antique stores to search for treasures. Heath was always fond of his history classes and loved anything with a past.

"Look at this spinning wheel," Heath had said, running his hands over the dusty relic. "I'll bet the woman who owned this put her kids through college by selling everything she ever made on it."

"Yes," I agreed. "And I'll bet she hated this old thing because of it. No wonder it's here, instead of being passed down as a loving memory through her family."

"Why are we doing this if you don't even like antiques?" Heath asked.

"I like antiques," I protested. "But if they're of value, I'd rather see them catalogued and presented in an aesthetically pleasing order in a museum, or even showcased in someone's home, instead of hap-hazardly strewn about some dusty old shop." Heath sighed, appar-ently giving up on me, so I added, "But since this is something you like to do, I'm happy to come along."

"Great. Just spare me the sarcastic comments. They're getting really old," he said, then brightened, adding, "just like the stuff in this shop!" As we laughed, Heath suddenly put a hand on my arm and pointed to a wall. "Look," he said.

It was the sunflower painting. Heath loved sunflowers and want-ed to buy the painting, but he didn't have enough money. I agreed to buy it with him because it reminded me of Van Gogh, who was one of my favorite artists. Plus it would perfectly match the colors in what we had begun to call *our* bedroom, though I was still officially Patrick's roommate. We hung it on the wall opposite Heath's bed, where the morning light would shine on it, illuminating a symbol of us as a couple.

After we'd separated, neither of us mentioned the painting when I began moving out the stuff I'd accumulated during my time with Heath. Although we bickered over who'd bought certain books and CDs, the painting was overlooked altogether. Even after we rekindled our friendship and I saw it hanging on the wall in Heath's apartment, it still surprised me to remove it from the box in his new house.

Heath saw me brushing my fingertips over the painting's surface and smiled. "Do you remember when we bought that?"

"That's what I was just thinking about," I said. "I was being a jerk, as usual, and this was the one thing we agreed on."

Heath looked confused and said, "You were being a jerk? That's not how I remember it. You kept finding things that reminded you of your parents' furniture. I was jealous because you grew up with all that family history around you. You helped me buy the painting so we could start making a history of our own."

"Hey, if you want to think of me in that misty, watercolored memory kind of way, who am I to argue?"

"You've always been too hard on yourself," Heath said.

"Are you sure you're not confusing me with some kinder, gentler ex-boyfriend?" I asked.

"Could be. There've been so many, who can keep up?"

"How many have there been?"

Heath had been on his way out of the room, but my question made him stop and turn around to look at me. "Are you serious?"

"Sure. We never talk about the missing years."

"Let's keep it that way," Heath said and left me alone.

He made me insane, and I said as much to Miranda the next day while she was bent over her work table, wire-wrapping stones as she listened. While I talked, I wandered through the open rooms, idly picking up things and putting them down, knowing she could hear me no matter where I was in her Craftsman Cottage.

I remembered when she'd first moved in. She was the only one of us to buy her own place after college. The Heights was enjoying a new wave of interest; many of its houses had been bought by lesbian couples, who appreciated the area's quiet appeal and liberal-minded residents. The Heights' building codes stayed true to the area's architecture; even newer houses were based on authentic Victorian homes. Miranda had been lucky to snap up one of the original houses before it was renovated and priced out of her range. I suspected her parents had probably bought the house outright and Miranda only paid for upgrades and refurbishing.

The downstairs was dedicated to her business, with work tables and orderly bins of supplies filling the built-in bookshelves of most of the rooms. She could accommodate several assistants when she was busy, but today she had the place to herself. Her own work space was in the original living room. The windows were large, and sunlight filled every corner of the room, which was made more inviting with dozens of plants in garishly painted pots. Area rugs scattered over the hardwood floors were chosen not only for their cheery appeal but to protect the wood from the spills and mishaps that were commonplace in jewelry-making. The former dining room was filled with display cases full of her beautifully crafted rings, bracelets, necklaces, and pendants. This shop wasn't open to the public, but she often invited buyers as well as an occasional wealthy customer in to look at her work.

The only parts of the downstairs that she reserved for her personal use were the kitchen and its sunwashed breakfast room. But even there, order reigned. It was only after you went upstairs that you could discern the true Miranda. Her bedroom was always cluttered with clothes, boots, and shoes. The waterbed was never made. Another bedroom was used for her television, stereo, and large collections of CDs and videotapes. Still another was a guest room, where I'd been known to crash a time or two. She had a few books scattered around, but Miranda wasn't really a reader, so most of them were on lesbian politics, jewelry, or nature and art that might inspire the creation of more jewelry.

Her bathroom was the house's masterpiece. She'd had a wall knocked out to extend its space, and it was all marble, glass bricks, and expensive tile, with a large glassed-in shower and a spa tub suitable for candlelit baths for two. I shuddered to think of how many women had seen their dreams of a commitment from Miranda swirl down the drain of that tub.

I ended up back in her workroom, watching while she focused on what she was doing. Once I shut up, I suspected she'd forgotten I was there, so I was allowed to study her at leisure.

She still had the same figure as when we first met as freshmen, a body she described as functional. She was too hard on herself. She wasn't petite, or even slender like Vivian, but she had what Heath called a "hardbody." Compact and sturdy. In college, she'd kept her dishwater-blond hair cut in a bob, but after graduating, about the time her parents had probably paid for her house, she'd shaved her head and gotten several more piercings in her ears. After she'd apparently horrified her family enough, and felt somewhat independent of them, she'd let her hair grow. And grow. She had a lot of it, and I always thought of it as a living thing in some Medusa-type fashion. She had a tendency to randomly tuck it into clips and clasps to get it out of her way, resulting in a disorder that was oddly appealing. Alexander said that Miranda's hair brought out his inner hairdresser; Patrick always professed to be afraid of it; and Heath was fond of playing with it. I liked it, and reminded her that Medusa, before she was demonized by one patriarchal society or another, had been a beautiful goddess, with all of nature at her command. Miranda simply rolled her eyes and said we all thought way more about her hair than she did, a conclusion that Vivian concurred with and bemoaned.

Miranda stopped working, looked at me with a frown, and began rolling her head to release tension. "This is my least favorite kind of work," she said.

"It's not what you usually do," I commented, pointing toward the more elaborate gold- and silver-set stones that made up the bulk of her designs.

"It's a new buyer. She owns a metaphysical shop a few blocks from here and pays way more than she should for it. Some people shouldn't be allowed to run their own businesses."

"Some people are dodging the subject," I said, bringing the conversation back to my frustration with Heath.

"Some people don't know why Heath's personal life is anyone's business."

"Some people don't understand why it's such a secret."

"Some people should respect Heath's privacy."

"Jeez, I'm not asking for state secrets. I'm just curious about the years when he and I were out of touch."

"Oh, good, we stopped speaking in third person. It was getting on my nerves."

"You're not going to tell me anything, are you?" I asked.

"Nope. If there's anything Heath wants to share about his life, that's his choice."

"Including David?"

"Who's David?"

"Never mind," I said, giving up.

"Seriously, I don't know about anyone named David."

"Fine."

"Why are you so interested?" she asked. "You're not thinking about having another go at a relationship with Heath, are you?"

"Oh, my God, I just asked a question."

"Aaron with Heath is the highway to hell," she said. "If you're on the feeder road, take my advice. Keep away from the on ramp."

"When did you turn into a traffic cop?"

"I've been in enough relationship wrecks to know—"

"Yeah, too bad you're not allowed to discuss that for a couple more weeks," I cut her off.

She laughed good-naturedly and began working again. I was glad we'd avoided an argument.

I thought about that the next day when I broke up a fight outside my classroom at St. Gregory's. Even though I knew I should send the two boys to the dean, I let them off with a warning to commemorate the spirit of harmony that had ended my visit with Miranda. When I was summoned to the office during my free period, I reminded myself that no good deed goes unpunished.

Edie, the headmaster's secretary, rolled her eyes when she saw me. "He'll see you in a few minutes," she said. "Is it a full moon or what?"

"I have no idea. Having a rough day?"

"Someone caught a table on fire in Mr. Stamp's chemistry class. Two girls shaved their heads in the locker room. A wandering tuba player managed to set off all the car alarms in the faculty parking lot. Two fetal pigs are missing from Ms. Rhodes' physiology lab. And my dentist just told me I need a root canal."

"Sounds like Monday to me."

She laughed as Bill Westin opened the door and motioned me into his office. I was surprised to find Dr. Joseph sitting in the guest chair. He stood to shake my hand, and I wondered if he'd come to the school because Khalid was having some kind of problem. He'd seemed much happier to me lately, but over the years I'd learned that kids were great at keeping secrets. At least from adults.

"Mr. Fisher, Dr. Joseph has been telling me about the interesting approach you've taken to teaching your students about the Trojan War," Bill was saying as Dr. Joseph nodded.

"Uh-huh," I said, unsure where this was going.

"I'll leave you two alone. Good job, Aaron."

That sounded promising, and I relaxed a little. Dr. Joseph moved to take his seat and motioned for me to sit in the other chair.

"Khalid says yours is his favorite class," Dr. Joseph said. "Perhaps I should explain a little about my son. Nahala and I think of him as our miracle. We tried for eleven years to have a child after we married. There was no reason why we couldn't have one, but she never got pregnant. You can imagine how happy we were when it finally happened. Khalid is the most important part of our lives, so perhaps we've been overprotective. It disturbed me that my son had so few friends. Now I see him running out the door to play soccer, hear him talking about other activities with his classmates. . . This makes his mother and me very happy."

"He's a great kid. Sometimes these things just take a little while," I said.

"And sometimes they get a little push. I want to find some way to show our gratitude. Mr. Westin suggested that I speak to you about what would be appropriate."

"All I did was present Khalid with a situation in which he could be himself," I said. "He made his own friends. Knowing he's feeling better about himself while he's learning is all the reward I need. I'm just doing my job."

"Which is what Mr. Westin told me you'd say. I was thinking of something like a donation. Perhaps to purchase some needed equipment or supplies for the school."

I thought it over and said, "Of course, we're always having fundraising drives, but St. Gregory's is well supported by parents like yourself. The public schools have a tougher time. I have a friend who's part of the Houston ISD Community Partnerships program. He could give you great information on the needs of some underfunded schools."

"Perhaps I could even involve some of my colleagues," Dr. Joseph said thoughtfully. He handed me his business card. "If you could fax me his information, I'll arrange a meeting with him. You don't mind if I tell him that you referred me?"

"Not at all," I said. "It's easy to see why Khalid is such a great kid."

He smiled to acknowledge my compliment, and I walked him out. After he was gone I looked at Edie, who was grinning at me.

"Not what you expected when you walked in, huh?" she asked.

"No. Now if I could just find those missing fetal pigs—"

"You'd be my hero."

I laughed and walked back to my classroom to get the information to fax to Dr. Joseph. Some days it felt great to be a teacher. I couldn't imagine doing anything else.

I remembered how shocked I'd been as a college senior when I did my student teaching. I'd listen to the "real" teachers in the staff room, horrified by how cynical they sounded. It had taken me a long time to understand that they were blowing off steam. Once they walked out those doors and into their classrooms, most of them dedicated themselves to their professions heart and soul. Even the least idealistic of them kept a place in their hearts for their students, no matter how they grumbled. In fact, over the years, I'd done plenty of grumbling of my own, though it was rarely about my kids. They were fine. Sometimes I just felt I had too little time to teach because of the meetings and paperwork I had to deal with. But I knew I was lucky; public school teachers had it much tougher than me. And St. Gregory's had a great headmaster, which made a lot of difference.

By Friday, it was hard to remember why my week had started out positively. I was so tired that when I got home, feeling rumpled, my tie askew, I was glad that Patrick was already at Dinks. I didn't want to go anywhere or see anyone. I took a shower, opened a beer, and planted myself in front of the television, ignoring my phone when it rang.

It wasn't until the next day, when I picked up my phone and heard the rapid dial tone, that I remembered I'd gotten a call. I dialed in to get my message.

Aaron, it's Miranda. Where are you? We're all at Dinks. We were going to have a spontaneous Love Sucks meeting, because next weekend we're all supposed to attend the debut of Tragic White Men. I'm not going to compete for attention about my sex life—or lack thereof—when Alexander has not only an adoring audience but access to a microphone. After much juggling of social calendars, we've chosen Tuesday to get together. Vivian says it's Susan B. Anthony's birthday. I figure that's appropriate. Didn't she try for like fifty years to be allowed to vote, only to die before women could cast their ballot? Sounds like my love life. Not that I'm complaining. So put your hair in a bun and show up at Dinks on Tuesday night at seven. We know it's a school night; we'll be gentle on you. Bye.

I deleted the message and dialed Alexander's number.

"Wha-huh?" he mumbled.

"Sorry, I always forget everyone's not an early riser," I said. "Late night, dear?" He muttered something inaudible. "You told me you wanted to go to the gym with me. I'm ready!"

"Whozis?"

"It's Heath!" I said, cracking myself up.

"Aaron? Whazzit, like seven o'clock?"

"It's eleven. Eat something small with lots of carbs. I'm picking you up in half an hour."

"ButIdonwanna—"

"See ya!"

Not long after we'd graduated from college, Alexander and I joined the YMCA in downtown Houston. I'd recently broken up with Heath, and Alexander had broken up with Mr. Love-of-His-Life Number 412. Suddenly single, we decided to reinvent ourselves by joining a gym and becoming healthy, buffed, and beautiful. Not only would we become objects of desire, but when we ran into our respective exes they would rue the day they let us go.

In an attempt to cut our membership rates in half, Alexander and I posed as brothers when we submitted our membership to the Y. We'd worked out an elaborate story beforehand to explain our different last names, but we needn't have bothered. The Y employee who processed our application for family membership barely looked up after checking our IDs and running my credit card. Alexander, who'd spent hours rehearsing our family tree, said he felt like Susan Lucci being passed over for an Emmy award. But he was quickly sated when he discovered that the photo on his membership ID had turned out flawless.

Our dedication to health, beauty, and the perfect body lasted only a few months. At first, we went every day. I'd meet Alexander after work and we'd diligently work out for two hours. If we took a day off, we'd feel guilty and vow to make up for it the next day. I began to notice a change in my moods, my sleeping habits, and my body. Standing in front of my mirror, I was aware that my body was taking on a more toned appearance.

Unfortunately, Alexander's interest in the gym quickly began to wane. He'd say that he only had time to work out for an hour. Eventually that evolved into not having time at all.

"Maybe tomorrow," he'd say, like a lackluster Scarlett O'Hara.

If the YMCA was a soap opera, Alexander quickly became a

recurring character who made appearances once or twice a month. And I had to admit that I had off-seasons as well.

However, like so many people at the dawn of a new year, I'd made a resolution to make the most of my gym membership. I wouldn't make myself feel guilty if I didn't have the time or energy to go. But I would try to attend at least four days a week.

I found it easy to keep the promise I made to myself and fell back into a regular routine. This time, it wasn't about looking good for other people. Or narcissistic revenge. I simply felt better after a good workout. It gave me time to reflect on my day or mentally prepare for tomorrow. But I often spent my time thinking about my friends. Since we couldn't discuss the ins and outs of their relationships, I found myself spending a lot of time on the treadmill. Alone.

I'd decided the gym would be a lot more fun if I could get my workout partner back. Not only would having Alexander around quell the monotony of running on the treadmill and lifting weights, but we could spend more time together not talking about his love life and strengthening the bond of our friendship.

Alexander fell into the passenger seat of my car, as lifeless as a bag of dirty laundry. In fact, he appeared to be wearing clothes that hadn't seen a washer in weeks. He had on sandals, worn jeans that had holes and coffee stains in several places, and a T-shirt with a picture of the Clash emblazoned across the front of it.

"Why do you look like hell?" I asked.

"I was rehearsing with Tragic White Men last night. I think I got four hours of sleep," he moaned. "Thanks to you."

"You're welcome," I said.

"I'd tell you to go to hell, but you're already driving me there."

"Don't you want to work out?"

"Not particularly," Alex admitted.

"But you got in the car," I pointed out.

Alex shifted in his seat, rubbing his eyes as if he was trying to rip them out of his skull so he could rinse the red off. "I have that performance coming up," he said. "Call me vain—"

"You're vain," I interrupted.

"—but I want to look good onstage," he finished. "No. Not just good. Hot."

"I'm sure that's exactly what Keith Richards says before his performances," I teased.

Alex looked at me in horror. "I do not look like the walking dead," he gasped.

"Only because you're sitting down."

I managed to find a parking space directly in front of the YMCA, which was housed inside an old brick building nestled between the chrome and glass skyscrapers that made up downtown Houston. We shouldered our gym bags—me with a skip in my step, Alexander walking like a beleaguered washer woman carrying a fifty-pound basket on her shoulders—and went inside to change into our gym clothes.

Once we were out on the floor of the gym, Alexander seemed to finally wake up. I jogged briskly on a treadmill and watched him pedaling furiously on a stationary bike while scanning the other members of the gym. I glanced around us too and noticed a few good-looking men on various machines around the room. I was glad Alexander's eyes were getting as good a workout as his legs.

He leaned over to me and said, sotto voce, "Look over there. That guy is totally cruising me."

"Which one?" I asked. "And I'm right next to you. How do you know he's not cruising me?"

Not that I knew who he was talking about. There must have been thirty other men in the gym. It was like pointing to a forest and saying, "Look at that tree."

"The hot one," he said.

"I'm going to push you off that bike if you don't—"

"The one working his abs. In the blue shorts."

Finally noticing the man Alexander meant, I made a low noise of appreciation. It was difficult to tell how tall he was, as he was seated in the ab machine, but his legs were long and solid, like a runner's. His torso was encased in a tight, filmy white tank top, which showed off his solid chest and tight abs.

"Dark hair, nice body, and Tom Cruise good looks," I observed. "Looks like a winner to me."

"Definitely," Alexander agreed. "Blue ribbon all the way. He keeps looking over here."

I pretended to watch CNN on the television suspended from the wall but noticed, out of the corner of my eye, that Blue Shorts was periodically glancing in our direction between each set on the abdominal machine. I wondered which one of us he was looking at. From time to time I'd been told I was handsome, and I knew Alex was, but we had different styles. Alexander, with his dark, disheveled hair, ice-blue eyes, and angular bone structure, often looked like a fashion model who woke up under a table in a gritty bar. Which would make me the conservative one. I was Mary Richards to his Rhoda Morgenstern. If the two of us were in a crowd, anybody's eyes would go directly to him.

We continued our routine, taking turns on the various machines, until we worked our way to what I called Muscle Beach, a room off to the side of the cardio-fitness room where the free weights were located. It reminded me of old movies from the '50s, where muscle-bound men would pose and lift weights that were conveniently located in close proximity to a beach. Just like in the movies, the free weight room was filled with guys lifting, curling, and pressing bar-bells and dumbbells. However, instead of the beach, they were lined up in front of mirrored walls, watching themselves or spotting each other on the benches.

Alexander and I paused momentarily at the door to Muscle Beach. Walking into a room full of bodybuilders was intimidating. Not to mention that the sight of all those muscles was a bit breath-taking.

"If I can't control myself and get hard, I'm skipping the weights and running straight to the sauna," Alex whispered.

"You couldn't run straight if you tried," I joked. "And don't forget, the YMCA is a Christian organization."

"Please," Alex said, sounding miffed. "I practice Christian values. I give good head and expect to receive it in return."

After finding a spot in front of the mirrors, we each picked up two thirty-pound dumbbells and began doing arm curls. By our third set of twenty repetitions, Alexander was red-faced and I was doing my best to hold back some un-Christianlike curse words. Suddenly Alexander seemed to get a second wind and began lifting his weights with gusto.

"Blue Shorts," he said quickly under his breath.

I dropped my weights in front of me and looked around the room while I stretched my arms. Blue Shorts was on the other side of the room with his back to us, but he could still see us in the mirror.

"Tell me if he's watching," Alexander said and set down his weights. As he did, he elaborately stretched out his back. I glanced across the room and saw Blue Shorts's eyes riveted to Alexander's ass in the mirror's reflection.

"He's definitely watching," I reported. "His eyes are rolling around in his head like a slot machine. Now he's salivating. Oh. Now steam is jetting out of his ears, and his jaw just hit the floor."

"Oh, shut up," Alexander said, raising up and smacking me on the back of the head. "Let's hit the showers. I'm over this place."

We went upstairs to the locker room, where we ditched our clothes and wrapped towels around our waists.

"I'm gonna sit in the steam room for a bit," Alexander said.

"I can't breathe in there," I complained. "I'll be in the sauna."

We split up, and I took a shower before I went into the sauna, which was the size of a walk-in closet. I relaxed and felt the heat seep into my body, slowly loosing up my muscles. The door had a Plexiglas window, and I watched men of various shapes, sizes, and ages as they walked by. After a while, I closed my eyes and rested my head against the wall. But I soon grew bored and went to look for Alexander.

I found him amid the swirling mists of the steam room, sitting next to Blue Shorts, who could now be called White Towel. Close up, wrapped in a towel, and enveloped in steam, his body was even more spectacular than it had appeared under the bright lights of Muscle Beach. I guessed him to be in his late thirties and noticed, since he was laughing at something Alexander had said, that he had perfect teeth.

"Hey," Alexander said, noticing that I was standing in front of them. "I didn't see you there."

"I'm not surprised. It's foggier than a Woody Allen movie in here," I said.

"This is my best friend, Aaron," Alexander said, heavily emphasizing the word *friend*. "Aaron, this is Zachary."

Zachary, né Blue Shorts, né White Towel, smiled affably and shook my hand. "It's nice to meet you, Aaron," he said. "I was trying to ask Alexander out on a date, but it's not very easy."

"Oh, no," I said. "He's easy."

Alexander sneered at me and said, "What Zachary means is, I'm rehearsing all the time with my band because of the gig we've got coming up. I don't have any nights free until after that."

"Why don't you do something during the day?" I asked.

"Maybe," Zachary said, sounding hopeful. "That would almost be better for me. Even though I work during the day, but I could take a half-day, I guess. Why don't I call you?"

"Yeah, sure. Let me get my pen," Alexander said, putting his hand underneath his towel.

Zachary laughed, then said, "I'm a CPA. I'm good with numbers. I'll remember."

Alexander recited his phone number, and I resisted the urge to tell Zachary that he could probably find it written on the walls of Houston's finest bars and bathhouses. They agreed to speak soon and shook hands before Zachary left, since hugging in a steam room at the YMCA would be a social faux pas.

As he stood to leave, Zachary's towel slipped from his waist. He caught it before it hit the floor, covered himself, and bashfully said, "Whoops. I'll talk to you soon. Nice meeting you too, Aaron. Bye."

When he was gone, I sat down beside Alexander in Zachary's place. We turned to look at each other, then burst into a fit of giggles.

"Did you see that?" I asked.

"What am I going to do with *that*?" Alexander asked, a little taken aback.

"Where there's a will, there's a way," I said, trying to gasp for air and coughing because of the steam heat.

"We have to stop at the drugstore. Apparently, I need to stock up on lube," Alexander said, and we both screamed with laughter again. When we calmed down, he said, "It's not often that I get to see my dates' dicks before the date."

"It looks like you'll have a *lot* to talk about at the next Love Sucks meeting," I pointed out.

"I love the gym," Alexander said.

Unfortunately, like most of his affairs, if they could be called that, Alex's fling with the gym was passing. He managed to evade my Sunday morning wake-up call, and I didn't talk to him again until I went to Dinks on Tuesday night.

When I'd asked Patrick why he suspended the "No Whining at Dinks" rule, he told me that, like any good businessman, he was multitasking. I figured he couldn't justify listening to people complain about their personal lives when his business needed his attention.

Once again, the rest of the gang had arrived ahead of me. I'd had parent-teacher conferences that lasted until five, then I had a late appointment at my dentist's office for a cleaning.

I slid into the only empty chair at the table in time to hear Miranda say, "An accountant? Haven't you been down that road before?"

"That was you," Alexander reminded her. "I've never dated an accountant."

"Oh, yeah, I get our exes mixed up," she said.

"Between the two of you, the only careers you've missed are royalty and wrangler," Patrick commented.

"Uh, I dated a calf-roper once," Alex said, and we all stared at him. "It was rodeo season. I was a poor college student. He got me into the Astrodome to see Patti LaBelle."

"I guess that gave you a new attitude about the rodeo," Heath said.

"And about bowlegged cowboys," Alex agreed.

"Say no more," Patrick ordered, pouring me a beer from the

pitcher. Our drinks were usually comped at Dinks if Patrick was around and we were willing to drink cheap. None of us had a problem with that.

"So am I to understand that you've actually seen Blue Shorts since Saturday?" I asked.

Alex blushed prettily and said, "*Zachary* and I spent yesterday together."

"Are accountants like hairdressers?" Miranda asked. "Mondays off?"

"Wow, he moves fast," I spoke over her.

"Quite the opposite," Alex said with dignity. "Zachary thinks I'm very interesting, and he wants us to get to know each other before we take things to the next level."

This was met by a deafening silence that was finally broken when Vivian asked, "So, what did the two of you do?"

"We met at Lobo for coffee, then we went to the Cockrell Butterfly Center." Even Vivian couldn't respond to that, and we all stared at him. "What?" Alex finally asked. "Is it so amazing that I might enjoy looking at exotic butterflies in a rainforest setting?"

"Who are you?" Heath asked. "And what have you done with our Alexander?"

"He's channeling Rachel Carson," I said.

"Who's Rachel Carson? Was that Miranda's homecoming date senior year?" Alex asked.

"Rachel Carson was an environmentalist who—" Vivian began.

"Oh, no," Miranda interrupted. "This is definite boyfriend crap. And I can't even get a date. The only thing I have to celebrate is Susan Fucking B. Anthony's birthday."

"I keep telling you, it's not a competition," Heath admonished.

"I think it's sweet," Vivian pronounced.

"Totally," I said. "What's next? You buy matching sets of binoculars and go bird watching?"

"How rude," Alex sniffed. "I share the details of my tender first date with you all, and you act like Heidi Fleiss has joined the convent."

"It's *your* analogy," I said. "Did you make a second date?"

"He's going to call me," Alex said. "It's tax season, so he's not sure about his schedule over the next few weeks."

"You mean you have to wait two months for a second date?" Miranda asked in a hopeful tone.

"No. I just have to be a little accommodating about last-minute plans. He'll definitely call."

"I, for one, couldn't be happier," Patrick said. "I hope you enjoy many drama-free years together. So tell us about your upcoming debut with Tragic White Men."

While Alex talked about the band, I met Heath's amused eyes and could tell that he, like me, was finding it impossible to picture Alex waxing rhapsodic about butterflies. I was sure that Heath remembered the time when Alexander's attempted murder of a tiny moth with Paul Mitchell hairspray had been accompanied by high-pitched squeals. Every dog in the neighborhood had joined in with sympathetic howls.

Later, when I walked Heath to his car, he brought up the same incident, and we laughed about it. "You were yelling, 'For God's sake, Alex, it's a pump, it only shoots three inches!'" Heath said.

"And he was flailing around, acting like he was being attacked by killer bees," I said.

"That cost me more than ten dollars!" Heath bellowed, imitating me.

"I did not say that," I argued.

"Oh, but you did. We were poor college students," Heath insisted.

"Can you believe he saw Patti LaBelle and never told us?" I asked.

"Selfish little shit," Heath agreed. "So do you think this Zachary guy is good enough for our boy?"

"From what I saw, he's more than good enough," I leered.

"Ah, I knew it had to be more than butterflies that held Alex spellbound," Heath said. I held out my hands to give him an approximate measurement, and he laughed.

"You know, I've been going to the Y, both sporadically and faithfully, depending on the season, forever," I said. "I've never picked up a guy at the gym."

"Those who can, do," Heath said. "Those who can't—"

"Work out." We were at his car. "Are you all unpacked?"

"Mostly. So I guess I'll see you at the performance of Tragic White Men, huh?"

"I'll be there," I said.

He kissed me on the cheek. I waited until he'd pulled away, then remembered that my own car was parked on the next street over. As I rounded the corner, I saw a couple in the distance. Two guys, one leaning against a car, while the other, who was much taller and heavier, had his hands propped on either side of him, as if he was holding him prisoner. As I got closer, I realized how accurate my assessment was.

"C'mon, Paul, it's late. I need to go home," the smaller guy was saying.

I groaned inwardly, now recognizing the bulky man as Paul Nettles, the speech teacher and debate coach at St. Gregory's. Paul was the only other gay faculty member that I was aware of, and we took great pains to avoid each other, as neither of us wanted to be compared to the other. I wasn't sure what his problem was with me, but Paul had almost every quality I detested in a teacher. He rarely shut up, expressing his cynical opinion on any subject in a whine that went right up my spine. He complained about everything and shirked any school duty that he disliked, which seemed to be most of them. I'd also seen him drive his poor students to tears. Paul believed that humiliation was one of the more effective teaching methods. He survived because he did turn out a first-rate debate program— whatever the cost to his kids—and he knew how to ingratiate himself with parents and administrators.

As I got closer to them, I could see that the guy he'd trapped looked like he was still a teenager. Paul had to be pushing forty.

"Just get in the car, Bobby. I said I'd take you home," Paul said in his usual aggrieved tone.

"Bobby!" I said cheerily. "Is that you?"

Paul dropped his arms and gave me a belligerent stare, while Bobby looked confused, since he'd never laid eyes on me before that moment.

"Oh, it's Miss Fisher," Paul said. "Shouldn't you be home grading papers or something?"

"It *is* you," I said, slipping an arm around Bobby's shoulders as he slid beyond Paul's reach. He must have decided I was the lesser of two evils, because he didn't pull away from me. "I haven't seen you in weeks. Do you need a ride home?"

"Yes," Bobby said gratefully.

"I'm taking him home," Paul said.

"Oh, I'm sorry. I didn't mean to interrupt your date," I said.

"He's not my date," Bobby assured me. "I'd appreciate a ride. We can, uh, catch up."

"That would be great. And now you can go home and hone your fellating—I mean, debating skills," I said to Paul.

"See you around," Bobby called back happily as I guided him toward my car.

When we got in, I looked at him and said, "What were you thinking, hooking up with that old troll? Do you know him?"

"I see him at the bars," Bobby said. "I was trying to get away from him."

"You shouldn't have gone near him in the first place," I scolded. "How old are you?"

"Twenty-one."

"I didn't ask what your fake ID says."

"Twenty."

"Again."

"Eighteen."

"Is that your final answer?"

"It's the truth," he swore, and I believed him. "Are we going to your place?"

"I'm taking you home. Where is home?"

"I live with my brother. In an apartment on Greenbriar."

I shook my head at him and started my car. "Does your brother know you come to the bars to hustle?"

"I do not hustle," he said angrily. "I hang out here with some of my friends."

"All right. Just be more careful, would you?"

"I hope I didn't cause any trouble for you with Paul."

I laughed and said, "I'm not even slightly worried about Paul."

"Well, you don't have to worry about me, either. I can take care of myself."

"Yes, I saw," I said.

"I wasn't going to get in the car with him."

I sighed and said, "He's pretty harmless. With his type, you just have to go for the ego, and they'll crumble."

"I'll remember that."

"It would be better if you didn't get yourself in situations where you had to remember it," I said.

"So you're a teacher too, huh?"

"What gave me away, my authoritative tone?"

"Paul said something about you grading papers."

"Oh, yeah. Yes, I'm a teacher. And you're not much older than my students. Or his, for that matter. Seriously, Bobby, stay away from dirty old men."

"What's your name?"

"Aaron," I said. "Aaron Fisher."

"Bobby Wallace."

I followed his directions to a set of modest, red-brick apartments and pulled up to let him out.

"Thanks for the ride, man."

"You're welcome. Take care, Bobby."

I pulled away when he was out of sight inside the apartment complex. I knew Paul would find some slimy way to make me pay for interfering with his attempted conquest, but it was worth it.

"Eighteen," I muttered. "Why do they want to grow up so fast?"

St. Patrick's Day

Heath's BMW was in the shop for servicing, and he didn't want to park his loaner car outside a bar, so I agreed to drive us both to Tragic White Men's coming-out performance. I deliberately got to his house earlier than I was supposed to, remembering my treacherous intention to snoop through his stuff.

Heath frowned when he opened the door, looking at his watch. "You're so early. I haven't even showered."

"I was bored. I'll hang out here and bug you while you get ready."

"Lucky me," Heath said. "Fix yourself something to drink. Make yourself at home."

He puttered around while I got a Coke from the refrigerator and gave myself a tour of the house. As I'd expected, everything was in perfect order. The kitchen looked great, with Heath's colorful dishes gleaming behind the glass cabinet doors. His copper-bottomed cookware, hung on the wall, looked burnished. I thought of my mother's pots and pans, with the copper blackened by years of use, and smiled. Heath's painstaking care of his possessions showed how hard he'd worked to buy them.

Not even a single unpacked box was left. The pictures were hung. The linen closet was neatly stocked. There was even wood stacked in the fireplace, though I was pretty sure it was merely for decoration. For one thing, there was only a small window of opportunity in Houston to have a fire, unless you ran the air conditioner while it was burning. For another, most of the older houses in the area had either gone to gas logs or had their chimneys sealed off.

"Well?" Heath asked.

"It looks terrific," I said. "Are you buying this house or renting it?"

"Renting with the option to buy."

"Do you think you will? Have you found any major flaws yet?"

"No. It's a perfect little house. I get the morning sun in my bedroom, and when I wake up it feels all cozy and right."

"I like the way you hung the antique windows in front of your windows in there," I said. "I'm sure it does look good when the sun shines through them."

"Thanks. I'm not sure about buying it; the price tag is steep. All the houses in this area are ridiculous, when you think of what you could get in the suburbs for the same price."

"Yeah, but then you'd be in the suburbs," I said.

"Exactly," he said and laughed. "Anyway, the cost isn't going to drop. Since improvements were already made to the kitchen and bathroom, the house doesn't need anything but a little landscaping to make it perfect."

"And he lived happily ever after," I said.

"I'll be in the shower. Put on some music if you want to."

I pretended to be looking through his CDs, but I had no intention of playing music. I needed to be able to hear him in the bathroom. Once the water was running and I heard the shower curtain hooks scrape across the rod, I hurried to the spare bedroom that he'd turned into an office. Stifling a single twinge of guilt, I quickly scanned the contents of the pigeonholes in his old secretary. Nothing but bills, a couple of notices of gallery openings, and an invitation to some black-tie event benefiting Texas Children's Hospital.

The water was still running, and I quietly started opening and closing drawers, finding only the usual office supplies and blank paper. Until I hit the bottom drawer, which had an enticingly thick manila envelope in it. I squatted down to peer at the labels. It had been sent to Heath's old Clear Lake address and had a New York City postmark. I was sure I'd hit pay dirt when I saw the yellow stick-on note with "contract renewal" in Heath's neat handwriting.

"I knew it," I muttered. "He does have a publisher."

As I reached for the envelope, the water shut off. When Heath came out of the bathroom, a towel wrapped around his waist, I was just hitting PLAY to start a Sarah McLachlan CD.

"Find what you were looking for?" Heath asked.

I could have sworn he knew exactly what I'd been up to, then I realized that he was only peering so hard at me through narrowed eyes because he wasn't wearing his glasses.

"*Fumbling Toward Ecstasy,*" I said.

"I heard you fumbling, but I don't have any ecstasy. Are you PMSing?"

"I like Sarah," I said defensively.

"Obviously I do too, or I wouldn't have the CD."

He pattered into his bedroom. I gave him enough time to finish drying off and slip on a pair of underwear before I followed him, throwing myself on the bed to watch him get ready.

Which might have been a mistake, because water was still glistening in the fine gold hairs at the small of his back, and I felt again that strange urge to pull him to me and see what happened. I rolled over on my stomach, so there'd be no chance of him noticing the effect he was having on me.

"I've been thinking over the Alexander situation," Heath's muffled voice came from the closet.

"And?"

"I probably worry too much. But you know what I hate?" He turned around to look at me, and I waited. "Why is it that when people start a relationship, they pretend to be something they're not?"

"You mean like going to look at butterflies when in reality you think of them as big, nasty moths?" I asked.

"Right."

"Maybe some people would see that as a compromise. Don't we all do things for the other person in our relationships?"

"Yeah, most of us do. And I know in the overall scheme of things, spending a date doing what makes the other person happy isn't a big deal. Like I said, I worry too much."

"No, I see what you mean," I said. "We're more honest in our friendships, because we expect them to last."

"That's it!" Heath said. "If you start out a romance by faking enthusiasm for something, sooner or later you'll get tired of it and start being yourself. Shouldn't you be yourself from the beginning, in any relationship? If you expect it to last, I mean."

"Longevity would be a new concept for Alexander," I said. "I guess he has to learn it through trial and error. Then again, don't we all?"

"OK," Heath said, dropping on the bed next to me. "Let's argue this out."

"Argue? About Alex?"

"No. I'm not stupid, Aaron. Ever since New Year's Eve, you and I have been dancing around something. I don't know if you have hard feelings from our breakup after all these years, or if you feel the attraction that's still between us, or what, but from time to time I get these weird vibes from you."

"What did Miranda tell you?" I asked, wishing she was in front of me so I could shake her.

"This isn't about Miranda," Heath said. "It's about you and me. I'm willing to go out on a limb and tell you how I see things, but only if you don't play games with me. You hurt me, Aaron, and I can't let you hurt me again."

"You weren't the only one who got hurt," I said.

"I believe that. You make me crazy sometimes."

"Likewise," I said.

"OK. We don't have to do this. Forget I said anything."

"Why do you give up so fast?" I asked. "For that matter, why did you eight years ago?"

"We were kids. You were the first guy I ever loved, and

sometimes we were happy. But I kept trying to make myself into who I thought you wanted me to be. Everything seemed so easy for you, but it was hard for me. I wanted to be like you, so you'd love me as much as I loved you. No, to be more honest, so you wouldn't leave me. I couldn't do it. You were so cocky and carefree. But you were also careless, Aaron. If I'd been a different person, it would have rolled off of me. But instead, it wore me down. So I left you before you could leave me."

"And I let you go. I was as dumb and confused as you were, Heath. But I honestly thought it was just a fight, and we'd make up. Only you moved away. I was too proud to do anything about it. We were *both* kids."

"And now we've got eight years, and I don't know how many relationships, between those kids and who we are now. I still think you're one of the sexiest men I've ever known."

"But?" I asked.

"But I find myself doing things with this little voice in my head that says, 'This'll show him.' Or 'Now he'll see what he gave up.' I don't want to be trapped in a time warp. Like I'm still twenty-two years old and trying to make one of us over so we can be together. I'd rather have your friendship—which, whether or not you know it, has become one of the sustaining forces of my life since my mother died—than screw everything up again by forcing us into something we're not very good at."

"You sound so rational. Is love supposed to be like that?"

"Maybe not, but it's who I am. And it's one of the things that you don't like about me."

"As a lover," I admitted. "But as a friend, I really do value it."

"And I appreciate the way you're willing to put yourself out there. To say, 'This is who I am. This is what I do. This is what I love. These are my flaws. Love me or hate me, but don't try to fix me.' There's nothing wrong with that. The man who loves you and wants to build a relationship with you should be willing to close his eyes, dive in, and go with the flow."

"And that's not you?"

He stared at me for a long time before he shook his head and said, "I don't think it is. You have no idea how much I wish it could be."

"Maybe," I said, trying to think my way through it as I spoke, "most couples only split up after things have broken down between them to the point that they really hate each other. I never felt that way about you."

"Then that's one more difference between us. Because I hated you after we broke up. Those feelings faded over time. Now I love you. But I'm still cautious with you. I'm careful about how much of me I give to you."

"You don't trust me," I mused. "Even as a friend."

"I don't know about that. It's more likely I don't trust myself. Because I know how easy it is to lose who I am just to be with you."

"I think you underestimate yourself. You left me, Heath. I'm the one who made the announcement that it was over, but you're the one who let it happen, then made it impossible for us to work it out. You were determined to make our last few meetings as acrimonious as possible. Except for your correspondence with Miranda, you vanished. Except for your mother, you wouldn't have come back. And for all your friendliness, you're still closed off from me. What I know about your life is less than what you'd put on a résumé."

"What do you want to know?"

"Who's David?"

Heath's eyes looked huge behind the lenses of his glasses, and he asked, "David? What do you know about David?"

"You talk in your sleep."

"And I said something about David in my sleep? What?"

"You called me David."

"How funny," he said, looking away. "I wonder what I was dreaming?"

"Do you intend to answer me?"

"David is—no one."

"You dream about no one?"

"He's not real. David is a fictional character."

"You mean all this time—" I broke off.

"You were jealous?" Heath laughed. "Sorry. I know I shouldn't laugh at you."

I pulled him to me. His shirt was still unbuttoned, and while I kissed him, I began pulling it off.

Heath broke away and said, "Bad idea. *Bad* idea."

"Shut up," I said. "If you didn't want me to want you, you wouldn't have slept with me and paraded around half-naked, and—"

It was his turn to shut me up, by kissing me back. In our haste, we were clumsy and awkward about undressing each other, but when that part was done everything familiar and easy came back like eight years hadn't happened.

Afterward, we rested side by side on Heath's bed, not touching. It was as if there was a glass wall between us and the slightest sound would cause it to shatter and pierce our fragile egos. I stared above me and noticed a crack in the plaster that extended from the light fixture in the center of the ceiling. It was hardly noticeable, but a flaw all the same in Heath's seemingly perfect home.

I turned my head, and my eyes met his. His lips parted, as if to speak, but he said nothing. Instead, he raised his hand, palm out, to me, and I mirrored his. We pressed our palms together, dissolving the glass wall between us. Our fingers curled around each other's, locking our hands together.

"No regrets?" Heath whispered.

I shook my head the best I could, since I was lying down, and said, "Not yet."

Heath pulled his hand away and sat up on the bed. "I knew this was a bad idea. I said it was a bad idea," he complained. "It was—"

"A bad idea," I said. "Thank you very much, Heath."

"That's not what I meant. The sex itself was good—"

"How very kind of you," I interrupted, not knowing why I felt so angry but unable to stop myself.

"But I feel like it was a mistake to give in," Heath finished. "We've only succeeded in complicating things between us. I like our friendship. I don't want things to be awkward."

He turned around and sat on the bed with his back to me, so I got

up and stood in front of him. Unsure what to say and, more worri-
some still, knowing anything I said would probably make things
worse, I began to run my fingers through his hair. Heath reached out
and wrapped his arms around my waist, pulling me to him and
pressing his head into my stomach.

"We should get going," I finally said. Heath said nothing, so I
kept running my hands through his hair and said, "You know how
you hate to be late."

"OK," he said, but he didn't let me go.

After a minute, I said, "I don't think what happened was a bad
thing. I care about you. I love you. But as long as we both know that
reviving our relationship wouldn't work—"

"Which it wouldn't," he agreed.

"—then neither of us is going to get hurt," I said. I wasn't sure
that I believed myself, but I sounded awfully convincing.

Heath must have thought so too, because he lifted his head, his
chin pressed into my stomach, and said, "I hope so."

He looked adorable, and I couldn't help but think back to fifteen
minutes earlier when we were wrapped around each other in an
enjoyably sweaty moment of passion. My body reacted accordingly.

"Aw, hell," Heath said with a devilish gleam in his eye. "I guess
we can be a little late."

Tragic White Men were sharing the bill at Numbers nightclub
with two other bands. When we arrived at the crowded venue, the
first band, Tyz That Bind, was already playing. If the grinding noise
churning from their instruments could actually be called playing.
Heath grabbed my hand, pushed his way into the crowd, and yelled,
"Don't let go!"

"I won't let go, Jack!" I shouted, quoting *Titanic,* but my words
were lost in the noise of the club. Heath dragged me through the
crowd of college students, punks, and rockers. Even in my jeans and
black T-shirt, I felt out of place. As if I'd had GUPPIE stamped on my
forehead at the door, instead of the number sign on my hand that
indicated I was over twenty-one. But nobody paid any attention to us
as we muscled our way through the crowd in search of our friends.

We found Miranda and Patrick near the front of the stage, but off to the side of the room, so they wouldn't be pushed or struck by anyone on the dance floor. Not that there was much danger of that happening, since Patrick wore a look of defiance crossed with amusement as he stood against the wall, one hand stuffed in his pocket, the other holding a beer in a plastic cup.

"Hey!" Miranda yelled, spotting us and waving us over while trying not to spill something red in a huge plastic cup.

"It's about time you guys got here," Patrick bellowed. Pointing at the band onstage he said, "If I have to be subjected to this crap, it's only fair that you should too. What kept you? Were you two fucking or something?"

I had forgotten how blunt Patrick could be when he was drinking. Miranda, who'd been sipping her drink, stopped, her eyes bulging like a frog's. Unsure if I should answer Patrick and, if so, how, I simply rolled my eyes. Then Heath said, "Patrick, if we did, you'd be the first one we'd tell. In graphic detail, no less."

Patrick winced and made a face like someone had peed in his beer. Which I found surprising, since he was the one who'd bought me my first gay porn video. We'd even watched it together, pointing and laughing while mimicking the stilted dialogue.

"I'm going to the bar," Heath said. "What do you want?"

"Beer," I answered. Then, hoping he'd hear me, I shouted after him, "In a bottle!"

I glanced at Miranda, who was furtively scanning the crowd, most likely looking for a partner in her competition with Alexander. The crowd wasn't exactly rife with women. The ones that I could see were hanging on to men. Or each other. Then something occurred to me.

"Where's Vivian?" I asked.

Patrick and Miranda both started looking around the room. Miranda raised up on her toes, pointed into the crowd, and said, "There she is!"

I looked and saw Vivian, who was suddenly lifted from the writhing crowd above everyone's heads. As she surfed over the pulsing throngs of bodies, she saw us. She waved wildly with both hands, her mouth open with glee, as if saying, *Hey, look, Ma! No hands!*

"That's my girl!" Patrick yelled, then finished off his beer in one He-Man gulp.

Heath returned with two beers, both in bottles, and gave me one. Patrick belched loudly and said, "My turn."

"Hurry up," Miranda admonished. "Alexander's going on soon."

When he returned, Tyz That Bind finished their set and there was a break in the program while their instruments were taken off the stage and replaced with Tragic White Men's equipment. Everyone either stood in place, talking above the music on the sound system, or went to the bar for drinks.

Vivian pushed her way to us. When she reached our group, she said, "Hi! I think twenty different guys just touched my breasts. This place is great."

"Aren't you jealous?" Miranda asked Patrick. Patrick only shrugged and went back to the busy task of looking bored.

"I don't think the Girls have seen that much action in weeks," Vivian said, repositioning her bra.

Heath and I turned to the stage to see if Tragic White Men were anywhere near ready to play.

Miranda looked at the Girls, impressed, and said, "Mine haven't seen much action either. You'd think they would, since a Democrat is in the White House."

"Since he's been in office," Vivian said, "breasts everywhere have been on guard."

A voice took over the sound system and said, "Ladies and gentlemen, Tragic White Men!"

"C'mon!" Patrick said, suddenly becoming animated. He pushed us forward, and we elbowed our way toward center stage. Alexander and the rest of Tragic White Men strode onstage and picked up their respective instruments. They were a six-person band: bass, lead guitar, synthesizer, saxophone, and drums, with Alexander standing center stage. He picked up a guitar, which surprised me. In his old bands, he always played keyboards and sang harmony vocals, never the lead.

"I didn't know Alex could even play the guitar," Heath said. I just shrugged, since I had never seen his new band rehearse.

"Is this thing on?" Alexander asked, speaking into the microphone and adjusting a guitar strap over his shoulder. "All right. Let's go."

They launched into a raucous instrumental that showcased each performer as they took turns playing a central blues riff. The crowd was clapping to the driving beat, hooting and hollering while they played. Finally, the lead guitarist took over the rhythm and Alexander abandoned his guitar for a harmonica that he took out of his pocket. We cheered them on as the song grew louder and more insistent. I felt people pushing me into the lip of the stage and turned around to see a large majority of the audience dancing.

Everyone kept dancing, cheering, and singing along once they learned the choruses of songs like "Butterfly Guy," "Hate Me Or Mate Me," and "Emotional Baggage Claim." As the crowd grew increasingly active with each song, Heath was soon pressed into my backside. We watched the rest of Tragic White Men's performance with his hands holding onto my shoulders and his groin pressed into my ass. I wasn't complaining, and neither was he.

Vivian and Miranda were next to us, with Patrick standing behind them, keeping the crowd at bay.

"They're great!" Miranda hollered in my ear as Alexander led the band into a cover of "Ode to Boy" by Yaz. Then she noticed Heath's hands on my shoulders and raised an eyebrow.

"No," I said. "It's not like that."

She offered a sarcastic nod and returned her focus to the band. Actually, her eyes were riveted on Tragic White Men's female drummer, who looked like Miranda's type. Petite, yet butch, with short blond hair and a rosebud mouth set in grim determination as she pounded on her drum set.

"I'd like to thank you for coming to Numbers tonight," Alexander said, breathing hard after their rock version of "Ode to Boy." He wiped the sweat from his brow with his shirt sleeve as he continued speaking. "But more important, thanks for staying. This is Tragic White Men's first performance, and you've all been great. I hope you've had fun."

The crowd started yelling, and Alexander used the moment to take a drink from a bottle of water and tune a string on his guitar.

"OK! Great! This is our last song. It's called 'Keep the Deal.' I sort of wrote it for some friends of mine. Hope you like it."

He counted off to four, and the band started playing. Alexander looked down and flashed a grin at us before starting to sing.

> We're the kind of people who feel the loneliness of the crowd
> And even when we're together we know we're still alone
> It's only when we find ourselves that we know that we're at home
> 'Cause our fate is sealed without the deal
> We talk about it, laugh about it, but it all stays the same
> We try so hard to work it out, but we know we'll never change
> When boys love boys who love themselves there's never room for
>   your pain
> Keep your head held high, don't cry, don't whine
> You know you were right, she was never your type
> It could never work out, there are other fish in the sea
> And you may not have her, but you'll always have me
> I am for real, I'll keep the deal
> I watch myself with shame as I try to play the game
> She paints her lips with pride, but I know she feels the same
> He's lonely since he left, but he tells me there's no pain
> I'm hiding what I feel, but I know it's all in vain
> We keep our heads up high, we don't cry, or whine
> Never know if we're right, we are nobody's type
> It may never work out, there are other fish in the sea
> We may never have them, but you'll always have me
> I am for real, I'll keep the deal
> Are you for real? Please keep the deal

When the song was over, Alexander and the rest of Tragic White Men took bows while the audience roared in approval. They left the stage, leaving their instruments behind, presumably for the stage crew to remove, but the audience kept cheering so they returned for an encore.

"Can we play another song?" Alexander asked, shielding his eyes from the stage lighting and looking above our heads. "I'm getting a nod in the affirmative. It's a go, kids!"

With that, Alexander cleared his throat and launched into the opening line to the Eurythmics' "You Hurt Me (And I Hate You)." Alexander gave the cover song his all, his voice growling and spitting like a wounded animal caught in a trap.

"Annie Lennox would be proud," Heath said into my ear.

"I know I am!" I said.

When the band made their final exit, we pushed our way through the crowd to the balcony, where Alexander had promised to meet us after their performance. We knew it might take a while, since they had instruments to pack into cases, so we got more drinks from the bar and managed to find seats at a table.

"They were great," Vivian gushed. "I never knew Alexander was so talented. He's always taken a backseat in the bands he's been in before."

"I know," Heath agreed. "I had no idea he could play the guitar. I mean, he's got three of them. But I always assumed they were for decoration. I've never heard him play."

"I have," I said, thinking back to our college years, when Alexander used to play his acoustic guitar in his dorm room. "He taught himself. He doesn't think he's that good, so he doesn't usually play in front of people."

"I'd guess that since he has no control over his love life these days," Patrick surmised, "our boy Alex is taking charge of the one part of his life that he can. His music."

"Don't forget, he has a date with Blue Shorts. I mean, Zachary," I pointed out. Seeing Miranda frown, I said, "Sorry, hon."

"Don't worry about me," Miranda said, suddenly sitting up straight in her chair and running her hands through her hair. "I think you've got enough on your own plate to worry about, Aaron."

I tried to mask my nervousness by assuming an air of confusion, which was echoed by Vivian and Patrick. I didn't dare look at Heath. Instead, I asked, "Miranda, what are you talking about?"

"Oh, look. There's Alexander," she said.

Alexander bounded up to our table, obviously still riding high on a sea of adrenaline from Tragic White Men's performance. We all congratulated him on an excellent show, which he tried to wave away in a moment of bashful humility. But he thanked us nonetheless.

"I really messed up the chords of the bridge in 'Hate Me Or Mate Me,' but I didn't think anyone could tell. I mean, it's not like anyone knows the song. But it was so great to be onstage again. The manager said we could play here again next week. Plus, we'll get a cut of the profits at the door."

"That's great," Miranda said.

"Yeah," Alexander agreed, obviously pleased. "Just walking up here to find you guys, tons of people stopped me to tell me they liked our band. I think a lot of people will show up next week too."

"Will Zachary?" Miranda asked coyly. I was as curious as she was to know the answer.

"We'll see. He's a busy man. And we're playing Thursday night. Since he has to work the next day, it might not be possible. Our schedules are so different; he works during the day and my life happens at night." Alexander trailed off, lost in thought, until his eyes focused on Patrick and Vivian, and he said, "But you guys are in the same boat."

Patrick snorted and resumed his interest in his beer.

"Don't rock the boat, baby," Vivian said to Alexander.

"So, Alexander," Miranda piped up, "about this song you wrote for us."

"Not for you," he said, shifting uncomfortably. "About you. Us, I mean. What about it?"

"Nothing, really," Miranda said. She smiled and ran her finger around the rim of her cup. I assumed that her only intention was to make Alexander uncomfortable and, having succeeded, she would change the subject. She didn't disappoint me when she said, "I thought it was good. Were you nervous about playing tonight? I mean, you just put the band together a month ago."

"Yeah. We all were," he said. "Except Joey, of course."

"Which one's Joey?" Vivian asked.

"Our—" he began, but broke off when Tragic White Men's drummer strode up to our table. Miranda's eyes lit up, but she retained a calm and unaffected air when Alexander said, "Guys, this is Joey Mitchell. Our drummer."

"Yeah. We were there when she played drums with you," Patrick said.

"You guys were fantastic," Miranda said.

Joey nodded at Miranda with an air of indifference and said to Alexander, "The gear's all loaded in Kevin's van. I put your guitar and keyboard in my truck, just in case. Do you need a ride?"

Alexander looked around the table, and Patrick said, "I have to check on the bar. I'll drop you off on the way, buddy."

"You are not drinking and driving," Vivian admonished. "If you have to go to the bar, I'll take you. And I'll drop you home on the way, Alexander."

"Looks like I'm in good hands, Joey," Alexander said.

"Good hands and great tits too," Joey said.

"Thank you," Vivian said, pretending to adjust the Girls and laughing.

Miranda frowned briefly but quickly shook it off, resting her chin on her hand and resuming an alluring pose.

"I'll see you tomorrow," Joey said, clipping Alexander on his shoulder with a light punch. "Good show, man."

"Thanks, Joey," he said. "You rocked."

"I know," she said with a wicked grin and loped away from the table.

We stayed a while longer, rehashing the finer points of Tragic White Men's performance and listening to Alexander wax rhapsodic about his triumphant return to rock and roll. After about an hour, Patrick insisted on going by Dinks to check the receipts and make sure his bar was still standing. Since Vivian had designated herself Patrick's driver, she tossed his keys to Heath.

"Aaron drove you here, right? Would you baby-sit Patrick's car tonight? He can pick it up tomorrow," Vivian said.

"If there's one ding in my car, I'll kick your ass," Patrick slurred, leaning over the table and pointing a finger in Heath's face.

Vivian grabbed Patrick's hand and said, "If he does, call me and we'll rake him over the coals in court."

When they'd gone with Alexander, I stood and said, "I think I'm going to call it a night too. It's pretty late."

"Yeah," Heath agreed. He finished the rest of his drink, also stood, and said, "I have a lot of work to do tomorrow."

"I'll be grading tests all day tomorrow," I said.

Miranda snorted and sipped her drink.

"What did she say?" Heath asked me.

"I think she said—" I imitated the noise Miranda had made.

"What does that mean?"

"It could be a lesbian mating call; I'm not sure," I said. "If it is, it doesn't seem to be working."

"Very funny. You two don't fool me," Miranda said. "I know what's going on here."

"It's painfully obvious, isn't it? We're standing," I said derisively.

"People do that before they walk out of a bar, you know," Heath added.

"No. I mean the two of you and your grand charade," Miranda said, pointing at us and narrowing her eyes.

I knew she was trying to get us to slip up and admit our guilt. Not that I felt guilty about what had happened. But I didn't know if Heath wanted anyone to know about it, so I looked to him for a cue. I hoped Miranda would interpret my expression as *What is she talking about?* Instead of *What are we going to do?*

"Miranda, I think you've had enough to drink," Heath said. "Do you need one of us to drive you home?"

"I'm fine," she said. "Deny it all you want, but I've got your number."

"Good. Call me," I called after her as she walked away from us.

When she was gone, Heath said, "Do you think she's really on to us?"

"Do you really care?" I asked, trying not to sound offended.

"I feel like you and I are putting enough pressure on the situation between us," Heath explained. "We don't need everyone else adding to it. Besides, we both agreed that it was a one-time thing."

"Twice, actually," I corrected.

"Right. Twice. Whatever. But you know what I mean. It's not like it's going to happen again. Anyway, I don't know how Miranda could suspect anything."

"She gave me a look during Alexander's performance," I said. "I think she saw you holding on to my shoulders and drew her own conclusions."

"That's preposterous," Heath protested. "I was only hanging on to you for stability, because of the crowd. It was nothing more."

"Sure," I scoffed. "I could feel your stability pressing into my butt. You weren't enjoying yourself at all."

"It was an instinctual animal reaction," Heath said. "Anyway, I'm going. I'm sure she's gone now. Are you leaving too?"

"Yeah," I said, and we walked out together. In the parking lot, Heath found Patrick's car and, as we awkwardly stood beside it, I said, "I had a lot of fun tonight."

"Me too," Heath said. "Well, good night."

He reached out to embrace me, so I folded myself into his arms and said, "Good night."

I kissed his cheek and was about to let go when I felt him hug me a little tighter, so I didn't move. Eventually, he let his arms move lazily down my back and pulled away, our waists still touching. Heath bit his lower lip, then moved forward, kissing me tentatively. He drew his head back, but I reached up and pulled him to me again. Our tongues met, and he held me tightly against his body, moving his hips against mine.

I half expected Miranda to jump out from behind Patrick's car like a paparazzi photographer trying to get a picture of Kim Basinger and Alec Baldwin. But the only witness to our kiss was the moon.

Breathing hard, Heath said, "Follow me home?"

"I'll race you there," I said.

The next few days provided me plenty of challenges in regard to keeping our secret. For the first time in months, Patrick was coming home from Dinks instead of staying at Vivian's. Since Heath and I seemed to have developed an insatiable lust for each other, he'd come to my apartment and dash out before Patrick got home. Or I'd spend hours in his bed, then come home and sneak past Patrick, who'd be snoring on the sofa with the TV blaring. I felt like an unfaithful husband.

On his end of things, Heath said that Miranda had developed an annoying habit of dropping in on him without calling first. He wasn't sure if she was trying to catch him with me or if she was just enjoying the novelty of having him live so close. Somehow both of us managed not to get caught with each other, but we knew it was only a matter of time until our friends knew what was going on.

After we left Tragic White Men's second performance separately, I drove around for a while and finally ended up back at his house.

"I'm exhausted," Heath said, letting me in. "How do unfaithful spouses manage this?"

"I don't know." I yawned. "I spent this whole week at school forcing myself to stay awake until three o'clock every day."

"You!" Heath said. "I was drooling on my keyboard. When Dr. Voss asked me for some research material on stem cells, I told him it was in 'Aaron's apartment' instead of 'Anne's department.' I've got to start getting to bed earlier."

"Just one more workday this week," I comforted him, "then it's the weekend. And next week is spring break for me, thank God."

We undressed and climbed into his bed. We held each other a while, then Heath started laughing.

"What?" I asked.

"I just realized that neither one of us wants to have sex. Are we getting old or what?"

"We're pathetic," I agreed. "But this is nice, actually. Just holding each other."

"I like it too." When I yawned again, he did too. "What are you going to do next week?"

"I don't know. No plans. I never make a big deal out of spring break. It's too bad you just started your job. You could take a few days off. We could go somewhere together. Galveston, or something."

"It'll be packed with partying students," he said.

I held him until he started snoring, then I stared at the ceiling for a while. I knew I should go home, but I was too comfortable.

The next thing I knew, Heath was shaking me awake, saying, "Aaron, you'll be late for school!"

"Shit," I said, sitting up and looking around to orient myself. "What time is it?"

"Six."

"Oh. I'm OK then. I've got plenty of time to get home and shower. I can't believe I fell asleep over here. I wonder if Patrick stayed at Vivian's last night?"

"Beats me." He found his glasses and crawled out of bed. Then he turned around to look at me. "You could shower here."

I made it to St. Gregory's just as the first bell rang. When I hurried down the hall, trying to adjust my tie, I nearly ran into Paul Nettles as he stepped out of his classroom.

"Cutting it a little close, aren't you, lover boy?" Paul asked, leering at me.

"You know what it's like to fuck and run," I snapped, grateful there were no students nearby. "Or maybe you don't. It's probably your prospective tricks who do all the running."

My adrenaline was going full blast when I called roll, as much from the exchange with Paul as from barely making it to class. I knew I was living dangerously to taunt such a vindictive old queen.

I was limp by the time I got home that evening and listened to my messages. My mother wanted me to call her back, as did Heath. I called him first.

"Just wanted to warn you," Heath said, "Miranda's coming over for dinner. She usually stays late. I don't mean to sound like I'm assuming you wanted to get together—"

"It's OK," I said. "Thanks for the heads-up. Why don't I call you tomorrow?"

"I wanted to run an idea by you," Heath said. "I'm driving to San Antonio Sunday night to take notes at a medical conference for Dr. Voss. I'll be there until Wednesday. If you still don't have any plans…"

"I'd love to," I said. "In fact, I'm thinking about spending the weekend with my folks. I don't have to tell Patrick how long I'm staying with them."

"Perfect," Heath said. "I'm starting to get off on this furtive stuff. Do you think that says something awful about my character?"

"I hope so."

He laughed and hung up, and I dialed my parents' number.

"Hi," my mom said. "I've got news."

"Good news?"

"Of course. Stasi and Tad found out the sex of their baby today. It's another boy."

"Are they excited? Did they want a girl this time, so Sister could have someone to play Barbies with?"

My mother laughed and said, "They don't care. You know them. If they gave birth to a fairy, they'd adjust."

"Our family does have the gene," I said.

She snorted and said, "You know I didn't mean that. Are you still driving out tomorrow?" I loved the way she always said it as if I lived thousands of miles away instead of twenty.

"Would you mind if I came tonight?" I asked. "I was going to stay until Monday, but now I need to leave Sunday night. I'll explain when I get there."

"Your room's all ready," she said.

Once I was stuck in outbound, rush-hour traffic, I remembered why most of my friends refused to venture outside the 610 Loop. If you looked up "urban sprawl" in the dictionary, the definition was probably Houston. It was the land of concrete, with one discount superstore/nails and hair salon/furniture/liquor store–clogged shopping center indistinguishable from the rest. Once you drove beyond these tributes to commerce, you hit the residential sections, planned communities with their cookie-cutter houses and sparse trees, all baking under an unrelenting sun.

My parents lived in Champions, one of the older northwest suburbs, so there was more foliage to offset the sameness of the homes, but Miranda had aptly described it years before as "tract housing for the rich." My parents weren't wealthy—certainly not the way Miranda's River Oaks family was, or even Alexander's family, who owned a beautiful home in the West U area, both of which were Houston's older, more distinguished neighborhoods. But we'd lived near a golf course, the schools had been good, and I had no resentment about growing up as a middle-class suburban kid.

That night after dinner, while my father was glued to the Discovery channel, my mother came upstairs and sat on the bed next to me. "Why do I get the idea you have a secret?" she asked.

"Because you're my mother. I'm not supposed to get away with anything."

"Are you up to something?"

"I am," I admitted. "Mom, Heath and I have sort of started seeing each other again." I held up a hand to stop her from saying anything. "I don't know what will come of it. We're just enjoying this for whatever it is."

"I like Heath," she said. "I'd hate to see the two of you hurt each other again. Be careful, Aaron."

"Hopefully since we're a little older, we're a little smarter," I said. "The thing is, we're trying to keep it simple, so we aren't telling our friends yet. He's invited me to San Antonio for a few days the beginning of the week, and I'm letting everyone think I'm hanging out with you guys."

My mother laughed and said, "It's been years since I covered for one of my kids."

"I don't remember you *ever* covering for one of us," I complained.

"I just didn't let you know it," she said.

I spent Saturday helping my father clean out the garage. Kelly, Stasi, TP, and Tad came for dinner. The next morning, I stayed in bed while my parents went to church. It was just like old times.

When Heath picked me up, we ate an early dinner with my parents. I could tell that my mother had warned my father not to pry, but they both treated Heath with extra-special care, as if they were afraid I was going to make him disappear like I had eight years before.

When we were finally on the road, Heath glanced at me and said, "I love your family."

"I know. They love you too. Heath, no matter what happens between us, I never want you to feel like you're not part of the Fishers. You always will be."

He reached for my hand, and we rode in silence for a while.

"I broke the rules Friday night," Heath said.

"The rules?" I asked, feeling a sense of panic. I didn't remember agreeing to any rules, but I wasn't prepared to hear they'd already been broken.

"I let Miranda whine."

"Oh," I breathed. "I didn't know what the hell you were talking about. Another conquest gone bad?"

"More like one who won't give her the time of day," Heath said. "She's completely infatuated with Joey."

"Joey!" I yelped. "She's interested in a *guy*?"

Heath laughed and said, "The drummer for Tragic White Men. Where is your head?"

"I know where it'll be in a few hours," I said. "Is Joey a dyke?"

"I'm pretty sure her fascination with Vivian's cleavage is a clue," Heath said. "She didn't even look at poor Miranda."

"Poor Miranda, my ass," I said. "Serves her right, after all the women she's dumped."

"Aaron—"

"I know. Rally 'round our friend, and all that."

"Actually, don't tell her that I told you. I don't think she intends to bring it up at the Love Sucks meeting on Thursday night."

"What? That'll be a first."

"I get the idea she doesn't want Alex to know. Not only would he torment her about it, but he might say something to Joey."

"Miranda has never kept anything about her love life to herself," I noted. "Yours are the only secrets she keeps. Did you tell her about us?"

"Nope."

"You really are enjoying sneaking around, aren't you?" I teased.

"It's fun," he admitted.

Fun was definitely the theme of our time away together. While he attended the conference, I languished by the pool at the upscale hotel, enjoying all the perks of vacationing on someone else's money. At night, we ate dinner together and strolled along San Antonio's River Walk, feeling a little bit like honeymooners. As a special treat, we found a place where we could get a couple massage, lying on tables placed side by side. While water trickled into a nearby fountain, our muscles were kneaded and soothed into complete relaxation. After our therapists were finished, we were told to lie still and enjoy the aromatherapy for a while.

I turned my head to look at him, and he held out his hand. We lay there for another half hour without saying a word, just enjoying our clasped fingers.

"I wish we didn't have to go back tomorrow," Heath finally said.

"It's been incredible. You're free to come up with all the brilliant plans you want to."

That night was the first time I'd have described our sex as lovemaking. It was as if the massage had broken down a final barrier between us and surrounded us with magic.

"What are you doing to me?" Heath whispered, keeping his eyes closed, even though the only light came from outside our windows.

"It isn't just you," I promised. "It's me too."

He smiled but kept his eyes closed. I moved over to rest my head on his shoulder, and we fell asleep wrapped around each other.

When he took me to my parents' on Wednesday afternoon, we agreed not to talk again until the next night. I stayed in the suburbs, getting back on Thursday night in time to meet the rest of the gang and celebrate St. Patrick's Day together with a Love Sucks meeting.

Heath and I didn't have to worry about anyone catching on to us, however, as our own Patrick seemed to have nothing to celebrate. Apparently I'd missed some sort of drama during my days away from my roommate. But Patrick's drama was like a silent movie. He'd go through the motions, moping quietly around the house, or sitting in front of the television, but he'd never voice his problems to anyone. Unlike the rest of us, who would practically rent a billboard or pay for airtime during the Super Bowl so everyone could hear about our latest agony.

Miranda, like a country doctor in *Little House on the Prairie,* often made house calls for her wealthier clients, taking her jewelry into their homes if they had a special occasion. Or if the special occasion was a new credit card with no limit, Miranda would be at their home faster than you could say "Charge." One of these clients, who had friends in the publishing industry, had worn some of Miranda's pieces to a magazine launch party. Not only was the socialite photographed wearing the jewelry, but the magazine's fashion editor ran a mention in the March issue.

"Look," Miranda said to us, pointing to the magazine and passing it to me. "This is my jewelry, on page thirty. And they list all the places in Houston that carry my stuff. Isn't that cool?"

We passed the magazine around our table outside of Crossroads Market and Books. Patrick barely glanced at the magazine before passing it to Heath, who oohed appreciatively over the glossy photograph then passed it to Alexander, who said, "So this is why you're going to New York next week? I don't get it."

Miranda took the magazine back and said, "I've been getting all these calls from buyers in Manhattan who want to sell my jewelry in their stores. I'm going to meet with some of them and see if it's worth it."

"Face it, babe," Alexander said. "You're hot!"

"If only the lesbians in town thought so too," Miranda said.

"And so it begins," Patrick moaned.

"Nope," Miranda said. "That's it. I've had no dates since our last meeting. No flirtations, no flings, no nothing. I'm not going to whine about it, either. I'm going to remain positive, because at least my career seems to be picking up. Maybe it's for the best that I'm a frigid, neglected single woman."

"At least you're not complaining about it," Alexander jested.

"Anyway, I'd rather hear about your suit-and-tie butterfly guy," Miranda said to Alexander, pointedly ignoring his sarcasm.

"There's not much to tell, really," Alexander said, which I found hard to believe. Whenever Alexander started a new romance, he'd shout it from the rooftops. And whenever he got fucked over by a man, he'd shout that from the rooftops too. "Zachary has been really busy lately, so we haven't been able to get together much."

"Much?" I repeated. "What exactly is the measurement of 'much' these days? One, two dates a week? An hour in a public bathroom?"

"I've met him for lunch a few times. Nothing major," Alexander explained. "But he bought me this great watch. Look."

Alexander pulled back the sleeve of his denim jacket to reveal a G-Shock watch that looked like it could launch missiles if you pushed the right button. Knowing the watch was expensive, we all masked our silent skepticism of Zachary's motives with words of approval.

"It's really nice," Heath said, then cut his eyes to me with an expression of concern.

"It looks really cool," Miranda said. "Where does Zachary live? Has he had you over for dinner yet?"

"Not yet. I've been busy with the band, and he's been working late anyway. I don't know where he lives, now that you mention it. It hasn't come up," he said.

"That answered my question," I said.

"Oh, no," Alexander laughed, "*that* has come up. I blew him in the car on the way back from lunch."

"Dude! Way too much information," Patrick protested, pushing his chair back from the table. Two guys at the next table, overhearing Alexander's confession, tittered with laughter. Patrick turned to them and joked, "What are you guys talking about? Can I join you?"

"Get back here!" Alexander insisted, grabbing the arm of Patrick's chair and dragging him back to our table. "Anyway, we're still taking it slow. So I don't have anything to talk about either."

We sat in silence, drinking our coffee and watching the traffic drive down Westheimer. During our conversation, I had pointedly avoided any eye contact with Miranda. If eyes were, in fact, windows to the soul, I wanted to keep the blinds drawn so she wouldn't see what was going on between Heath and me. Neither of us wanted to talk about our assignations with the rest of our friends, especially not during the Love Sucks gatherings. Besides, our clandestine meetings were about lust, not love. At least that's what I kept telling myself.

Miranda flipped through her magazine, Patrick seemed lost in thought, Alexander was watching the other people seated on the patio, and Heath was repeatedly humming a television jingle, which I knew would be stuck in my head for the rest of the day. I kept expecting Patrick to leap from his seat and make up an excuse to leave, but he didn't. I could tell something was wrong, but I couldn't think of what it would be. I wasn't sure if Vivian had a spring break too, but since she wasn't with us I figured law school was either keeping her busy or she'd gone out of town. Considering Patrick's mood, it seemed best not to ask.

An elderly man in an electric wheelchair appeared from around the corner of the building, lazily gliding along with a smile. His chair was decked out for the holiday like a float in a one-man parade, with bright green shamrocks, streamers, and balloons. He wore a green hat on his head, a green cardigan sweater, and oversize green elf shoes. Every three minutes, he'd honk a horn and throw confetti in the air, shouting, "Happy Paddy's Day, everybody!"

The people at the tables around us smiled and returned his greeting, until a bus came by and picked him up. I waited five minutes, then said, "What the hell is wrong with you people?"

Four heads snapped up and stared at me in confusion.

"What the hell is wrong with you?" Patrick asked.

"I just asked you the same thing," I said. "You were sulking before I went to my parents', and I see nothing's changed."

"I never sulk," Patrick said, then resumed sulking.

"Did none of you see the wacky man on the wheelchair who just went by?" I asked. "He was here for a good fifteen minutes, and not one of you made your usual sarcastic comments. On a normal day, Miranda would've said something like, 'That sweater does *not* match those shoes.' Alexander would've sung, 'When Irish Chairs Are Rolling.' But you guys are sitting there like—like—"

"A shamrock on a log?" Heath offered.

"A bump on a leprechaun's ass?" asked Patrick.

"That's gross," Miranda said.

"Whatever. This has been the most boring Love Sucks meeting yet. I can't believe neither of you has anything to tell us," I said, indicating Alexander and Miranda. Pointing at Patrick, I continued, "And obviously something is wrong with you, because you have nothing to say at all. Which is not in your nature."

"If something is wrong," Patrick said, "I'm not going to whine about it in these insipid little meetings. And I'm sure as hell not going to broadcast it on the patio of Crossroads."

Hearing that, several of the guys at neighboring tables stopped eavesdropping and resumed their own conversations.

"So you admit there's something going on that you're not telling us?" I asked him.

"No. I admit nothing," Patrick said. "You worry about your own problems, Aaron, and I'll worry about mine. OK?"

I made the mistake of glancing at Miranda, whose eyes caught mine in a scrutinizing stare. "If anyone here does have something they're not sharing," she said, sounding like an Army officer interrogating a prisoner of war, "maybe they'll bring it up in the next Love Sucks gathering. Until then, if nobody has anything they'd like to get off their chests, I think our meeting is over." We all exchanged questioning glances, except for Miranda, who kept her eagle eye on Heath and me, but nobody appeared to have anything else to say. "All right, then," Miranda said. "Let's go to Dinks and get wasted in true Irish spirit."

Earth Day

I kept a close eye on Patrick over the next couple of weeks, waiting for an opening to ask him what was going on with him. Since I worked during the day, I wasn't sure how often he and Vivian saw each other. He was always at Dinks at night, but the two or three times I stopped in there was no sign of his girlfriend. Heath agreed with me that Patrick wouldn't respond well to being pushed for explanations. I figured that sooner or later he'd break down and tell me the reason for his ill humor.

The other disadvantage of his bad mood was that I didn't feel as if I could talk to him about Heath and me. Patrick never reduced serious things to scintillating gossip. Instead, he'd take an approach that would give me fresh insight, and I missed that.

On the other hand, it wasn't like I saw what was going on with Heath and me as a problem. After San Antonio, we'd stopped feeling like we were racing to get in all the good times we could before the other shoe dropped. So far, complications had not set in. We talked about work and our friends, shared dinners, and made love without worrying about where we were going.

Alexander's grandmother had asked for and been given a performance by Tragic White Men. Alex had dropped hints about the band making a demo, and he was sure it was only a matter of time until Grandma Casey coughed up a check. Rehearsals, performances, and sporadic meetings with Zachary kept him away from the gym, but he'd gotten into the habit of calling me in the early evenings to catch me up on what was going on with him.

Miranda called Heath after her New York trip, but only to let him know that she was going back with a couple of proposals for some major orders. She promised to fill everyone in at the next Love Sucks meeting. Heath and I were both grateful that her preoccupation with her work kept her from quizzing him about me. Or maybe, like I had so many times, she'd just hit a stone wall when it came to getting answers about his private life from Heath.

Except for Patrick's moodiness, I was enjoying a prolonged period of contentment. So I was completely unprepared for disaster when it did strike, and I was scared enough to bypass everyone from whom I usually sought advice and run straight to Vivian.

My phone call had prepared her for something serious, so when I met her for dinner at one of Houston's few quiet restaurants, she'd gotten there before me and ordered for both of us, promising our waiter she'd tip him double if he'd keep the host and other service people away from us. She was in full lawyer mode.

"Just talk," Vivian ordered, "and if I have any questions I'll jump in."

"My headmaster, Bill Westin, called me in for a conference today," I said. "To ask me about a situation that's been brought to his attention. Bill's been at St. Gregory's as long as I have, and he's always known I'm gay. It's a nonissue for him. And in all these years, it's never been an issue with any parents either. I've had a couple of colleagues who've made remarks from time to time, but Bill has always let me know that nothing matters to him but my work."

"OK," Vivian said when I paused.

"One of the newer teachers at St. Gregory's, Leslie, came to us from Lamar High. This week, she got a call from a teacher there, who mentioned me by name and repeated a rumor she'd heard. Leslie thought about coming to me, but she decided Bill would be my best ally. I'm glad she talked to him, because if this becomes a problem, I'll need him in my corner. Apparently, someone has implied that I'm dating a student."

"One of *your* students?" Vivian asked.

"No. That would be too improbable, since I teach the middle grades. As far as I know, Lamar's where the rumor started, so I guess it must be a Lamar student. I assured Bill there was absolutely no truth to it, and he believes me. The problem is, this is the kind of thing that doesn't need to be true to blow up in my face. As Bill said, in cases like this, perception is reality. Bill advised me to be a bit proactive just in case it turns into something. He wasn't specific about what he meant, and his opinion was that our discussion was private and doesn't need any follow-up. But I thought maybe I should talk to an attorney, just in case."

"Aaron, you know I'm just a law student—"

"Oh, I know, and I don't expect you to give me legal advice. But I figured you can get me the name of an attorney who not only has experience with situations like this but would be, I don't know…"

"Gay-friendly?"

"Exactly."

"I can do that," she said. "Meanwhile, you need to figure out any possible situation you've been in that could have been misconstrued by someone."

"Are you kidding? It's all I've been thinking about. And I can't come up with anything. I know I have to be more careful than most teachers to avoid even the appearance of impropriety. I only meet with students during school hours. Usually a parent or another staff member is present. If not, we meet in the classroom, and I keep my door open. Any outside activities I participate in always involve a group of students and other teachers. Vivian, this is like my worst nightmare. I'm scared shitless, and I haven't even done anything wrong."

"Was there any indication that it's a student who's saying this about you? Do you even know any Lamar students?"

"Not that I can think of. Nor can I think of a way any of them would know me. I'm just a teacher, Vivian. At a private school, so I'm not exactly high-profile in the district. As for my personal life, hell, you know about that. I go out, but always with friends, and the bars I go to are just as likely to be straight bars as gay bars. I don't pick up tricks, young or otherwise. I can't figure out where this got started."

Vivian frowned and said, "That's why these kinds of things are so insidious. When your only weapon is the truth, and it's your word against someone else's, you have to know who the someone else is. I'm so sorry, Aaron. I know this must be awful for you."

"It makes me sick. Because even if nothing ever comes of it, if it's never more than just an ugly rumor, it could still affect my career. I love what I do. From time to time, Bill has suggested that I get an administrative credential, but I don't want to leave the classroom."

"For what it's worth, I agree with your headmaster. About you being proactive, I mean. An experienced attorney may even have some insight into how these things get started. I'll talk to some of my professors and other contacts and get a list of names for you. But let me caution you about a couple of things. Don't choose counsel based on cost. And I mean that either way. The most expensive attorney's not necessarily any better than the cheapest. Also, don't assume your attorney has to be gay to understand the situation or fight for you. You want someone whose only agenda is *you*. And your case, if it should ever come to that."

"I hadn't thought that far ahead," I said. "I'm still in the shocked phase, I guess. Hoping it will all go away."

"It very well could. You know what they say: Hope for the best; prepare for the worst."

"At least I feel better after talking to you. Bill was great, but he's in a delicate position. He has to look out for the best interests of the school, no matter how much he may like me personally. With you, I feel like someone's on my side, no matter what."

"Anyone who knows you, Aaron, knows you'd never do anything improper with a student. Hell, with anyone. You're probably one of the most trustworthy, honest people I've ever known."

I thought about Heath and me and felt like I'd forfeited my right to her assessment of my character. Which I knew was ridiculous. Heath and I were adults and entitled to our privacy, even with our friends.

"God, I've been so freaked out since I talked to Bill. Let's talk about something else," I suggested.

"Patrick?"

"Now that you brought him up, yes," I agreed.

"Has he told you anything?"

"No. I just know he's in a bad mood, and he sleeps at home every night. I don't want to pry, but it's obvious something is wrong with you two."

"You could say we're on a break," Vivian admitted. "My idea. You guys always joke about me being Superwoman, but I'm not. I didn't know how much I was overextending myself until I realized I was in danger of getting a *B* in Environmental Law. I can't do that. I've only got one more year. If I have to sacrifice my social life to get through it, then that's what I'm going to do."

I could tell by her defiant tone that this was an argument she'd already had with Patrick. As an undergraduate, I would probably have been on Patrick's side and urged her to relax. But I was a little older and wiser now, and I could remember well the damage these same arguments had done to my relationship with Heath.

"I think you should do what you have to," I said. "Patrick will come around."

"I'm not so sure about that," Vivian said. "I didn't know Patrick when he was caught up in the corporate world. I don't hold it against him that he left it to open his own business. Patrick thinks I don't respect him. Or that I think he doesn't work as hard as people who put in twelve hours in an office every day. I'm not some kind of snob, Aaron. I can see that he's happy with his life. I even understand why he wants more of my time and attention. But our timing is off."

"But like you said, you've only got another year—"

"And then what? Even if I get a job in Houston, I'll be busting my ass at some law firm. Patrick's at a point where he's thinking of moving to the next level. Buying a house, starting a family. That's not in the cards for me for a while. When one person works all day, and the other works all night, how do you fit a marriage and kids into that? I know people do it. But it overwhelms me to think about it. I need some breathing space."

"I see what you mean," I said, a little surprised by what she was telling me. I'd obviously fallen into the usual trap of underestimating Patrick. Somehow I'd thought the two of us were going to drift along as roommates for years.

"Honestly," Vivian added, "I can party as hard as the next person. I like to cut loose now and then. I don't want to jump from the rigors of law school to juggling a career with a family. Don't get me wrong; Patrick understands all of this intellectually. But that doesn't mean it makes him happy."

"No, it sure doesn't mean that," I said, thinking of his moodiness. "But he loves you, Vivian. I really believe it's something you can work out. If you both want to."

"You and Heath didn't."

"We gave up too easily," I said. "And we were a lot younger than you and Patrick. Besides, a gay couple has an entirely different set of pressures."

"Don't be so sure of that."

I decided not to go down that road with her, not wanting to cross any boundaries in my friendship with Patrick by learning too much about their problems. In any case, she didn't seem inclined to say anything else. It made me respect her even more; she knew she was walking a fine line by confiding in me, because I was both Patrick's roommate and one of his oldest friends.

However, she'd made me feel better about my situation, so that when I told Heath the whole story in bed later, I was much calmer than I had been. When I finished, I tried to decipher his frown.

"What are you thinking?" I finally asked.

"I'm not sure how to put it into words," he said. "Give me a minute."

I got us both some water, then crawled back into bed. "Well?" I asked, needing to hear his perspective.

"My mother told me something once," Heath said. "I was taking a writing class at Ole Miss, and I showed her one of my stories. It was pretty bad. I was trying to mix my fiction with my politics, and it was coming across heavy-handed. I wish I could remember exactly what she said, because it made a big difference in how I began approaching things. But she talked a little bit about what it was like to be a single mother. An unwed mother, in fact. She said that she always felt like she had to be better at it than other mothers. She put all this pressure on herself because she perceived that society automatically regarded her as…less than. If that makes sense."

"I can understand that."

"Sometimes, that's what we do as gay men. You know, *I've got to be better than everyone else. I'm starting out with this strike against me. So I have to be more circumspect, more driven, more perfect.* You remember what a lady my mother was. But in essence, she said to me, 'Fuck them, Heath. You are not less than anybody because you didn't have a father. And you are not less than anybody because you're gay. Don't make it an issue, because it isn't one.' At the time, I thought she was being naive. Just because it's not fair doesn't mean it's not real."

"Right."

"But when I started working, I began to see what she meant. I know my field has different pressures from yours. But I had homophobic managers who didn't want me on projects because they knew I was gay. There were times I knew I was treated unfairly. But what I came to understand was that a lot of times I was buying into it. I carried this irritant inside of me that made me think I deserved that kind of treatment. Assholes know how to use that little bit of shame against us, Aaron. That's what somebody's doing to you. You know damn well that you've done nothing wrong. And you know that any teacher, straight or gay, can't afford these kinds of accusations. But you're *grateful* that your colleague went to Bill. You're grateful that Bill wants to give you his support. You're even *grateful* that Vivian doesn't think you're some kind of child molester. Do you think a straight teacher would say what you're saying? Why should you be grateful? You're innocent, and you're a great teacher. Isn't that enough to entitle you to their support? They're not doing you a favor. They're doing the right thing. Which is exactly what you deserve."

"All I'm saying is that I'm happy they're doing the right thing."

"No, it's not. You're saying that you're happy they're doing the right thing even though you're gay. Well, I say what my mother said. Fuck that. Being gay is not a flaw. The reason you're not perfect is because you're human. And so is everyone else."

"That all sounds really pretty, Heath, but I *am* at greater risk. That's just a cold, hard fact."

"Only if you let it be. If you're going to buy into Bill's 'perception is reality' bullshit, then your perception is just as real as the next person's."

"This is getting way too serious. I don't want to fight about it."

"I'll bet you don't," Heath said.

"What does that mean?"

"It means you'd rather be *grateful* to me for reacting the way you want me to and saying the things you want to hear."

"You don't have to get nasty."

"Sure I do. That's the only way you'll have an excuse to run away."

"Who said I want to run away?"

Heath laughed and said, "Look at yourself. Your whole body is tensed, ready to spring from this bed, get dressed, and leave angry. Just like old times, huh?"

"Maybe I'm tense because you're pissing me off."

"Maybe I'm pissing you off because I'm right."

"God, I *hate* these kinds of arguments."

Heath shrugged and said, "You hate any arguments. Get a lawyer. Do whatever you think you should to protect yourself. But if you're doing it from some position of moral inferiority, you've already lost."

"Thanks, Heath, now I feel a lot better."

"Oh, no you don't," he said, gripping my arm when I swung my legs out of bed. "We can kiss and make up, or you can stay here mad, but you are not walking out on me."

I glared at him, but he seemed unperturbed. When I saw that little twitch at one corner of his mouth, I felt angry all over again.

"Don't laugh at me."

"Stay here," Heath said. "I'll be right back."

When he came back from the kitchen, he held out a bowl of ice cream. "You can eat it in bed. You can even lick the bowl."

"I'm not a kid."

"If I were treating you like a kid," Heath said, sitting on the edge of the bed and taking a spoonful of ice cream, "I'd do this."

When he tried to put the spoon in my mouth, I jerked my head away and the ice cream trailed across my cheek. We both started laughing, and Heath leaned forward to lick the ice cream off my face.

"I want to stay mad," I whined.

"You're so easy," he whispered in a taunting voice. "You can resist me, but you can't hold out against mocha fudge."

"You just better be glad you didn't bring any wimpy vanilla in here," I said.

"Nothing vanilla in this bed tonight," Heath assured me.

He was as good as his word, and we made a huge, sticky mess of ourselves and the sheets before we were done.

"It's killing you, isn't it," I asked later, "to lie here in all this. You want to change the sheets and take a shower."

"Not as bad as it's killing you that I got around your bad temper," he retorted.

"Uh, considering that those weren't exactly complaints you heard a few minutes ago, I wonder who's maneuvering whom?"

"Nice try," he said.

I kissed him and sat up, saying, "I really do have to go now. I'll be in a foul mood tomorrow if I don't get some sleep."

I laughed as I let myself out. I could hear that he was already pulling the sheets off the bed.

Vivian came through for me, and early the next week I told Bill that I needed a personal day and asked for a substitute so I could meet with the attorney she'd recommended.

Grant Coker was a partner in a large downtown firm, and I felt better as soon as I walked into his office. In his mid-forties, he was the epitome of conservatism, with his dark blue suit, subdued tie, and salt-and-pepper hair. He even passed the ultimate test of a successful member of the Texas old boy network—he was wearing expensive, but authentic, cowboy boots with his suit. After giving me a firm handshake, he sat next to me on a sofa in his office, a legal pad propped on his lap, and listened as I gave him all the details that I knew. When I finished by telling him that Vivian had thought he might be able to speculate about the source of the rumor, he nodded briskly.

"Most often, it's a case of wires getting crossed," Grant said. "Let me give you some hypotheticals. A couple of teachers at Lamar are whispering about a teacher who's dating a student. In this case, it's a little racier because of the same-sex factor. Another teacher comes in, and they start telling her the gossip. A fourth walks in just as the third teacher says something like, 'I wonder who it is. I only know a couple of gay teachers. Like what's-his-name, Aaron something, over at St. Gregory's.' The fourth teacher finds out what they're talking about, only now he's connected your name to the story. The next time it gets repeated, suddenly you're the guy who's dating a student. See how that works?" I nodded. "Another possibility is that the rumor is a malicious attempt to get back at you for some perceived wrong."

"Like a student with a bad grade or something?"

"Depends on the age of the student. For example, in cases of molestation, young children seldom lie. Teenagers—well, I've known them to lie about a teacher just because they didn't get to leave class when they wanted to, or they didn't like a homework assignment. But the sad fact is that sometimes it takes an adult to be that vindictive about another adult. Someone who got passed over for a promotion that went to you. Someone who got in trouble because you blew the whistle about something he or she did. In your particular situation, it could be somebody who has a moral issue with your being gay. Or maybe you just pissed off somebody. You have any enemies?"

"Me? I don't—" I broke off, thinking of Paul Nettles. "Maybe."

I told him about my acrimonious relationship with Paul and how I'd humiliated him that night with Bobby.

"Do you know if Bobby is still in high school?" Grant asked.

"He didn't say. He said he was eighteen; he could be a senior. He doesn't live far from Lamar. So now what?"

"First of all, keep in mind that we're dealing with two separate issues. One, your homosexuality. So far, you don't perceive a negative consequence of that on your employment. Second, a rumor that you're dating a student. Your headmaster gave you a heads-up without advising you what to do about it. Right now, my best advice would be to do nothing. Rumors blow over, especially if there's not a party—Bobby or anyone else—who feels wronged by you. If the student is Bobby, and he was telling you the truth about being eighteen, there's no legal issue. He's of age. However, just in case it becomes an ethical issue because some of your school's parents hear the rumor and demand that action be taken, I'd like for you to write an account of your meeting with your headmaster. Get him to sign it if you can, though I doubt he will. People tend to be shy about signing things that could end up in court. If you're asked to sign anything, don't. Let me see it first. Send me a copy of your employment contract and your school's policy for employees, grievance procedures, or any other documents you think may be relevant. If your headmaster asks for another conference, don't meet with him alone. I can give you more informed advice on that after I read St. Gregory's policies. Meanwhile, there's no charge for this initial consultation. If it becomes necessary for you to retain an attorney, and you want me to represent you, we'll discuss my fee then. Fair enough?"

"Yes," I said with relief.

"One other thing. Don't discuss this with your colleagues. Even ones who seem sympathetic to you. Especially not with Paul. Sometimes my clients are their own worst enemies. Just do your job, carry on as best you can, and hopefully you and I won't have to talk about this again."

I left his office wishing I had my gym bag with me, since I was already downtown. I knew a good workout would help me get rid of the last of my stress. I drove home to get it and found Patrick staring at a dark television.

"Did the TV die?" I asked.

"Nope. I was watching a *Full House* rerun and realized that when Michelle says, 'You got it, dude,' she sounds just like me. I turned it off. You're home early."

"I had an off-campus meeting, so I took the day off. I'm going to work out."

"I've been meaning to ask you about that," Patrick said. "How much is your membership at the Y?" After I told him, explaining that it was a family membership because Alex was on it, he nodded and said, "Mind if I tag along? I'm thinking of joining."

"Great," I said. "I could use another workout partner, since Alex always flakes on me."

I wondered if Patrick wanted to get himself in better shape because he felt like Vivian had made him single again. Or maybe he was like I used to be, determined to flaunt my remade self in front of anyone who'd rejected me.

I left Patrick with a Y representative at the front desk and went downstairs to work out. It was still early enough to be slow, so I didn't have to wait for any of my favorite machines. By the time I finished and headed for the locker room, the place was filling up with all the corporate drones who used the gym to delay hurling themselves into suburb-bound, gridlocked traffic. Texans love their cars, so I wondered if we'd ever actually get the public transportation that had been in the "planning" stage for as long as I could remember.

I caught up with Patrick in the whirlpool. "Rough workout, dear?" I asked. "I didn't see you downstairs."

"I came through on my guided tour," he said. "You were busy leering at some weasel in gray shorts. A few guys I know from Dinks were playing basketball, so that's where I stayed."

"To watch or to play?"

"Baby steps," Patrick said with a grin, then closed his eyes and leaned his head back.

I did the same, letting the water finish the job of washing away my problems, refusing to think about lawyers and vicious queens.

Over the next few days, I found it possible to shove the entire incident to the back of my mind. Neither Leslie nor Bill said anything else about it to me. I sent the requested documentation to Grant Coker. Heath brought it up once, apologizing in case he'd seemed unsupportive and telling me that he was always willing to listen if I needed to talk. But I was hopeful that Grant was right and the whole thing would blow over.

It was Alexander who came up with the idea for our next Love Sucks meeting. In celebration of the fact that Houston had achieved the dubious honor of becoming smoggier than Los Angeles, he suggested we throw caution to the wind and have a picnic on Earth Day, inviting mosquitoes and UV rays to take their best shot at us. We agreed to spread our blankets under the live oaks outside the Menil Museum, and Heath handled the logistics of who would be responsible for Frisbees, food, and beverages.

He and I went together to Disco Kroger, so named because it was the grocery store closest to the heart of gay Houston—the intersection of Westheimer and Montrose—and was a great place to cruise any time of day or night. We were standing in a checkout lane, enjoying the tabloid headlines, when I got the uncanny sensation that someone was watching me. I glanced around and saw Ramon a couple of registers over. He pantomimed a swoon and mouthed Heath's name at me. After making sure that Heath was engrossed by a story about another alien baby, I flipped up my middle finger at Ramon. He clutched his heart in mock despair, and I started laughing.

"What?" Heath asked, looking up.

"Laura Dern's mother can't believe Billy Bob is leaving Laura for Angelina Jolie," I said quickly.

"I thought Angelina was dating her brother," Heath said.

"Dating your brother is so last month," I said.

After we parked on a shady side street, Heath and I each took a handle of the cooler and began walking, keeping an eye out for any sign of our friends. Heath came to a sudden stop, nearly causing me to lose my grip on the cooler, while the ice sloshed around inside.

"What the hell is she doing?" he asked.

I followed the direction of his curious stare. Miranda was sitting on a quilt, frantically digging through Alex's backpack while casting hurried glances in the opposite direction from where we stood. We watched until she apparently found what she was looking for, pulling out his cell phone and rapidly pushing buttons.

"Making a phone call?" I asked.

"Then how come she looks so sneaky?"

"Making a phone call to Australia?"

Miranda wrote something on a piece of paper, which she shoved into the pocket of her denim cutoffs. Then she returned Alex's phone and the pen to his backpack and assumed an innocent expression.

"Strange," Heath said.

"I know what she was doing," I said. "I'll bet she was looking at his directory to get Joey the drummer's phone number."

"Good work, Sherlock," Heath commended me.

"Thank you. She's a clever one, that Miranda."

When we joined her, she gave us one of her piercing looks and said, "What a surprise, seeing you two together."

"You know how Heath is about arranging things," I said. "He figured he'd make sure I was on time for this meeting, since I've been late for the other ones. And since *I* don't have a cell phone, I can't be reached any time, anywhere."

At the words "cell phone," Miranda blanched and quickly changed the subject. "Vivian said she couldn't make it today, because she has to study for finals. Or something like that. I wasn't exactly paying attention. I get the feeling there's something going on between her and Patrick."

"There is," I said, sitting on the quilt and leaving Heath to deal with the cooler. "They're dating. It's been going on for quite a while now."

"We didn't know if you could handle it," Heath said, joining us on the quilt but sitting a safe distance from me. "We know you've had a crush on Patrick since college."

"The whole lesbian thing is just an act, isn't it? The jig is up, Miranda," I said.

Miranda scowled at us and said, "You two are *so* funny. Whenever you guys make fun of me together like that, it takes me back to college when you were dating. It's almost like you never broke up."

"If that's the case, why am I paying so much rent?" Heath asked.

"And where's my ring?" I asked, just as Patrick walked up.

"I hope you guys didn't start whining without me," he said. "Did anyone have the fortitude to bring libations?"

"Uh-oh," Miranda said. "Not only is he drinking during the day, he's using big words."

"There's soft drinks and beer in the cooler and a thermos of margaritas somewhere," I said, ignoring Miranda and hoping Patrick would too. She was right, though. Whenever Patrick was feeling especially insecure or troubled, he had a tendency to be verbose in order to make himself feel intelligent. "And no, we haven't started the meeting, because Alex isn't here."

"Where is Alexander?" Heath asked, looking around.

"He had to go to the bathroom, so he went inside the Menil," Miranda explained. "He said he has some great news. I can only imagine what that means."

"Maybe he finally had sex with Zachary," Heath guessed.

Miranda made a snorting noise.

"You disapprove of his relationship with Blue Shorts?" I asked.

"I'm not sure you could call it a relationship," Miranda said. "From what we've heard, they've hardly seen each other. Maybe something's changed since our last meeting, so I hesitate to draw my own conclusions, but—"

"You already have," I finished for her.

"Here he comes," Patrick observed.

We turned our heads toward the museum and saw Alexander approaching us. Patrick started telling us one of his infamous "so there was this drunk at the bar" stories, while Heath and I unpacked cold cuts, bread, chips, and bananas from the picnic basket Miranda had brought.

"Hey, guys," Alex said in greeting, then plopped down on the quilt beside me. "Sorry I took so long. I started looking at art and got sidetracked."

"Who's Art?" Patrick asked.

"You shouldn't do that in public rest rooms, you know," I teased.

"You two should take that act to the stage. Want to open up for Tragic White Men next week? After you guys, we'll look like geniuses," Alexander said. "So who wants to start?"

"Why don't you? What's this good news you wouldn't tell me about before?" Miranda asked.

"Zachary and I had a real date two weeks ago," Alexander gushed. "After our last meeting, I started thinking about how he and I never really do much together. Then I wondered if he bought me that watch in order to pacify me."

"Oh, no," Miranda said, with all the sincerity of an insurance salesman.

"Yes," Alexander insisted. "So I confronted Zachary, who assured me that I was wrong. He bought me the watch so I'd think of him whenever I looked at it."

Patrick, true to his character, groaned out loud, while the rest of us sat with poker faces or fake smiles.

"Tell us about the date," I prodded.

"I'm getting to it," Alexander assured me. "A week went by, and we still hadn't had a real date. Finally, we went to the movies, and I blew up at him afterward. I accused him of being ashamed to be seen with me, seeing someone else, and all those other scenarios your mind creates when you're insecure. Zachary told me that he'd been especially busy but promised to take me out to dinner the following Friday. And he did! He took me to the Steakhouse."

"Isn't that in Galveston?" Patrick asked.

Alexander nodded his head so furiously that I thought it would fly off his shoulders and land in the cold cuts.

"Isn't that a little out of the way for dinner?" Miranda asked.

"That's what I thought," Alexander said. "But during dinner, he asked me if I had any plans for the weekend. I didn't have any gigs lined up, so I said no. It turned out that Zachary had reserved a suite for us at this bed and breakfast in the historic district. It was this beautiful old Victorian inn, and we were in the 1816 suite, or something like that. It had a huge brass bed, Jacuzzi, television, stereo, and a little sitting room."

"Sounds like the perfect room for Rachel Carson and her butterfly guy," Miranda said.

"*Who's* Rachel Carson?" Alexander asked.

"You guys spent the night?" Heath asked.

"We spent the weekend!" Alexander exclaimed. "At first, I felt a little uncomfortable and insisted we only spend one night. I mean, as far as dates go, it was pretty excessive. And I'd never be able to reciprocate. But he'd paid in advance for the weekend, so it would have just gone to waste if we didn't stay. I thought, 'Fuck it, Alexander. This may never happen again, so go for it.' And I did. It was really relaxing. We went to Moody Gardens, explored the stores on the Strand, and went out to a few bars. It was so fun."

"How did you sleep?" I asked coyly.

"Like a baby," Alexander answered. Then he added, "Especially after Zachary fucked me."

Heath and I howled with laughter. Patrick winced but betrayed himself by smirking before drinking his beer. Miranda, however, wore an insincere smile, which I attributed to her competitive nature. It seemed Alexander's love life was on an upward turn; she was probably eating her heart out just as ferociously as she was attacking the bag of pretzels.

"I'm glad you had a good weekend," I said to Alexander.

"Me too. The only drawback was that Zachary kept checking into work a lot."

"Did he spend a lot of time on the phone in your room?" Miranda asked.

"No," Alex answered. "He used his cell phone."

"His what?" I asked, and Heath looked down to hide a smile, while Miranda pretended she hadn't heard me.

"His cell phone," Alex repeated. "But usually only if I went to the bathroom or downstairs to get something to drink. Or if I was out on the veranda. Never when I was around, because then I had his undivided attention." Miranda nodded her head and munched thoughtfully on pretzels, not saying a word. "I guess it's good that he kept checking in with the office. If that's what it takes for me to spend a weekend being pampered like a celebrity, I'm all for it." Alexander beamed. "That's enough about me. How was your trip, Miranda?"

Miranda brushed pretzel crumbs from her T-shirt, swallowed, and said, "I had a great week in New York City. In fact, you are now looking at a member of the Mile High Club."

"No way!" Alexander exclaimed, probably upset that she'd beat him to it.

"Yup. This flight attendant gave me the eye while we were boarding the plane and getting ready for takeoff. Of course I couldn't be sure, but when she brought the beverage cart by and gave me my Coke, she touched my hand in a way that answered all my questions. A little while later, I got up to go to the bathroom and she saw me, made eye contact, and slipped in with me."

"You did it with a stewardess?" Patrick asked in awe.

"A flight attendant," Miranda corrected, "but yes."

"Forgive me," he said, "but I may have dreams about you tonight."

"It really set the tone for the rest of my trip," Miranda continued, pointedly ignoring Patrick. "I'd meet with whatever buyer during the day, but at night I'd cut loose, exploring the bars and clubs. It was fantastic. I found this incredible lesbian bar. It was a hole in the wall dive, in this nothing neighborhood, but it was packed with people having fun. Everyone was so nice too. I danced, drank, and had a ball. Every place I went to was like that."

"Were there any more encounters?" I asked.

"Oh, yeah," Miranda said and grinned. "I picked up this woman in a bar and brought her back to my hotel room. I felt like a man. I fucked her and asked her to leave. It was great."

"I'd hardly say—" I started to protest.

"Yeah, right," Miranda interrupted. "Anyway, I had a few one-night stands. It was great to get laid, but it's not like I met anyone serious. I'm not going to date someone who lives thousands of miles away."

"Yeah," I agreed. "If you did, can you imagine the phone bill? You'd have to get one of those *cell phone* plans with the three thousand weekend minutes."

"That's pretty much it," Miranda said, glaring at me. I suspected that if she'd had super powers my head would have exploded on the spot. "I sold my jewelry to a chic department store uptown and to a funky boutique downtown. The department store buyer said that if the first order sells well they'll want to order for their Beverly Hills location too."

We all congratulated her, and I searched for yet another reason to bring cell phones into the conversation.

"Do any of you boys want to tell us about your love lives?" Alexander asked Heath, Patrick, and me.

Miranda looked at me and smiled wickedly.

It had occurred to me to make up a phantom lover to throw Miranda off the scent. Or, after seeing him in Disco Kroger, I considered telling them about Ramon. Even though I hadn't planned to talk to Heath about him, at least it might get Miranda off my back. However, I was spared having to come clean—or lie—when Patrick suddenly spoke.

"I hadn't planned on divulging this information to anyone," Patrick said somberly. "Especially not during these frivolous monthly assignations. But I have to get it off my chest."

Ignoring his wordy insults, I tentatively said, "Go ahead, buddy. We're here for you."

"I anticipate that Vivian and I are about to sever our relations," he announced.

"What?" Alexander yelped, looking dismayed by the bad news.

"He said they're breaking up," Miranda explained. "Really, Patrick. I know it sucks, but can you stop talking like an Emily Brontë novel?"

I tossed a slice of pimento loaf at her and said, "Ignore her, Patrick. Go on."

"I don't know what happened," he said, paying no attention to Miranda when she peeled the pimento loaf off her face and bombarded me with pretzels. "I thought things were great between us. Then one day she came to Dinks and said, 'We need to talk.'"

"Uh-oh," Alexander said.

"Exactly. When a woman says that, you know things aren't good. So we talked. She said all this crap about needing time to finish her degree. I don't see how that affects our relationship. Then she started talking about the future and how our schedules aren't conducive to raising a family together."

"I didn't know that was on your mind," Heath said, echoing the thoughts I'd had when I'd spoken with Vivian.

"I do think about it," Patrick said. "It's private, though. It's not something I bring up in everyday conversation. I thought she and I were on the same page, so I mentioned it not too long ago. And I got shot down because of it."

"Don't say that," Alexander begged. "If you want something, you have to ask for it."

"Speaking as a woman—" Miranda began.

"Instead of what?" interrupted Alexander. "A water buffalo?"

"Speaking as a woman who could kick Alexander's ass with one hand tied behind her back, I think you should be patient, Patrick," Miranda said. "She's trying to prove herself in a career that a lot of people still see as a man's profession, and she's not even out of law school yet. Give her some breathing room, but be supportive of her. Because she is a woman, Patrick. Just because you had that one conversation doesn't mean it's all over. Women process everything. I guarantee that every little detail, word, and nuance is still churning in her brain."

"You're saying that I can change her mind?" Patrick asked hopefully.

"Weren't you listening? I said she's a woman. No. Of course you can't change her mind," Miranda said. "I'm saying that no decision is set in stone. If she's worth holding on to, and I think she is, you'll keep talking to her. Keep giving her encouragement. Let her know it's important to you that she graduates with honors and gets a job with the best law firm in the city. Tell her how much you value her friendship. Give her what she needs, and she'll see how important you are to her. Make a place for her in your life, and she'll keep you in hers."

Patrick weighed her words, then said, "Thanks, Miranda. I'll think about that. I have to admit, this has really shaken me up. I love Vivian. And I'm willing to do whatever it takes to keep her in my life."

"Good," I said, though I couldn't help but feel that his last words were a bit ominous. "If you need to talk, we're here for you. You don't have to hold this stuff inside until you burst."

"I do feel a lot better now," Patrick said. "But don't think I'm going to be bitching and moaning at every one of these monthly PMS festivals like you losers."

"Oh, no," Miranda assured him. "We wouldn't dare think that. But doesn't it feel good to get it all out of your system? Aaron, Heath, if either of you has something you'd like to talk about, we're more than happy to listen."

Heath nonchalantly said, "No. I'm good."

I shrugged, declining with a shake of my head, and began humming AT&T's "Reach Out and Touch Someone" jingle.

"If you ever want to talk, Patrick, any time, just let me know," Alexander offered.

The rest of us echoed his statement and Patrick said, "That's cool. But enough of this heavy stuff. Let's play."

The rest of the afternoon was spent playing Frisbee, laughing, and listening to Alexander as he played his acoustic guitar. His proficiency with the instrument far surpassed his self-critical assessment of his musical abilities, which was reflected in the number of passersby who stopped to listen. They smiled, enjoying the music, often asking him where he performed, where he studied, where they could buy a CD. He'd politely answer every question, his fingers never leaving the strings, and when people tossed dollar bills at his feet he laughed and begged them to take it back.

"I'm playing because I love music. And I need the practice," he said to a group of college students. "I'm not looking for a handout. Keep your money. If you have to part with it, give it to some organization that really needs it."

The kids laughed, flashed him a peace sign, and walked away. I lay on my back next to him on the quilt, listening to his guitar while watching Patrick and Miranda play Keep Away from Heath with the Frisbee.

"If you don't want their money, I'll take it," I said.

"These days, it's not like when we were in college," Alexander said. "Kids today are issued gold cards for their Sweet Sixteen birthdays, while we were returning bottles and cans for money."

"This from the man who still takes checks from his grandmother," I said.

"Not always," he feebly protested. "I mean, I always take the checks, but it's not like that's what I live on."

"What do you live on?" I asked. I was curious and wondered why the subject had never come up between us. "As far as I know, you've never had a job. At least never longer than a couple of weeks."

"I'm a free spirit. I can't be pinned down," he said.

"Pinned down? Like one of your precious butterflies?" I teased. "Seriously, what's the secret? How do you manage?"

"Promise me you won't tell anyone," Alexander requested.

"You act like it's a matter of national security," I said. "OK. I won't tell."

"A musician likes to keep an air of mystique about him," Alexander explained. "If people know that I do have a job, my credibility as a dedicated artist will plummet."

"What do you mean you have a job?" I asked.

"Do you recognize this tune?" he asked, and plucked out a repetitive melody on his guitar.

"No. I can't say that I do," I said.

"That's funny, since it's the theme song to one of your favorite movies," Alexander said with a sly smile. "It probably sounds different on a keyboard."

"You write songs for movies? That's incredible. Why wouldn't you want anyone to know? Why don't we know? If I wrote songs for movies, I'd tell every stranger on the street," I said.

Alexander laughed, then said, "Maybe. But if you wrote the theme song for *Randy Ranch Hands* or *Shakespeare in Heat,* would you tell all your friends?"

"You write music for gay porn movies?" I exclaimed and curled up on the quilt, holding my sides while laughing.

"Shut up! Not so loud," Alexander admonished. "Yes. I write under the name Al Camino."

"Why Al Camino?"

"The first time I submitted music for a movie, they wanted a name to put in the credits. I didn't want to use my own name, so I had to make up something fast. I looked out the window, and there was an El Camino parked outside," he explained.

"I can't believe this," I said. "How did you ever get involved with the porn industry?"

"Remember Trevor Chapman, from college?" he asked. When I nodded, Alexander continued, "He was from Los Angeles, right? His cousin was visiting and mentioned how he was an associate producer for a gay porn film. He was telling all these crazy stories, then he mentioned how the producer he was working with was looking for someone to write music for their latest film. So I gave him a few tapes I'd made, nothing special, but they called a few weeks later because they wanted to use what I wrote."

"Incredible," I said, in awe. "It's not every day that my friends surprise me. Just when I thought I knew everything about you, I hear this."

"Do you think less of me because of it?" Alexander asked anxiously.

"No. Not at all," I said. "In fact, I'm proud of you for being so industrious."

"I'd hardly call myself industrious," he protested. "It helps pay the bills. But never assume you know all there is to know about me, Aaron. I may not be the sharpest tool in the shed, but I am multidimensional."

"Multifaceted," I corrected.

"Whatever," he said, drawing out the last letter of the word.

As Alexander started playing the full theme song to *Randy Ranch Hands,* I stretched out on the quilt to admire Heath's golden good looks while he ran and jumped, and to think about secrets.

Chapter 5

BEVERAGE DAY

I really did have good intentions about not divulging Alex's secret life as the maestro of porn music. It was Heath who started a discussion about our friends during our next round of pillow talk by bringing up Miranda.

"Remember how bizarre she was at the picnic?" Heath asked. "Not that you helped matters any. Maybe you could have mentioned cell phones a couple of hundred more times."

"Admit it. You thought I was funny."

"I admit nothing. Anyway, she's been acting weird ever since. And forgive me if I sound politically incorrect, but have you ever once, any time that you've flown, seen a flight attendant that you pegged as a lesbian?"

"Only some of the guys," I said.

"I think she made up that whole mile-high thing. And exaggerated her sexual exploits in New York too."

"Aw, come on. She may not have a grip on love, but she's never had a problem bedding women. Why would she make that stuff up? Just because Alex is in a potential boyfriend situation?"

"I don't think it had anything to do with Alex. At least not in the way you think. I got nervous that day too. With no Vivian there to dominate the conversation, and with Alex all gushy about Zachary, I had this uneasy sense that there wasn't going to be enough to talk about. I started wondering if I should make up something in case Miranda started getting too inquisitive about you and me."

"Funny," I said, "I was doing the same thing. I'd even decided to make up a lover to throw her off track."

"That's exactly what I think *she* was doing," Heath said triumphantly. "Of course, nobody realized that Patrick was going to chime in with a tale of woe. I think Miranda was scared that you were going to tell Alex about the cell phone and I was going to tell everyone about her crush on Joey the dyke drummer. So she made up a bunch of stuff to keep that from happening."

"Man, Patrick would be really pissed if he knew she was making up shit to whine about!"

"But she didn't whine," Heath reminded me. "Which is the strangest thing of all. Do you suppose these meetings have really helped Alex and Miranda see how much they focus on the negative parts of their love lives?"

"Maybe," I said. "It's funny how things have evolved. First I couldn't handle the silence. Then I got used to the one-time-a-month thing. Now they don't complain. Alex talks about Zachary, and Miranda talks about work."

"I still think it's odd that Zachary hasn't seen Tragic White Men perform. Maybe he will, though, if his life has gotten less hectic after income tax season. I'm beginning to think he doesn't exist."

"He exists," I assured Heath. "Unlike the rest of us, Alex has no reason to make up a boyfriend."

"I'm pretty sure Alex has his secrets too," Heath said. I opened my mouth, about to blurt out the one secret I knew, then closed it. Heath propped his head on one arm and pinned me with his stare. "Spill."

"I promised I wouldn't."

"I told you about Miranda and Joey."

"And I've been good. Miranda has no idea that I know."

"I'll be good too," Heath promised. "Don't make me force it out of you."

"That might be fun," I said. When he maintained his stern and expectant expression, I caved, telling him everything Alex had told me about where he got his income.

"I figured it was something like that," Heath said. "Even though Alex's family has money, I know they try not to give him too much in hopes that he'll take a more 'respectable' career path." I sighed heavily, and Heath gave me a curious look. "What?"

"Why is it that nobody has secrets but you?"

"I'm an open book," he insisted.

I rolled my eyes and said, "Speaking of books…"

"I don't have one published. Is that good enough for you?"

"No. I want to know about the fictitious David. And where you make your extra income. And why you always talk about writing but never tell anyone what you write."

"I'm not telling you! You just proved you can't keep a secret."

"That is so low," I said. "I've kept lots of secrets."

"Tell me some more, and maybe I'll consider it," Heath said, laughing at my scowl. "It's not that big of a deal. Haven't you ever had some little private part of your life that you just wanted to keep to yourself?"

I thought about Ramon. Though there had never been any reason for keeping his place in my life from my other friends, I'd always liked the separateness of what we shared. I could tell Ramon anything and know it wouldn't become material for my friends' gossip. He confided in me the same way. And it was always nice that neither of us had our own opinions about the other's friends. It was almost like writing in my journal, except Ramon could talk back. But when he did, he'd always be on my side, because my side was the only one he knew. And we provided great, uncomplicated, uncommitted, uncalculated physical pleasure to each other. It worked for us, and we both knew if we got tangled up in all the other parts of each other's lives, it would change things in a way neither of us wanted.

"You're right," I said. "Everyone is entitled to something that's just theirs. But jeez, Heath, you never tell anyone anything. I don't know about your romances. You hardly ever talk about work. I don't even know what gym you go to."

"Bally. Always have."

"Thanks," I said. "I feel so much closer to you now."

"When I was in graduate school, a writing professor introduced me to one of his former college roommates," Heath said. "This guy was a poet. A great poet. I had an intense affair with him that lasted about a year and a half. Thanks to him, I got to see a lot of the places I'd only heard about. Key West. Provincetown. Fire Island. You can see the theme. He was successful. He had lots of money. Everybody knew him. But not because of his poetry. He was head writer for a soap opera. It earned him a comfortable income and a place among a certain set of sophisticated gay men. But it totally overshadowed his true gift.

"When our relationship ended, we remained friends. We're still friends. A few months after we broke up, he got in touch with me. The soap wanted to introduce a new character. A gay priest. It was a safe way to do something innovative. After all, if the character was celibate they didn't have to get into the sexual side of his life. What they really wanted was a powerful AIDS storyline and a character of good conscience who could guide it. Do you know much about soap writing?"

"No," I said.

"There's usually a writing team, and different writers are responsible for different characters and storylines. Anyway, my friend suggested that I develop this character. The gay priest. He gave me some guidelines on how to write for the soap, and I did it. My friend's name is Terry. My character's name is David. David was a big hit, so about once a year the show brings him back, gets him involved in a storyline, then writes him out again when the storyline is resolved.

"I'm the only person who's ever written David. It was Terry's idea that I use a pseudonym. So that just in case I ever wrote something more literary, I wouldn't be cursed the way he felt he had been. Now you know. That's my secret. Kind of similar to Alex's, isn't it? It may be a soap, but I put a lot of thought and energy into David. I didn't want him to become a joke among my friends. Because of the soap angle."

"It amazes me how long you've been in my life, yet there's so much I don't know," I said. "Alex writes scores for porn films, and you write a character on a soap opera. What's next? Miranda is a CIA agent?"

"That wouldn't really amaze me," Heath said. "If she sold Avon door to door, *that* would amaze me."

There was a lull in our conversation, and I sat up on the pillows and pulled Heath against me. He lay with his head on my chest, and as our breathing synchronized I gently messed up his hair, smoothed it down, then messed it up again, while my mind wandered. Because he'd opened up a door and let me into an area of his private life that few people were allowed to see, I should've felt closer to him. But I didn't.

"You're going to ask me which soap it is, aren't you?" Heath said.

I laughed and said, "It really doesn't matter. I mean, yes, I'm curious. But you told me the character is a gay priest, and the name of another writer. It would only take a quick search online to find out which soap it is."

"I guess you're right," he said lazily, still not telling me the name of the show.

"I think it's great, though," I said. "I mean, it's great that you're a working writer. I find myself feeling jealous."

"It's not jealousy," Heath said. "I know you. It's competition."

"Could be," I said. "It does make me feel like I should be doing something too. Alexander is not only on stage with a new band, but he's writing music for films. Miranda has sold her jewelry to department stores in New York and has been featured in a magazine. Patrick owns his own bar. Vivian—well, she doesn't have her law degree yet, but she may as well be Wonder Woman."

"Yes," Heath agreed, reaching up to gently grab my wrist, so I'd stop playing with his hair. "And don't forget, Patrick and Vivian are in love. That's quite an accomplishment in and of itself."

I thought back to New Year's Eve, when Heath had told me in

his sleep that I'd never been in love. "I should feel closer to you, but I don't," I finally spoke my thoughts aloud.

"What?" Heath asked.

"Because of what you told me," I explained. "About the soap job, your old lover, the whole kit and kaboodle. You let me in to a private part of your life, but I don't feel any closer to you. In fact, I don't even know that it's a private part of your life. I could be the only one who doesn't know."

"Aaron, stop," Heath said, suddenly sounding very tired.

"No. I don't even know why you told me," I said.

"Because you asked," Heath said slowly, as if it was taking every fiber of his being to be patient with me.

"But not because you love me," I surmised. Heath didn't agree or disagree, so I drew my own conclusion. "I thought so."

"Don't make assumptions about me," Heath said, sitting up.

"I knew this would happen. I knew one of us would get hurt. If there's one thing I've learned from Patrick and Vivian, it's that there are no guarantees when it comes to matters of the heart."

"You can't compare us to them," Heath said. "It's different."

"Why? Because they're straight? Or is it because they're in love?" I asked. "I'm sorry. That was mean. I know; it's because everybody's different. Everybody loves in their own way."

"Yes," Heath agreed. "Also, because they haven't really broken up. I hate to say I told you so, but I did say that this was a bad idea."

"This isn't the best time to always be right," I muttered, then we both laughed. "I knew it was a bad idea too. But I had this tiny spark of hope that maybe things would be different this time. That we'd work out."

Heath smiled at me. He leaned forward on his hands, kissed me lightly, then said, "I did too. Maybe we're getting ahead of ourselves."

"Maybe," I agreed. "It's obvious that we love each other. And we've proven over and over that we're sexually compatible." I opened my arms, and Heath wrapped himself around me.

"I'm kind of surprised that you're still here," he said.

"That was uncalled for," I said. Then I realized what he meant. "Oh. That I'm not running out the door at the first sign of conflict?"

"Yeah, that," he said.

"I'm tired of running. If this is just a sexual relationship, it's better to know."

"I wouldn't say that," Heath said. "I *am* your friend."

"Yes. You definitely are," I agreed. "I'll try not to have a lot of ridiculous expectations and just enjoy this for what it is."

Heath's eyes almost sparkled when he kissed my ear and said, "So I can do this?"

My breath caught in my throat as his warm breath tickled my ear. "I guess that's OK," I said.

"What if I did this?" he asked, and drew the sheets over our bodies while rolling on top of me.

"That's fine," I said, laughing.

Later, during my drive home, I opened the car windows. As the wind rushed around me and blew into my eyes, I hoped it would sweep away the nagging feeling of doubt I had about Heath. If ours was just a friendship with sex, why couldn't I tear myself away from him? Why was he the natural answer to my libido's yearning questions? If I had Ramon to turn to for unapologetic, wanton sex with no expectations, then what was Heath's place in my life?

Normally, I would've casually brought up the subject with Patrick when I got home, and he'd sum up the situation in a trite but profound statement and offer me sage advice in the form of a pithy answer. But when I entered our living room and found him asleep on the sofa, with the television on and the remains of a six-pack scattered haphazardly on top of the coffee table, I knew he wasn't the one to turn to. He had his own problems to contend with.

During the first week of May, I went through my paces at school as if I was on autopilot. But in the back of my mind, between classes, the situation with Paul Nettles kept rearing its ugly head. I'd eye the other faculty members suspiciously, certain they were giving me strange looks and whispering behind my back. No matter how many times I told myself it wasn't true, that it was just my mind playing tricks on me, I couldn't be sure that I was right. Or wrong, for that matter.

Just like my relationship with Heath, the worst part was not knowing what was going to happen. I wished there was a way to control it, but I didn't want to make any waves, especially so near the end of the school year. I decided to wait for the outcome patiently and alleviate the pressure by confiding my worries to Alexander.

We met for drinks at Dinks on the first Saturday of May. In addition to telling Alexander about my situation at work, I also wanted to keep an eye on Patrick. However, he was nowhere to be seen. The bartender told me he was in the office going over invoices and payroll.

I was facing the door and saw Alex walk in. He spotted me, but as he made his way over, people kept stopping him to talk. Apparently his recognition quotient had gone way up because of Tragic White Men. That made me happy, but what made me even happier was seeing how appealing and lighthearted he looked. I thought of the months that had led up to New Year's Eve, when he and Miranda played their running game of Misery with each other. I wasn't sure whether his changes were because of the band or because of Zachary. Maybe the reservations about his new boyfriend that Heath, Miranda, and I seemed to share were unfounded. Alex was obviously in such a good space that it made me rethink my decision to confide in him. I didn't want to bring him down.

"Sorry," Alex said, rolling his eyes as he plopped down next to me. "Where's Patrick?"

"Working in the office," I said. "But that's OK. I really just wanted to catch up with you."

"What did I do wrong?" Alex asked. "I know I haven't been to the gym in a while—"

"Jeez, am I that big of a hardass?" I asked. "Relax."

He continued to look a little skeptical and said, "Let me get a drink."

When he came back, I listened while he told me how things were going for the band. They were working with a couple of booking agents, which had netted them some upcoming appearances in Austin and Dallas.

"I'm so proud of you," I said.

"It's about time I got serious about something, don't you think?" Alex asked. "At least this is music I can share with Grandma."

"I don't know, a little gay porn might perk the old girl up," I said.

Alex started laughing and said, "Can't you hear the conversation at the dinner table? 'I don't know, Warren,' she could say to my father, 'I think his music in *Rimbo* had much more depth.' Then Mom would argue that *Boys on the Slide* was my magnum opus."

"Let me write those titles down," I said, pretending to search my pockets for a pen.

"Like you don't know the video room at Lobo by heart," Alex said.

"How are things with Zachary?"

"I haven't seen much of him lately," Alex admitted. "We talk all the time, but he's had family visiting from out of town. I know he feels guilty, though, because we went to Soundwaves one day so I could help him find some new CDs. He must have been listening to every word I said, because after he paid and we went to his car he'd also bought all the CDs I'd talked about wanting and gave them to me."

"That was generous."

"Yeah. I felt a little weird about taking them. It's not like he has to buy my love."

His words triggered all of my mental alarms, and I asked, "You're in love?"

Alex shrugged and said, "How do you know when you're in love?"

"Don't ask me. Heath tells me I've never been in love."

"That's just his bitterness talking," Alex assured me. "Because you're the man who got away." I dropped my eyes and played with my beer bottle. "Uh, you *are* the man who got away, aren't you?"

"Not exactly," I said, wondering why it was so hard to tell Alex the truth.

"Aaron, what's going on? Are you and Heath getting back together?"

"Definitely not," I said. I finally met his eyes and saw that he was genuinely concerned and not just looking for gossip. "Honestly, I thought that's where we were headed. But now I'm not so sure. I don't think it's what he wants."

"What do you want?"

"If you'd asked me a couple of weeks ago, I might have said Heath," I admitted. "We've had this intensely hot relationship going on since right after he moved to his new place."

"Yeah, I kind of picked up that vibe," Alex said. "Plus Miranda was dropping hints like Wile E. Coyote drops anvils."

"Don't forget who gets the worst of that deal," I said. "Miranda needs to stay out of it. It's been a lot harder not talking to you and Patrick about it."

When I told him about my last conversation with Heath, Alex looked sad. "I'm sorry, Aaron. I really am."

"At first I was too," I said. "But I can definitely say one good thing has come out of it. Those unfinished feelings from the past… some of them hard feelings…they're gone. I think we'll come out of it better friends."

"So it's over?"

"I don't know," I confessed. "I'm accepting it for what it is, though, and not looking to make a till-death-do-us-part future out of it. In the overall balance of things, I'd say I deserved to suffer a little at Heath's hands, wouldn't you?"

"No. He's not the only one who got hurt all those years ago." He raised his hands as I started to say something. "All right, you remember it your way; I'll remember it mine. You know what's depressing about it?"

"You want a list?"

"I mean to me. And maybe to your other friends. You and Heath are both sane, stable men who have it all together. If you can't make a relationship work, what hope do your crazy friends have?"

"First of all," I said, "those qualities don't have anything to do with falling in love and making it last. And second of all, I'm not so sure I have things any more together than the rest of you. Your career is taking off. Miranda, the jewelry queen of the Southwest, is expanding to both coasts. And Patrick has been successful in two different careers. Whereas I'm having my own Wile E. Coyote moment at work, teetering on the edge of a cliff that may be crumbling. The next sound you hear may be that little *poof* as I hit bottom."

"You're no poof," Alex said in an exaggerated British accent.

"As if that's not enough, I just realized I'm in a bad Monty Python skit with my best friend."

"There's no such thing as a bad Monty Python skit," Alex said. "What's going on at work?"

His expression was incredulous when I told him about the situation at St. Gregory's, including my suspicion about Paul Nettles's role in it.

"Nothing more has been said about it," I finished, "but I'm definitely ending the school year on a sour note."

Alex gave me a sympathetic hug and said, "That's awful. Who is this asshole? Why didn't you tell us what's going on? Patrick will beat him up. And I'll do something a lot more devious. We'll destroy him!"

"Calm down, Alexis," I said.

"You said it," Alex said. "I'll go Joan Collins all over his ass."

"Please, I don't want to think about Paul's ass," I begged.

"I think it's terrible," Alex said.

"It *is*," I agreed. "That's why I don't want to think about it."

"What a frickin' nightmare," Alex said, ignoring my effort at humor. "How are you coping with it?"

"Mainly by leaping into bed with Heath, I guess," I said dryly.

"Say no more. I get it," Alex said. "I need another drink. Let's move to the bar."

We traipsed across the room and leaned on the bar, ordering two more drinks. As we waited, Alex said, "Do you think that's the only reason you've been sleeping with Heath again?"

"Because of the situation at work?" I clarified. When Alex nodded I said, "I hadn't really thought about that angle, but he does have a way of taking my mind off things. I'm so drawn to Heath, it's ridiculous. He's like a drug."

"Just don't overdose," Alex advised, slapping a ten-dollar bill on the bar to pay for our drinks. "It's possible. It's happened before."

"Let's change the subject, OK?" I begged.

A man seated on a barstool next to us said, "Please do. In fact, why don't you go to one of your own bars?"

"Excuse me?" I asked.

"We don't own a bar," Alexander said. "So this one will have to do."

Alexander sat down as daintily as possible, crossing his legs at the knee and batting his eyelashes with a radiant Miss America smile.

"Get the fuck away from me, faggot," the man growled.

"I can't. I think I love you," Alexander teased.

"Is there a problem here?" Patrick asked, suddenly appearing behind the bar with a stack of books in his hands.

"Yeah, there is," the bigoted man insisted. Several of the people at the bar had their eyes glued on us. Nervously looking around the room, I noted that we had the attention of half the bar. I was more embarrassed than afraid. "I'd appreciate it if you'd kick these fags out of here."

"I can't do that, sir," Patrick said. He pointed to Alexander, and said, "This one is my best friend." Then Patrick gestured to me and said, "And this one has my heart wrapped around his little finger."

Before I knew it, Patrick leaned across the bar, grabbed my head in his hands, and planted a big, wet kiss on my lips. Alexander nearly fell off his barstool, he was laughing so hard.

"Keep it up, boys! You're turning me on!" a voice behind me exclaimed. When Patrick came up for air and let me go, I turned and saw Vivian behind us.

"You people are deranged," our detractor spluttered, getting up from his stool to leave.

"Hey, guys!" Patrick boomed. "Drinks are on him!"

I cringed, while Vivian and Alexander shrieked with laughter. We knew, as did the regulars at Dinks, that this was Patrick's favorite way of eighty-sixing customers who got out of hand. Before the belligerent customer knew what was happening, everybody around him began tossing their drinks in his face, until he was drenched.

"Get your hateful, closed-minded, intolerant ass out of my bar!" Patrick ordered.

"Bye, bye! Y'all don't come back now, y'hear!" Alexander sang sweetly, while the man, seething with anger, stormed away. He pushed past Heath and Miranda, who had just entered the bar, as he bulldozed his way out the door.

"Aw, shucks," Miranda said as she and Heath approached us. "Did we miss all the fun?"

"Only someone who didn't know about our No Bigots policy," Patrick explained, while he helped the bartender replace the drinks that had been thrown.

"What are you guys doing here?" Alexander asked.

"Heath and I were at my place, watching Lifetime," Miranda said. "Then we realized we were watching Lifetime, so we came here as quickly as we could. Fancy meeting you guys here. What is this, a Love Sucks meeting?"

"It might as well be," I said, shrugging with indifference to the idea.

"Maybe I was too hasty about throwing that guy out of here," Patrick said. "Now I want *you* to leave."

"Drinks are on Patrick!" Alexander yelled. "Just kidding!"

"Speaking of Love Sucks, I'm sorry I've been missing the meetings," Vivian said. Nobody said anything tangible, so she said, "Patrick has filled me in on everything, though. Alex, have you seen Zachary since your weekend in Galveston?"

"Not really," he answered. "We've mostly just talked on the phone."

"Damn it, Alex," Miranda interjected, "he's not treating you right. I'm sorry, but I have to say it. You deserve more attention than he's giving you."

"For those about to whine," I interrupted, "let me remind you that we just met about a week ago. If you complain now, you'll have to go another month, maybe more, until you can bitch and moan again about love."

"No problem," Alex assured us. "I'll admit that I wish Zachary would pay more attention to me. But when he does, he does it well. If this is the price I have to pay for dating someone who has a nine-to-five job, so be it. It takes a little adjusting on both sides, and I'm willing to compromise."

"I don't have to like it," Miranda said.

"That's fine," Alex said.

"Alex is right," Vivian said. "When two people are in a relationship, and they have different schedules and different goals, it's tough to make the relationship work. But 'relationship' is synonymous with the word 'work,' in my opinion."

"Hypocrite," Patrick said.

"Excuse me?" Vivian said, sounding astonished.

"Who are you to preach about relationships and how they take a lot of work? Especially after the way you've been running from me when the going gets a little tough."

"That's not why, and you know it," Vivian said. "Yes or no, Patrick? Did I not tell you that I have a lot of work ahead of me to get my degree? And that nothing is going to stand in my way?"

"Yes, you did," Patrick said. "It's not my intention to get in the way of that."

"A simple yes will suffice, Patrick," Vivian said. Heath cringed at that remark, while Miranda and I stared at the jukebox on the other side of the room with rapt fascination. Alex, however, watched Patrick and Vivian while they verbally sparred as if they were trapped in a rerun of *Moonlighting*. Vivian continued. "But let the record show that when I said that between making time for you and pursuing my degree, I was left with little time to study, you said that maybe I should take a year off. How is that being supportive and not standing in my way?"

"All I meant was that I would like to see you," Patrick stated. "It's hard on me too, you know. What do you want me to do, sell my bar?"

"You shouldn't have to," Vivian said. "It's not my place to tell you what to do. I'm just doing what I have to do to make it through school. What's wrong with that?"

"And you're going to sacrifice our relationship so you can graduate with honors? Does that make any sense?"

"I'm not sacrificing anything," Vivian stated. "I'm not breaking up with you."

"It sure feels like it," Patrick said. Noticing Alexander's scrutinizing stare, he said, "Can I get you some Goldfish crackers, Alex?"

"No. I'm good," Alexander said. "Don't let me interrupt you. Go on."

"I just need a break, Patrick," Vivian said, ignoring Alexander.

"I don't see why," Patrick said. "Besides, summer is almost here. You won't have classes, so we can be together and fix whatever it is that's wrong between us."

Vivian let her patrician-lawyer facade falter for a moment when she looked down at the floor.

"What is it?" Patrick asked. "What aren't you telling me?"

"I've been accepted for a summer internship with a law firm downtown," Vivian explained. "It's a twelve-week program. Basically, I'll be doing paralegal work and assisting with corporate law cases. Real cases, Patrick. They'll be working me like a dog. I'll probably end up doing twelve-hour days. Not only will I get great experience, but I'll get paid about two thousand dollars a week. My student loans and I can't turn down that kind of salary. I can't say no."

Patrick stared at Vivian with a blank expression. Finally he shook it off and said, "Then don't. Good luck with that."

"That's all you're going to say?" she asked.

"What more can I say?" he asked. "You've presented an airtight case, Madam Counselor. Congratulations."

"Could we all step back a minute and calm down?" Heath pleaded.

"Let's see how calm you are when we discuss your fuckfests with Aaron in front of the entire bar," Patrick snapped.

Heath and I looked at each other and simultaneously asked, "You told him?"

"I only told Alex," I protested.

"I didn't tell anyone," Heath assured me.

"I've got eyes," Patrick muttered. "And you two have put off enough hormones—"

"Pheromones," Vivian corrected.

"Like silkmoths," Alexander added.

"Rachel Carson speaks," Miranda said. "I'd like an apology." Since she was the only person who'd thus far endured our impromptu meeting unscathed, we all turned dumbfounded looks her way. "You always talk about my lesbian dramas, but I seem to be the only one here whose life is under control."

"If screwing your way across the Eastern seaboard is your idea of control—"

"Hey," Miranda cut Vivian off, "at least I'm not emasculating some poor guy for the sake of a grade and a few bucks."

"I am not some poor guy!" Patrick bellowed.

"He didn't seem emasculated when he kissed me," I spoke quietly, drawing everyone's eyes to me. "Don't you all think we've entertained Dinks' clientele long enough?"

"I know I don't," a guy said from the end of the bar. "I'll buy you all a round if you keep talking. It is Beverage Day, after all."

"Is there some kind of conspiracy by Hallmark and American Greetings to turn every damn day of the year into a holiday?" Miranda asked. "When is Dysfunctional Friends Day? I'll volunteer to host that meeting."

"I'm out of here," Vivian said.

"Don't do it," Heath said, catching her arm as she turned away from us. "Seriously, it's hard to repair the damage once you walk away pissed off."

"Good advice," I said. "Could we all sit down and act like adults?"

We moved away from the bar as a group, much to the chagrin of our number one fan. No one said anything as the bartender brought us a pitcher of beer and glasses. Miranda poured for us, apparently looking too self-satisfied for Alex.

"I don't see how you can say yours is the only life under control," he said to her. "Things are going great for me."

"Wake up and smell the perfume on Zachary's collar," Miranda said. "Is it obvious to everyone but you that your boyfriend is married?"

"Are you nuts?" Alex asked. "He's just busy. I've been screwed over enough to know that I'm the only man in his life."

"I don't doubt it," Miranda said. "Married, Alex. To a woman."

"What?" Alex gasped. "You really have been watching too much Lifetime. Is that where you get this stuff?"

"No, I get it from public records," Miranda said. "Zachary Simmons, right?" Alex nodded. "Works at Hammond Hill and Larson, CPAs. Lives in Friendswood with his wife of nine years, Alicia Simmons, and their two children, ages seven and five. I don't know the kids' names, but if you give me some time—"

"He is not married," Alex said firmly. "Trust me, I'd know." He glanced around the table, waiting for one of us to back him up. "Aaron?"

"I don't know," I admitted. "It would explain a few things. You should ask him."

"Are you allergic to other people's happiness?" Alex asked Miranda, standing up. "I don't need this crap from someone who's supposed to be my friend."

Miranda watched him walk out, then turned to face the rest of us. "He had to find out sometime," she defended herself.

"Maybe not in front of everyone," Heath said with a hint of reproach.

"We've aired everybody else's dirty laundry tonight," she said. "Aren't we supposed to be here for each other? Isn't that the real point of these meetings? Are we only supposed to talk about what's comfortable? And get each other through meaningless events like— like—I don't know like what. But you get what I mean."

"I vote that we adjourn," Patrick said. "And no more meetings this month. We could all use a break."

"I'm sorry I made a big scene in front of everybody," Vivian said to him. "Will you call me?"

He nodded. After he and I exchanged a glance, I followed the others from the bar. We made sure Vivian and Miranda got to their cars OK, then Heath and I looked at each other.

"I hope you're not pissed that I told Alex about us," I said.

"Not at all. What would be the point, when Patrick told a large percentage of Montrose tonight? You want to come over?"

"I don't think so." I shook my head. "I should check on Alex. I didn't like the way he looked when he left."

"Me, either," Heath said. He gave me a hug, and we separated and headed to our cars.

I was glad to see Alex's truck parked outside his garage apartment. I'd been afraid, since it was Saturday night, that he'd go out drinking somewhere. He opened the door after I knocked and gave me a surprised look.

"What?"

"I thought you might like some company," I said.

"Not really," he said. "I'd actually like to be alone."

"Are you sure?"

"I'm fine, Aaron. She's wrong, you know."

"All right. Call me if you need to talk."

I went back to my car and briefly considered driving to Heath's. Then I decided that I too would rather be alone. Although grading papers didn't make for an exciting Saturday night, I was ready for a little peace and quiet.

I threw myself into the last three weeks of school, fighting my students' customary end-of-the-year tendency to slack off. Heath and I saw each other occasionally, but everyone else seemed to be laying low.

On the last full day of classes before finals, I had my eighth and ninth graders choose from two topics on which to write a paper in class. They could either title their papers "The Most Important Thing I Learned This Year" or "The Most Significant Change in Me This Year." Although they groaned about having to do anything, especially when it wasn't for a grade, it made for a relatively calm finale to our time together. I watched them write, wondering if their assessment of themselves would match the ways I'd seen them grow and change after nine months.

I sat in bed that night, music playing softly in the background, a glass of wine on my nightstand, and began flipping through their papers, looking for one in particular. When I found it, I settled back to read.

"The most important thing I learned this year," Khalid had written, *"was that I'm not a big geek. I made a lot of friends and found out it's okay if I look a little different and talk a little different. It started in my English class. But then I found out there were people in all my classes who would be nice to me and accept me. My parents say I have more self-confidence and they're proud of me. I've always wanted them to be glad I'm their son. Now I know they are. Having a good family is important, but the best thing about this year was making friends. My friends and I have made plans for a killer summer. And the ones I don't see over the summer I'll see again when school starts next year. So not only did I learn that I'm not a big geek. I learned that having friends is one of the greatest things in the world."*

"You got that right," I said aloud, then took a drink of my wine.

As I read through the other papers, I grinned a lot. Some were obvious attempts to suck up one last time, just in case I'd lied and was assigning grades to what they'd written. I gave a little sigh when I got to Justin Woodhill's paper, wondering what great athletic feat he'd chosen to write about. But after the first sentence, I was riveted.

"My most significant change," Justin wrote, *"is about the word 'gay.' Everybody I know uses that word to mean lame or dumb or geeky. We say you're so gay, or that's so gay, or stop being so gay whenever we want to make fun of someone. Well, I stopped doing that. You know people say you're gay, Mr. Fisher. I guess you are, since you're so old and you never got married. But you're not lame or dumb or geeky. This was the coolest English class I ever had. The Shakespeare's Villains part was cool, but the coolest was being a lawyer for Khalid when we studied the Trojan War. That rocked. In fact, even though I've always wanted to play pro baseball, maybe for the Braves or the Mets, now I'm thinking that maybe I'd also like to be a lawyer. My mother says that's okay as long as I never tell my father if I vote for a Democrat. Are all lawyers Democrats, I wonder? Anyway, the thing about using the word 'gay.' Khalid and Jason and Ashley and some other kids talked it over, and we decided we wouldn't use it in a bad way. I even asked guys on the team to stop. At first they thought I was gay.*

But some of them saw this show on MTV about hate language. So we made a deal. If somebody used the word 'gay' in the locker room to put somebody down, the first person that socked him on the arm got a free combo meal from McDonalds. At first we were lifting a lot of cheeseburgers with sore arms, but lately we don't seem to be going to McDonalds as much. Either the habit got broke or our wallets did. Ha ha. Thanks, Mr. Fisher, for being a great teacher."

I didn't know whether to laugh or cry when I got to the end. I'd forgotten how one kid could surprise me and make every bad teaching experience irrelevant by reminding me why I wouldn't consider doing anything else with my life.

I finished my wine, shoved the rest of the papers aside, and stared at the ceiling, taking a little time to relish what Khalid and Justin had taught me. I felt sorry for teachers like Paul Nettles, who might never understand the value of real friends or the miracle of seeing a mind open up and make choices that the heart dictated. What I'd said to Alex was wrong; I wasn't ending the school year on a sour note after all.

Chapter 6

FATHER'S DAY AND INTERNATIONAL PANIC DAY

I had just walked through the door after a grueling midmorning workout and dropped my gym bag on the sofa when I heard the phone ringing.

"How does Patrick sleep through this?" I asked aloud. "Hello?"

"Hey, it's me," Miranda said.

"Hi, me. How's it going?"

"I finally finished the last of my jewelry orders," she said. "It seems strange to me that they'd want orders at this time of year, but who am I to argue? Hopefully, it means they'll want more as they gear up for the holiday season in the fall. I had three people working for me full-time; can you believe that?"

"I hope they were legal," I said. In the past, whenever she got too busy, Miranda was known to pay wages under the table to people who barely spoke English. Heath had warned her never to run for political office.

"Anyway," she ignored me, "I finally have some time on my hands, and I wanted to know if you have plans today."

I had planned on calling Heath to see if he was interested in a nooner, but I hadn't seen Miranda since our verbal brawl at the last Love Sucks meeting at Dinks. I decided a good friend would forfeit an afternoon of sensational sex to spend time with a friend who was reaching out.

"What did you have in mind?" I asked noncommittally. Though I wanted to be a good friend, there was a lot to be said for sensational sex. Plus I was still riding high on endorphins and wanted to put them to good use.

"I haven't seen you in a while," she said. "I want to catch up. We haven't done anything together outside of Love Sucks in ages. Can I pick you up? We can drive around and talk while looking at houses."

One of Miranda's favorite pastimes was looking at houses she couldn't afford, dreaming about her life in them if she suddenly won the lottery or accepted her trust fund. She'd get in her car and visit them over and over, as if they were pieces of art in a museum.

"Sure," I said. "I'll be waiting. Honk when you get here."

"OK," Miranda said, and from outside I heard the sound of a car horn.

"That was fast," I said, and she giggled.

"I'm on my cell phone. Get your butt out here."

Five minutes later we were on the road with the radio cranked up, laughing and singing as Miranda wound her green Mustang through the streets of Montrose. When I realized we were turning onto the street where Alexander lived, I became suspicious.

"What are you doing?" I asked, turning down the volume on the radio.

"I'm driving, Aaron. What does it look like I'm doing?"

She pulled over and stopped her car a couple of doors down from Alexander's apartment and said, "I love this house. It's so charming. If I lived here, I'd plant rosebushes by the front door. Instead of those hideous shrubs. I'll bet those shrubs make the house sad. And I'd—"

"This house has stucco," I said flatly, interrupting her. "You hate stucco. What are you up to, Miranda?"

"Nothing! Jeez, Aaron. We're looking at houses, like I said we would. Maybe I've changed my mind about stucco. A person can change her mind, you know. Even about stucco. Stucco's not *so* bad. It's a perfectly acceptable exterior, and the texture is actually kind of inviting." Miranda's voice lost its conviction when she noticed a black Saab back out of Alexander's driveway. "Duck!" she yelled.

"What?" I shrieked.

"Just do it!" she ordered and grabbed my shirt, pulling me down in the seat with her, as if fearing a hail of gunfire.

"Who did you screw over now?" I asked, but Miranda paid me no attention. Instead, she peered over the dashboard. After a minute, she sat up, threw the Mustang in gear, and lurched away from the curb.

"You can get up now," she said.

"Fuck that," I said. "Let me out."

"Drama queen," she muttered.

"Something tells me we're not looking at houses," I said. I sat up and realized we were following the black Saab. "What exactly are we doing?"

"We're following someone," Miranda said.

"I can see that. Who are we following? Alexander?"

"He drives a truck, Aaron. You know that. Use your head."

"If we're not following Alexander, and that was Alexander's driveway back there, then we must—" I broke off when I remembered the bomb Miranda had dropped the last time I saw her. "We're following Zachary, aren't we?"

"Bingo! Give the boy a prize," Miranda exclaimed. "I also give you partial credit for your first answer. It looks like Alexander is with him."

As the black Saab turned a corner, allowing us full view of the passenger side window, I could see Alex seated inside.

"You're scaring me, Miranda. I fear for your sanity. Why don't we make a left up here and go to Crossroads? We'll have a nice cup of coffee and talk. Check that. You probably shouldn't have caffeine. We'll get you a decaf."

"We're not going to Crossroads," Miranda said. "We're following Zachary's duplicitous, cheating ass so we can make Alexander see him for who he really is."

"It's been a month since you told Alexander that Zachary's married. He must have confirmed it by now," I said.

"Obviously not! There's Zachary driving the Saab in front of us. And there's Alexander in the passenger seat," Miranda said, pointing. "Alexander is either still kidding himself that Zachary is single, or he's been duped into thinking that Zachary will leave his wife for him. Or, like you and Heath, he's with him for the sex."

"I've seen Zachary naked. If that's the reason, I can understand," I said.

"This isn't the time for jokes, Aaron," Miranda said, hitting the accelerator so she wouldn't get caught at a red light. "At least I care about not letting our friends get hurt."

"I haven't seen any proof that Zachary *is* married," I said, suddenly feeling like Vivian and looking at every angle of the situation. "In fact, this whole escapade could be some grand scheme to wreck their relationship so you'll win the deal."

I paused, since that was the moment when if Heath was there, he'd yell, *"It's not a competition!"*

"I don't have physical evidence," Miranda said. "But trust me, he's married. And do you really think so little of me that you believe I'd arbitrarily decide to ruin Alexander's relationship just to win some stupid bet?"

"Considering the circumstances at the moment, I'd think twice about asking that if I were you," I said. "Oh, and when you're arrested on charges of stalking, I'm adding kidnapping to the list."

We followed Zachary's Saab to Baba Yega's, one of Alexander's favorite restaurants. Miranda parked her car a block away from theirs and watched as they went inside.

"What now, Calamity Jane?" I asked.

"I guess we follow them inside," Miranda said.

When we got out of the car, I pointed up the street and said, "Nope. I'm not playing Ethel to your Lucy. I'm going to J.R.'s to have a drink."

"It's barely noon," Miranda said. "Come on."

She crossed the street, and I tried to make up my mind whether or not to follow her. I didn't want to be linked to her when she faced the wrath of Alexander and Zachary. Because it was almost certain that she'd be seen. However, if I went with her I could help smooth over the wrinkles of the situation. Not to mention that I'd have a ringside seat when the shit hit the fan. Making the obvious choice, I ran to catch up with her.

When I walked through the door of Baba Yega's, Miranda was saying to the host, "Could I please sit there, behind that fern?"

"Is it a table for two?" I asked.

"I thought you were calling the police or something," Miranda said.

"I figured you'll get in less trouble if I keep both eyes on you," I said, following the host to our table. "Besides, I'm sure there's a phone at the bar."

We were seated inside the restaurant on the edge of the outdoor patio. I could see why Miranda chose the table. Not only was it hidden behind a large fern, it afforded a view of Alexander and Zachary's table on the patio.

When our waiter arrived, Miranda blandly said, "I'll have an iced tea."

Our waiter rolled his eyes and rested them on me. After my morning workout I was famished, which I'd forgotten during Miranda's cloak and dagger routine in the car, so I ordered a steak.

"Medium rare, please," I said. Pointing at Alexander and Zachary's table, I said, "And can you send that table two Mai Tais with a note that says *Run like hell*?"

"Don't you dare," Miranda warned the waiter. "He's kidding."

Neither of us spoke before my food was set down in front of me. Miranda was too intent on watching her prey to maintain a conversation. When I ate my last bite of steak, I finally said, "I'm done. Now what?"

"They're still talking," Miranda said, peering through the fern. "I'm not leaving until I know, once and for all, that he and Alexander aren't—"

She broke off, emitting a high-pitched scream that miraculously failed to shatter Baba Yega's windows. She batted at the fern, which rocketed an enormous palmetto bug across the room.

"Is it June already?" our waiter asked as he dropped our check in front of me. "Those things always come in here looking for water at the beginning of summer."

Unfortunately, the palmetto bug had landed in the middle of someone's table, which caused more screaming. I looked toward the patio and saw Alexander craning his neck to see what all the commotion was about.

"I think you're about to be busted," I said to Miranda. "How does it feel to be foiled by a giant cockroach? And you were so brave when faced with the same situation at Café Adobe. You disappoint me."

"Pay the bill, and let's get out of here," Miranda said.

"Oh, no, you don't," I said, pushing the check at her. "You kidnapped me. You pay the bill."

"Aaron, we don't have time for—"

"Hey! What are you guys doing here?" Alexander asked, appearing at our table with Zachary in tow. "Zachary, do you remember Aaron from the gym? And this is my friend—"

"Miranda?" Zachary asked. "I didn't know that you knew Alexander. What a pleasant surprise."

"You two know each other?" Alexander asked, casting a startled glance Miranda's way.

"Uh— well—" she stammered.

"Miranda is a client of mine," Zachary said.

"He's helping me stay in compliance with my payroll taxes," Miranda said quickly. "As I tried to tell you, Aaron, when you accused me of hiring illegals."

"Gosh, I can't believe I suspected you of doing something wrong," I said. "You're the most ethical person I know, Miranda. In fact, not only is your own life above reproach, but you watch out for all the rest of us too."

"Oh, shut up," she muttered, while Zachary looked from me to her with a bewildered expression.

Alexander, on the other hand, looked annoyed. He'd obviously deduced that we were stalking him. He glared at Miranda, then shook his head at me, as if he couldn't believe I'd been sucked into her delusion about Zachary.

"We should go if we want to make that matinee," he said to Zachary. "I'll talk to you two later."

"It was nice to see you both again," Zachary said, then turned to follow Alex, who was already halfway to the door.

"Let's go out through Wild Earth," Miranda said, referring to the herb shop that adjoined the restaurant. "I'd rather not run into them again."

"Sure. Maybe they sell something in there that will balance you," I suggested.

Miranda stopped outside the back door of the patio, as if she was admiring the waterfall that spilled into the garden pond, and said, "I'm not wrong, Aaron. Zachary has a wife and two kids."

"Which you already told Alex," I pointed out. "Whether or not he believes you, he's a big boy. He's entitled to make his own mistakes."

"So you *do* think he shouldn't be involved with somebody's husband," Miranda said triumphantly.

"It's none of my business. Besides, how do you know there aren't mitigating circumstances?"

"Now you sound like Vivian."

"I'll take that as a compliment," I said. I sat on a bench and pulled her down next to me. "OK, what if Zachary is married? What if he's lying to Alex? Or what if Alex knows but thinks they're separated or something? All you've done so far is piss him off. If this relationship crashes and burns, that just makes it harder for him to turn to you, maybe to any of us, for comfort. Deep inside, you have to know I'm right. It's just like me and Heath."

"What is?"

"You drove yourself, not to mention the two of us, crazy trying to find out what was going on. Once it became public knowledge that we were involved, you backed off. Why? Because you think we're headed for a disaster, and you want us to be able to turn to you when it happens. Which neither of us would do if we were mad at you and didn't want to hear 'I told you so.'"

"It's not the same thing at all," Miranda argued.

"The only difference is that you haven't been stalking us all over town—" I broke off as she blushed and dropped her eyes. "Good grief, Miranda, you need a life."

"I *do,*" she agreed, looking pathetic. I wasn't sure if it was a blatant attempt to gain my sympathy, but it was such an unusual expression for her that it worked.

"What's wrong?" I asked in a gentler tone.

"It's Joey!" she wailed.

"The girl from the New Year's Eve party?" I asked, pretending not to know who she meant.

"That was Jodi," she corrected me. "And the word for her is *woman,* not *girl.* I'm talking about the drummer for Tragic White Men."

"You're dating Alex's drummer?"

"I wish. She treats me like I'm a leper."

"Maybe she's straight," I said.

"She's definitely not straight."

"You've been stalking her too, huh?"

"Stop calling it that. I don't stalk people."

"Not very effectively," I agreed. "Have you asked her out?"

"Only about twenty times."

"And she says?"

"No, obviously. At first she acted pissed that I was bothering her. Then she'd just laugh at me like I couldn't be serious. Then she started looking annoyed again, so I stopped asking. I've never had this problem, Aaron. *I'm* the one who says no."

"Maybe that's why you're being so persistent," I suggested, trying not to sound unkind. "Rejection is new to you, and you see it as a challenge. If she said yes, after one date you'd magnify her flaws and—"

"Not this time. Trust me, I've seen her at her worst. Wearing clothes I hate. Being a bitch at the bars. Flirting with women. I've even seen her falling down drunk. And she wears all that black eye makeup! But when I think of her, I think of how hot she looks when she's playing the drums. Or how she puts off great energy when she dances. And one time, I saw her at Borders—totally by accident, I swear—and she was reading a biography of Virginia Woolf. Does that sound like someone I'd date? Normally I'd write that off as either boring or pretentious. But no, I went and bought the same book."

"That is sobering," I teased. "Did you enjoy reading it?"

"I didn't get past the first chapter," she admitted. "But I liked the pictures."

I couldn't stop myself from laughing and hugging her. I pulled her up and we went inside Wild Earth, where we were accosted by a guy asking to read tarot cards for us.

"No, thanks," I said, trying to guide Miranda away.

"C'mon, Aaron, it's only ten dollars," Miranda said, pulling money from her jeans pocket.

"You can," I said. "I don't want to."

I wandered through the shop, sniffing oils and playing with a Tibetan bowl, worried that I might turn into Lily Tomlin. I kept trying to remember the name of the movie where she and Steve Martin switched bodies.

"*All of Me,*" Miranda said when she found me.

"That's it!" I said. "Thanks, I was going crazy trying to remember that. Well? Is there a drummer in your future?"

"He didn't say," she answered vaguely.

"Oh, jeez," I said. "You asked about Heath and me, didn't you?"

"Surprisingly, you're not the most pressing matter in my life," she said.

"Is it going to end badly?"

"Things are progressing as they should," she answered cryptically, and I considered bouncing the brass bowl off of her head. "Now I'm starving."

"You should have eaten when I did," I said.

"I was busy. Let's go somewhere else."

She drove us to Empire Café, a coffee shop/restaurant that looked out at Westheimer, where the usual mixed crowd strolled the sidewalks. Suburban wives pushing strollers and looking for deals on antiques in the many open-front shops and cottages-converted-to-stores that lined the street. Gay boys and girls wearing everything from leather to cutoffs. Black-clad teens proudly displaying new piercings and tattoos. Corporate types grabbing a late lunch. Given my company and the day I'd had, I wondered who was spying on whom in the crowd.

I went to a table while Miranda stood in line to order. She brought an iced coffee for me when she joined me.

"So you think I backed off of you and Heath, huh?" she asked. "We just haven't had an opportunity to talk about it. But I have plenty of opinions on the subject."

"I know. You told me a while back that any relationship between us was doomed."

"I never said doomed. I said it was the highway to hell. Maybe I was wrong. If it's working for you two, who am I to argue?"

"It depends on what you mean by working," I said. "If you mean that we're madly in love and planning to stay together forever, that's not where we're at. But we're OK with that."

"Both of you?"

"Both of us," I said emphatically.

"I know that Heath doesn't express himself the way Alex and I do," she mused, "but he's still the kind of guy who wants someone to come home to. A relationship. He seems so practical, but he'd love to be swept off his feet and find himself madly in love."

"And me?" I asked, deliberately not reacting to her assessment of Heath.

"You like being single. You don't share all of our romantic illusions. You're self-sufficient and content to be on your own. Really, it would suit you if you and Patrick stayed roommates forever. That's as close as you want to get to a committed relationship. You're probably the smart one. Since you don't have unrealistic expectations about love, you'll never get your heart broken."

"Interesting," I said, grateful that her food was ready. The interruption gave me a chance to change the subject. When she began eating, I said, "I'm going out of town for a week or so. With my family."

She frowned and asked, "Don't y'all usually do that in August?"

"Yes, but Stasi's baby is due in August. So we changed it to June this year. We're not going anywhere exotic. She wants to stay close to her doctors. A friend of my parents owns a beach house in Galveston. Dad's renting it for the whole month, but I'll only be there part of the time. Until Father's Day."

"I thought that was the date of the next Love Sucks meeting," Miranda said.

"It is. I'm coming back that afternoon. Don't worry; after the last one, I wouldn't dream of missing this one. I fear what might be said about me behind my back."

"Do you think Patrick and Vivian will have worked things out by then?"

"I don't know," I said, trying not to sound pessimistic. Patrick's moods and actions had given me no reason to believe things had improved between my roommate and his girlfriend.

"Wouldn't it be funny if, when our deal is over, you and Heath were together, Alex and I had significant others, but Patrick and Vivian were finished?"

"It wouldn't be funny at all," I said. "It would be awful. The part about Patrick and Vivian, I mean."

"Well," she shrugged, "like Alex sang in his song, there are other fish in the sea."

Her comments left me feeling contemplative. When Heath fell asleep that night at my apartment, I got out of bed and pulled out my journal, trying to sort through my feelings while I wrote. But I mostly found myself chewing on my pen and staring at him. Something about Miranda's assessment of the two of us was bugging me. I finally gave up and crawled back into bed, making enough of a commotion to wake him.

"Are you OK?" he asked, squinting at me.

"I'm fine."

I kept nudging closer until he finally turned over and wrapped his arms and legs around me. I could tell he didn't want to wake up, so even though I wished I could talk to him, I let it go, lying sleepless when he resumed his light snoring. At least we no longer had to sneak away from each other in the dead of night to keep our friends from knowing about us.

I took my quiet mood and my journal with me to Galveston. Kelly was the only one at the house when I arrived. After I put all my stuff in my room, she and I walked to the beach together, arranging our towels and helping each other slather on sunblock while seagulls screamed overhead.

We made small talk, catching each other up, then she dozed while Miranda's words replayed in my mind. Just when I felt like I was on the edge of some realization, I heard TP screaming my name. I sat up and saw the whole family descending on us. Any hope of peace and quiet was swallowed up in the logistics of arranging umbrellas, chairs, coolers, and TP's toys. I was exhausted after ten minutes.

However, thanks to Kelly's engineering expertise and oversight, I helped Tad and TP build the world's greatest sand castle, complete with enough roads, bridges, moats, and turrets to horrify any architect, housekeeper, or flood insurance salesman. My parents and Stasi occasionally interrupted their lazy conversations under the shade of the umbrellas to request modifications or remind us that it would all be gone the next day, victim of either the tide or marauding teenagers.

By the time I crawled into my bed that night, worn out from the sun, my nephew, and a marathon session of Trivial Pursuit, I'd forgotten all about writing in my journal. I awoke the next morning to the fragrant smell of coffee and TP's overloud conversation, a lot of which seemed to consist of *But why do I have to be quiet?*

I threw on some shorts and a T-shirt and stumbled downstairs. My mother guided me to a chair and set a cup in front of me without asking questions. Not that she'd have been able to get one in, as I was bombarded with *Is the sand castle still there? Do sharks dream? If I got a dog, would it be bigger than a shark? Could a shark eat a dog?* and *What do sharks eat for breakfast?* before I'd even taken my first swallow of coffee.

"Don't worry," my mother softly said. "We're going to the beach as soon as he's finished eating his cereal."

"Uh-huh," I said, giving her a bleary look.

It was more than an hour later before they finally left the house with all their beach accoutrement. Even though the clock said 8 A.M., I was by then irreversibly awake, so I took a shower and settled myself into an Adirondack chair on the deck. I made sure to take my journal with me, so I could stare helplessly at it just as I had at home. But at least now I was undistracted by the beauty of a sleeping Heath.

Finally I wrote down the gist of what Miranda had said.

Heath wants someone to come home to. Seems practical but wants to be swept off his feet and to be madly in love.

Aaron has no romantic illusions. Self-sufficient. No unrealistic expectations about love. Will never get his heart broken.

After I stared at the words a while, I figured out why they kept bothering me. I was perfectly willing to fall in love with Heath. I had millions of romantic illusions and expectations about him. It was Heath, not me, who'd tried to head off the resumption of our love affair. It was Heath who held *me* at arm's length. It was Heath who stayed closed off, remote, and private, even when he was sharing a passionate physical relationship with me. No wonder I'd told him that knowing more about him didn't make me feel any closer to him.

I remembered Alexander saying that Heath hadn't been the only one who was hurt all those years ago. Not that Alex had much credibility in matters of love. In all the years I'd known him, he'd never taken responsibility for a single heart he'd broken. *I never lie to them, so if they get hurt, they have no one to blame but themselves,* was his mantra.

As for Alexander's heart, as much as he grumped and groused about the men who did him wrong, I couldn't recall a single one who'd broken it. Alex did not fall in love. At least I'd once been in love with Heath. Maybe I still was, a little, although it would be disingenuous to say that I'd spent the years since he left missing him or letting it stop me from having other relationships. After the initial shock of our breakup had worn off, I'd put him behind me, with little expectation of ever being with him again.

"What are you doing?" Kelly asked, yawning from the doorway.

"Brooding."

"That sounds like fun. Or you could watch Sister's belly with me."

I put my journal on the table and followed her inside, where Stasi was lying on the sofa, laughing at her stomach.

"I don't remember TP moving around this much," she said. "Oops. There he goes again."

"If this one's going to have more energy than TP, you better start feeding him Ritalin as soon as he's born," I said. I sat on the floor next to her and pressed my hands to her stomach. "Good grief. Does that hurt?"

"Nope. Sometimes, when a hand or foot presses against my ribs. But I think he's dropped, which puts more pressure on my bladder. We had to stop five times coming down here."

"As fascinating as your urinary habits are, I think I'll cook breakfast," Kelly said. "Aaron, come make yourself useful."

"Do you ever think about getting married and having a baby?" I asked her while we cooked.

"Sometimes," she said. "Then I listen to the women at work and change my mind. I don't know if I feel like balancing a career with a family. And childcare costs are ridiculous. Sister is lucky that she can stay at home." She listened as I told her what was going on with Patrick and Vivian, and finally she said, "I guess if I was really in love, I'd find a way to make it work. But I understand Vivian's hesitation. Do you think they'll stay together?"

"I hope so," I said. "Patrick's not the kind of man who proclaims his emotions. But I know he loves her. She's lucky to have him."

"Not if he expects her to make all the sacrifices."

"What's he asking her to sacrifice?" I asked. "He adores her and wants to build a life with her."

"Depends on his vision of a life. Like the guys I work with? Most of them are Neanderthals when it comes to relationships. Even the ones who are married to women with professions. If their wives keep working, they're still the ones who have to run the household, worry about the kids, stay home if the kids are sick, yada yada yada. I couldn't handle that. I doubt Vivian can either. If Patrick wants to hold on to her, he should come up with solutions that don't run her ragged while he gets to keep living the same way, only with Vivian instead of you as his roommate."

"Hmm," I answered, not wanting to admit that she made sense.

"Your life wouldn't change much if you moved in with a boyfriend," Kelly said. "You'd both go to work, come home, eat out or cook dinner, watch TV, go to bed, and do it all again the next day. It's a lot simpler."

"You think so?" I asked, laughing. "I'll be sure to tell that to some of the gay couples I know."

She shrugged and said, "At least you don't start with the preconceived notion that one of you is more entitled than the other."

"Right," I said, rolling my eyes.

"Y'all are both full of crap," Stasi said, chiming in from the doorway. "Neither of you has ever had a relationship that lasted more than a few months." She looked at Kelly and said, "Most fights are about power and respect, even if they seem to be about kids, money, and sex. I don't see how gay couples have any advantage over straight couples. But y'all don't have to worry about it. You've never committed yourselves to a goldfish, much less a significant other. I'm starving."

Though it was hard to find a better time than bickering with my sisters and playing with TP and Tad, who was basically a larger version of his son, I managed to tear myself away a few nights later for some Aaron time. It was too early for much action at Evolution, so after a stop in the Boulevard Saloon, with its impressive view of the Gulf, I went to Kon Tiki, which offered a dance floor for the patrons as well as dancers on cubes in the middle of the bar, pool tables, and a drag show. I was a little surprised not to run into anyone I knew, but it didn't matter. I had plenty of chances to dance and flirt. It was a nice break, and I was gratified by several offers to extend my evening into more intimate moments. It wasn't until later that night, when I wrote in my journal, that I realized Heath had never entered my mind when I declined those offers.

By Father's Day, I'd decided my time away constituted our cooling-off period. I was sure Heath was thinking along the same lines. On my drive back to Houston, I found myself feeling a little smug about how we'd managed to come through our affair with no damage done. Things would get back to normal, with our friends providing all the drama.

Then he opened the door after I knocked, our eyes met, and the next thing I knew we were on the sofa in his living room, trying to catch our breath after a robust reunion. Apparently, *cooling off* had been the wrong term for where things stood.

"Miss me?" Heath finally asked.

"Not at all."

"I could tell. Shall we get cleaned up?"

I let him unpeel my sweaty body from his leather sofa and asked, "Where is this evening's whine fest? And why did we choose Father's Day? None of us is a father."

"It's International Panic Day," Heath explained. "Don't ask me; Patrick picked it. We're going to Crostini's. Feel like a little Italian?"

"Sure, lead me to him."

Heath laughed and said, "Overachiever."

"I'm still a virile young man."

"For a few days, babe, until you hit the big three-oh."

"*You* haven't slowed down. Much."

"I'll make you pay for that later," Heath said, laughing and ruffling my hair.

"Don't threaten me with a good time."

We were at the restaurant before everyone else, but there wasn't a crowd, so they seated us and brought our wine while we admired the artwork on the walls. Crostini's was one of my favorite places, with its highly polished wooden bar, vases of miniature roses on every table, and subdued lighting. I was dipping a warm slice of bread into an herb-flavored olive oil when Patrick and Vivian arrived. I was happy to see that they were together, even if they did seem a bit strained when they sat down.

"How was Galveston?" Patrick asked. "I actually missed you."

"If you missed me, why didn't you greet me the way Heath did?" I asked.

"Dude, I don't wanna know," he said, raising his hands in mock horror.

I talked about the Fisher family vacation, masking my surprise when Patrick ordered iced tea and Vivian sipped daintily at a glass of water. If the first step to fixing a broken love affair was actually twelve steps, then Heath and I were doomed, since we'd ordered wine almost before the host could hand us our menus.

"Did you hit the bars?" Vivian asked. "Was it lively down there?"

"Once or twice," I said, darting a quick glance at Heath to see his reaction. He was reading his menu with a look of intense concentration. Either he wasn't listening, or he wanted to prove that I didn't make him feel jealous and possessive. "I had fun. It was crowded, but not miserably so. I saw a couple of good drag shows. Danced with some hot guys. All in all, I'd say the vacation was just what I needed."

"Drag shows, huh," Patrick said. He looked like he was about to comment further, but at that moment Miranda appeared, somehow creating a stir just by walking through the restaurant.

"Hello, how's everyone, kiss kiss, how was Galveston, where's Alexander?" Miranda asked in one long breath.

"Did you two switch bodies?" I asked, looking from Miranda to Vivian.

Vivian gave me a blank look, and Miranda said, "Huh?"

"Usually it's Vivian who's a dynamo of energy, but she's cool and collected tonight. Whereas you're coming in like gangbusters."

"You mean *I'm* usually cool and collected?" Miranda asked, delighted.

"More like woeful, melancholy, and aggrieved," Patrick said. Which answered my question. If Patrick was still speaking in his created language of Victorian Synonymese, things were not resolved between Vivian and him.

"I just have a lot on my mind," Vivian said. "I forgot to tell you. Alex isn't coming."

"Why not?" I asked, apparently sounding a bit aggrieved myself, because all eyes turned to me as if I'd said something outrageous. "I mean…well, why not?"

"He didn't give a reason. Just left a message that he wouldn't be able to make it tonight."

"Why should he come?" Patrick asked. "The whole reason for Love Sucks meetings is for him and Miranda to complain about their love lives. Apparently, *he* has no complaints."

"Neither do I," Miranda said. "So we can all enjoy a nice, peaceful dinner together."

"Did Joey finally say yes?" I asked.

As soon as the words were out of my mouth, I regretted them. Even before Miranda gave me a look that could curdle milk. The waiter stepped up to take our orders, and I sent a pleading glance Heath's way, hoping he would rescue me. Unfortunately, since I'd never told him that Miranda had confessed about her crush on Joey, he thought I'd betrayed his confidence. His expression was even more annoyed than hers.

"Who's Joey?" Patrick asked, getting right to the point as soon as the waiter was gone. I considered kicking him under the table, but I figured that would only get me in more trouble.

"Joey as in the drummer for Tragic White Men?" Vivian asked Miranda. "Is that who you've got your eye on?"

"Thanks, Aaron," Miranda said.

"Yeah," Heath said.

"What are *you* thanking him for?" Miranda asked.

"Because I didn't tell him about Joey," I said quickly, before Heath could admit that he'd told me Miranda's secret before she had.

His eyes looked big and innocent behind his glasses as he took a swallow of wine.

"Oh, he already knew," Miranda said. "And thanks to you, so does everyone else."

"Not Alex!" I reminded her. "He's the one you didn't want to tell."

"Why's it such a big secret?" Patrick asked. "After the production you made telling all of us that Alexander's boyfriend is married, why are *you* entitled to secrets?"

"Joey's been turning you down, huh?" Vivian surmised.

"I don't want to talk about it," Miranda said.

"Isn't that what these meetings are for?" Patrick asked. "For you to pontificate about your misery?"

"Her misery over not being able to find The One," I pointed out. "But now she thinks she has, only The One doesn't want her."

"Wow, Aaron, you're a real cheerleader tonight, aren't you?" Miranda asked. At that moment, she caught sight of Vivian's speculative gaze and grumpily asked, "What?"

"In all the time I've known you, I never remember a woman turning you down," Vivian said. "What's wrong with her?"

If at first Miranda seemed startled by Vivian's words, her expression softened with gratitude. "Thanks for not asking what's wrong with me," she said.

"Please. Any woman would be lucky to have you. You have a good time, but you're smart enough to run your own business. Successfully, I might add. You've got tons of friends. You know practically everybody in this city."

"Including Zachary," I murmured, and Miranda narrowed her eyes at me, then turned back to Vivian, dying to hear more praise.

"Everybody likes you. And besides that, you're good-looking." At these last words, Vivian seemed to be struck by something. "You know, the times that we've gone to see Tragic White Men, the girls Joey hangs out with are all…" When she trailed off, we waited breathlessly for her next comment. "Well, they're all kind of waifish and helpless-looking."

"Femme," Heath provided helpfully.

"I am not turning into a lipstick lesbian for some bleached-blond brat," Miranda yelped. "I am what I am."

"You shouldn't have to," Vivian assured her, and fixed Miranda with another stare as our salads were set in front of us. She bit into a tomato, chewed a moment, then said, "There's nothing wrong with emphasizing your more feminine qualities, however. You know, a little more attention to accessorizing or grooming—"

"That sounds like a cross between Elizabeth Taylor and a French poodle," Miranda whined.

"Miranda's makeover, courtesy of the incomparable Vivian," I said, giving the gayest hand clap I could muster.

"Can this lesbian be saved?" Heath intoned and shook his head sadly as he lowered it in a Phil Donahue imitation.

"You guys are assholes," Miranda said, then turned back to Vivian. "Tell me more."

"A good hairstylist for a cut and highlights—"

"I could start that process with a weed whacker," Patrick volunteered.

"—a facial with eyebrow waxing. A little makeup wouldn't kill you. And we can go shopping together and feminize your wardrobe."

"I'm living in hell," Miranda said, but she looked intrigued.

"Put yourself in my hands, and I swear, you'll still be you. Just the you who's dying to get out."

"Wasn't that the plot of *Alien*?" Patrick asked, and Heath choked on his wine.

The girls ignored us to discuss Vivian and Miranda's Excellent Shopping Adventure, so we opted to stop the witty repartee in favor of male bonding. This entailed shoveling as much food into our mouths as quickly as possible, and caused our waiter, who'd been born more femme than Miranda ever would be, to ask us in his sweetest voice if we wanted to see the menu again. He obviously heard the sound of his tip decreasing, since he comped us a round of coffee and a dessert to share.

The next day I tried to call Alex, leaving a message when he didn't answer. Since I couldn't torment him with questions about Zachary, I turned my attention to Patrick, who was munching on a bowl of Cheerios while watching *The Young and the Restless*.

"How's your love life?" I asked, draping myself over a chair.

"At least nobody's stealing my sperm," he said, nodding toward the television. "Who writes this stuff?"

I smiled, thinking of Heath's confession, and said, "Don't dodge the question. You and Vivian were together last night."

"We're still on a break," he said. "And I'm OK with that."

"Really?"

"Yep. I decided to focus on other things. Like Dinks."

"When do you not focus on Dinks?" I asked.

"Thanks. You sound like Vivian. Going to clubs to see Tragic White Men has given me an idea."

"You want to start a band? Get some groupies? Make Vivian jealous?"

"I'm thinking of knocking out that wall between the bar and the back room to expand my space," Patrick said, ignoring my questions. "Putting in a stage. Maybe having a show now and then, or a band. Nothing fancy, just changing the pace a couple of nights a week. I mean, why should everyone else be making money off of Alex's band? I'm his friend. That entitles me to be first in line to exploit him."

"But you don't really have a club kid crowd," I pointed out.

"I could. I could have entertainment on nights that are slow now, and build a new and different clientele." He looked at me. "Go ahead. Play devil's advocate. I know how you hate change."

"I do not. Why do people always say that about me? I just subscribe to the belief that if it ain't broke, don't fix it."

"Like I said, I'm thinking about the slow nights. Besides, if I don't put some of my profits back into the bar, the taxes will eat me alive."

"That makes sense," I conceded. "Just do your research."

"Aaron, when have I ever not done my research?" Patrick asked. "People thought I was nuts to give up a big salary with a growing company to open my own bar. I proved it was the right move. But it's getting a little stale. Maybe if things were different between Vivian and me, I wouldn't be bored. But I am, so I'm looking for a new challenge."

I thought it over, deciding that he was probably being smart. Other men might have sought a new relationship as a diversion. I hoped Vivian appreciated Patrick's patience and devotion. If the two of them could just hold on through this uncertain period, they'd probably end up together for life.

When a nagging voice inside me pondered applying those same philosophies to my relationship with Heath, I jumped up and browbeat Patrick into going to the gym with me.

RAT CATCHERS DAY

I had to admit that I was hurt when Alex not only returned none of my calls over the next couple of days, but didn't acknowledge my birthday. Heath joined me for a birthday dinner at my parents' house, awed by the size of Stasi's stomach. He seemed worried that she might go into labor any moment and kept his eye on her the entire time we were there, which amused her.

Later, when we were alone, he gave me my present. Somehow he'd found a different sunflower painting by the same artist, which touched me beyond belief. His eyes grew wary as mine filled with tears.

"Are you getting all sentimental on me?" he asked.

"I can't believe you found this," I said. "Thanks, Heath. I love you."

"I love you too," he said. If he'd only left it at that, everything might have been different, but for once he decided to open up. "These last few months have been incredible, Aaron. We've connected in a way I never thought was possible for us." My heart started racing as I waited for his next words. "I suppose I've felt adrift ever since my mother died. My friends are my only family. But you're more than a friend."

"I feel the same way about you," I said. "But don't forget, the Fishers are your family too."

"It's so great to spend time with them. I hope, when the day comes that you fall in love, I'll still be part of your family. He's going to be a lucky guy, but he'd better be an understanding one too. Because I'm not running away from our friendship again. You're my soul mate, Aaron." Although I felt like my face was frozen into something akin to a death grimace, Heath seemed to regard it as a smile, because he gave me a hug and said, "Happy birthday."

My first instinct was to scream, cry, and hit him with the framed painting. His *friend*? His *soul mate*?

When I closed my eyes, I could see little flashes of white lights. Since I'd always heard that anger made a person see red, I decided maybe seeing white meant I was having a stroke. It would serve him right if I died on his fucking leather sofa and left him with a mess to clean up. Or better yet, I'd be paralyzed, unable to walk or talk, and he'd be stuck taking care of me for the rest of my long, disabled life.

Then again, I wondered why I should have to suffer just so he would. I decided I'd rather kill him. I'd spent months warning myself not to fall in love with him again. And now that I had, he thought of me as his *soul mate*?

When his attempt to kiss me was met with a clenched jaw and gritted teeth, it dawned on him that I might not be skipping down the sunflower-strewn path to best-buddy nirvana with him.

"Did I say the wrong thing?" Heath asked, pulling back to look at me.

"Not if that's how you feel," I managed to voice from my locked jaw. I sounded like a cross between Jack Nicholson and Jack on *Will & Grace,* which horrified both of us.

"Aaron, talk to me. What's wrong?"

"That was not the declaration I've been waiting for," I said.

He was too smart not to understand me, and he dropped his arms and backed away from me. "I told you from the start that I was not the man who could dive headlong into love with you," he reminded me.

"And that it was a bad idea," I agreed, hating him as much as I loved him, if that was possible.

"I was afraid one of us would get hurt."

"And now I have been. Are you happy, Miss Cleo? You were right again."

"Aaron," he said, reaching for me.

"No," I said, and he dropped his arms. "Since you're the one breaking my heart, I don't want you to comfort me. You're going to have to let me be angry and upset. I'm sure I'll get over it. You did."

He shook his head at me but merely said, "All right."

I picked up the painting and left his house, wondering why I couldn't cry. I wanted to cry. It hurt not to. But I needed to feel safe somewhere and not so alone. I couldn't go to Miranda. It still stung that she'd completely misread my relationship with Heath, certain that I'd be the one who would hurt him. Patrick and Vivian had enough troubles of their own. If I went to either of them, we'd just feed off each other's misery.

Since I'd been dumped after celebrating the birthday Alex had ignored, I decided the least he could do was give up one night of band rehearsals or dalliances with Zachary. I'd certainly given him enough nights over the years to have one coming to me.

His apartment was dark, but I knocked anyway. Of course he didn't answer. For all I knew, he and Zachary were on a Princess Cruise, drinking bellinis and toasting each other's sexual prowess. At least that was the explanation that made my spirits plummet further downward.

I was glad I had a grip on the wrought iron banister when I heard a quiet voice quaver from the garden, "Alexander is not home."

After clutching my throat—why did gay men turn into starlets when their hearts were broken?—I saw the shadowy outline of Mr. Bryant leaning on his cane in the dim light spilling from the back porch of the main house. Mr. Bryant was Alexander's ninety-two-year-old landlord. Alex called him "Montrose's Founding Queer," and he did have some amazing stories to tell about decades of gay Houston. But I wasn't feeling particularly conversational at the moment.

"Thanks, Mr. Bryant. Could you tell him that Aaron came by?"

"Certainly, Aaron. It's a hot one, isn't it? Ten o'clock and still ninety degrees."

I really wasn't up for either of Houston's main two conversations—the first being the weather; the second, when the weather would change—so I said something innocuous and hurried to my car. I could think of only one other person who might offer a shoulder to cry on, and I drove to Ramon's house with the slimmest of hopes that he would be there.

"Oh, baby," Ramon said after one look at my face. He pulled me inside and asked no questions while I blubbered against his shoulder. After I calmed down, he pushed me toward the sofa and went into the kitchen, coming back with something that tasted like cherry Kool-Aid.

"What is this?" I asked, making a face.

"Cherry Kool-Aid. It's all I have. Tell me what happened."

"Heath and me. It's over. Or maybe it never got started. I just hoped it would."

Ramon listened, his large brown eyes liquid with sympathy, while I told him what had been going on between Heath and me. I wasn't sure if it was because of crying or talking about it, but I felt better after I finished my pathetic tale. It definitely wasn't the Kool-Aid.

"And on your birthday," Ramon said, shaking his head. "He's a beast."

"My actual birthday was a few days ago; we were just celebrating it tonight. Heath's not a beast. I think he was as surprised as I was by my reaction. I don't know what I was thinking. People only get back together in books and movies." A couple of suitcases stacked next to the door finally penetrated my self-absorption. "Are you going somewhere? Did I come at a bad time?"

"Mmm." Ramon appeared to be lost in thought, so I took the Kool-Aid into the kitchen and poured it down the drain, filling the glass with tap water, though I normally drank bottled water. When I went back to Ramon, he smiled and said, "Before you say no, hear me out."

"What?"

"I am going somewhere. Some friends and I are flying to Portland in the morning."

"Oregon?"

"Maine. There were supposed to be six of us, but that idiot Frederick got appendicitis. Two of the guys are flight attendants, so between frequent flier miles and companion passes, everyone's flying free. We're staying in a big old house owned by one of the guy's aunts. If you're willing to kick in for your share of the groceries, you can escape this heat and heartache and enjoy a week in coastal Maine."

"In a house with you and four strangers? That would be kind of weird."

"I hear the house is huge," Ramon said. "You could get lost in it. You might even like my friends. But if you don't, you can stand on the rocky shore and stare tragically out to sea, like the French Lieutenant's woman. No one will mind. We're not planning a high-energy vacation. We're just running away from the heat."

I'd never been to Maine, and I had to admit the idea sounded appealing. Especially since my only other option was wallowing in self-pity while my friends struggled not to say *I told you so.*

"Do you think we'd be blurring our boundaries?" I asked.

Ramon laughed and said, "Aaron, I'm your friend. I think friends can take a trip together. If you just had a birthday, that makes you a Gemini. Isn't a Gemini supposed to be spontaneous?"

"I have no idea," I said. But I did know that leaving for a few days would keep me from returning to the scene of the crime. Time away from Heath might be exactly what I needed. "When do we leave?"

"That's the spirit. Like the princesses we are, we have a limo service picking us all up in the morning. Could you be packed and ready by nine?" I nodded. "Good. Be sure and throw in a sweater or two."

"Are you nuts?"

"My friends say Maine nights can get into the lower sixties. That's like winter here."

"It sounds great," I admitted. "I guess I should go home and pack, huh?"

"And get to bed so you don't oversleep."

He walked me to the door, and I said, "Thanks, Ramon. You're right. You are my friend."

I went home to pack and write a note to Patrick explaining my whereabouts. I thought, briefly, of calling Heath. Instead, I changed my message to explain that I was out of town for a few days. If he called, he'd know. If he didn't, then it didn't matter anyway.

The next morning, I didn't even try to sort out the faces and names of my traveling companions. I figured there would be time enough to do that during our week together. Since we had two flight attendants in our group, there was a lot of laughing and joking around with the crew, and we were treated like royalty. I mostly spent the trip dozing against Ramon's shoulder, comforted by the fact that no one really knew me or how lousy I felt inside. But that was something else I could sort out over the week.

When we arrived at the Portland International Jetport, a name that struck me as odd since the airport was smaller than St. Gregory's, we found our luggage. Then Brett, our host for the weekend, rented a car. We all tried to pitch in for the cost, but he wouldn't hear of it.

"If I came up here on my own, I'd rent a car anyway. It's the same thing, in my opinion, so let me do this. It's no big deal. Really," he assured us, smiling warmly.

Brett had straight hair, the color of sand, which was cut a little long in the front. When his bangs fell into his blue eyes, he'd push his hair back over his head, which would last for five minutes, then he'd repeat the process all over again. His peaches-and-cream complexion was dotted with a light five o'clock shadow. Brett's demeanor was affable and made me feel like I was in good hands. I liked him right away.

"Girl, you won't hear any arguments from me," Shaun said. "I still have rent to pay, and bills up the wazoo."

Grover said, "The only thing that should be up that wazoo of yours is—"

Shaun shrieked and clamped his hand over Grover's mouth while the rest of us looked on and laughed. Shaun and Grover, our two flight attendants, had met two years before on a red-eye flight from Las Vegas to Manhattan, fallen in love, and set up housekeeping in Houston. They were like two peas in a pod, carbon copies of each other, a condition known to occur in many gay male couples. They dressed in similar attire, both had buzz-cuts, and they were wearing the exact same Diesel sneakers. The only difference I saw was that no matter how much he tanned, Shaun would never be an African-American like Grover.

We piled our luggage into the back of the SUV Brett rented. Ramon jumped into the front seat, Shaun and Grover sat together in the middle of the vehicle, and I found myself in the last seat with Larry. Or Harry. I couldn't be sure, since I had only heard his name once.

Worn out from our trip, we took a vote and decided to eat in and settle into Brett's aunt's house instead of going out to eat in our rumpled, travel-weary state. Brett drove us to a grocery store, where we had fun choosing food for dinner and breakfast. We figured we'd worry about the rest of the week at another time. Afterward, I marveled at the old houses we passed on the tree-lined roads on our way to Brett's aunt's house.

"Be on the watch for a sign that says Randall," Brett announced. "I always miss it. It should be somewhere on the right side of the road."

"As opposed to the wrong side of the road?" Grover asked.

Our copilot, Ramon, spotted the sign, and we turned onto a private driveway that cut into a forest of pine, ash, and elm trees. Beyond the trees were rolling fields of green grass, a small apple orchard, and several flower gardens positioned around huge rocks and tree stumps.

"Here we are," Brett announced. "Welcome to Captain Randall's farmhouse."

"Farmhouse," Ramon repeated. "This doesn't look like *Green Acres* to me."

The Randall house was a stately, three-story Colonial home with an ell joining it to a carriage house and an immense barn. The clapboards were painted a gleaming white, and the trim and wooden shutters were black. Perched on top of the roof was a widow's watch, and on either side of the house, two chimneys rose to the sky.

"It's huge," Grover observed.

"Enormous," Shaun agreed.

"I'll bet you say that to all the boys," Brett said. "But what do you think about the house?"

We all groaned in unison, then followed Brett into the entry hall. I was expecting the interior to be dark and imposing, but the floors were a polished, butternut brown wood, the walls were a soft, glowing white, and small whimsical items were hung on walls or scattered about the room. A barometer hung by the door, two buoys leaned in a corner, and several small silhouette portraits were framed on the wall opposite a grand staircase.

"I'd give you a tour, but I'm tired, and I'll bet you guys are too," Brett said. "I'll show you to your rooms and you can explore on your own, if you want."

I was taken to a room on the second floor. It had a weathered iron bed with fluffy pillows on a patchwork quilt. The walls were papered with a blue-and-cream flowered pattern. I dropped my bags by a chest of drawers and parted the ivory lace curtains. I could see a manicured lawn, flanked on either side by tall, wild grasses and reeds that sloped down to a rocky beach and the ocean.

A gentle knock prompted me to turn around to see Ramon leaning against the door frame. "Your room is beautiful," he commented, as if I had decorated it myself. "It's bigger than mine. I'm on the third floor. I guess Brett didn't know that we're…" He trailed off, unsure how to define our relationship.

"Actually, I'm kind of grateful to have some time alone," I gently said. Then added, "No offense."

"None taken," he assured me. "I completely understand. That's why I asked you to come along. I'm going down to explore the beach with Shaun, Grover, and Barry."

"Barry!" I exclaimed. "Thank you. I didn't catch his name on the plane. He's a quiet one, isn't he? Not that I've offered much sparkling conversation either."

"I met Barry through an old friend. Barry works as a paralegal at the same firm as Brett," Ramon explained. "He's fun, but he takes a while to warm up to new people."

"How do Grover and Shaun fit into this mix?"

Ramon laughed, and said, "Brett, Barry, and I met them last year on our flight to Miami. They were a lot of fun, and we ended up spending nearly every night with them. Speaking of which, they're probably waiting on me. Sure you don't want to come?"

"You go ahead," I urged. "I'll go up to the widow's watch and await your return."

"Or you could help Brett with dinner," Ramon casually said as he walked away.

"So that's why everyone's so anxious to see the beach," I said.

Ramon reappeared in the doorway and asked, "By the way, do you have your own bathroom?"

I looked around my room until I noticed a door, which revealed a small bathroom with a claw-foot tub.

"I guess I do," I answered.

"Damn it. I have to share a bathroom with Barry," Ramon muttered and walked away again. I heard his footfalls as he went downstairs.

I briefly considered unpacking but instead left my room in search of the kitchen. I wandered through a parlor, a living room, a sun room, and a music room, until I found the kitchen through a door off the dining room.

The kitchen was quite large, with a rustic-looking post-and-beam interior. The walls were stark and made of swirled, white plaster. The beams were stained a deep, dark brown and had large pots, pans, and dried herbs hanging from hooks. Off to the side of the room, near a bay window—through which I could see a rose garden in the backyard— was a small round table with six ladder-back chairs.

Brett was fussing over an old cast-iron, wood-burning stove, setting a trivet underneath a steaming pot. The kitchen was a mix of modern appliances with touches of days gone by. While I could see the need for the microwave on the counter, I wondered how often the hand-operated meat grinder was used.

"Need a hand?" I asked.

"I think I have everything under control," Brett said. "Could you open a window? It's getting hot in here."

I opened windows on both sides of the room, which created a salty cross-breeze, and said, "I nearly got lost trying to find the kitchen. This place is incredible, Brett. Thanks for allowing me to tag along."

"No problem," he replied. "The more the merrier. There's certainly enough room. Can I offer you some wine?"

"You can," I insisted. "And I'll accept."

Brett disappeared into a pantry and returned with a bottle of white wine. While I opened it, he found two glasses and set them on the butcher block island for me to pour.

We made small talk until the others returned from their walk on the beach. Dinner was served at the table in the kitchen, and we ate fresh corn, potatoes, lima beans, and lobster.

"I'm stuffed," Ramon said, pushing his chair away from the table and resting his hands on his stomach.

"Me too," Shaun agreed. "So that was lobster? It wasn't bad."

"I can't believe you've never had it before," Grover said to him. "I never knew that about you."

"It's so expensive in the South," Shaun drawled. "Mama couldn't afford it. Isn't it great that we've been together so long, and you're still learning new things about me?"

"I think I'm going to be sick," Barry said.

"Lobster can do that to you," Ramon said. "It's so rich."

"No. It's not the lobster," Barry protested. "It's those two Southern-fried love birds," he added, pointing at Shaun and Grover, who stuck out their tongues at him and moved their chairs even closer together so they could kiss. I decided Barry could use a good Love Sucks meeting.

Brett rose from the table and said, "C'mon, Aaron, let me show you the beach. Since we fixed dinner, the others can clean up."

Even though he'd made the dinner and all I'd done was pour wine, I stood to follow.

"Where's the dishwasher?" Grover asked.

"You are the dishwasher," Brett said. "Have fun."

I followed Brett across the lawn and down to the rocky beach. A long wharf stretched over the water, with a sailboat tied to the end of it.

"Where am I?" I asked. "Club Med?"

Brett laughed, and said, "Yes. The Maine branch."

From the beach, I could see a few houses nearby in either direction. They were more modern and not as large as the Randall home.

"Did you grow up in Maine, Brett?"

"No, I didn't," he answered, pushing back his bangs, which had been blown into his eyes by the winds off the ocean. "I'm originally from Connecticut. But we spent our summers here with my aunt when I was young. I used to hate it, though."

"Why?" I asked. It was so picturesque, and the house so beautiful, that I couldn't imagine anyone hating to be there.

We stepped onto the wharf, walked out to the end, and sat down, dangling our feet over the edge. My toes hung a foot above the water.

"When I was younger, it was boring here," Brett explained. "I'm an only child, and there were no kids around to play with. I suppose my parents could have taken me to activities in town, but the thought probably never crossed their minds."

"Didn't you have cousins here?" I asked, thinking of my extended family, and how whenever I visited my grandparents I'd always meet a new relative.

"My aunt never married," Brett said. The gentle thudding of the incoming tide against the side of the boat underscored his voice as he spoke. He asked, "Are you ready for a story?"

"Always."

"Captain William Randall guided British Navy ships into the Boston Harbor. At that time, there was no Maine, since this land was part of Massachusetts. Like many seafaring men, my first ancestor in the colonies built a home here. The kitchen was the original house, and the rest was added on as time went by. Captain Randall also ran lumber to Boston as a side business. As he grew older, he gave up sailing ships and began building them, right here in Cape Elizabeth.

"Captain Randall's son, Harrison, had no interest in the sea. Instead, he founded a granite quarry, which provided much of the stone that was used in the Brooklyn Bridge. Not to mention several buildings in Washington, D.C."

"That's amazing," I said.

"In those days, the granite mine was run by my great-grandfather, Thomas Randall. By the time my grandfather took over this house, the granite was gone. So he taught at Harvard's school of business and agriculture. Do you see a theme here?"

"The Randall House is always given to the first-born male of your family," I surmised, to which Brett nodded. I added, "And your family is loaded."

Brett threw back his head and laughed, which caused his hair to fall into his eyes again. His teeth were perfectly straight, not to mention gleaming white. I resisted the urge to brush his bangs back with my fingers and sat on my hands.

"I guess we are," Brett said. "Money, but no time for family, unfortunately. However, my grandfather never had a son. He had three daughters; the youngest died of smallpox. My grandmother died too, and he never remarried. My mother couldn't wait to leave, and never came back after she graduated from Radcliffe. However, it wasn't the money she wanted to leave, so she was lucky to fall in love with my father, an investment banker.

"My aunt never left this old house. Never married, and took care of my grandfather until he died. She was a nurse, which was fortunate; she fulfilled his wish to die in this house."

"Spooky," I said, hoping he hadn't passed away in my room.

"He was a stoic old bastard," Brett said. "He didn't trust modern medicine. I liked him. Anyway, my aunt inherited the house. She and my mother barely tolerate each other, so I don't know who'll get this place when she passes on."

"No wonder you hated coming here," I said. "If your mother and aunt didn't like each other, why did she bother coming here for the summer?"

Brett laughed, then said, "I guess my parents felt obligated. Or it was an act in hopes of one day getting the house. In any case, this place is big enough for them to spend a month in it yet hardly see each other. And usually my aunt would take off to tour some city in Europe for a month, which is where she is now. She likes me, though, and was disappointed to hear that I'd be using the house while she's not here."

"Should we be here? I don't want to get you disinherited," I said.

"Oh, no. I meant she'd like to see me," Brett clarified. "She's got great stories. For Pete's sake, listen to me. I've been rambling on and probably boring you. Who needs my aunt around? I probably sound just like her. No wonder I never get a second date."

"Your family history wasn't boring to me at all," I insisted, placing my hand on his shoulder. I withdrew it immediately, as if his skin was hot to the touch, even through his shirt. "Besides, my friends tell me I'm a good listener. For some reason, people open up to me and tell me everything. Sometimes even things that they shouldn't."

"You could cultivate some great stories out of what they say. You should be a writer," Brett said.

"I suppose so," I said. I turned away from him, pretending to follow the path of a seagull, while I rolled my eyes, frustrated with myself for not being able to say that I was, in fact, a writer. Except for my journals, I hadn't written so much as a letter in years.

"It's getting dark," Brett observed. "And chilly. Let's go back."

We all retired to our rooms relatively early, after talking and sipping Scotch in the parlor. The alcohol made me feel warm and sleepy, as did the fire Brett prepared in the fireplace, so I crawled into my bed on the second floor and fell asleep instantly.

The next morning I found my way to the kitchen, where Ramon and Barry were seated at the table eating breakfast.

"Good morning, starshine," Ramon sang to me.

"The earth is aglow," Barry joined in, then added, "because of the depletion of the ozone layer and the burning of fossil fuels."

Barry's surly attitude seemed to have readjusted itself overnight, which I acknowledged and encouraged with a smile.

"Sit down," Ramon ordered. He deposited his dishes in the sink and began pouring pancake batter into a skillet. "I'll fix you some blueberry pancakes. There's bacon too. Here's your coffee," he said, suddenly swooping by me and depositing a cup on the table.

"Thanks, Alice," I said to him.

"Well, kiss my grits," he exclaimed.

Barry corrected, "I could be wrong, but I think Flo said that."

While Ramon finished preparing my pancakes, he explained that Brett was out getting groceries. The others planned to hike down the beach to Portland Head Light, a working lighthouse. I declined their offer to join them, since I still wanted time to myself. Barry tried to change my mind, but Ramon dragged him out of the room, saying something about giving me space to breathe.

After I cleaned the kitchen, I decided to explore the house. I didn't get far, though, because the first room I peeked into turned out to be a study that was lined from floor to ceiling with books.

I ran my fingers over the spines, noting titles by Dickens, Twain, and Hawthorne among business texts, agricultural essays, and outdated encyclopedias. I opened a tattered, dusty hardcover and smelled the pages. I noticed the title, *Gone With the Wind,* and said, "It sure doesn't smell like peach blossoms."

I turned around, intending to leave, but found myself in front of a leather-topped desk with an old typewriter. I pressed a key; the resounding snap pierced the muted serenity of the study.

I sat down in the chair and opened the right-hand drawer of the desk. As if someone knew I'd look there first, I found a sheaf of typing paper. I rolled a piece into the antique machine and, without thinking, began typing the first ideas that entered my mind. Time was lost while characters and dialogue traveled from my mind and through my fingers as they danced over the keys.

I paused only when the door to the study opened and Brett slowly poked his head into the room. Seeing me behind the desk, he said, "Jesus! It's you."

"No. It's me, Aaron," I said. "People get me and Jesus mixed up all the time. They get upset when I can't turn water into wine."

"I heard the typewriter while I was putting away groceries," explained Brett. "I thought everyone was out exploring and I was all alone in the house. So I freaked out when I heard typing."

"As far as I know, spirits don't type. Or take dictation, for that matter," I said. It made me feel good that Brett was comfortable enough in my presence to groan audibly in response to my bad jokes. Hoping it wasn't too presumptuous of my houseguest status, I apologized for using the typewriter.

"That's OK," he assured me. "As long you don't break it, it's fine. Even if you did, I'm sure it could be fixed, so whatever. What are you working on?"

I felt my body try to shrink into the chair. I sounded almost apologetic when I said, "I'm writing a story."

"I didn't know you—" He cut himself off, then said, "Oh, man. I just remembered that comment I made on the dock last night. When I said you should be a writer."

"It's OK. In fact, thank you for that. It gave me the kick in the pants that I've needed to get myself writing again. I teach, so I find myself occupied with work and my students. When I'm not working, my friends take up a lot of my time. As a result, writing has kind of fallen by the wayside over the years."

Brett sat on a settee that faced the desk, rested his elbows on his knees, and clasped his hands together as he looked at me. I felt like I was being interviewed. Only the one being questioned rarely sat behind the desk. After a moment, he asked, "Can I read it? Or will you read it to me?"

I fidgeted and felt my face flush as I said, "I just started it. It's not in a place where I'd feel comfortable—"

"It's OK," he said, interrupting me. "I understand."

"It has nothing to do with you. I feel really vulnerable about my work if it's unfinished," I said.

"So, Aaron, why didn't you join the others at the lighthouse?" Brett asked.

For a second, I was grateful for the change of subject. But then I realized that it put me in another awkward situation. As charming and likeable as Brett was, I hesitated at the idea of explaining why I wanted time alone. I didn't want to come off as whiny or have him regret my presence in his family's home.

However, before I realized it, I found myself telling him everything. I told him about the deal my friends and I made on New

Year's Eve, the monthly Love Sucks meetings, and how they led to me getting close to Heath again, until my birthday, when I was left feeling more alone than ever.

"I guess I came up here to lick my wounds rather than enjoy the view," I said after I finished the whole story.

"There's nothing worse than having a crush on or being in love with someone who can't, or won't, return the feeling," Brett said.

"You said it," I agreed. We both sat in silence for a minute, until I said, "I really didn't mean to talk about this. Now that I have, I realize that I don't want to be alone as much as I thought I did. Is there something we could do? Or somewhere we could go?"

"Let me show you where I like to go when I want to be alone," Brett said.

After Brett hoisted the sails and tied off the rigging, we were coasting over the waves of the ocean in his family's sailboat. The wind rushed through my hair, and the boat seemed to hop over the waves when Brett steered us into them. With the warm sun on my face, and the occasional spray of saltwater, I felt more relaxed and carefree than I had in months.

Sailing took Brett's attention, so I was able to scrutinize him without his noticing. It struck me that if pushed for a description, I couldn't say much about the others I was sharing a house with. Other than Ramon, of course, because I'd known him intimately for years. But I'd be hard-pressed to give more than a rudimentary description of Shaun, Grover, and Barry, yet Brett's image was already so imprinted in my brain that I felt like I'd known him for even longer than I'd known Ramon. Maybe it was because he was different from me, with his blue eyes and untamable blond hair.

Finally it clicked. Brett reminded me of Heath. Golden boys. They'd be a beautiful couple. I found the thought disconcerting. Not because I didn't want to imagine Heath with another man, but because I found it strangely exciting to picture the two of them together. I tucked that thought away for later use and forced myself to stare at the horizon with what I hoped was an expression as innocent as a choirboy's.

"Hey!" Brett called. "Want a lesson in crewing?"

I nodded agreeably and made myself as useful as I could. From time to time, as our bodies brushed against each other's, I felt the way I had the day before, like his skin was hot to the touch and I shouldn't get too close. I chalked it up to his similarity to Heath. Maybe I was already learning, again, to think of Heath as my ex and to start the weaning process.

That night, after dinner and a boisterous poker game, I took my filched copy of *Gone With the Wind* to my bedroom and settled in to enjoy the trials of the beleaguered Southern belle. I'd been reading about an hour when I heard the first clap of thunder. I loved storms and hoped that if the Atlantic coast was going to provide one, it would be profound. I slid out of bed and opened my window to the high-voltage breeze off of the ocean, then returned to the novel. I was just considering closing the book to indulge myself in a fantasy of the Tarleton twins—or maybe the Heath and Brett twins—when my door quietly opened and shut before Ramon slipped onto the bed next to me.

He looked at the title, said "The Yankees win," and removed the book from my hands. He then proceeded to drive all thoughts of the Old South out of my head. For that matter, I didn't think of Heath, Brett, or any combination thereof. At least not until later, when the lights were out and the only tempest was the one still raging outside my window.

"What did you say Brett does? He's a paralegal?" I asked, while Ramon yawned against my shoulder.

"Nope. Barry's the paralegal. Brett is an immigration attorney."

"Ah," I said, with understanding. Ramon was a court reporter, so I assumed he must have met the two of them through his work. "Does Brett have a boyfriend?"

"I hope not."

I tried for a minute to decipher that and finally asked, "Why do you hope not?"

"Because he's straight."

"Brett is straight?" I yelped, then lowered my voice. "Are you kidding?"

"No." Ramon laughed. "Brett and Barry are both straight. Your gaydar might need a tune-up."

"Apparently." I was quiet a few minutes, readjusting my perceptions with this new information. "How is it that you're all friends? I mean, good enough friends to take vacations together?"

"This from a man whose main social life is with his straight roommate and a lesbian?"

"You're right," I said. "I don't know why I assumed this was an all-gay weekend. I guess because Shaun and Grover are so rampantly—"

"Don't even try to cover your ass," Ramon interrupted and laughed again. "You think of me as some fey disco debutante and can't imagine that my life story doesn't play on the all-queer-all-day network."

"I just don't know that many straight guys who'd take their vacations with a gay man they met through work."

"Who said we met through work?"

I sighed and said, "Second strike, and the bases are loaded. Rather than further humiliate me, can you pitch me some backstory?"

"That's not usually the position I play, but anything for the boys of summer. Barry's brother, Russell, was a friend of mine. He was gay. I met Barry and Brett through him."

Past tense. For someone our age.

"AIDS?"

"Yep. Barry was a good brother. After Russell died—have you been through that with anyone close?"

"No."

"Some straight people, once they enter our world through that channel, find it hard to go back. That's the way it was for Barry. The whole experience was so intense—not always in a bad way, but with good things too—that he had a hard time being around people who think of AIDS as something they read about in *Time*."

"Like a loss of innocence."

"Exactly. Barry couldn't let us go. At first because we kept him connected to Russell and his memories. In fact, after Russell died, we got back together because we made a Quilt panel for him. Then we went to Washington in '96 for the last full display of the Quilt, to see Russell's panel."

"Gosh, you've been friends that long?"

"Russell died on Christmas Eve in '95. Anyway, a group of us went to D.C. Barry, Brett, Frederick, and I shared a room."

"Frederick being the one with appendicitis whose place I took this week," I surmised.

"Right. It was our first trip as a group, and in spite of all the emotions involved, we had a good time. Since then, we've taken several vacations together. Frederick was Russell's boyfriend. He's from Germany and originally came to the States on a student visa. Brett helped him when he decided to stay. That's how Brett became part of our group. Later, he got Barry the paralegal job at his firm. Russell was the way we all met; I think he'd like it that we stayed friends. Were you getting a little crush on Brett?"

"I think he's sexy," I admitted. "He reminds me of Heath."

"The beautiful Heath. What do you think is going to happen?"

"Nothing. If you mean between Heath and me. I'm going to get over it, and we'll stay friends."

"You make it sound easy."

"I know it won't be easy. But I'm willing to try to take the long view of things. Maybe this is something Heath and I had to get out of our systems so we could move on. It's not like we haven't dated other people over the years, but I don't think we ever got over each other."

"Makes sense. I know lots of gay men who stayed friends after their romances fizzled out."

"I do want him in my life." I looked at him. "Like you. If one of us decides to put an end to the sex, I hope we can stay friends."

"I'd like that too. In the meantime, the seventh inning stretch is over. Ready to take the field?"

"Baseball has been very, very good to me," I said enthusiastically and pulled him to me.

I wasn't sure if Ramon told the others that I knew more about their history, or if I just picked up on things I hadn't before, but over the next few days I realized that Russell's name came up from time to time. I thought it was a good tribute to their lost friend and brother that they'd stayed friends with each other, as well as bringing others, like Grover, Shaun, and now me, into their dynamic.

It made me think of my friends and how a piece of us had always seemed to be missing after Heath moved away. What I'd told Ramon was the truth. I wanted to keep our group intact, even if it meant swallowing my anger, disappointment, and pride so that I could keep Heath as a friend instead of a lover. Maybe that was easier to envision when I was a thousand miles away from him, but I was willing to try.

With that in mind, I called Heath as soon as I got back to Houston, asking him if we could get together a couple of days before the scheduled Love Sucks meeting. I thought I detected wariness in his tone, so I suggested we meet at Crossroads for coffee on Thursday evening.

I deliberately arrived an hour early, getting an iced coffee and sitting at a table with my journal so I could write down some of my memories and impressions of Maine.

But while I was trying to collect my thoughts, my gaze rested on a man with black hair and blue eyes who was working on a laptop across the shop. Which led me to contemplation of the still-elusive Alexander, who'd left me a message while I was away.

I'm sorry I missed your birthday. I'll make it up to you. I've just had a lot going on, and now you're out of town. It must have been some spur-of-the-moment trip? I'll probably have to miss the next Love Sucks meeting, because the band has a gig in Austin. But I'll call you. I promise.

If I knew Alexander—and I couldn't think of anyone who knew him better—the real message was in what he wasn't saying. He was definitely avoiding me. Maybe all of us. And he didn't say *when* Tragic White Men would be playing in Austin; the "probably" gave him away. He hoped I would assume the band was playing on Saturday.

Alex had never been the kind of friend who held a grudge. No matter how annoyed he'd been with Miranda and me for stalking him and Zachary, he wouldn't be punishing us more than a month later. I was sure the reason he was avoiding us was because Miranda had been more accurate than he wanted to admit about Zachary, and Alex wasn't ready to heed her wisdom. Or anyone else's, for that matter.

It bothered me a lot that he didn't want to confide in me. While I might not see things exactly his way, he and I had never had a bite-your-tongue kind of friendship. Or maybe I had it all wrong. Maybe he was just in the boyfriend phase where a person neglects his friends. Since this was the longest I'd ever known him to date one man, I couldn't hold a little thoughtlessness against him.

The problem was, I needed him. Though it had helped to unload my drama on Ramon and Brett, no one could substitute for Alexander in his role as my confidante. Other people listened. Alexander, like Patrick, also talked, with knowledge of all my attributes, including my flaws. But sometimes, even though I knew he didn't mean to, Patrick could sound like he didn't take gay relationships as seriously as straight ones. I couldn't really blame him, since the three gay men he knew best—me, Alex, and Heath—hadn't exactly excelled in long-term commitments.

"Where are you?"

I snapped back to reality and saw Heath standing next to my table, chewing on a coffee stirrer while he watched me. I couldn't believe I'd been so lost in thought that I'd not only missed his entrance, but he'd had time to order, pay, and doctor his coffee.

"I don't know," I said, and he sat down.

"Where have you *been*?" he asked.

"I went to Maine with some friends."

"You're still mad."

I shrugged. Heath stretched out his long legs and slid down in his chair as if settling in for the long haul. I'd defiantly dressed in rumpled shorts, a T-shirt, and sandals, determined to prove that I was secure enough not to try to look fabulous so that he—and every other gay man in the vicinity—would know what he was throwing away. But as usual, Heath, with his white ribbed T-shirt tucked into his jeans, managed to look just as casual but also gorgeous.

"I don't know how I feel," I finally disagreed.

"I don't know how you feel either. And I wouldn't tell you what I think you should feel. But I'm willing to give you my perspective, for what it's worth."

"Go ahead."

"Circumstances haven't changed. From the beginning, it was not our intention to turn what we had into any kind of relationship beyond friendship. We both said that's what we wanted. The sex is great." When I made a face, he paused, then went on. "I don't mean just because it's great physically. It's great because we connect on so many levels. Emotionally and intellectually as well as physically. I'm comfortable with you, but it's also exciting. Anyway, I've been honest with you. I never said I wanted the sex to stop. But I'd rather give it up than risk losing your friendship. At some point, you have to figure one or both of us will get involved with somebody who wouldn't feel like sharing with an ex-boyfriend."

"Everything you say makes sense, and if I didn't have feelings—"

"I know, Aaron, and I'm sorry if I've hurt you. But I honestly— no, never mind."

"You can't start something and not finish it," I said. I wasn't sure if I meant us, or what he'd started to say.

"I really think what you feel is hurt pride more than a broken heart," he said slowly, obviously wishing I hadn't forced it out of him.

"I really think what you're doing is more about payback than anything else," I countered.

"If that's true, then I'm an asshole, and you're better off without me."

I watched the pigeons bob and weave on the sidewalk outside, while Heath went back to chewing on his coffee stirrer. I knew he was right. He had been honest with me from the beginning. And I didn't think he was vindictive enough to hurt me just because of our past. Maybe it *was* my pride that kept me from letting him off the hook and assuring him everything would be OK. I might as well bow to the inevitable…

I looked up, expecting him to be waiting for my reaction, but he was staring toward the next table. I glanced over and saw a man trying to balance a bottle of water and a piece of cheesecake while letting his backpack slide from his shoulder to the table. Once I saw that he could manage it, I looked back at Heath to continue our conversation. But Heath's eyes were still riveted to our neighbor, so I took a second look.

He was cute, and if I hadn't been busy trying to make Heath feel guilty I might have noticed him myself. It was hard to tell what shade of brown his hair was, because it was shaved close, obviously by choice since there was no evidence of a receding hairline. He was wearing a chambray shirt, sleeves rolled up to just below the elbow, khaki shorts, and sandals. From what I could see, he had good muscle tone. Cute, but not devastating.

He glanced our way, but I didn't have to stop staring, because his eyes locked on Heath. He smiled, and I looked at Heath, who smiled back and nodded. They kept up the eye-play for a few seconds, then both of them looked down. Heath seemed to find his mangled coffee stirrer fascinating, and the other guy uncapped his water and took a bite of cheesecake. He glanced at Heath again, realized I was watching him, and reached into his backpack to pull out a book.

"Oookay," I said softly. Heath looked up at me and blushed. "I think I'll head to the gym before I grab something for dinner. I guess we're all getting together on Saturday?"

"That's the plan," Heath said.

"I'll see you then."

"Aaron…"

"I'm fine," I said. I stood quickly and put a hand on his shoulder before he could move from his slouching position. "It's OK, Heath. Really." I squeezed his shoulder and walked out of Crossroads.

To say that I didn't give Heath a second thought after that day would be a lie. I wanted to get him out of my system, as if he was a flu bug causing me to feel achy and lethargic. Since aspirin and water didn't alleviate poor judgment and unrequited love, I gave into indolence and took to the sofa, watching every movie that aired on the Sundance Channel for the next three days.

I was halfway through the movie *Maurice,* sympathizing with the title character, when Patrick swept in front of the television and neatly turned it off.

"Hey!" I exclaimed. "I was watching that."

"I know. You've been watching it for days. I assume you're living on the sofa because of Heath."

"Yes, thanks for warming it up for me the past couple of months," I said.

I tried to glare at him but had to rub my eyes first. They felt strained and tired, and I had to wonder if my mother had been right so many years ago when she told me that too much television was bad for you. Or was it that sitting too close would make you blind? No, maybe it made you sterile. I couldn't remember.

"You don't need to answer me now," Patrick said. He crossed his arms over his chest and smiled slyly. "Just get up and come with me to Katz's Deli, then you can tell us all about it."

"Katz's Deli? Why?"

"Because love sucks, my friend, and that's where this month's meeting is. Besides, misery loves company. You look like you could use some company. A little kvetching and noshing will do you good."

I was too annoyed at myself to bother with Patrick's attempt at humor. Internally, I was berating myself for wasting my time by wallowing in despair because of Heath. I'd never thought I was an overly dramatic person, but parking my ass on a sofa like Winona Ryder in *Reality Bites* was fairly extreme. At least I didn't spend hours dialing 976 numbers and pouring out my heart to the stranger on the other end.

"Winona could've used a good Love Sucks session in that movie," Patrick said when I told him how I was feeling on the way to Katz's Deli.

"You're being surprisingly dedicated to these meetings for somebody who berates his friends for whining once a month," I said.

Patrick negotiated a turn at a busy intersection, then said, "I know what you're going through, Aaron. It sucks to devote your energy to someone then find out they're not on the same page as you."

"It does," I agreed, "but your relationship with Vivian is far more serious than anything that was going on between me and Heath."

"Which time?" he asked, with a derisive snort.

"Fuck you," I said.

"Seriously," Patrick said and hit my knee lightly with the back of his hand, which was one of his fraternal gestures. "I won't deny that these meetings are making me feel better about the stuff that I've been going through lately. Knowing that my friends have similar problems, and that you all support me, is a great help. But I will deny all this if you bring it up tonight."

"Of course you will," I said, then added, "you macho pig."

Patrick answered by grunting.

Vivian was waiting for us when we arrived at Katz's Deli and Bar, a two-story restaurant that brought the New York deli experience to Houston. We secured a table for six, ordered drinks, and settled in to wait for our friends.

"How have you been, Aaron?" Vivian asked. "I feel like I haven't seen you in a while."

"That's because you haven't," Patrick pointed out. "You've been too wrapped up in your summer law program."

I bristled internally. Though they were seated next to each other, and had even hugged when we arrived, it seemed to me like there was a Grand Canyon of distance between them.

Vivian surprised me by admitting, "Yes, that's fairly accurate. I have been really busy. I'm sorry I haven't called or anything, Aaron."

"That's OK," I assured her. "I've been out of town, anyway. I'll tell you all about it when the others get here. I can't wait to see Miranda."

"Why?" Vivian asked.

"The makeover you were going to do on her," I answered. "I'll bet she looks—"

"Like that?" Patrick interrupted, pointing to Miranda as she walked toward us after being guided in the right direction by the host. She had on her best Diesel blue jeans, which were designed to look like they had been worn by a pit crew in the Indy 500, her chunkiest work boots, and a black T-shirt. Her wild blond hair was tied back so it wouldn't get in the way of displaying one of her necklaces. Which, on her, looked like a last-ditch attempt at femininity.

"Where are Alex and Heath?" Miranda asked, sitting down hard in a chair and promptly slouching.

"They're not here yet," Patrick said.

"Well, duh, Einstein," Miranda said. "I want a beer. Which one is our waiter?"

"My God, Vivian. She's a changed woman," I said, pointing at Miranda. "You should ditch law and dedicate your life to doing makeovers."

Patrick laughed so hard at my sarcasm that he had to cover his mouth with his napkin to keep from spewing beer all over our table.

Vivian sighed, then said, "Go ahead and laugh at me. I admit, I tried and failed."

"She did try," Miranda assured us. "We went to the Galleria and visited countless makeup counters. Remember those stupid Barbie heads?"

"Come again?" Patrick asked.

"You know," Miranda said. "Those big Barbie things that were just her head and shoulders, so you could put makeup on her and style her hair, with different earrings and all that crap?"

"Yes!" Vivian exclaimed with a broad smile. She all but clapped her hands at the memory, and I suddenly felt like I knew what she looked like as a six-year-old. "I had two of those. My friend and I would play beauty salon with them. You had one too?"

"No! Are you kidding?" Miranda said, recoiling in horror. "I had Barbies. But mine all had shorn heads and wore fatigues that I made myself. They kicked G.I. Joe's ass."

"At least you could sew," I said.

"Funny, that's what our maid said," Miranda said. "Anyway, the makeover thing was a nice idea, Vivian, but I felt like one of those stupid Barbie heads with all that makeup on. It's just not me."

Our waiter came and we ordered, since it was obvious that Alexander and Heath weren't going to show. I told them about my vacation and the friends that I'd made at Captain Randall's House on the rocky coast of Maine.

They were all jealous of my time away. The department store in New York had asked Miranda for a second order on her jewelry. Vivian was logging inhumane hours in her summer law program. Patrick was already working with an architect to redesign Dinks. I quickly discovered a common theme among us.

"Each one of us is escaping our love lives by devoting every waking minute to our careers," I stated. "That way we don't get hurt."

"Aaron, you're not exactly furthering your teaching career by watching movies from the sofa, you know," Patrick said.

"You did the same thing when you and Vivian started having problems," I pointed out. Patrick quickly cut his eyes to Vivian, obviously embarrassed by the information I'd revealed. Vivian pretended not to notice and suddenly found her fries extremely intriguing. I continued, "But I didn't avoid my love life by working too much. Instead, I went thousands of miles away to get away from it. From Heath."

"Do you think Alex is touring Texas with his band to get away from Zachary?" Miranda asked, sounding somewhat hopeful.

"It's possible," Patrick replied.

"But why?" Vivian asked, waving a French fry in the air for emphasis. "Why go from town to town just to get away from Zachary? Why not just break it off? End the relationship with a rash of excuses like he usually does?"

"Maybe he's attached to the idea of things working out between them," I speculated. "I mean, when Heath and I were—"

"But that doesn't make any sense," interjected Miranda. "I can't say this enough: Zachary is married. Alexander obviously realized that things won't work out between them and is literally putting distance between them."

"Or maybe," Patrick said, pausing for effect, "he's actually touring with his band."

"Sounds scandalous," Vivian joked. "I'll bet you're right. But I have to wonder why he's still in that relationship."

"If you really like someone, you look past his faults," I said.

"Sometimes you don't see it when things aren't going to work out. That sure happened with me and Heath. When he told me that—"

"That's bullshit," Patrick interrupted. "Alexander and Zachary haven't known each other long enough to have those kinds of feelings for each other."

"I don't know," Miranda said, frowning into the remains of her Reuben sandwich. "That Zachary's obviously a real con artist."

"If you're right, and he is married," Vivian said to her, "then he's nothing but a rat."

Miranda steeled her eyes and said, "Then you can call me the rat catcher."

They ignored my sulking as thoroughly as they'd ignored my efforts to talk about Heath, so I gave it up. I would follow through on the decision I'd made in Maine and eviscerate him in some future story I'd write about us.

Bad Poetry Day

August had always been my least favorite month. The weather was unbearable, and life became a logistics exercise wherein I tried to figure out how to rush from one air-conditioned space to another. In the few seconds it took to get from anywhere to my car, my body would be limp from heat and wet from humidity. The weather was the reason my family had always taken our vacations in August, and I resented my baby sister for not planning her pregnancy better. When I called her with another of my daily complaints about the way she was stubbornly resisting going into labor and getting the whole ordeal over with, she speculated that the term "dog days" was invented because of people like me. I just growled and hung up.

I also disliked August because I thought of it as the in-between month. Summer fun was mostly behind me, and the new school year was three weeks away. I felt like I was in a holding pattern. It was the perfect metaphor for my relationship with Heath. Carnality was a thing of the past, and we hadn't figured out what would happen next. So we avoided each other, and I found myself going to Ramon's more often.

But even there, I sensed a shift. Maybe it was the heat, but we seemed to spend more time talking and less time hitting the sheets.

Although I liked talking to Ramon—he was entertaining, and I could indulge my campy side with him—being sexually stalled with both of my lovers was making me want to turn back time. It seemed like being thirty wasn't such a good thing.

I came home from the YMCA on a steamy Friday and hurled my gym bag into a corner of my bedroom, determined that it could sit there and smell until August was over. I was too disgruntled to give myself pep talks about how working out was about feeling good, not just looking good. I also didn't see the point of taking a shower after a workout if I was going to have to take another one, since the short drive home didn't allow enough time for my car's air conditioning to kick in.

The cool water streaming over my body felt too good for me to run for the phone when it rang. If it was important, they'd leave a message. But the second time it rang, I dripped my way to the phone and picked it up, snarling when I heard one of those stupid record-ed messages pleading with me to send our governor to the White House. I wished they'd give me *his* home phone number, so I could call and relay my opinions on AIDS funding, the Employment Non-Discrimination Act, school vouchers, and the shortsightedness of gearing the state's teaching curriculum to standardized tests.

Still dripping, I dialed in to check the message from the previous call and was shocked to hear Alexander's voice. He hadn't gotten in touch with me since I'd returned from Maine.

Hey, it's me. I'm at the Galleria with Grandma. The woman is a shopping fiend; she's wearing me out. I was hoping you'd meet me here, grab a bite, and drive me back into Montrose. But if you don't get this within an hour—it's five—no sweat. I can catch a bus or get a cab. If you do get it, call me on my cell phone. Shit, my battery's dying. Meet me at the ice rink by six, if you can.

I was groomed, dressed, and in my car ten minutes later. There was no way I was going to miss the chance to see Alexander after so many weeks of fretting about him. Besides, it was significant to me that he'd chosen the ice rink. Back in our college days, on a trip to the Galleria, we'd dared each other to ice skate. It was not a normal part of Texas childhood, but both of us had proved surprisingly adept. I'd learned to glide over the ice without falling or making a fool of myself. Alex had actually gotten good at more complicated spins and movements. The rink became "our" place, one we didn't share with our other friends. I suspected that skating was the only time Alex allowed himself to exercise without hunting new quarry, since he always cruised on his rare forays to the gym.

I parked in the garage closest to the rink and walked inside, my nose wrinkling at the smell of chemicals from a hair salon, then scanned benches and bistro tables for any sign of Alex. Finally I spotted him on the ice. He was in the middle of a group of girls whose ages appeared to range from five to fifteen. While Britney Spears regretted, over the speakers, that oops, she'd done it again, Alex was going through her dance routine with the giggling girls.

I sat in a spot where I'd be least likely to catch his eye, grinning while I watched him do his Britney imitation. One tiny girl in a pink leotard kept flubbing it, and Alex knelt beside her so she wouldn't have to struggle to keep her balance while looking up at him. I glanced toward the parents sitting on the bleachers at the rink entrance. Some were on cell phones, some were talking to their neighbors, but all eyes were glued to Alex, and they wore an array of expressions ranging from amused to smitten.

I wasn't surprised. Alex had always had charisma, but he was also looking very put together, something he'd have done for his grandmother, who did not tolerate sloppy men. I assumed Grandma Casey had already gone, her ever-faithful Shreve at her side. We never knew if Shreve was his last name or his first and whether he was her employee or her suitor. He lived in what they called servant quarters—actually a luxurious apartment—behind Grandma Casey's elegant old home in West U, and he seemed to exist for the sole purpose of making her life comfortable. Alex was sure they were lovers, an opinion that scandalized his parents. Though I had a hard time believing their relationship was sexual—Shreve was many years younger than Caroline Casey—I did think he filled the role of host, companion, and assistant. I found him likable, and I'd tried several times in the past to engage him in conversation, but he never let his attention stray long from Alex's grandmother.

I'd once predicted that Alex was going to be just like her—a rich old matriarch with some toady to do his every bidding. He'd just stared at me and said, "Why wait until I'm old?"

After Alex and his fan club had gone through their routine several times—all of them laughingly indifferent that at least three other songs had played since Britney—they whooped as Janet Jackson began singing "Nasty," and Alex showed them that he had that routine down cold as well. I stood and walked to the Plexiglas wall surrounding the rink. If I didn't stop him soon, he'd morph into every video diva in existence. He saw me, waved, and finished the routine before skating to the entrance to exchange his skates for his shoes.

"Hi," he said, giving me a big hug. "Long time, no see. Is Bennigan's OK?"

"Sure," I said, although we rarely went to chain restaurants since there were so many great locally owned dining spots in our neighborhood.

"I'm sorry we have to eat so early, but I've got rehearsal after this."

"No problem. I was beginning to think of you as the Invisible Man." He frowned, and I decided to find a safer subject. "You've been shopping with your grandmother all day, but you have no packages?"

"Are you kidding? I won't have to buy clothes or underwear again for five years. She's having everything dry-cleaned or laundered and delivered to my place. She went all out. Emporio Armani, Gucci, Levi's, Saks, Banana Republic."

"Spoiled brat," I said fondly.

"I know. Has Sister had her baby?"

"Not yet."

We continued the harmless small talk until we'd been seated, gotten our drinks, and ordered. Then Alex leaned back in his chair and said, "So. Tell me everything."

"I'd rather talk about what's going on with you."

"Later. Vivian tells me you went to Maine?" I told him about my trip, frustrated because his face showed nothing beyond interest in what I was saying. My suspicion that he was keeping the focus on me until he could insist that he had only minutes to get to rehearsal was confirmed when he said, "OK, OK. Maine is beautiful, the company was excellent, you had the time of your life. Why aren't you talking about Heath?"

"This isn't a Love Sucks meeting," I said. "Besides, since you seem to be getting your information from Vivian these days, I'm sure you already know. What's going on with you and Zachary?"

"This isn't a Love Sucks meeting," he mimicked me.

I stewed for a minute, then asked, "Does it suck? Are you no longer seeing him?"

"I didn't say that." He rolled his eyes at the look I gave him and said, "Miranda was right, OK? He's married. Sort of."

"How is one 'sort of' married? They did it in Vegas with an Elvis impersonator presiding?"

"Technically they're married. But they don't sleep together."

"Do they *live* together?"

"He stays because of the kids. They have an arrangement."

"Arrangements are for flowers. And bowls of fruit. But I don't think he qualifies."

"Gosh, I can't imagine why I was reluctant to explain this to you."

"I'll shut up. Go ahead."

"He thought he could stop being gay. For a while it worked, especially when the kids were little. But she's more into being a mother than a wife. They grew apart. He got the urge to stray."

"And he chose you?"

"I'm not the first. They haven't lived as husband and wife for years. When the kids are older, he'll leave, and they'll get a divorce."

"And you believe all this?"

"Why wouldn't I? He doesn't have to lie to me to see me. I'm not looking to marry him, after all. What do I care where he sleeps? I'm the one he loves. Zach says no one has ever made him feel the way I do."

"It must be mutual. You've never dated anyone this long." Before he could make a size joke, I added, "I need to apologize for that day at Baba Yega's."

"No, you don't. I've gotten at least twenty phone messages from Miranda that exonerated you of guilt. I was so gullible that I honestly thought running into the two of you was a coincidence. Until I found out Miranda had hired him to do her accounting. Don't you think that's a little creepy?"

"Yes. It's not like Miranda to be fiscally responsible." Alex's laugh encouraged me to think maybe I could make a point. "She's concerned about you. We all are."

"Now you've seen me. You can tell everyone I'm fine."

"Why don't you tell them yourself?"

"I don't feel like putting my relationship with Zachary on the table so it can be dissected by my friends."

"But you've always told us—" I broke off, frowning at him. "Is that because you love him or because you don't feel right about what you're doing?"

Alex held his knife toward me and said, "Scalpel?" I stared into his brilliant blue eyes, trying to find answers, and he shook his head. "You, of all people, should understand. You didn't talk to us about Heath. Some relationships are off limits."

"That's different. For one thing, Heath is part of our group. For another, I'd love to talk about him now, but they won't let me. I assume because he's one of us."

"I did ask," Alex pointed out. "I *can* listen to you and understand that there are two sides to every story."

"There are," I agreed. "I wonder what Zachary's wife's side is?"

"Ask Miranda," Alex said. "By now, they're probably best friends."

"I found out that I can't be physically involved with Heath without becoming emotionally involved as well. That's not what he wants. So it seemed best to go back to being friends. No harm done."

"No harm?" Alexander asked.

"Nothing lasting," I said.

"I'm sorry. I really hoped he wouldn't hurt you. Again."

"I'll survive. I'm a big boy."

"So am I," Alexander pointed out.

"Point taken. Alex, I miss you. I want you back."

"I haven't gone anywhere. I just needed a break."

"So you and I, we're OK?"

"We're OK."

I didn't feel like we were, but I decided to have faith that we would be. And I knew I had to back off the subject of Zachary. I agreed with Miranda's and Vivian's assessment of him; I definitely caught the scent of rodent in the air.

I said as much to Patrick when I went by Dinks after dropping off Alex at Tragic White Men's rehearsal.

"So what are you going to tell the girls?" he asked, looking as if he had nothing more on his mind than the wine glasses he was polishing.

"Either of whom would scream at you for calling them girls," I pointed out. "I don't have to tell them anything. They know he's a rat. But hopefully they also know that, for now, he's Alex's rat, and that's the way it is. What the hell is that stack of papers on the bar?"

"That's my call list. Or rather, it's Vivian's call list. To solicit votes for Al Gore. She's so bogged down with work that I figured I could at least take one thing off her hands."

"I thought you were a Nader man."

"For that matter, Vivian likes Nader too. But please, he doesn't have a chance, and we have to keep Dubya out of the White House."

I couldn't argue with that, but I suspected Patrick had ulterior motives.

"Mmm-hmm. You're just trying to score points with Vivian, aren't you? I've heard nothing from you about the election before now."

"Aaron, was I or was I not a political science minor in college?"

"You were."

"Did I or did I not demonstrate with you and ACT UP at the Republican National Convention at the Astrodome in '92, nearly getting myself trampled by a police horse in the process?"

"You did," I answered, noting that Patrick had picked up some of Vivian's argumentative skills.

"Do I or do I not have in my office an autographed *Texas Monthly* cover with Ann Richards astride a motorcycle?"

"You do," I said, leaving out Patrick's admission that he'd found the picture of our former governor oddly arousing when it arrived in our mailbox.

"Was I or was I not the only one of us who campaigned for Clinton and Gore in '96?"

"You were."

"Do I or do I not come from a family of Yellow Dawg Democrats?"

"You do."

"Of course I'm doing it to impress Vivian. A man has to work with what he's got."

"You know, Patrick, if you were gay…" I trailed off.

"Yes?"

"Our apartment would be a lot cleaner," I said.

He let out a roar of laugher, high-fived me, and said, "I knew a smart-assed comment was coming. Thank you for not disappointing me."

"Any time," I said. "How are the renovation plans coming along?"

"Slowly but surely. I've been getting estimates. Most of the work can be done during the day, so I probably won't have to shut down. If I do, I could use a vacation, so it's no big deal. I think once the job is finished, and the stage has been built, I'll have a night where contractors come in and give estimates in front of an audience."

"It could be like a combination of *The Price Is Right* and *To Tell the Truth*," I suggested.

"With a little *Gong Show* thrown in for good measure," Patrick added. "The winner gets to do the job without me breathing down their neck the whole time."

"But if you already had a stage, that would be moot," I said. "On the other hand, you could host a Love Sucks night."

"And what, have half of Houston in here whining about their love lives? Forget it."

"Patrick, we were just talking about the election and politics. What's more American than stealing an idea from your miserable friends and profiting from it?" I asked. I was on a roll. "It could be like a game show. You get three guys and three women from the audience on the stage. Each of them explains why their love lives suck. The audience decides which guy, and which girl, has the suckiest love life. The two who are chosen get an all-expense paid date and the chance to turn their rotten dating luck around."

Patrick stared at the wall, soon to be ripped out and replaced with a stage, and stroked his chin with two fingers. I could almost see the wheels turning in his head as he pondered my idea.

"Love sucks, but it doesn't have to," he said absently, as if reading a flyer.

"At Dinks," I added.

"I'll think about it," Patrick answered halfheartedly.

Although my fate as a club promoter lay in Patrick's hands, I did have control over my career as a writer. I decided to revisit the story I'd started during my trip to Maine. I didn't want to work at home, where I'd be distracted by the telephone, the television, and the stereo. I collected what I needed and decided to work at Lobo, a gay bookshop and coffeehouse in the Montrose area. I rarely ran into anyone I knew there, so it seemed like the perfect place to get some work done.

I opted to sit inside, not only because of the heat, but because conversations at the outdoor tables would be too distracting. I dropped my knapsack on one end of an old couch, then went to order coffee and a brownie, certain that a caffeine and sugar rush could only enhance my writing. When I turned around from the counter, I ran into Miranda. Literally.

"Oh, my God! I'm so sorry, hon. Are you OK?"

"Hot! Very hot! Very fucking hot!" Miranda screamed, as she pulled her T-shirt away from her body in an attempt to keep the scalding to a minimum. A nearby lesbian raised her eyebrows in appreciation and tried to steal a glance down Miranda's shirt, which was totally lost on Miranda, who was glaring at me and pressing napkins against her breasts.

"I think there's a woman at the other end of the counter who'd like to help you with that," I suggested.

"I'm not amused, Aaron," Miranda said. "I got this T-shirt in New York. It's Earl."

"My underwear, Billy Joe, is pleased to make your T-shirt's acquaintance," I said.

"Earl is a designer, you moron," she said.

"I'm sorry. I'll have it cleaned for you. Seriously, are you OK?" I asked.

"I'll live," she answered.

Lobo's barista, who was adorable but too young to be datable, refilled my coffee free of charge. I tipped him a dollar and offered to buy Miranda whatever she wanted to compensate for my clumsiness. After assuring her that an impromptu performance of "I'm a Little Teapot" in my Billy Joe underwear was not on the menu, much to the dismay of the barista, she settled for a chocolate shake and joined me on the couch.

"What are you doing here, anyway?" I asked. "You don't read."

"I read!" she protested.

"Magazines, fast food menus, and road signs don't count."

Miranda laughed, then her smile froze in place, her teeth still bared as if she'd been possessed by a rabid Osmond.

"What's wrong with you?" I asked.

Miranda said nothing, and a flyer was suddenly thrust under my nose.

"Hey. You should come to my reading, man," someone said. I extracted the flyer from the hand in my face and followed the arm until I realized it belonged to Joey, the drummer from Alexander's band.

"Oh. Hi," I said lamely. Miranda was still smiling like a game show hostess. With the wet coffee stains on her T-shirt, she looked like a lactating Vanna White on a bad hair day. "I heard Tragic White Men played some gigs in Austin," I said. "How'd that go?"

"It was OK," Joey said, shrugging her shoulders and looking bored. She waved the stack of flyers in her hand and said, "I'm doing a poetry reading on the eighteenth. You should definitely come. It's gonna be deep, man."

"Yeah, OK," I said. I resisted the urge to say, *Far out,* and instead added, "We'll definitely be there."

Joey glanced at Miranda as if noticing her for the first time. She looked appalled, then laughed a little, as if Miranda was a joke she didn't quite understand, then waved at us before loping off to pass out more flyers.

"If you don't stop, your face is going to freeze that way," I said.

Miranda relaxed and looked forlornly at her chocolate shake. "I don't know what it is about Joey, but whenever I'm around her, I act like..." She trailed off, searching for a comparison, so I thought of one for her.

"A dummy without a ventriloquist?"

"Pretty much," she agreed.

"Dan Quayle on *Jeopardy*?"

Miranda laughed then said, "Yes. Thank you. I feel better now."

"Farrah Fawcett on *Letterman*?"

"OK! That's enough. I get it," Miranda said. "I'm going to have to admit that Joey and I will never be a couple. She's way out of my league."

"What league is that? The League of Tongue-tied Lesbians?" I asked. Miranda stuck her tongue out at me, perhaps to prove it wasn't knotted. "I've never known you to admit defeat. But maybe you're right. Maybe Joey isn't the one for you. She might be *beneath* your league. Kind of like how Zachary's beneath Alexander's league."

Against my better judgment, with the intention of getting her mind off Joey, I told Miranda about my encounter with Alexander. I confirmed that she'd been right all along and expressed my concern that Alexander was eventually going to be hurt by Zachary.

"I'll get him," Miranda assured me. "By giving up on Joey, I'll have a lot more time to pin the tail on the adulterer."

"I think it'd be best if we just keep out of it," I said. "At least, I'm going to stay out of it. I know you'll do what you want."

Like the perfect spy, Miranda said nothing. I flipped open my notebook.

"What's that?" she asked, craning her neck to get a look.

"It's a story I started writing a while ago," I said, frowning at the typed pages I'd stuck between handwritten notes in the bound notebook. I'd started a period piece based on Brett's New England family, but it wasn't working for me. I put the pages together, tore them in half, and said, "So much for that."

"If at first you don't succeed," Miranda said.

"Get drunk and call it a day," I said, revising the cliché.

"That sounds like a good idea. I'll leave you to your work," she said, rising from the couch. "Though I'm sure this is just a ruse of yours to attract men who are drawn to quiet, literary types. The end of the year is getting closer. You might want to think about finding a boyfriend."

"If your performance this afternoon was any indication of how our deal is going to turn out, I think my status as a single gay male will remain untainted," I said.

"That's about the only part of you that's untainted," Miranda said and walked away.

I took my journal from my knapsack, read through a few pages, then turned back to my notebook. Although the story about Brett's family was a bust, I had the beginning of another one. The main character was infatuated with a man who was a physical composite of Heath and Brett but with all the nasty qualities of a man like Zachary.

I wrote furiously for a couple of hours, stopping occasionally to get a coffee refill. When I finally took a break, I glanced at the flyer Joey had given me. Maybe I could talk the others into going to the poetry reading, then holding our Love Sucks meeting afterward. It would give Miranda an opportunity to gape at Joey without Alex catching on. Assuming Alex would actually attend the next meeting. For that matter, I wasn't sure Heath would either. I wondered if our little group was falling apart, or if we just needed to spend some time away from one another because of all the emotional complications. I didn't want it to be permanent, especially not if it was partially my fault because of the rift between Heath and me. I needed to find some way to bridge the distance between us.

My baby sister provided it a few days later. I called Heath to tell him the news.

"Sister had her boy. Six pounds, eight ounces," I announced when he answered his phone at work.

"That's great," Heath said. "Are they both doing OK?"

"That's what I hear. I'm driving to The Woodlands to see them at the hospital this evening. If you want to go with me, I'm sure the entire family would be thrilled."

"Traffic will be vile," Heath said. "I'll drive."

I didn't argue, remembering that I'd always made him nervous when I drove in heavy traffic. I figured my efforts at peacemaking might as well start early.

In any case, our night began calmly enough. While he drove, I brought Heath up to date on the news about Patrick, Alex, and Miranda. Although he was definitely listening, since he added a comment from time to time, he seemed preoccupied. Again, I held my tongue, determined to let sleeping dogs lie.

As I'd promised, my entire family was at the hospital, delighted to see Heath. We had to pose for pictures with the baby, Ryan James—although I knew he was destined to join his initialed brother and become RJ—in every combination possible. When Kelly shot one of me and Heath with the two boys, I no longer had to speculate about Heath's mood. He was definitely uncomfortable.

In the car on our way back to Houston, I finally said, "All right. Out with it."

"What?" Heath asked, probably hoping I'd think his distracted tone was because he was focused on driving.

"I guess I'm not surprised things are strained between us, but you never seemed ill at ease with my family until tonight."

"Shit," Heath said. He took an exit and pulled into the parking lot of Greenspoint Mall, letting the car idle.

"Uh, you know this used to be called Gunspoint, don't you?" I asked. "I mean, I've heard it's better than it was, but—"

"All right, all right," Heath said, driving around until he found a Denny's with about twenty pickup trucks parked outside.

"Do you *want* to get our asses kicked, or what?" I asked.

"Try not to act like a big sissy, and we should be safe," Heath groused, getting out of the car.

"I'll do my best," I said meekly and followed him into the restaurant. We asked to be seated as far from everyone else as possible and ordered coffee. I stared at Heath until he finally met my eyes. "Just tell me."

"I'm seeing somebody."

"I figured. The guy from Crossroads?"

"Damn—is Miranda stalking *me* now?"

"No. Ray Charles could have seen that you two connected that day. Details, please."

"His name is Logan Musgrove. He's a geologist. He works for Shell. He's thirty-two."

"At least he's older than me. Who's better in bed?"

"Aaron," he warned.

"Good answer," I said, and he laughed. "Is it serious?"

"I've only been seeing him a couple of weeks," Heath said.

"Some of the greatest love affairs I've known have run their course in two weeks," I said. "Have you had your first fight yet?"

"Would you stop?"

"I can't. Pettiness and jealousy are the first reactions listed in the scorned lover's handbook."

"How long before you move on to resignation and support?" Heath asked.

"You're not supposed to impose a timetable on grief." I smiled at him. "Did you have to get over me so fast?"

"Fast?" Heath asked. "*Fast?* It's taken me eight years to stop comparing every man I meet to you. To their detriment, I might add."

"Please do add it. My ego needs the stroking."

"I'll always love you, Aaron. I know the chemistry's good. Maybe

I'm just a coward. Because I'm not willing to risk our friendship for love. I can't go through that loss and hurt again. I can't." I nodded and dropped my eyes to my coffee cup. After a long silence, Heath said, "I know this is going to sound like I'm trying to excuse myself. And I know I've said it before. I'm too cautious, and you deserve someone who's willing to leap into the unknown with you. To risk everything for a shot at something that might not last but will be extraordinary while you have it. And I deserve to find someone that I'm willing to do that for."

"Is Logan the one?"

"It's too early to know that."

I felt slightly mollified by his answer, sure that if Logan was the one, Heath would already know it. Unless he was trying to spare my feelings.

"I'll be fine," I said. "I guess what upsets me the most is that I feel like we didn't really try."

"Which is exactly my point. I'm not willing to try. Because if we tried and failed—"

"I get it," I said. "I'm not stupid."

"No, but you can be awfully dense sometimes."

"What does that mean?"

"Nothing. I shouldn't have said it. I miss everybody. I miss those stupid Love Sucks meetings. I don't want to do what Alex did and vanish. But I wasn't sure how you felt about seeing me."

"Avoiding each other won't make me feel any better. And frankly, I'm worried about our friends. Everything seems so fucked up. I feel like you and I should do what we have to for their sake. Not that I feel like we can fix everything. But we don't have to add to the strain."

"I agree," Heath said. "There's nothing new about Alexander's and Miranda's love lives being a mess. It's just that they're usually the ones making it that way. Now they seem to be on the receiving end. And with Patrick and Vivian also unstable…"

"I know." I told him my idea about the poetry reading. "Who knows whether or not Alex will show? But since I think Miranda will go to the reading anyway, if for no other reason than to hear Joey's poetry, we should be with her."

"You're right. I'll be there."

"Just don't bring Logan. I'm not ready for that."

"I wouldn't do that to either of you," Heath said with a smile.

We paid for our coffee, then spent the rest of our ride back into Montrose talking about the most harmless things we could. When he stopped outside my apartment, I turned to look at him.

"No matter how pathetic I act, you know I wish you the best, Heath."

He pulled me to him and held me. I desperately wanted him to kiss me, but I knew if he did I wouldn't let him leave, and we'd undo whatever progress we'd made. It was over, and I had to let it go. I broke the embrace and got out of the car.

Two hours later, I was flailing around my bed, sweaty and angry and hating him, when the phone rang. I picked it up, welcoming any distraction. Maybe I'd get lucky and it would be a heavy breather.

"This is so hard," Heath moaned. "Why is it so hard?"

"I was *hoping* for an obscene phone call," I said.

We talked for hours, recalling memories of our first attempt at love, comparing our interim lovers, and finally reliving every moment of our most recent attempt at a relationship. It was as candid as he'd ever been with me, and I had no idea what it cost him, but I managed not to cry more than two or three times.

"I'm exhausted," Heath finally said. "But I feel better. How do you feel?"

"I finally feel that closeness I've been wanting from you. Like you pulled down the barriers between us. Don't worry. I know this doesn't change your decision. But I feel like we're on the other side of it now, instead of in the middle. You just showed me that as my friend, you can share things that you wouldn't as my lover. We'll always be friends, Heath."

"I'm counting on it," he said. "I love you."

"I love you too."

I slept like a baby after we hung up. My improved state of mind was still there when I woke up, and it persisted over the following days, in spite of the noncommittal reactions of everyone except Heath to the next planned Love Sucks meeting. I refused to let them get me down and devoted myself to planning lessons for the upcoming school year and continuing the story I was working on.

Although I'd originally intended to use the love interest to purge myself of bad feelings about Heath and Zachary, I found that as I wrote, the villain became less interesting to me than my main character, who slowly began to embody all the qualities I admired about Alex. He was sexy, funny, and edgy, with a big heart, and creating him took some of the sting out of Alex's absence.

Heath and I agreed to meet early the night of the poetry reading, wanting to test our newfound goodwill in person, without the pressure of everyone else's scrutiny. We both grinned like idiots when our eyes met, and I felt like a huge weight had been lifted from me.

"Thank you," Heath said, hugging me.

"I'm as relieved as you are," I assured him. "We did it. We survived."

"I think you're right," Heath said.

"How's, uh…"

"*Logan* is fine, and so am I. Thanks to you."

"I'm fine too."

Vivian was the first to arrive. She looked stressed and tired, and her eyes darted between Heath and me as if she expected a fight to break out at any moment.

"They've been working you to death, haven't they?" Heath asked sympathetically.

"Yes. But this was my last week. I made so much money it's ridiculous, and now I just want to get on a plane going anywhere and forget law school."

"By next week, you'll be raring to go again," I assured her. "You're in the home stretch. Your final year. Then you'll be doing what you love."

"If I survive another year."

"You will," Heath said. "We'll all be here for you. It's amazing what you can get through with the right friends helping you out."

We smiled at each other, and Vivian heaved a sigh of relief and said, "At least you two seem OK."

"We're great," I said.

"Are you back together?"

"Not as a couple," I said cheerfully.

"You don't have to sound so happy about it," Heath teased.

"If we're lucky, one of tonight's presenters will read maudlin poems, and you can all watch me cry."

"Bad poetry does that to me too," Heath said.

"Do you think tonight's poets know it's Bad Poetry Day?" Vivian asked. "Or will it just be coincidence if they all sound like bad imitations of Alanis Morissette?"

"Are there *good* imitations of Alanis Morissette?" Patrick asked, dropping down next to us.

"There are good parodies of Alanis Morissette," Heath said. "There's even a Web site devoted to them."

"Sign me up, dude," Patrick said. "I don't get enough whining from my friends. Good God, is she wearing makeup?"

We followed the direction of his gaze and saw Miranda pausing inside the door while she looked for us. She was indeed wearing makeup; her hair had actually been tamed into something resembling a hairstyle; and she looked sexy and slim in low-rise Capri pants and a black T-shirt. Her sandals exposed painted toenails. Heath and I exchanged a baffled glance.

"She looks fantastic," Vivian said. "Now why couldn't she do that for me?"

"Buy a strap-on, cop an attitude, and join a rock band," I suggested.

"Hello," Miranda said brightly. "Not a word from any of you. Do you think Alex is coming?"

"No one knows," I said.

"I do," Patrick said with a smirk, and nodded toward the door. Alex grinned at us, went to get something to drink, then sat down next to me.

"Miranda, you look great," he said. "What's different?"

"Thanks, I think," she said.

Everyone got quiet for a minute, then all eyes turned to Heath and me. "What?" I asked, receiving only blank stares in return.

"Everything's good," Heath said. "Relax. Damn, Alex, your hair is so long. I don't think I've ever seen it this long."

"My hair hardly rates a mention in light of Miranda's. What did you do?"

"I traded the most fabulous onyx bracelet to a client's stylist," Miranda said. "She has him flown here from L.A. He has a shop on Rodeo Drive and does zillions of celebrities. He said he was truly awed by my hair, since he usually has to use extensions and weaves to get this much volume. In fact, he thinned it out for me."

"This is the dowdiest I've ever felt in my life," Vivian said.

"The theme is Love Sucks, not Hair Sucks," Patrick reminded her.

"The theme for this part of the evening is bad poetry," Alex said. "I'm ready, and it looks like our bards are too."

It wasn't as bad as I'd feared it would be, or maybe I was just reserving my most venomous criticism for Joey. I knew Alexander, clueless about Miranda's feelings, would expect us to applaud his drummer like seals on crack. But I couldn't shake the image of the way Joey had looked at Miranda that day at Lobo. She could expect no mercy from me.

Alexander was enthralled by one of the poets—a stunning brunette with great arms set off by his tattoo of Bob Marley—and didn't notice our group stir when Joey came in and sat down alone, her fingers drumming her table in what I assumed was a nervous rhythm. Although she pretended not to notice Joey, Miranda sat up straighter and attempted to radiate some kind of glamour girl/earth mother vibe. She definitely had it bad.

Joey was the last presenter. She read a poem that wasn't awful. At least it was short, less Alanis Morissette than Kurt Cobain. Patrick gave me a look and turned up his wrists, as if to say, *Do you have a razor blade handy? I left mine at home.* I grinned at him, and he sighed heavily while Joey waited for the polite applause to die down so she could read her next poem.

"This one's about why some love sucks," Joey said.

We turned as a group to look at Alexander. Someone had been talking. He kept his eyes glued to Joey, so we settled back, wondering if we were about to have our dirty linen aired publicly. At least that's what I was wondering, so I assumed the others were too.

Joey began to read.

This is her world, the world she walks through
Never caring where she puts her foot down
Whose heart she leaves her footprint on
She expects her victims to lie down for it
To thank her for it, to want it
Like worshippers of some ancient goddess
She bestows her favors on mere mortals
Leaves them to eat what's left of their hearts
After she sends her crowning glory out like snakes
Like some power-crazed Lady Godiva
Or Rapunzel
Or the dead redhead in a Spanish novel
Wraps it around her prey
And then weeps—weeps!—
Because no one understands her
Or loves what will not be loved
Only endured and survived

When the rest of the room applauded, our table remained quiet, none of us looking at one another. I finally shifted my eyes to Alex, who had the grace to appear uncomfortable. He must have felt my gaze, because his hand dropped under the table and rested on my leg. I felt sorry for him; it couldn't be easy to be caught between opposing Sapphic forces. I rested my hand on his reassuringly, and he finally looked at Miranda, as did I.

"I can't hold it in any longer," Miranda said with a brilliant smile. "One of my parents' friends wants to do me the biggest favor. I've designed a line of jewelry called 'Good Bad Girls,' and she's going to send some pieces to her friend, Sarah Ferguson. Can you imagine seeing exiled British royalty wearing something of mine in her Weight Watchers ads? This could be huge!"

"Just like Fergie's ass used to be," Heath said, and we all laughed with nervous relief.

"But Fergie looks terrific now," Vivian said. "Proof that a woman can bounce back from anything and be better than ever."

"Definitely a good bad girl," Miranda agreed.

While they talked about it, I went to the coffee bar to get a refill. At least that was what I hoped everyone would think. Joey was there, sucking down a bottle of water, and I couldn't resist the opportunity to speak to her.

"What'd you think?" she asked, making it easy for me.

"You made me think of Maya Angelou," I said.

Joey looked confused and asked, "One of her poems? Which one?"

"No, one of her books. I think it was called *I Know Why the Lesbian Drummer Is a Bitch.*"

"Excuse me?"

"Did I hurt your feelings?" I asked, not sounding at all sorry, then walked away without giving her a chance to react.

"Joan Collins," Alex was saying when I sat down.

"Shannen Doherty," Vivian suggested.

"Donna Mills," Alex said.

"Morgan Fairchild," Miranda countered.

"It's always faded, prime-time soap vixens with you people," Heath commented.

"I can't help it," Alex said. "What about you, Aaron? I'm sure you know a good bad girl from classic mythology."

"Maleficent from *Sleeping Beauty*?" I asked.

"Or from fairy tales," Alex said, giving me an exasperated look.

"Oh, come on, the ultimate good bad girl is Madonna," Patrick said. "Why does it take a straight guy to remind you of that?"

A lively discussion ensued of what elements made up a good bad girl. I tried not to be obvious as I kept my eye on Miranda, waiting for a crack in her composure, but none was forthcoming. When our group finally broke up, deciding the poetry reading was as much of a Love Sucks meeting as we needed, I managed to get her alone for a few seconds.

"Are you OK?"

"I'm fine. Why do you ask?" I didn't say anything. If she'd somehow missed the point of Joey's poem, I saw no reason to clarify it for her. "Are you referring to Joey and the less-than-literary arrow she sent my way?"

"Uh-huh."

Miranda laughed and said, "Not a problem. In fact, it's the first indication I've gotten that I've left an impression on her."

"You mean like a *footprint on her heart?*" I asked.

"I mean she's not as immune as she pretends to be. Writers don't usually waste words on someone they're indifferent to, do they?"

I thought about the way Heath and Alex had found their way into my most recent efforts and admitted, "No. I guess they don't."

"She's afraid of me," Miranda said. "Fasten your seat belt—"

"I am not going stalking with you again," I yelped.

"You won't have to," Miranda said and laughed. "I'm in, Aaron. Wait and watch."

"Lesbians have weird mating rituals."

"Whatever works," she said.

"Patrick was wrong. *You're* the ultimate good bad girl."

"I'm just getting started," she assured me with an evil gleam in her eye.

Confucius's Birthday

When I was very young, I'd gone with my mother and Kelly to see a play called *Up the Down Staircase*. The character I remembered most was the school librarian, a dour woman whose love of order and organization mandated that the library stay closed most of the time. Years later, I fondly recognized some of her qualities in Heath, with his alphabetized CDs and color-coordinated closets. And in an eerie example of life imitating art, the first librarian I'd known at St. Gregory's was strikingly similar. The only time she seemed truly happy was the week before classes started. The empty hallways and classrooms ensured that her shelved books—there was never any doubt that they were hers—maintained the stiffness and precision of soldiers at perpetual attention.

When she retired, her replacement, Dale Campbell, became one of my favorite faculty members. Young and enthusiastic, with a love not only of books but of kids, I'd found that she was an English teacher's greatest ally. She also shared my sense of the ridiculous; she and I often conspired to be on the same committees and were drawn to each other at meetings.

So I wasn't surprised when she settled next to me at our first faculty meeting in the days before our students returned to St.

Gregory's. She arranged her donuts and coffee in front of her and said, "The theme is 'What I Did on My Summer Vacation.' We'll take turns as they come through the door."

I looked expectantly toward the back of the room. When one of our fresh-out-of-college teachers came in wearing crisp khakis and an obviously new blue shirt and tie, I said, "Learned to shoplift at the Gap."

Dale muffled her snicker when the next person through the door was our headmaster, Bill Westin, looking tanned and fit. After a pause, she said, "Accepted a gift membership to the Houston Yacht Club."

I nodded, then I perked up when the evil queen Paul Nettles walked in. He looked like he'd dropped twenty or so pounds, and his hair, which he'd always allowed to curl messily over his ears and collar, was cut short and had been bleached to a somewhat orange hue.

"Fucked his hairdresser." I looked again at the color and amended that to, "Fucked his hairdresser badly."

Crumbs of the donut Dale had just bitten spewed across the table, followed by a dusting of powdered sugar that landed on my organizer. "I have to get away from you," she said, trying to choke back her laughter while Bill gave us a bemused look from the front of the room. "You're an awful influence."

"Your game," I said in a blasé tone, blowing the sugar off my organizer.

"I'd say it was *your* game," she said, turning her face away as if to deny knowing me.

I grinned and continued jotting notes in my organizer. When I glanced up again, I realized that Paul had sat across from us and was giving me what I could only describe as a sickly smile. That scared me even more than his new hairdo, and I quickly shifted my gaze to Bill as he began his annual welcome speech.

My apprehension seemed justified when Paul approached me during our first break to ask, "How was your summer, Aaron?"

"Great, thanks," I said. "Yours?"

"I think it gets hotter every year," he whined. "Must be global warming. I did manage to spend a few days in Cancun. Did you do any traveling?"

Who *are* you, I wondered, but said, "I spent time with my family in Galveston and took a trip to the coast of Maine."

"I'm sure it was beautiful," Paul said.

"Gorgeous," I agreed, still edgy about Paul's uncharacteristic friendliness. There had to be an angle I was missing.

When his congenial mood persisted over the following teacher workshop days, I chalked it up to one of those anomalies I had to accept in life, like crop circles, Easter Island, and Michael Jackson. But I began to wonder if there was something sinister in the Montrose water supply when I heard the latest from Vivian about Alexander.

"He says he's either going to Southern Decadence or Last Splash this weekend," she told me over the phone.

"Alex?" I asked skeptically. "He's never exactly been a circuit queen."

"I'm just telling you what he said," she insisted. "Maybe his interest in such debauchery means he and Zachary broke up."

"Did you ask him?"

"He's too touchy," she said. "That's why I'm calling you."

"You'd rather he bite *my* head off," I theorized. "You've been talking to Miranda, haven't you?" Her silence spoke volumes. "Oh, all right. I'll call him."

When Alex answered his phone, I got right to the point. He laughed and said, "It doesn't take much to get everybody's tongues wagging. Vivian called my cell phone while I was with Zachary. I wanted to see what he'd do if he thought I was making steamy Labor Day plans."

"And?"

"I'll be spending Labor Day and most of the following week in Fredericksburg with Zachary," he said smugly. "Enjoying the hill country, going to wineries, having great sex. No parties, no boys, no drugs. Just me and Zachary soaking up the local color."

I bit back a retort about the advantages of being the other woman and said, "Speaking of color…" I then proceeded to tell him about Paul's new hair and his bizarre attempts at friendliness.

"Don't trust him for a minute," Alex warned. "You always say he's treacherous. If you want my advice—"

"This should be good."

"—stay away from him. You know those people who sell candy at intersections?"

"Who buys candy through a car window?" I asked. "You have no idea what's in that stuff."

"Exactly. Lock your doors and roll up your windows. If you see Paul, change gears and reverse. A treacherous man is married to lies, and he'll never—"

"Leave his wife?" I interrupted.

"I'll call you after I get back from Fredericksburg," Alex muttered.

I didn't have time to think about Alexander or Paul when school started in earnest after the holiday. I'd agreed to teach a semester-long freshman class in Elizabethan drama. I had to provide an overview of the subject, teach one of Shakespeare's plays, and help the class complete a group project.

Several of my freshmen were familiar to me, since I'd taught them in earlier grades. I was less than thrilled to see Jeanne Baxter. I'd had her as a seventh grader and remembered her as the ADD poster child. However, Jeanne's parents were unable to think of their little girl as anything less than perfect, so she wasn't on medication. Even though I hadn't taught her for two years, her name still haunted me. I'd prefaced innumerable requests or directions with it. *Jeanne, sit down. Jeanne, stop talking. Jeanne, get back to your desk. Jeanne, don't sharpen your pencil again.* I hoped age had mellowed her. Or else her parents had come to their senses and medicated her.

In spite of its R rating, most of my students had seen *Shakespeare in Love,* so their reading choice was *Romeo and Juliet,* and we spent a couple of days brainstorming ideas for their class project. Their final decision was to shoot a movie of selected scenes, with flat paper characters along the lines of *South Park,* but rather than using animation, they wanted to film the paper puppets moving on the stage of the school's miniature model of the Globe Theatre.

As they divided into a crew including a director, costume and set designers, lighting and sound techs, and cinematographers, I was amused when Jeanne came up with an idea for casting. She intended to take celebrity pictures from the Web and magazines, cutting out faces that depicted different emotions to use for the heads of the paper characters. I couldn't wait to see how it all worked out, trying to imagine a sitcom favorite like Lisa Kudrow portraying the moods of Juliet. I had a feeling we were all going to have a blast and come up with unwittingly hilarious results. In the meantime, they'd have to prepare themselves by reading and understanding the play.

As happened every year, I had a non-joiner, a freshman named Colt Roberts. His name was unusual among a group of students whose parents filled out their birth certificates with an eye to distant Fortune 500 letterhead, and I thought it must be short for Colton. When I asked, he corrected me from his back-row seat; it was just Colt.

Because he was a new student, I couldn't ask any of his former teachers if he'd always been a loner. He looked like all the other boys in his navy or gray slacks with white Oxford shirts and school tie. He was tidy, and his shoes were expensive and polished. The only thing that set him apart was that he had the face of an angel and eyelashes that wouldn't quit. Although I normally would have sat Jeanne right under my nose in some vain attempt to control her, I put her in the back row next to Colt. She was as pretty as he was, and I figured if anyone could charm him out of his shyness, it would be Jeanne.

I kept my eye on them as we settled into the second week of classes. Although Jeanne was as gregarious as ever, by Friday Colt was still warily scrutinizing everyone around him. During my planning period, I went to the records room and pulled his file, which gave me the answer I'd been looking for.

Each year, St. Gregory's awarded several scholarships based on financial need and academic excellence, and this had been Colt's means of admission. He lived in a single-parent home. His mother had listed her occupation as "the entertainment industry." I had no idea what that meant. But I did know that our need-based students often required a period of adjustment, until they found out that even though St. Gregory's certainly had its share of snobs, most of the students cared more about whether someone was into Limp Bizkit or 'N Sync, Buffy or Sabrina.

As I closed the door of the records room behind me, Bill Westin was coming out of his office. He tilted his head back to indicate that he wanted to see me. After I followed him in, he shut the door and said, "I was just about to come to your classroom. This is your planning period, right?"

"Yes," I said, wondering which school activity I was about to be hit up to support. I'd have to make sure it didn't interfere with the Love Sucks meetings. I didn't want to miss the denouement of my friends' minidramas as we approached the end of the year.

Bill's gaze absently fell on my legal pad, then his expression sharpened and he said, "Colt Roberts?"

"One of my freshmen," I said. "I was checking his records."

"Sit down," Bill said, and after we both sat he went on. "Colt may not be a student of yours much longer."

"Is he changing schools?"

"No, his mother asked me to take him out of your class."

When I heard this, I was dumbfounded. I couldn't think of any reason why Colt might complain about me so early in the semester. Maybe Jeanne was driving him crazy. Or maybe he just wasn't excited about Shakespeare. When I asked Bill if that was the problem, he said, "Nope. She wants Colt out of your class because she's heard that you're gay. Before I make a decision about how I'm going to handle it, I wanted to know if you'd detected any attitude from Colt, exchanged words with him, anything like that."

"No," I said, still dazed. "He's quiet. Awkward. I was curious; that's why I checked his file. I figured it might be because he's a scholarship kid. Like he's afraid the other kids will look down on him. But he's been a model student so far."

"That pretty much confirms what I suspected," Bill said. "I don't think Colt has a problem with you. I think it's just the mom. Parents. How come I have to start every school year trying to choose which battles to fight?"

"Don't turn it into a battle on my account," I said. "No reason for Colt to get caught in the crossfire. There are other good English courses."

"So we remove him from a challenging class led by an excellent teacher because his mother's intolerant? That's a slippery slope. What's next? Do I have to take him out of Patsy Butler's class because she's in a wheelchair? Or Ms. Rhodes's class because she's over sixty?"

"You did say last year that there might be fallout from those rumors about me," I reminded him.

"That old gossip? Totally different situation," Bill assured me.

"Unless Colt's mother heard it," I said.

Bill shrugged and said, "She'll get her chance to meet with the dean, the chaplain, and the guidance counselor. I'm sure they'll tell her the same thing I did. Her son is lucky to have a teacher like you."

When I left Bill's office, Paul Nettles was complaining to Edie about the inferior chalk in his classroom. He broke off to stare at me, but I brushed past him without saying anything. Just as I sat behind my desk, he strolled through the door of my classroom.

"You look upset," he said. "What's up?"

"I didn't realize you cared," I muttered.

"Is this about Colt Roberts's mother?"

"What did you do," I asked, "bug the headmaster's office?"

"Westin was asking you about me, wasn't he?" When I gave him a blank look, he went on. "Althea Swanson was in Westin's office when he got a call from Colt Roberts's mother. She was so loud that Althea heard her say something about no fag teaching her kid. Colt is in my speech class. So what did Westin ask you? What did you tell him about me?"

"Your name never came up," I said. When Paul gave me a skeptical look I explained, "Apparently, she wants Colt pulled out of my English class." The look of relief on his face would have been laughable if it hadn't made me loathe him even more. "You're safe. You can run along."

"What's Westin going to do?" Paul asked, making no move to leave.

"I don't know. Why don't you ask Althea to update you? Or maybe you could speak a few words in Colt's mother's ear and finish the job you started last year."

"Huh? What are you talking about?" he asked in that nasal voice that so annoyed me.

"Give me a break. I gave a kid a ride home from a bar last spring, and the next thing I knew you'd started the rumor that I was dating a student. You could have cost me my job." The bell rang, and I stood up. "You need to take off before my students get here."

He left without a word, and I realized my fists were clenched. I took a deep breath and smiled at the first kids who walked into the room.

By the time the school day ended and I'd run my errands, I was hot, tired, and more than a little irritable. I considered going to Dinks for a drink. Or to the gym. Instead, I went to Ramon's. As usual, he read my mood as soon as he saw my face, and he gave me a more exciting workout than I'd have gotten at the YMCA.

He ordered pizza later, and we ate it in bed, fans blowing on us while the TV blared some mindless sitcom. Until he muted it and sat up, giving me a serious look.

"Uh-oh," I said. "Which one is it?"

"Which one is what?"

"Number one: I think we shouldn't see so much of each other. Number two: I really value your friendship. Or number three: There's someone else."

"Number three," he admitted. "Although I really value your friendship."

I smiled and reached out to ruffle his hair, saying, "Are you in love?"

"Maybe. He says he's in love with me. He wants to be exclusive while we're, you know, figuring it all out."

"There's nothing wrong with that," I said. "Except I'll miss you. A lot."

"You and I agreed we'd become friends," Ramon said, sounding a little panicked.

"There's no way I'm letting you vanish on me," I said. "We're already friends. Besides, I need you. I can always count on laughing with you."

"And crying," Ramon reminded me.

"That was the Kool-Aid. Never serve it to me again, or it's over."

"Too late," Ramon said, snuggling next to me in spite of how hot and sticky we were. "You practically admitted you can't live without me."

I grunted, and after a long silence I could tell by his breathing that he'd dozed off. Maybe it was my destiny to watch men sleep after they dumped me. I carefully pulled away, not wanting to wake him, and feasted on the sight of his smooth brown skin, dark hair, and sensual mouth. I'd known that, sooner or later, this goodbye would come, but it didn't have the same power as Heath's to hurt me. It felt more like a change than an ending, and I'd prepared myself for it almost from the beginning.

I smiled and settled next to him again, deciding against leaving. I'd liked waking up with him in Maine, and I wanted to experience it one last time, maybe as a way to mark this new milestone in our relationship.

While he cooked Southwestern eggs the next morning, Ramon admitted that the man in his life was actually an old friend— Russell's widow, Frederick. This new facet of their relationship had taken them both by surprise. They were hesitant to take things to the next level, so they had tormented each other with longing phone calls and dire warnings about doing irreparable damage to their friendship. They weren't sure how their friends would react. They both felt a little guilty about Russell.

"Not that I knew him, but Russell probably would say life is too short to worry about all that other crap. When you think you've found The One, you should grab hold and never let go," I said.

"Sounds like good advice," Ramon said. "I wonder why you never took it?"

"I never found him," I said. "But I did have Heath. We're proof that if a love affair doesn't work out—twice—you can be friends again. Go for it. I'm sure Brett and Barry will tell you the same thing."

"Love is torment," Ramon said in a languid voice.

"No. Jalapeños are torment." I gasped and frowned at my empty juice glass while I frantically fanned my mouth.

Ramon jumped up, got me a bottle of water from the refrigerator, laughed when I drank until it was empty, then said, "This is why you and I would never have fallen in love. You can't handle anything too hot."

"Yeah? Which one of the Spice Girls are you?" I wheezed. "Grumpy? Dopey?"

"Gidget," he said. When I gave him a vacant look, he explained, "Gidget is the Taco Bell dog. Yo quiero a kiss."

"Please don't mangle Spanish. And since you think you're so hot, I don't want you anywhere near my mouth. It's already on fire."

I was in a lighthearted mood when I bounded down the stairs later, rounding the corner of Ramon's building to visitors' parking and coming face to face with Alexander. He was walking from the opposite direction, cell phone against his ear, and his eyes widened when he saw me. "Gotta go," he said. "Call you later." He flipped the phone shut and returned my stare.

"Since I know I'm not stalking you, you must be stalking me," I said. "You never called."

"I was busy with Tragic White Men after I got back from Fredericksburg."

"What are you doing here?"

"Seeing a friend. What are you doing here?" he countered.

"I was seeing a friend too. Who's your friend?"

"Don't worry. It's not the same friend."

"How do you know?" I asked.

"Because my friend's name isn't Ramon," he said. When I glowered at him, he went on. "Good grief, Aaron, he's been a part of your life for years. Up until I got the band together, I danced at the same clubs that he did. Went to the same parties. How could I not know he was your 'mistress'?"

"I think you may be uncertain about the definition of mistress," I said. "Which is ironic, considering—"

"Let's just pretend we didn't run into each other this morning. Will that work?" Alex asked, shifting his sunglasses from his forehead to cover his eyes. "I'll call you later."

I watched him go to a downstairs apartment and knock, then I walked to my car. I sat there a minute, turning the air conditioner higher until the gust of air cooled my car. In spite of the fact that I needed to shower and shave, I decided to drive to Miranda's so I could vent. I knew I'd never find a more willing accomplice when it came to making scathing remarks about Zachary and his effect on Alexander.

When I rang her doorbell, I heard the window above me open, and I looked up.

"I'm in the tub," she said, looking like an unkempt Rapunzel. "The kitchen door is unlocked and there's fresh coffee. Make yourself at home. I'll be down in a few minutes."

I nodded and walked around back, but got a bottle of water instead of coffee, still trying to soothe the jalapeño burn. I was idly glancing at what looked like sample invitations on her table when the doorbell rang.

"Jesus Christ!" I heard her bellow from upstairs.

"I'll deal with it," I yelled, then went to the front door, opening it to find Alexander standing there.

"Would you stop turning up everywhere?" I demanded. "You're making me jittery."

"I didn't see your car," he said, looking abashed. I noticed that he'd parked in Miranda's driveway, so it was plausible that he hadn't noticed my car across the street.

I rolled my eyes and walked back to the kitchen with Alex on my heels. He poured himself a cup of coffee and sat at the table just as Miranda joined us, a towel wrapped like a turban around her unruly hair.

"How Nora Desmond of you," Alex commented.

"Norma," I corrected. "You're thinking of Carol Burnett's version."

"Whatever," Alex said.

Miranda cast a wary look at the two of us while she poured a cup of coffee and said, "Who pissed in your Meow Mix?"

"He's mad because I caught him at his bed buddy's apartment a while ago," Alex said.

"Oh," Miranda said. "Ramon?"

"Do you two work for the CIA?" I asked. "Who the hell were you visiting at such an ungodly hour? You never got up this early to go to the gym with me."

When Alex ignored me, pretending to be engrossed by the clutter on Miranda's table, she said, "Alex was visiting a buddy too. But not a bed buddy." He shot her a warning look, which she pretended not to see as she went on. "He met his buddy through AFH."

"The AIDS Foundation?" I asked. "I don't get it."

"Could we drop this?" Alex asked. When I continued to give him an expectant look, he said, "He's just a guy that I help out from time to time."

"He takes him to Stone Soup and Thomas Street Clinic, helps him do his laundry, makes sure he gets his prescriptions from Walgreens, that kind of stuff," Miranda explained.

"That's great, Alex," I said, astonished by this new information. "How come you never—"

"I told you not to assume you know everything about me," Alex said, and abruptly changed the subject by picking up some cards from the table and asking, "What's all this?"

"I'm ordering invitations and organizing address lists. Don't mess up my system," Miranda barked.

"Invitations? Isn't that premature? You haven't even gotten her to say yes to a date yet," I said.

"Party invitations," Miranda said, frowning at me.

"What party?" Alex asked indignantly. "You never told us about a party."

"Good grief, it's not until December. Plus, it's a business thing. I didn't think you'd want to spend an evening hobnobbing with a bunch of River Oaks luminaries." We listened as she explained that one of her mother's friends was hosting the party to launch her holiday line to a new group of buyers and possibly even potential investors.

"You should invite my grandmother and her friends," Alex said. "She may be a little older than most of these socialites, but she knows everybody in West U, and she's loaded."

"If you think she'd want to come," Miranda said agreeably. "I always like seeing her and Shreve. Power up my laptop, and you can put her address in the data base."

While he was occupied, Miranda and I exchanged a little eye play, which led her to say, "Aaron's starting me on a new fitness regime today. We're going jogging in Memorial Park. Want to join us?"

Alex gave her a horrified look and said, "Are you nuts? In this heat?"

"Sweatin' off the pounds," Miranda chirped. "Come on. We'll have fun."

"I gotta go," Alex said. "I only came by to, uh… Anyway, I've got a bunch of stuff to do today. You two have fun."

"Evidently sprinting is more his style," I said, after we heard the front door close behind him.

Miranda laughed and said, "That's the fastest exit I've ever seen him make. What's on your mind?"

"You sure you wouldn't rather jog?"

"Oh, please. I get dizzy if I move too fast from my front door to my front seat."

"Isn't that a Bruce Springsteen lyric?"

"Hello? Why are you here so early on a Saturday?"

"Brace yourself. I need to whine."

"Outside of Love Sucks?" she gasped with mock horror.

"I didn't come to complain about love. I mean, it's true that in the past year Heath renewed his ex-boyfriend status and Ramon jilted me because he found a new love. Also, the only other guy who somewhat rocked my world turned out to be straight. Patrick has been a less than optimal roommate while he and Vivian do their tango of torment. Alex is in denial about adultery, and you're chasing the meanest dyke in Houston. But this is not about love. I'm starting to wonder if it's time for me to change careers."

Miranda looked startled and said, "Are you kidding? You love teaching."

"Something happened last year, and now it's starting back up this year."

After I told her the whole story, she thought for a few minutes. Then she said, "I guess we can't chalk this up to a seven-year vocational itch since this is, what, your ninth year? I could tell you to go back to school and take some administrative courses. Or chuck it all, move to the shore, and write the great American novel. Or get an advanced degree and teach English at the college level in a more liberal environment. But it's not like you, Aaron, to let a couple of bumps in the road detour you."

"Maybe all this is a sign. You guys are always telling me that I resist change. Maybe it's time for me to accept that change can be good."

"I'm all for being happy. If you told me you hated teaching and you only did it for a stable income, I'd tell you to change jobs. But why walk away from something you love? Besides, somebody has to be a gay role model for teenagers. We lesbians can't shoulder the entire burden."

"What lesbians?" I asked.

"Melissa. k.d. Ellen. Amy and Emily."

I laughed and said, "Trust me, my students wouldn't have a clue who any of those women are. Miranda, I think we're getting old." I shifted and caused a stack of addresses to slide. As I made a quick grab for them, I saw a name I recognized. "Why are you sending an invitation to Zachary Simmons? You have to stop this stalking stuff."

"I'm not stalking anyone. You know Zachary is my accountant. I'm looking for investors, Aaron. Do the math. Or rather, understand that Zachary does the math and can vouch for my ability to turn a profit."

"You need a different accountant. It's a bad idea for you to get too close to Zachary. I have this feeling it'll mess up your friendship with Alex."

"I told Alex the truth about Zachary. He decided to go on living in a fool's paradise. I'm done with it. Anyway, maybe everybody else is right. Maybe Zachary and his wife really are just some weird version of roommates. Since he knows Alex and I are friends, maybe Zachary will even bring him to my party. Which would serve Alex right," she added with a giggle. "He'd be bored out of his mind."

"You're playing with fire. Don't say I didn't warn you. Weren't we talking about me?"

"We're done," she said. "Stop being a pussy and worrying about vindictive old queens and bitchy mothers. You've got a job to do; do it."

"I can't wait until our next Love Sucks meeting," I grumbled. "One complaint out of you and I'm—"

"I have nothing to complain about," Miranda interrupted. "Joey's a lock for the future. Business is booming—"

"Speaking of vindictive old queens and bitchy mothers, are you still trying to get Sarah Ferguson to wear your jewelry? Will she be at your big party?"

"I haven't heard back from my contact yet," Miranda said. "If you're going to stick around, now that I've resolved your crisis you can help me put all these addresses in my database."

I spent the rest of the day typing in addresses from Miranda's organizer, since she said I was faster than her. It was really because Miranda had a gift for getting other people to do things she didn't like doing. As we worked, I tried to ply her for information about Heath and his new boyfriend, but Miranda wasn't very forthcoming.

"It's not that I don't want to tell you," she said. "Or that he swore me to secrecy. I'm just out of Heath's loop, I guess."

"Why do I find that hard to believe? I know how close you two are."

"It's the truth," she insisted. "Stop talking. You're wasting time."

When I went home that night, I found Patrick in the middle of his own mailing list frenzy. Our coffee table was littered with Gore campaign pamphlets and stacks of envelopes. Patrick sat in the midst of the mayhem, stuffing envelopes while watching CNN.

"Hey! I didn't hear you come in," he said when I sat down on the sofa. "What have you been up to?"

"I don't believe this. I just left one mailing list sweatshop, and now I'm in another one."

"Wanna help? It's fun," he said with a grin.

"Nice try, Tom Sawyer. That rhetoric hardly ever works. How's the campaign trail?"

Patrick's eyes radiated enthusiasm as he said, "It's great. I've been canvassing neighborhoods every day, spreading the word about Gore."

"You sound like a politico Freddy Krueger."

"What?"

"Nothing. I'd love to help you, but I have a hot date with a frozen lasagna and homework to correct."

"Speaking of hot dates," Patrick intoned.

"You've got a date with Vivian?" I asked hopefully.

Patrick winced and said, "No. I was going to ask if you have anything lined up for next Thursday. I'm organizing the next Love Sucks get-together."

"*You're* organizing it? How did that happen? Since when do you organize anything?" I asked, thinking about the chaos in Patrick's bedroom.

"Not only do I run a thriving bar, thank you, but I'm expanding it. Remember?" Patrick said, looking genuinely hurt. I immediately regretted taking potshots at him. Until he said, "I only asked if you have a date to be nice. Dating means you're ready for commitment."

"Excuse me?"

He turned away from his envelopes and looked me in the eye. "I'm not saying this to be an asshole. I'm just being honest, Aaron. You're not that great at letting people in. I don't know. Maybe you're not ready. Maybe that's why you pine away for Heath."

"I don't *pine.*"

"Whatever. But I'm guessing that's why you went back to him. It was safe and easy."

"Trust me, there was nothing easy about it," I grumbled.

"Give me a break. What's easier, reverting to the old or braving the new?"

I thought about it and realized Patrick was right, which annoyed me. It was easy to slip into my old patterns with Heath. But what had I gone back to, besides good sex? It was like jumping back on a merry-go-round and expecting to get somewhere new. Sure, a ride on the horsie was entertaining for a little while, but wouldn't a roller coaster be more exciting?

And speaking of stallions, it was the same situation with Ramon. Losing my fuck buddy was like being pushed off the merry-go-round. I knew we'd continue to be friends. I was more upset by the thought of having to find someone new. It was easy to open up to Ramon, because I didn't think anything would ever change between us. Neither of us wanted a relationship, so it was safe and comfortable.

Unlike Heath. If relationships were an amusement park, and love was a roller coaster, there was always the possibility that one of us might suggest we buy a ticket to ride. Maybe I wasn't ready for anything but the merry-go-round. Or the Ferris wheel. Or any of those rides that went in circles and never got anywhere, until they stopped. Or until you threw up and realized the ride wasn't for you.

"Besides," Patrick continued, "if you really were in love with Heath, then why all the secrecy when you got back together? And how can you shift from love to friendship? I can't see myself settling for friendship with Vivian."

"Enough," I said. My head suddenly hurt and I massaged my temples. "Stop the ride. I want to get off."

"Then you're on your own," Patrick said, returning to his mission to get Gore elected. "As liberal as I am, I don't think I could—"

"You know that's not what I meant," I said and went into the kitchen.

It didn't take me long to grade my students' homework, and soon I was staring at my empty dinner plate, feeling less than satisfied. I kept replaying my conversations with Miranda and Patrick in my head, trying to apply their insight to my love life and my job. I couldn't seem to come to any conclusions.

Over the following week, I continued to keep a low profile at work, taught my children well, and didn't make any waves. I was between classes on Thursday when I checked my messages and heard a reminder from Patrick about that night's Love Sucks gathering.

Patrick says, Man who come to Ming's tonight will not whine alone. I laughed, thankful that I was the only person in the staff room. *Seriously, bro. See you around eight. Oh, uh, sorry about being so brutal with my honesty the last time we talked. You know how I get. Between my problems with Vivian, the bar, and this campaign stuff, maybe I'm overloaded and I took it out on you. I don't know. But there you go. That's all the complaining I'm going to do. But don't let that stop you tonight. If anyone needs to do some talking, it's you. I know you've got a lot on your mind, and you need to open up, man. It's not good to hold it all in. See ya.*

Later that night, after my post-work workout, I managed to find a parking space a block away from Ming's Cafe, a Chinese restaurant in the heart of Montrose. Patrick had probably chosen the location because of its close proximity to Dinks.

When I reached the parking lot outside Ming's, I stopped short at the sight of Heath and his new boyfriend, who I recognized from the day they'd flirted at Crossroads. Heath was standing next to his car, and the new guy, whose name I'd blocked from my memory, was sitting on the hood. He was cuter and more muscular than I'd remembered.

I took a step back, feeling awkward and uncomfortable. It was true; Heath had moved on. But the longer I stood there watching them, the more I realized how relieved I was. They looked good together. Maybe Heath had finally found someone who was into roller coasters. Maybe I could be happy for them.

I found myself moving on as well, and I walked toward them. At the sound of my footsteps they stopped kissing, and Heath saw me.

"Oh. Hi," he said awkwardly and blushed. He gestured toward his handsome hood ornament and said, "This is Logan."

"Of course you are," I said. Now I remembered thinking that his name sounded like a sci-fi action movie hero. Or a porn star. "I'm Aaron. It's nice to meet you."

"You too," he said. Returning his attention to Heath, Logan asked, "How 'bout it? Can I use the car?"

Not *your* car, but *the* car, I observed.

"Logan teaches karate on Thursday nights. He has a class, but his car is in the shop," Heath explained.

Correction. A sci-fi/action/kung-fu/porn movie character. Alex could write the music.

Heath made a big production of warily handing over his keys, but he grinned when Logan leaped off the car and gave him a bear hug. I politely wished Logan a good class and watched Heath's eyes follow him as he drove away.

"Sorry about that," Heath said.

"He's got a ticket to ride," I said.

"And you don't care," Heath added.

"No. That's not true," I assured him. "He seems nice. He's hot. You seem happy. I'm fine with it. And this is just from seeing you together for five minutes. The possibilities for the future are infinite. Now tell me, is he good in bed?"

"I can't believe you want to know that," Heath said incredulously. "Or that you think I'd answer you."

"Maybe you'll tell us during the Love Sucks—" I broke off when I saw a handwritten sign affixed to the door of Ming's, informing us that they were serving take-out only, as the restaurant was reserved for a private party. "Now what? What time is it? I wonder if the others know about this yet."

"Relax," Heath said. He held open the door for me and urged, "Go in."

I stopped inside the door, overwhelmed by familiar faces. Miranda, Vivian, Alexander, and a beaming Patrick were seated in the middle of the restaurant. Ramon, Brett, and the rest of the guys I'd met during my trip to Maine crowded around an adjacent table. Stasi, Tad, Kelly, and my parents waved from their seats. Bill Westin, Dale Campbell, and a few of St. Gregory's more liberal teachers were there too. New friends and old friends were everywhere I looked. What overwhelmed me most, even more than everyone applauding and cheering, was the sight of several of my former students, Khalid Joseph and Justin Woodhill among them.

"What is this? Isn't Chinese New Year in February?" I asked, once everyone had settled down.

Patrick stood up and said loudly, "Patrick says, He who has this many friends is loved by all." Everyone in the room cheered again. "Patrick also says, When Aaron stops gawking from door, everyone gets to eat faster."

"What the hell is going on?" I asked as Heath pushed me toward a chair next to Patrick. "Hi, Brett. Hey, Dale. I don't get it. I thought we were—Carla Baker? I haven't seen you in five years. Aren't you in college now? Would someone tell me what this is all about? This is like *It's a Wonderful Life*."

"The gay version," Alexander said.

"Combined with that last scene in *Longtime Companion*," Miranda added.

"But nobody here is dead," Vivian pointed out.

"Except for Aaron's sex life," Miranda said.

"That's dormant, not dead," Heath corrected.

"Is that it? You brought everyone I know here to mourn my sex life?" I asked. "If that's the case, you could've left my family out of it. Not to mention my boss and my students."

Patrick said, "Patrick says—"

"What's with all this 'Patrick says' crap?" I interrupted.

"Today is Confucius's birthday," Patrick explained. "Everyone is here tonight because we have one thing in common. A really good friend."

"He means you," Miranda explained.

"Thank you. I wasn't sure," I said.

Speaking loudly, so everyone could hear, Patrick said, "Confucius said, 'To be able, under all circumstances, to practice five things constitutes perfect virtue. These five things are gravity, generosity of soul, sincerity, earnestness, and kindness.' That sounds like you to me, man, and everyone else in this room agrees. You're loved. Let's eat, damn it."

Our regularly scheduled Love Sucks meeting was replaced by a Life's Not So Bad party, as everyone circulated around the room or took plates of food to the outside deck and talked. I eventually ended up next to my parents and Bill Westin, and Bill gestured for Alex to join us.

"This is the gentleman who put all this together," Bill said. "We had quite an entertaining time calling a few of your old students."

"*You* did this?" I asked Alex, too amazed to let myself worry about my boss spending time with my wildest friend. "I thought it was Patrick who organized tonight."

"It was Patrick," Alex agreed.

"Patrick picked the place and kept you from finding out," my mother said. "But it was Alex's idea and his phone calls that got us all together."

"Why?" I asked, thinking about how Alex was continually surprising me lately.

"Miranda told me you were having a rough time at work, wondering if you're in the right place."

"Which you are," Bill said sternly. "Don't even think of leaving St. Gregory's."

"Also…I still feel bad about letting your birthday get by me this year. I wanted to do something special for you," Alex said.

"You succeeded," I said, touched to hear him acknowledge that his absence might have hurt me. "Thanks, Alexander."

"I'm glad you're not mad. I know how you compartmentalize your life."

"I'm not mad. It's weird, but it's OK."

"Of course it's OK," my father said, "because you've always lived your life honestly, son. You've never done anything you had to hide."

The lump in my throat kept me from answering, and Alex glanced away, his forehead wrinkling. I wondered if he was thinking about Zachary and the clandestine life they were leading. I watched as Vivian followed him to the tables where Brett, Ramon, and Stasi were sitting next to Heath and the rest of the Love Sucks crew. It gave me pause to see Heath and Ramon together, but it was out of my control.

My father looked solemnly at Bill and said, "Aaron's spoken to us about what's going on at school. I hope you're not the only one at St. Gregory's who knows what a fine teacher he is."

"The situation will be addressed at our governing board's regular first Thursday meeting, where the boy's parent will have her chance to be heard. I'm sure Aaron has nothing to worry about."

"It's funny how no one disapproves of opposite-sex teachers," my mother said. "By this woman's reasoning, shouldn't she be worried about straight women teaching her son?"

I noticed that Justin Woodhill had stopped on his way to get another Coke and was listening, so I said, "This is probably not the place or time to talk about it."

They changed the subject, Justin walked away, and I mentally rehashed the situation. I hadn't decided yet whether or not I would attend the board meeting. Bill wasn't even sure Colt's mother would be there, in which case the entire matter would be dropped. So far, Colt was still attending my class, which I took as a good sign.

After a while, I ambled over to the Love Sucks table and sat down. Alex was halfheartedly listening to Miranda tell Ramon and Heath about her new jewelry designs. I noticed that Patrick was wearing a surly expression. I followed his gaze to an adjoining table, where Vivian was in an animated conversation with Brett.

"Who *is* that guy?" Patrick grumbled.

Ramon glanced over and said, "That's my friend, Brett. It was his family's house where Aaron stayed when we went to Maine."

"Your boyfriend, did you say?" Patrick asked.

"No. Brett's straight."

I knew this wasn't what Patrick wanted to hear, so I quickly said, "Thanks, again, Patrick, Alex, for putting tonight together. I still can't believe it."

Patrick obviously hadn't heard me, as he was fixated on Vivian.

Alex tried to shrug it off. Ramon scooted next to me and said, "You have so many friends. It's nice to meet some of the people you've talked about over the past few years."

Alex stared at Ramon with an inscrutable expression, then his gaze went past me and he broke into a big grin, jumped up, and said, "You came!"

I turned around in time to see Zachary cast a doting smile on Alex. Before I could stop myself, I glanced back to meet Miranda's eyes. We managed to keep our faces blank while Alex introduced Zachary around. Even Patrick stopped scowling at Brett long enough to acknowledge the significance of the moment.

"I knew tonight meant a lot to Alexander's best friend, so I wanted to stop by and say hello, Aaron," Zachary said. I thought he sounded about as believable as a man in a bad toupee hawking condos to old people on late-night TV.

"Thanks," I said with as much enthusiasm as I could muster, hoping my pleasant tone masked the hostility I felt toward him. "It's nice to see you again."

Zachary's eyes went past me, and he said, "Hi, Miranda. What's the word on the Fergie deal? Is she going to be wearing your jewelry?"

Miranda's face fell and she said, "No. My friend wasn't able to connect with her. However, rumor has it that someone else is interested in my Good Bad Girl line."

Patrick said, "I hope it's not that semiliterate poet—"

"It's Anna Nicole Smith," Miranda said quickly, before Alex could take umbrage at Patrick's insult to his band's drummer.

My mouth dropped open, Patrick's eyes bugged out, and Heath said, "Anna Nicole Smith? Weren't her fifteen minutes of fame up about a million minutes ago?"

"She's planning a big comeback," Miranda assured us.

"You'd better give her some big jewelry then," Patrick advised. "Be careful about the length of her necklaces if you want anyone to actually see them."

"I can't believe your jewels will be next to Anna Nicole's skin," I said.

"Exactly what her late husband's sons said to him," Alex quipped.

When I met his eyes, we both began to howl with laughter, and I think I was the only one who heard Miranda mumble to Heath, "Isn't it amazing how Alexander always has a straight man feeding him lines?"

Almost Halloween

I'd just about convinced myself to skip the Thursday meeting of St. Gregory's governing board, although it was a teacher planning day so I had no students. Bill had made it clear that since I wasn't actually being accused of wrongdoing, my job performance wasn't in dispute, and I wasn't at risk for losing my position, my presence wasn't necessary. He still had not received any notification from Colt's mother that she would be in attendance, so he had a feeling her request for Colt's transfer would be taken off the agenda.

I stopped by the office to ask Edie if anything had changed, but no one was behind the desk. I scanned the visitors' area and felt the nerves on the back of my neck crinkle. A woman was watching me with a sour expression. Thin lips pressed together in her weathered face, stocky, early fifties—she had to be the judgmental crone who thought I was a threat to her son.

"Hi," I said as brightly as I could. "Have you been helped?"

"They know I'm here," she said and looked away as if I was annoying her.

I resisted the part of me that wanted a confrontation with her. It would serve no purpose, and in the long run it would probably be Colt who paid the price. But seeing her made up my mind for me.

She wasn't going to make innuendoes about me in a board meeting unless she had the guts to do it to my face.

I took the stairs two at a time to the large conference room. When I stepped inside, I stopped short, a little surprised. Bill was there, of course, with the guidance counselor, Terri Howell, the Episcopal clergy who were on the board, Don McBride, who was the dean of students, and several other board members. But I hadn't expected to see Grant Coker, the attorney I'd consulted a few months before, standing between Vivian, who hadn't told me she'd be at the meeting, and a woman who was probably Grant's assistant. Grant and Vivian were engrossed in conversation and hadn't seen me come in, but I must have caught Grant's assistant's eye, because she gave me a measuring look.

I did a double take. Not only did she have the Barbie doll figure and blond, blue-eyed, angelic looks of my little sister Stasi, but her casual attire reminded me of some of the girls I'd gone to high school with who were rodeo groupies. She looked like she'd been poured into her Western-cut shirt and Wranglers, and I glanced down to see that she was even wearing black roping boots. I was surprised to see someone who worked in Grant's office dressed unprofessionally. Go Texas Day was still months away, and it wasn't casual Friday, which I knew many offices observed.

As if in response to an invisible signal, everyone began finding places at the conference table. I slid into a chair against the wall as unobtrusively as possible, wondering when they'd summon Colt's mother from the office. Bill noticed me, but he just smiled and nodded, then one of the board members started the meeting.

After a few procedural matters were discussed, Bill took over, saying, "We have several visitors here today. After I introduce them, we'll take care of their business first, so they can leave and we can complete the rest of our agenda. Aaron Fisher," he nodded toward me, "is a member of our teaching staff."

While Bill went on to give a little bio about me, I looked at Vivian, who gave me a reassuring smile. Grant nodded at me, and his assistant, sitting on his right, narrowed her eyes as if trying to read my mind. I wondered if I should stop Bill and let him know that Colt's mother was downstairs. It didn't seem right to start the meeting without her; maybe Edie hadn't let the headmaster know she was waiting.

"Grant Coker is Mr. Fisher's legal counsel, although today, he and his colleague, Vivian Taylor, are here only as interested observers. To Mr. Coker's right is Tamra Roberts. Ms. Roberts is the mother of one of Mr. Fisher's students, Colt Roberts."

I gaped at her, certain I'd heard Bill wrong. There was no way Southwest Barbie was old enough to be Colt's mother. And no one could be more different from the woman who was sitting downstairs in the office.

It took me a few minutes to regain my senses. By then, Bill had already explained what Ms. Roberts's complaint was, and one of the board members was asking her questions.

"Has Colt expressed any dissatisfaction with his English class or Mr. Fisher's teaching methods?"

"No. Colt is fifteen years old. Kids can't always judge what's best for them. That's my job as his mother." Her Texas drawl was thick and her voice soft, but her expression made it clear that she considered herself a wild mare who wouldn't be broken.

"Ms. Roberts, the school can't make curriculum decisions based on your personal aversion to what you may perceive as flaws in Mr. Fisher's character. As Mr. Westin just told us, Mr. Fisher has an exemplary record at St. Gregory's. No parent or student has ever filed any kind of complaint about his behavior or his teaching performance. I simply don't see this as an issue."

The other board members seemed to concur, but before they could dismiss her request, she spoke up again. "Character? I have my own opinions about the character of men. When I was Colt's age, I got expelled when my school found out I was pregnant. I never finished high school; I got my G.E.D. Colt's father's parents sent him out of town quick, so he wouldn't have to take any responsibility for me or his child. I worked crummy jobs and saved every penny I could so that when I had my baby, I could pay my way at the hospital. We've never been anybody's charity case. When they told me I had a little boy, I was glad. Because I knew then, and I haven't changed my mind, that it's a lousy world for girls."

"Ms. Roberts, I don't see what this—" Dean McBride broke off when one of the other board members raised a hand to silence him.

"It's tough being a single parent," she went on. "But I never took anything from anyone. The only reason I let Colt accept the scholarship here was because I felt like he'd worked hard to deserve it. We don't take handouts."

"Colt has an excellent record," Bill Westin agreed.

"He's never given me any trouble. I was always there when he came home from school, and we did his homework together. My sister stayed overnight at our house, because since Colt was six, I've worked as a dancer. Most girls can't make it nearly ten years, like I have. They end up dead, in jail, on drugs, or with abusive pimps. I never had any illusions about what I was doing. I was making a living that gave Colt the best of everything. Clothes, toys, books, and anything he needed for school. On the weekends, we did things together. The zoo, Astroworld, every art and science museum. Art festivals, Greek festivals—if I thought Colt would have fun and learn something, I took him."

"That's commendable," one of the board members said.

"We have a nice house. Colt knows what I do, that it's just a job. It doesn't come home with me. My customers don't come home with me either. But after nine years, I know all about the *character* of men. Like I said, I was glad Colt was a boy. I didn't have to worry about him being pawed and used the way a daughter would have been."

I glanced at Vivian, who was looking at Tamra Roberts with admiration. Apparently she'd forgotten whose side she was on.

"Ms. Roberts," I said, keeping my voice as soft as hers, "I've never behaved inappropriately with a student. It's apparent that you've heard rumors that I'm gay, but I assure you, your son is completely safe in my classroom."

"In your classroom? Maybe. But outside of it? I heard you dated a male student. I don't want you near my son. We're not waiting until this is a story for Channel 11. I want him out of your class."

Grant had pushed his chair back so he could get a better look at her over the tops of his reading glasses. Just as he seemed about to comment, the door burst open. Everyone glanced around, startled, and I was bewildered to see several students, led by Justin Woodhill, file into the room.

"Perhaps you didn't realize there's a meeting going on in here," Dean McBride said sternly. "It's an in-service day. You can't be on school property unsupervised."

"We're here for the meeting," Justin said defiantly. "The handbook states in Section 4, Part B, that impacted students are allowed to attend open board meetings and speak when recognized."

"Any staff member who is up for disciplinary action is entitled to attend meetings with counsel. We're here to counsel Mr. Fisher," Khalid added, looking up from the piece of paper he'd been reading.

I didn't know whether to laugh or chastise them, wondering if our mock trial the year before had created these monsters. I glanced at Bill, whose face was twitching suspiciously.

"I'm Mr. Fisher's legal counsel," Grant said, speaking respectfully to Khalid. "However, he's not here for disciplinary action."

"Oh," Khalid said, his face falling.

"But we're impacted students, so we can be here," Justin doggedly went on, and the group behind him nodded as one.

"Are you Colt's mom?" Jeanne Baxter asked Ms. Roberts. "He's really cute. We tried to talk him into coming with us—"

"Miss Baxter," Bill said, "I'm afraid I'm going to have to ask you and your—"

"Let them stay," I heard a weak voice speak from the far end of the conference table. I looked that way and saw Reverend Bellamy, Rector Emeritus of St. Gregory's Church. "I'd like to hear what they have to say about their teacher."

"We don't think Mr. Fisher should be in trouble or lose his job," Justin said. "He's the best English teacher we've ever had."

"He treats everyone fairly," Khalid said.

"His classes are hard, but I feel like I learned more in them than any other class," Jeanne added.

"We don't know if he's gay, because he never told us. Mr. Fisher doesn't talk about himself like some teachers. That's because Mr. Fisher would rather listen to us. What we think about the things we read. How we see stuff," Justin said.

"Anybody is lucky to have him as their teacher," Jeanne added. "We just want to know when we go to English class tomorrow, Mr. Fisher will be there. We have a lot of stuff to do for our class project."

Khalid added, "When I told my father Mr. Fisher was in trouble, he said he might have to get on the school board himself to make sure the school doesn't fire good teachers."

"Thank you for your input," Reverend Bellamy said, and I could see his eyes twinkling. "It's been most enlightening."

The kids gave me little signals of encouragement when they filed out. After the door shut behind them, gentle laughter swept the room, and I turned back to Colt's mother.

"Ms. Roberts, if you really want Colt removed from my class, I have to accept that. But as I was trying to explain before, your son is not at risk in my company, on or off the school grounds. In the first place, I don't fraternize with students. I've never dated a student. I honor the school's reputation as well as my own. That's all I have to say."

"I'd like to make a few remarks," Vivian said. "Ms. Roberts— Tamra—I'm not here to give Mr. Fisher legal assistance. I've known Aaron for several years as a friend. I think you realize, in your heart, that all men are not—well, whatever word you want to use. One day, your son is going to be a man, after all. He'll look back at St. Gregory's and see what a great opportunity it was. Especially because he had dedicated, honorable teachers like Aaron Fisher."

"Speaking as Colt's guidance counselor, I think it would be extremely disruptive to move him out of Mr. Fisher's English class," Terri said. "Colt and I have discussed this. He said I was free to tell the board that he doesn't want to be moved. He's excited about his current English project, and he thinks Mr. Fisher is a good teacher. However, he also told me that what you say goes. What he said was, 'She's my mom. She's thinking about what's best for me.' I hope that you are, Ms. Roberts."

"Colt said that?" his mother asked. "I'm just trying to protect him."

"There'll be a lot of places in the world where you can't protect him," I said. "But I believe that school should be the one sure place children are safe." After a signal from Bill, I left the conference room followed by Grant and Vivian. I turned to speak to them. "It surprised me to see the two of you here. Why didn't you tell me you were coming?"

"Bill Westin gave me a courtesy call," Grant said. "I'm sure he was covering his ass in case things got ugly. He doesn't want you to end up suing the school."

"As if," I said.

"Grant asked me if I wanted to come along," Vivian said.

"So what do you think will happen?" I asked.

Grant shrugged. "Hard to say. Ms. Roberts is a woman who knows her own mind. She just doesn't know her mind is narrow."

At the foot of the stairs, Vivian took my arm and said, "Her story made me think about Heath."

"Why?" I asked.

"The unwed mother who busts her ass to give her kid a good life. She went a different route from Laura Temple, but she's only trying to protect her son. I don't agree with her, but I understand her. No matter what happens, Colt will be fine. Judging by what the counselor said, he's already learned to think beyond his mother's limitations."

After they left, I stopped by the office, where Edie tried to decipher my expression. When I just shrugged, she said, "One thing about teaching. There are a lot of wins you don't know about until years after they happen. But they do happen."

"You're right," I agreed. "I wanted to ask you something. Earlier there was some old battle-ax in here. She looked like a drill sergeant. I thought she was Colt's mother."

Edie burst out laughing and said, "She's the potato lady."

"The what?"

"In the cafeteria. She's always behind the baked potato bar. I guess you didn't recognize her out of the hairnet."

"Jeez," I said. "That's what I get for avoiding carbs. Not to mention the school cafeteria. I don't think I've eaten there in about five years."

"Now you know what you're missing."

"I think I'll just keep brown-bagging it," I said.

"That's probably what Mr. Potato Lady does too," Edie said with a straight face.

During my planning period the next day, Bill Westin came to my classroom. As soon as I saw his expression I knew.

"I'm sorry," he said. "She wouldn't budge. It seemed better for Colt's sake to give in. After all, she's free to take him to another school, and that would cheat him out of the entire St. Gregory's experience. You did have the full support of the board, if that helps."

"Thanks," I said, but it didn't ease the sick feeling in my gut.

"Do you want to talk about it?"

"No. I'll just hold on to a thought that Edie gave me yesterday. Sometimes we don't know about the wins for a long time."

"Isn't that the truth," Bill said. "My door's open, Aaron. Any time."

By the time my ninth graders came in, I was composed. After the bell rang Jeanne stared at Colt's empty seat, then sent me a stricken look. I gave her a reassuring smile and said, "Act five, scene three. *See what a scourge is laid upon your hate / That heaven finds means to kill your joys with love.* Let's talk about the meaning of that passage."

I spent the next couple of weeks keeping to myself. My friends probably thought everything had turned out OK, since I wasn't whining about it. I wanted to wait until the sick feeling went away before I turned it into conversational fodder.

It helped that everyone was caught up in their own lives, especially Patrick. Even at night, when he was at Dinks, people were constantly in and out of our apartment to pick up campaign materials and call lists. Several nights they spent hours on his phone, making calls for Gore. I bought a new television with a built-in VCR for my room and hid out, unwilling to be guilt-tripped into working with them. I cared about the election, and of course I'd vote, but I couldn't understand why everyone was getting worked up about it.

To me, it was a no-brainer. People would vote for Gore because the country, especially the economy, had been thriving under the Clinton/Gore administration.

Our next Love Sucks meeting was scheduled for Halloween, which fell on a Tuesday. Since it was a school night, I'd agreed to dinner, but I insisted that I couldn't go out afterward, nor was anyone to expect to see me in some lame costume.

The Thursday before our planned gathering, I was hunkered down in my room watching *Love Story,* of all things, when Alex charged through the door without knocking.

"Who the hell are all those people downstairs? Are you running an escort service out of—" He broke off to give the television a horrified look. "Ali McGraw. The woman who emoted by means of flared nostrils. Love means never having to say you're equine."

"Everybody's a critic. Those are Patrick's fellow Gore campaigners downstairs."

"That explains all the cars with bumper stickers lining the street. I need help."

"It's about time. First of all, that T-shirt should be burned," I said. "And why are you wearing a tie with it?"

"Not fashion help," he said, rolling his eyes. "We're taking a road trip this weekend."

"You and the band?"

"Me and you." When I didn't respond, he sighed and said, "You've already got that sullen, I-don't-want-to-leave-my-house-or-ever-do-anything-spontaneous look. How old are you? Sixty?"

"I'm as spontaneous as the next person," I insisted. "Where do you want to go? Austin? Galveston?"

"Actually, we fly out tomorrow night about eight, then drive back. The band can get a free van—for keeps!—if I just drive it back here."

Something about the strange lack of details set off my inner alarms. I wasn't sure what I wanted to know first, so I said, "Why don't you ask Zachary to go with you? Wouldn't that be more fun for you?"

"There are very few people in the world that I can spend hours on the road with," Alex said. "You're one of them."

"How many hours are we talking?"

"Don't worry. You'll be home in time to get plenty of sleep before work on Monday." He paused, waiting for the dozen shrill questions that he was sure I had, but I didn't speak. He decided to take a different approach, one that would disarm me with its seeming irrelevance. "Did you know Miranda won't be at Love Sucks on Tuesday because she's out of town?"

"No."

"I can't believe she didn't call you. She probably thought you'd be all negative and surly. I don't know *why* she has that opinion of you."

"Negative and surly about what?"

"Joey. They're a couple."

"That's impossible," I said. "If Miranda finally got a date with Joey, she'd have rented a billboard to let us know."

"I only know because Joey told me. Maybe Miranda wanted to see how it would work out before she told us about it. It must be going OK, because she and Joey went to see Joey's family. Miranda is meeting the folks. Doesn't that sound serious?"

I had to agree that it did, but it was clear Alex was leading up to details that were making me nervous. "You're making me nervous. Just spit it out."

"OK. Miranda and Joey thought it would be fun to take a trip. So they drove to Joey's parents'. Joey's brother owns a carpet cleaning service, and he's buying a new fleet of vans. He has several old cargo vans that he's selling, and he said he'd give Joey one—free!—for Tragic White Men. She just has to drive it back. But Joey and Miranda don't want to drive back separately. One of Grandma's friends is a Continental executive, and he's giving me travel vouchers so that you and I can fly there for free, pick up the van, and drive it back. Isn't that simple?"

"It sounds simple," I agreed. "Now tell me the rest of it."

"Joey's parents live in San Diego."

"Oh, for God's sake. You want me to fly to San Diego on Friday night and spend two days riding back in some stupid van that probably says *Hal's Carpet Cleaning: No Job Too Small* on the side?"

He glanced at the TV and asked, "What were you planning to do this weekend? Is it the American Not So Classic Movie Festival? Your big chance to see *Ice Castles? Arthur II? First Knight? Rhinestone? Mannequin?*"

"You do realize that the drive from El Paso to Houston is perhaps the dullest in the entire world, don't you?"

"That's why I need you with me. The hours will fly by while you share the tender details of all the romantic movies you watch on the sly."

"I confess. The porn thing's been a lie all these years. Which is why I'm unfamiliar with Al Camino's *Greatest Hits.*"

"I'm willing to bet Al Camino's movies gross more than *Bed of Roses,* Christian Slater notwithstanding. So will you go with me?"

"Of course. At the very least, I can see what kind of aliens spawned your dyke drummer."

The trip to San Diego was enjoyable, since we were treated like VIPs in first class. I'd always liked going anywhere with Alex, whose buoyant mood when he traveled was contagious. Midway into our three-hour flight, he turned to me and said, "Now that you've got nowhere to run, let's hear it."

"Hear what?" I asked blankly.

"Do you think I'm the only one of our group who gets talked about behind his back? I was chosen to get the story on Ponyboy."

"Pony—oh, Colt," I said. "I don't want to talk about it."

"They took him out of your class, huh? OK. *I'll* talk. Vivian told us enough that I can make assumptions. You feel like Colt's mother won. Even worse, you feel like Paul Nettles won, because his spiteful gossip started this whole thing. You feel like you and Colt lost. Colt didn't lose. He had a teacher and a class that he liked. Because of prejudice, a change was made. Thirty years from now, he probably wouldn't have remembered a freaking thing about Shakespeare except that it was hard to read. But he'll always remember what it felt like to be on the wrong end of an injustice. He sounds like a decent kid. This won't turn him into a bigot. It'll have the opposite effect. That's a win."

"Maybe," I conceded.

"You know I'm right; stop being stubborn. There's another win too. People from four corners of your life came together to show their support and friendship at Ming's. Your family, friends, students, boss. If you feel sorry for yourself after that, you should have your ass kicked. Beyond that, you sat in a conference room with Episcopalian ministers of all ages and a bunch of straight men and women who work with you or know you. According to Vivian, everybody in that room except the mother was on your side. That wasn't just a win for you, Aaron. That was a win for all of us. It means things are changing. They're getting better. Twenty years ago—maybe less—just a rumor might have meant your job. Instead, the truth about you being gay was irrelevant. They stood up for you because you're a good teacher and a good man. Stop seeing the glass as half empty. And speaking of empty," he finished, fixing his gaze on Tony, our flight attendant.

As Tony walked toward us with a fresh drink, I surprised us all by reaching over, catching Alex's chin in my hand, and kissing him hard.

"Girl, get a room," Tony said.

"Thank you," I said to Alex. "For putting that in perspective."

"You're welcome," Alex said. "Should we try that again with tongue?"

"I'm next," Tony said.

"You both wish."

Joey was driving Miranda's Mustang when they picked us up at the airport. One look at Miranda removed any lingering doubts I'd had about the accuracy of Alex's information. They were definitely an item. Although Miranda seemed smitten, there was an edginess to their interaction that I found reassuring. In the first place, I didn't want anyone to walk over Miranda, but I also knew she wouldn't be happy with someone she could push around. It appeared that she and Joey were finding the right balance.

"We grilled chicken tonight, so if you're hungry my mom's got food waiting at home," Joey said.

"Whether you're hungry or not, she's going to make you eat it," Miranda said. "She's an older version of Vivian."

"Too bad you got here after sunset. We could have gone to see the ocean," Joey said.

"The water's too cold to swim," Miranda said. "But look, I'm tanned!"

Joey laughed and said, "We've been going to a tanning salon. She refuses to go back to Texas from Southern California without a tan. You all need to come back in the summer, after June gloom goes away."

"I've been to San Diego before," I said.

"And got no farther than the Hillcrest bars," Alex said.

"I went to Black's Beach!" I protested.

"You got naked on the beach?" Joey asked.

"Why do you sound so shocked?"

"You don't seem like the type."

"Aaron'll drop trousers any time," Miranda said. "Back before he became celibate—"

"I am not—"

"He was quite the slut."

"I was never a—"

"Yeah, he's definitely slowed down over the past few years," Alex agreed.

As we took a brightly lit on-ramp, I could see Joey's kohl-rimmed eyes watching me in the rearview mirror. I was pretty sure she looked sympathetic, which was big of her since the last time she'd seen me I'd called her a bitch. Or maybe she was feeling sorry for me because of my alleged lack of a sex life.

I had no idea which of San Diego's suburbs we were in when Joey finally pulled into a driveway.

"Stucco," I noted. "Just like home. Did you know that some people don't like stucco?" Miranda turned around to glare at me, while Joey parked behind what I assumed was the van that would take me back to Texas. After I got out of the car, I saw the ad on the side for RAY MITCHELL'S GENIE-CLEAN: MAKING YOUR CARPETS AND RUGS MAGICALLY NEW! I took a closer look at the genie sitting in the middle of a flying carpet and said, "Hey, isn't that—"

"Yes, and there's nothing you can say that I didn't hear in high school," Joey said. "He has TV ads too, so my face is everywhere."

"Do you still have that *I Dream of Jeannie* outfit? I can totally see Miranda—"

"No. You can't, and shouldn't, if you know what's good for you," Miranda said.

We went inside and were introduced to Joey's parents, Glenda and Ray Sr., who were sitting in their living room surrounded by boxes. Glenda immediately hurried to the kitchen to fix us both a plate, and Ray Sr. said, "Glenda had a couple of spinster aunts who lived seventy years in a house in La Jolla. The last aunt died a few weeks ago, and we've been trying to sort through her stuff and figure out what to do with it."

"We're going to send a lot of boxes back in the van with y'all," Miranda said.

"Boxes of what?" Alex asked. "Do I have to unload them?"

"No. I asked my parents if you could park the van at their house until I get home. Just leave everything inside it, including the keys. They'll put it in their garage."

"The girls have been giving us fashion shows," Ray Sr. said. "I think some of these dresses were Joey's grandmother's."

"There's a ton of costume jewelry," Miranda said. "I'm going to use some to make Glenda a few new pieces."

"Hon, you can do whatever you want with that old junk," Glenda said, returning with two plates while Ray Sr. put up TV trays for us.

"Oh, yeah. I found something for you in one of the boxes," Miranda said to Alex. She started digging around and finally handed him a book. I craned my neck to see the title and started laughing.

"*Silent Spring?*" Alex asked. "I don't get it."

"The author," I pointed out, then Miranda and I both mimicked him, saying, "Who's Rachel Carson?"

"You guys are weird," Alex said.

While we ate, Joey and Miranda pulled out some of their treasures. Alex sneezed a few times, but I enjoyed watching the two of them.

When Miranda went to the bathroom later, I caught her as she came out.

"How'd you pull it off?" I asked. "I can't believe you told me nothing."

"I told you it was going to happen," she said. "Have you no faith in me?"

"Details."

"A bunch of my friends and I were out dancing one night. I saw her come in, but I ignored her. I guess she figured out that she liked being chased, so before I knew it I was dancing with her, she went home with me, and the rest is—"

"Munching the magic carpet," I said. "Then you decided to really put her sincerity to the test with a road trip?"

"We had a blast driving here," Miranda said. "Telling the stories of our lives, figuring out what we have in common, planning when she's going to move in with me."

"Seriously?" I demanded.

"No, I just didn't want to cheat you out of your chance to make U-Haul jokes. No one's moving in with anybody. But I'd definitely say we're girlfriends. I'm happy."

"Wow, you and Alex both beat the deadline by a couple of months," I said.

She made a disparaging noise and said, "Do *not* compare my relationship to his with that lying, sneaking—"

"Talking about me?" Alex asked, and we both swung around and tried not to look guilty.

"Paul Nettles," I said quickly.

Miranda and I followed him back to the living room, where we behaved the rest of the night. I revised my opinion of Joey. Not only was she fun and down to earth, but her easy relationship with her parents reassured me that she was not another of Miranda's dysfunctional dykes. Except for the crazy makeup and hair, she was pretty normal.

"I'm putting you boys in Joey's room, because the guest room is full of more boxes," Glenda said when she noticed me yawning.

"Where will you sleep?" Alex asked Joey.

"Miranda and I are roughing it in the den with sleeping bags," Joey said. "We figured you two needed the bed more, since you're starting a long drive back tomorrow."

"Thanks," Alex said.

"I hope you don't mind sharing a bed, though," Glenda fretted.

"Maybe they want to share a bed," Ray Sr. pointed out, obviously having decided we were a couple.

"We don't mind," I assured her.

"Both of them have always been able to sleep with anyone," Miranda said with an innocent expression. I scowled at her, and she said, "What? Men are like dogs. When they close their eyes, they're asleep."

"Isn't that the truth?" Glenda said, leading us down the hall. "Snoring as soon as their heads hit the pillow." She showed us where the clean towels were, everyone said good night, and Alex and I were finally alone.

"Before you start in on me, I admit it. I like Joey."

"I knew you would if you just gave her a chance," he said and looked at the bed. "Outside or inside?"

"Outside," I said. "You know I always have to be in the escape position."

Alex took the bathroom first. By the time I came back from my turn, he was already under the covers. I slid in and turned off the light.

"It's kind of weird," he said.

"Sleeping with me? Thanks."

"Hell, no. I've slept with you lots of times. It's weird to be on sheets of lesbian love."

"Just don't wake me in the middle of the night for some long conversation about your junior high P.E. teacher," I muttered, yawned, and closed my eyes.

When I opened them, the room was still dark, but I felt like it was morning. I peered at the clock and realized I still had another hour to sleep. Alex was glued to me. When we'd taken road trips with our friends in college, everyone but me had refused to share a bed with him. No matter where he started out, he ended up clinging to whoever he was sleeping with. I'd always seen it as an endearing reversion to childhood. I turned over and put my arms around him, and he scooted even closer without waking up.

The next time I opened my eyes, he was already up, standing in the doorway of our room, saying something incoherent about coffee and how the bathroom was all mine. When I got out of bed, he tried to get back in, but I gently nudged him into the hall, where we ran into Miranda.

"Keep him awake while I'm in the shower," I said. "You know how he is in the morning."

Even after eating breakfast and loading boxes, it was well before seven when we were ready to hit the road, and Alex was still in a stupor.

"Are you sure he's OK?" Glenda asked. "Does he have some kind of sleep disorder?"

"Maybe he's a narc," Joey said.

We all stared at her, confused, until Miranda exclaimed, "Oh! You mean a narcoleptic. I don't think so, although it would explain a lot."

"He's not a morning person," I said. "I'll drive the first few hours. He'll wake up by noon."

"Goodness," Glenda said.

"Joey," Miranda said, "why don't we let them take that other box too? The one in the bedroom?"

"Good idea," Joey said.

When she came through the kitchen with a well-taped box, I said, "What's that?"

"Some stuff we picked up to take back to friends in Houston," Miranda said, seeming evasive. "There's more room for it in the van than the Mustang."

"That better not be drugs," I hissed to her when Glenda left the kitchen.

"You caught us," she said. "Joey and I are major drug dealers. Don't tell Alex. I don't want him to bust us. No, actually, I'm having you smuggle illegal aliens back to Texas to work in my sweatshop. They're very small."

"Like Sea Monkeys," Alex said, opening his eyes. "Put them in water and they grow."

"He lives," I said. "But I'm still driving."

"Fine by me," Alex said, returning to his semi-catatonic state.

Glenda came back with handwritten directions. I glanced at the paper and said, "Wait, I thought I'd be taking Interstate 8—"

"No, no," she said. "You're in North County. Going south would put you in rush-hour traffic. You can shoot right up the 15 to the 10, and you'll be going against traffic."

When we were finally on the road, Alex dozed against the door. I found a station on the radio and tried not to think of the twelve to fourteen hours ahead of us. The next day's drive through West Texas would be even worse.

"Hey, look," I said, nudging Alex after I'd been driving a while. "We're approaching some place called Rainbow."

He opened his eyes, looked down the highway at a Border Patrol checkpoint, and said, "What's that? They stop you to make sure you're queer before they let you in?" I laughed, but it didn't seem so funny when we got waved over at the checkpoint. "It's the van," Alex said. "They have to make sure we're not smuggling anybody in from Mexico."

He dug in the glove box and handed me the registration and insurance card, both still in Ray Mitchell Jr.'s name. As the Border Patrol agent approached the car, I glanced in my mirror and said, "He's kind of hot. I've always been turned on by mirrored sunglasses. Maybe he'll have to frisk me. And do a body-cavity search."

"Great. All I want to do is sleep, and you're babbling a porn scenario. Al Camino never gets a vacation."

The agent greeted me, took the registration, insurance card, and my license, then said, "Are you an employee of the carpet cleaning service? You do realize if you're working in the state, you're required to apply for a California license within ten days."

"I'm still a resident of Texas," I said. "Mr. Mitchell gave his sister the van. We're just driving it home to Houston for her."

"You need to step out and let me have a look in the back." He nodded toward Alex and said, "If you'll step out too, sir, and come around to the back."

When we got out, I noticed he never turned his back to me as we all moved behind the van. Maybe we looked dangerous because we hadn't had enough sleep. When I opened the back of the van, he motioned for another agent to join us. While he looked again at the paperwork, the second agent said, "What's in the boxes?"

"Vintage clothes," I said.

The two agents looked at each other and the second one said, "We'll need to check the contents." When he opened the first box, he pulled out a tattered pink feather boa, a hat trimmed in the same pink feathers, and a dress that had probably been all the rage sixty years before. He stared at the clothes then looked at us as if trying to figure out which one of us was the drag queen.

We all maintained a stony silence as evidence that Alex and I were in touch with our feminine sides seemed to mount with the opening of each new box. Finally the only remaining box was the taped one that Joey had put in the van at the last minute. The second agent took out a pocket knife and cut the tape, and Alex and I leaned forward to see what the mystery contents were.

"Holy shit," Alex said and cracked up laughing.

"Those aren't ours," I swore. "But if you confiscate them, I'm guessing there'll be a lot of unhappy Houston homosexuals of one gender or another."

"I can take it from here, Mike," the first agent said, and the second agent shook his head and walked away. "I'm going to let you proceed with your cargo. But you should be aware that it's against the law to have more than two dildos in your possession in Arizona, and possession of six or more in Texas is illegal."

"I always heard that if they're for educational purposes—"

"Five are for educational purposes, but six are a Class A misdemeanor," the agent interrupted Alex.

"Wow, you Border Patrol agents are really up on the law, aren't you?" I asked.

He gave me a surfer-worthy white-toothed smile and said, "You boys drive safely—and don't do anything I wouldn't do."

"Is there anything you don't do?" Alex asked, perking up.

"I don't pick up cute guys when I'm at work," he said and handed me the van's paperwork and my license before he strode away.

Alex and I climbed back into the van, looked at each other, and burst out laughing.

"Personal pleasure devices shall henceforth be called Sea Monkeys," Alex declared.

"This trip will be forever known as Operation Sea Monkey," I agreed. "Only with you, Alex, would I escape being busted with contraband dildos by getting a gay Border Patrol agent."

ELECTION DAY

When I was a freshman in high school, I ran for vice president of my class. I spent days making buttons, posters, and speeches during lunch, trying to convince my fellow students that I was the man for the job. I may have been man enough, but my opponent, Trina Duvelle, was woman enough, because she won by ten votes.

I was crushed. High school elections were a popularity contest, so I felt like an outcast. Worse yet, I lost to Trina, who was a known nose-picker, so what did that say about me? My parents tried to console me by telling me that life was an uphill battle. Things like losing an election would only make me stronger.

"It'll all seem insignificant someday, son," my father said.

Of course, he was right. I ran for class president in my junior year, won, and eventually escorted Trina Duvelle to our senior prom. As the years went by, there were more important victories and failures to contend with. Exams were passed and failed. Lovers came and went. I made lots of friends and even some enemies. With each milestone, my vice-presidential blunder became a distant memory.

That is, until Patrick sold his soul to Al Gore. His enthusiasm and confidence that Gore would be our next president mounted as election day grew near, reminding me of my fourteen-year-old self in the year when I'd learned that elections were unpredictable. I was worried that Patrick was using the presidential race to determine the outcome of his relationship with Vivian, as if she'd run back into his waiting arms when Gore was elected. I tried to reason with him, just in case, but he wouldn't listen.

"An election is like gambling, Patrick. Like a lottery," I warned him. "You never know who's going to win."

"Thank you, Forrest Gump," he said, rolling his eyes. "Duh. I know how our government works."

I followed him to the kitchen. "I'm worried. I think you're putting too much stock in the election, and I'm not sure why. All I ever see you do is work on campaign mailings and surveys. If you go out, it's to canvass the neighborhood or pass out leaflets. When was the last time you went to Dinks?"

"Just the other day," Patrick said blandly as he extracted a beer from the refrigerator. "It's still standing, still making money, and still under construction."

"You're kidding. I thought it would be done by now." I followed him into the living room, where he flopped down on the sofa. I felt mildly consoled when he put his feet on the coffee table and took a swig of beer. At least some things stayed the same.

"It's been hard to stay on top of the changes," he said matter-of-factly. "But it's almost finished. Anyway, Vivian was right; I spend far too much time there. That's why I've been hitting the campaign trail. I'm not in it just for Gore, you know."

"You're not?"

"Nah. Don't get me wrong, I want him to win. But I've also been helping to raise campaign funding, visiting lots of corporations and business leaders."

"Really," I said.

Patrick swallowed another sip of beer and said, "Yeah. The contacts I've been making are unbelievable."

"Are you sure you're not a Republican?" I asked.

"Of course I'm not. But I've got three interviews scheduled the week after the election. I'm back in business, man."

"What about Dinks?"

"I'm keeping it. My manager and the staff can run it. If I'm working in the corporate world again, while earning income from the bar, I can build up quite the nest egg."

"Are you doing this for yourself or for Vivian?" I asked. "Because right now, you're the only one feathering the nest, my friend."

"I'm doing it for both of us. This is what she wants from me. I've given her room to do her thing. I'm working for the causes she believes in, and going back to the nine-to-five grind so our schedules will mesh. I'm saving money for our future," he said emphatically. "Mark my words, Aaron. She and I will be together again. I'm as sure of it as I am that Al Gore will be our next president."

Even though Patrick was certain that happy days would be here again, I wasn't convinced. I knew that Vivian had been spending a lot of time with Brett since our gathering at Ming's. She assured me that they were only friends. Brett was acting as her mentor, helping her study and guiding her toward her future career, although they occasionally went to the movies or dinner.

"He's living in a fantasy world," Miranda said about Patrick on election day. He'd invited our friends to our apartment to watch the returns. Originally, he'd planned to have everyone meet at Dinks, but I talked him out of it. Since he was taking the election so seriously, I didn't want him burning his bar in protest if Gore lost the race. Miranda glanced into the kitchen, where Patrick was showing Joey how to mix the perfect martini, and added, "That's what he gets for watching so many Disney movies."

"He only watches those because they draw the women so hot," I said, then made Miranda laugh as I did my best Patrick impersonation. "They're total babes, man."

Someone knocked, and I let Alexander in. "Hi," he said hurriedly. "I—"

"Alex," Miranda blared, observing his entrance and grabbing a bag of Doritos from the coffee table, "nice to see you. Are you alone?"

Alexander frowned at her and said, "I didn't bring a date, if that's what you mean."

"Joey's in the kitchen," she said. "Joey. My girlfriend, Joey." When Alex gave her a blank look, Miranda pointed out, "We're less than two months away from the end of the year. I've got one toe over the finish line, Alex. I'm poised to win."

"It's not a contest," Heath admonished as he came from the bathroom. "Alex, where's Vivian? I thought you were giving her a ride."

"I was trying to tell Aaron about that before *she* started in on me," Alexander said, pointing at Miranda. She stuck out her tongue at him, showing him a mouthful of chewed-up Doritos. "Ew! Nasty!" Miranda closed her mouth and swallowed, looking pleased with herself. Alex shuddered with revulsion one last time, then said, "Vivian called me and said she was getting a ride here from Brett."

"Brett?" Heath asked.

"The guy whose house I stayed at in Maine," I clarified.

"I know who he is," Heath said. "I just don't think it's in good taste for Vivian to bring her new boyfriend here."

"He's not her boyfriend," I said, reminding myself of a child who doesn't want to believe his divorced parent is dating.

"They're just friends," Alexander said. "At least, that's what she told me."

"I agree with Heath," Miranda said. "After all, *he's* not flaunting Logan in front of Aaron."

"He's at a crystal energy workshop," Heath explained.

"Whatever," I said indifferently. "If Logan was here, I'd be fine with it."

Miranda and Alexander both looked at me skeptically.

Joey returned to the living room with Patrick, saying, "This guy makes a great martini, Miranda. Want some?"

"No, I'm good," Miranda answered, licking orange Dorito dust from her fingers.

Patrick beamed at Joey, since he was always happy to find a new drinking buddy. He realized we were all staring at him and asked, "What?"

Before we could answer, someone else knocked, and Patrick said, "I'll get it." We watched anxiously as he opened the door to Brett and

Vivian. Before anybody could react, Vivian swept into the room, hugging Patrick and reintroducing Brett to everyone.

"Why isn't the television on?" she asked. "I can't wait to hear how Gore trounced Bush."

"You're so certain?" I asked. I glanced at Patrick, whose grimace quickly evolved into a grin.

"No doubt at all," Vivian said. "I don't see how anyone could buy into Bush's—"

"It's possible," Brett said, cutting her off. "Gore lacks a certain charm."

"Like Bush is so endearing," Heath said, wrinkling his nose.

"No," Brett admitted, "but his plans for the economy—"

"Are so full of holes!" Patrick interjected.

Vivian smiled at Patrick, then said to Brett, "Don't tell me you actually voted for him."

"OK," Brett said as he sat down, "I won't tell you."

"No!" several of us chorused. Joey wrenched the bag of Doritos from Miranda's hands and threw a handful of them at Brett.

"Who brought him here, anyway?" Vivian asked, looking around the room.

"You did," Patrick said, comically poking her shoulder.

"Shhh! Don't tell the lynch mob," Vivian stage-whispered.

Miranda sighed audibly, got up from the sofa, and sat on the arm of Brett's chair. She said, "I might as well join my countryman."

"You didn't!" Joey wailed in horror.

"Break up with her!" Alexander shouted, and I couldn't help but laugh. He'd do anything to one-up her with the deal.

"Oh, Miranda," Heath said sadly.

"I'm a business owner," she pleaded. "I need tax relief."

"We probably shouldn't discuss this," I said, watching Brett softly pat Miranda on the back. "How a person votes is way too personal."

"Don't tell me you voted for Bush too," Patrick said.

"Oh, hell, no. I voted for Gore," I said.

"Good boy," Vivian said.

"I voted for Nader," Joey said proudly.

"You *threw* your vote away?" Brett and Patrick chorused, then looked at each other adversely.

"A vote for the Green Party is not wasted. Our current two-party system could use a little diversity," Heath said. We all silently stared at him until he said with resignation, "Gore. I voted for Gore. Are you happy? Jeez."

Everybody turned to Alexander, who was sitting on the floor, absentmindedly toying with a chain on his wrist. He finally noticed us staring at him and said, "What? I thought we weren't—"

"That was then. This is now," Heath said.

"He's probably not even registered," Miranda said condescendingly.

"I know I'm not the most political one in the room," Alexander stated. "But I always vote in the presidential elections."

"And?" I prodded.

"Some things should remain private. Now hush. Let's watch CNN."

As the hours went by and each state's returns were announced, the presidential race grew more intense. Although the evening began with early states going to Bush, when Gore swept the vote in Michigan, Illinois, and Pennsylvania, it became obvious how Alexander had voted when he high-fived Patrick and jeered at Miranda. I didn't hold it against Brett when he arched his eyebrow and gave a moo of satisfaction when it was announced that Bush had won Gore's home state of Tennessee.

Later that night, after CNN and Florida kept seesawing, Miranda put her head in her hands and said, "What have I done?"

"Does this mean you're not a Republican anymore?" Joey asked.

"I'll get help," Miranda said with a crazed look in her eyes. "There must be a program I can go to or...*something.*"

"I can't believe this thing is still going on. I have to get to bed," I said.

"Me too," Brett said, standing up. "I have to be in court in the morning. I hope my political leanings won't keep you from inviting me back here. I had fun tonight."

"Don't worry," I assured him as I walked him to the door. "Democrats are a very forgiving people."

"Do you need a ride home, Vivian?" Brett asked.

Vivian shook her head, and Brett left alone. I had a thought that I voiced aloud. "Maybe we shouldn't choose our relationships. Maybe our friends should vote on our prospective suitors."

"That's ridiculous," Patrick said.

"Not really," Heath said. "When you and Vivian started dating, I never would've guessed it would work out. I probably would've voted against it."

"Don't make me kick your ass in front of everybody, Heath," Patrick said.

"Joey probably wouldn't have picked Miranda if she knew she was a closet Republican," Alexander stated.

"Hey!" objected Miranda.

"He has a point," Joey mused. When Miranda glared at her, Joey added, "For the record, my friends all agreed I should give her a shot. That was kind of like an election."

"Relationship elections would only work if your friends are objective," Alexander said, "and have your best interests at heart."

"Yes," Miranda said emphatically. "That's exactly right, Alexander. Exactly."

They stared at each other, stone-faced, until Vivian broke the silence, saying, "OK, then. Let's hear from the people. Going back to Patrick and me, what's the outcome? Should we stay together?"

"You want us to vote?" I asked. "Are you sure?"

"Yes."

"This is fucking stupid," Patrick said.

"They're still counting votes in Florida," Vivian said. "We need something to do."

"I thought you were going to bed," Patrick said to me.

"I'll stay up for this; then I'll go," I promised.

We each wrote our votes on pieces of paper, folded them, and gave them to Joey to tally, since she was named the most impartial in the room. With an air of solemnity, Joey went into the kitchen alone to count the votes and plunder Patrick's pitcher of martinis.

She returned, suppressed a hiccup, and said, "Vivian and Patrick should stay together. The public has spoken. Seven to none."

We all cheered, and Patrick looked smug. I went to bed as Vivian, to boos and hisses, pointed out that the popular vote didn't always determine the outcome of an election.

The next morning, I smiled when I went downstairs for breakfast and found Patrick and Vivian curled up together on the sofa underneath an afghan. According to the morning news, our next president was yet to be determined. Patrick, however, had apparently won his race.

There was little else for Vivian and Patrick to celebrate over the next couple of weeks. Whenever they were in the apartment, they huddled together on the sofa, muttering bitterly at ongoing TV campaign coverage. I, on the other hand, had to field all phone calls and provide ongoing couple coverage to our friends.

I was doing so one night to Heath when he asked, "What about Patrick's interviews? Does he have a new job yet?"

"The last I heard, Vivian was demanding that Patrick stay out of the evil corporate empire that poured money into Bush's pockets. She also swears she's going to work for the ACLU when she graduates. Right now, they feel like the only two liberals left in Texas."

Heath laughed and said, "It'll pass. At least they're together, but you need a night away from them. You and I never spend time alone anymore. That's not the way I meant for us to be. All or nothing."

"Me either," I agreed. "Should we meet for dinner or something?"

"Why don't you come here Friday night? I'll cook. We can enjoy a meal and conversation without Patrick and Vivian's politics or Miranda and Alex's constant challenges to each other over their deal."

"It's not a contest," I reminded him. "Speaking of Alex, did you hear about the project I roped him into?"

"No."

"Remember the video my kids are making of *Romeo and Juliet*? I figured with Alex's background in porn music, he was the ideal resource to help them score their movie."

After recovering from his laughing fit, Heath said, "I hope you intend to screen this for your friends. *Shakespeare in Heat* meets *Shakespeare in Love*. You guys are quite a pair."

I'd been enjoying having Alex in my classroom. His creativity and enthusiasm could be boundless when he was doing something he liked, and my students were reaping all the benefits. His presence also gave me an unexpected break from Jeanne Baxter's hyperactive behavior. She had such a crush on Alexander that she was struck dumb in his presence.

"I've never seen her like this," Dale Campbell agreed while she helped Alex set up the equipment we'd checked out of the library's audiovisual department.

"Stop. You guys are embarrassing me," Alex said.

"Please. You thrive on adulation," I said.

"Well, yeah, when I'm performing."

"I'm sure you have quite a stage presence," Dale said. "I'll have to come see your band sometime."

"That'd be great," Alex said. "Bring your friends and relatives. We need all the fans we can get."

I got out of their way so they could finish setting everything up before the next period, when my freshmen would descend on us. I was grading papers at my desk when I realized the room was quiet. I glanced up to see Alex sitting alone in the back of my classroom, watching me.

"Did Dale leave?" I asked. He nodded. "What are you doing?"

"Watching you and thinking about schoolgirl crushes," he said. "Do you get a lot of that?"

"Almost never. I'm just another boring adult authority figure to them. You're exotic and fun."

"Don't forget drop-dead gorgeous."

"You don't need me to tell you that."

"I don't?"

"You're drop-dead gorgeous," I said.

"Oh, you're just saying that."

"Yes. Under duress."

"Hi, Aaron." I heard the familiar nasal whine from my left. I turned to see Paul trying not to gape at Alex from the door of my classroom.

"Hello, Paul," I said in a voice so friendly that it caused him to dart a suspicious glance at me. "This is Alexander Casey. He's helping my ninth graders with their class project. Alex, Paul Nettles."

"Nice to meet you," Paul said, giving him a shark-like smile.

"Wow," Alex said. "That's a brave hair color. Not everyone can pull that off."

"I guess I'd better get back to my classroom," Paul said vaguely and drifted out of sight.

"Oh, Alex," I said, dropping my head in my hands and laughing.

"He looks like an orangutan."

"Sometimes I love you so much I can't stand it," I said.

"I'll take that as a compliment. I love you too."

I repeated that story to an appreciative Heath when I got to his house on Friday night. I was chopping vegetables for a salad while Heath put the finishing touches on our meal of spinach lasagna and his legendary home-baked bread. The smells made me so ravenous that by the time we sat at the table, I missed all the finer points of the candlelight, cut flowers, and the merlot that Heath poured. I was too caught up in my feeding frenzy to do much more than offer an occasional grunt while he talked about work and what he'd been up to lately.

He finally sat back and rested his elbows on the arms of his chair, while holding out his hands as if to encompass the scene in front of him, and said, "It's flattering that you react to my cooking with such gusto, but you might want to come up for air occasionally."

"If I thought all this was setting the stage for a seduction, I'd have better manners," I assured him. "But since your conversation has been liberally sprinkled with references to Logan, I figure I should satisfy whatever appetite I can."

"Does it bother you?" he asked. "I don't have to talk about him."

"I'm glad you're happy," I said.

"That isn't what I asked you."

"If I get a little jealous from time to time, you should just enjoy that," I said. "Would you rather I felt relieved that you dumped me?"

He laughed and said, "I didn't dump you."

"OK," I said. "Serious answer. The only thing that bothers me when you talk about Logan is that you don't tell me how you feel. It's like your walls are up again. I thought we'd gotten beyond that."

"What do you want to know?"

"What makes Logan special to you. Why you're happy."

Heath thought for a few minutes, then said, "I suppose what I like best about him is that he surprises me. He's full of contradictions. When I think I have him figured out, he shows me something new."

"Example."

"Like when he talks about rocks," Heath said. "His place is full of them. He can pick one up and tell me what it is, where it was mined, and what it's composed of. Everything technical that I never wanted to know about a rock, but when he talks about it I catch his enthusiasm. Then he can turn around and just as seriously tell me its metaphysical attributes. He's not limited by his passion for science. He's willing to explore things in ways that some people might think are utter nonsense. I like discovering new things about him."

"I know what you're talking about," I said as Heath began stacking our plates. "It reminds me of Alexander."

His head whipped around and he said, "How so?"

"As long as I've known him, he still surprises me. It's one of the reasons I enjoy his friendship so much."

"That is amazing after so many years," Heath said. "There's nobody like Alexander."

"There isn't," I agreed. "What do you think is going to happen with this Zachary mess?"

"I have no idea," Heath said. "If you remember, I was skeptical from the beginning. But in spite of everyone's doubts, this is the longest Alex has ever sustained a relationship. There has to be something there."

"Yeah, great sex," I said. Heath gave me a funny look, and I asked, "What?"

"There's something I've been wanting to ask you." He spoke slowly, as if weighing his words.

I wasn't sure why I was suddenly filled with anxiety, but I suppressed it and said, "Go on."

"I picked up a lot of signals the night we all went to Ming's." He hesitated, then went on. "What's the story with you and Ramon? If it's none of my business, say so. But I gather you've known him for a long time. It seemed weird that you never mentioned him. Before you answer, you should know that I asked Alex about him. It made him uncomfortable, which convinced me there's a story, even though Alex brushed it off."

"Ramon's a friend," I said.

"I got that. And that you met Brett through him, so I guess Ramon's the reason you went to Maine."

"Right. Ramon invited me."

"This is like pulling teeth. Straight question. Were you in a relationship that got screwed up because of what happened between you and me?"

"Straight answer. Ramon has been a friend for several years who I sometimes had sex with. He was never a boyfriend or a potential boyfriend. His choice and mine. He's got a boyfriend now, so he and I are just friends. It was comfortable when we were together, but I wasn't broken up when it ended. I didn't realize until recently that Alex and Miranda knew about him. I liked keeping it private, but I guess that made it seem like more than it was."

"When you and I were involved—"

"I wasn't having sex with him when I was having sex with you," I said. "Is that what you want to know?"

"It's not like you and I made any promises about that. But the possibility did bother me."

"Were you jealous?" I asked, trying not to sound too delighted.

"A little. Mostly it was strange to think that while we were together, you might have had another intimate relationship that you never talked about. But the worst part was worrying that getting involved with me again cost you someone you could have been happy with."

"I have no regrets about anything that happened between us, Heath," I assured him. "Maybe I had some unrealistic expectations, but I'm fine with where we've ended up."

"OK," he said. "That's all I needed to know."

I followed him into the kitchen and loaded the dishwasher while he cut cheesecake for dessert. We settled on his sofa, and he turned on the television, flipping through channels until he stopped on *The Thin Man*.

"I love this movie," he said. "Nick and Nora Charles are a fun couple."

"That dog is a scene stealer," I said. "None of the *Thin Man* movies were about the detective work. They were all about the dog and the snappy dialogue."

"Did you ever read the Dashiell Hammett book the movies were based on?" Heath asked.

"No. I read the other ones. The Mr. and Mrs. North mysteries."

"By Francis and Richard Lockridge," Heath said. "I liked those too."

"Did they ever make movies of the North books?" I asked.

"Radio shows," Heath said. "They were like *The Thin Man*. Not as much clever wordplay, but a lot of martinis and amateur sleuthing."

"And they had Siamese cats instead of a dog," I remembered.

Heath shifted on the sofa so that his head rested on my lap while we watched the movie. I played with his hair out of habit, feeling nostalgic. I'd been honest when I told him that I had no regrets, but I still wished there was something that was just ours, connecting us in a unique way. Sort of like skating with Alexander. Or driving around looking at houses with Miranda. Or being Patrick's roommate. Heath was the only one of our group that I'd ever made love to, but I wanted more than memories.

"They could never make this movie today," Heath mused. "Way too much drinking."

"Before I knew about your secret career as a soap writer, I used to think you wrote mysteries," I said.

"I always wanted to." He sat up during the commercial break

and said, "It's been a long time since I wrote fiction. Are you writing anything these days?"

"Sort of," I said. "Well, honestly, what I've got is a lot of starts. I lose interest and never finish anything. You've always been a more disciplined writer than I am."

"But you always wrote edgier stuff. I got too bogged down in political correctness. You knew how to take risks but keep things light."

"They're so light now you can't even see them on the page," I joked.

The movie came back on, and I waited for him to settle on my lap again, but he reached for the remote and muted the sound, saying, "Maybe we could do what Francis and Richard Lockridge did."

"Get married?"

"No, you nut. Write together. Create our own Mr. and Mrs. North to solve mysteries. Only ours could be Mr. and *Mr.* Something. A gay couple who stumbles over corpses like the Norths do and is urbane and witty like Nick and Nora Charles."

"Will our gay couple swill martinis like there's no tomorrow?" I asked, glancing at the TV.

"No, they'll be big wine connoisseurs," Heath said, holding up the glass of Madeira he'd poured to have with dessert.

"I don't know anything about wine," I said.

"It's not like I go around murdering people, you know. That's what research is for."

"Huh," I said, thinking it over. "I guess one advantage of writing together would be getting feedback. Writing is such a lonely activity."

Either Heath was getting excited or the wine was starting to have an effect, because he suddenly couldn't sit still. "Plus we'd push each other. Neither of us could slack off, because we'd be depending on each other."

"True," I said. "But how would we do it? Make an outline and take different sections?"

"What if I started it," Heath said. "I won't know who's going to get killed or how or who the murderer is. I'll set up our gay couple, then pass it to you. It'll be a cliffhanger for us each time."

"So we're not attempting to write great literature."

"Oh, I doubt we could ever get it published. It would get both of us back into disciplined writing habits, though, and it would be fun to create something together."

"Where would we set it? You want urbane, but Houston's the place I know best, and it's not exactly a cultural hotspot."

"I want urbane *characters,*" Heath said. "Translation: gay. We could set it in Galveston. Our couple could own a bed and breakfast. That would bring strangers into their lives. Murderous strangers!"

"And instead of Nick and Nora's histrionic dog or the Norths' Siamese cats…"

"They'd have a parrot with a commanding ability to rattle off bon mots," Heath said.

I smiled, liking it, and said, "How tropical. A big old Victorian bed and breakfast, right?"

"Of course," Heath agreed.

"And we'd give our couple last names that sound cool together. Like West and North, so they'd be Mr. and Mr. North-West. Except we can't use North; it's been done."

"You'll have to count on me to come up with something clever, won't you?" Heath asked. When I reached over and engulfed him in a big hug, he laughed and said, "What's that for?"

"Nothing," I said. "Sometimes I just wonder if you can read my mind."

"Of course," he said. "That's why we'll be a good writing team. However, there might be one problem."

"What's that?"

"You've got another big project to take on next year."

"I do?"

"Finding a boyfriend. Miranda's dating Joey, and Alexander has been with Zachary for most of the year. You made a deal, remember? If they've got someone on New Year's Eve—"

"Please," I interrupted, rolling my eyes. "There are still six more weeks until the end of the year. We're talking about Miranda and

Alex. I predict another year of contented bachelorhood for me."

"We'll see," Heath said. He turned the sound back on so we could finish watching the movie, although my mind was already racing ahead to a waggish whodunit. I couldn't wait to get my first installment from Heath.

New Year's Eve

I was trying to decide if I was in the mood for cowboys or a more mystical experience when I heard someone pounding on the front door. With a sigh, I dropped *Seven Queers in Tibet* on top of *The Bunslingers* and went downstairs. I opened the door just as Miranda was about to knock again, and her fist stopped in midair.

"I was afraid you weren't here."

"I occasionally enjoy a quiet Saturday night to myself," I said, thinking wistfully of my unwatched videos. As she strode inside, it occurred to me that she looked awfully put together. "What's with the glamour girl look?"

"Tonight was my River Oaks party," she reminded me.

"Oh, yeah. How'd that go?"

"We don't have time for small talk," she said. Then she added in a tiny voice, "He came."

I had to think about that for a few seconds before I asked, "Zachary?"

"Yes. But he didn't bring Alex."

"Oh," I said, realization dawning. "He brought the wife?"

"Alicia," Miranda said. "Her name's Alicia."

I waited, but Miranda gave me a defeated look, so I said, "Was she awful? Did she do something to embarrass Zachary in front of the River Oaks set?" Then a thought occurred to me. "Don't tell me that *you* did something and screwed up your own party."

"Nothing like that," Miranda said. She sank to the sofa. "She was lovely. I mean, she isn't drop-dead gorgeous, but she's attractive. She was dressed just right for the occasion. Elegant. No one would have guessed that she's a suburban soccer mom if she hadn't told them. She hit it off with some of the younger women at the party. Maybe they were comparing their kids' orthodontist stories or something. She seemed really nice."

"Then why are you acting so weird?"

"Zachary," Miranda spat. "It's totally obvious to me that he and his wife are not in any way estranged, no matter what he told Alex. Yet it didn't bother him to bring her to my party, knowing that *I* know what a lying philanderer he is. He's such a phony. He was *so* attentive to his wife. All smiles and pleasantries. Passing as the straight husband. One time I happened to meet his eyes when Alicia and her new pals were laughing, and he actually *winked* at me! Like we were sharing some great secret! He's a total dirtbag. It's plain his wife has no clue."

I sighed and said, "Miranda, you already thought he was a dirtbag; you just hadn't seen it with your own eyes. But it doesn't matter, because Alex doesn't think so. Why get worked up about it?"

"Because," and her voice was tiny again, "now Alex has seen it with *his* own eyes." I blinked but kept my mouth shut, and she went on in a more defensive tone. "How was I supposed to know Alex would escort his grandmother to the party? Before you say I told you so, I admit it. I should have listened to you. You told me something bad would come out of my association with Zachary, and you were right."

"So Alex saw the wife," I mused. "How'd that go?"

"He looked uncomfortable and miserable," Miranda said. "I mean, he had no idea Zachary would be there. He saw him right away. First he looked surprised, then he got this big, goofy smile. You could tell he'd thought bringing Grandma Casey to the party was going to be dull, but there was his hunky boyfriend standing across the room."

"Then what happened?"

"He made sure Grandma Casey had someone to talk to, then he headed toward Zachary. But before he got there, Alicia walked up to Zachary, who hadn't seen Alex. He put his arm over her shoulders. She said something, he laughed, and Alex froze with this awful look on his face. That's when Zachary saw him."

"And?" I erupted when she paused.

"Zachary smiled at him. With that same complicit expression that was on his face when he winked at me. He looked so smarmy. Alex just stood there for what seemed like a thousand years. Then he turned around and went back to his grandmother. When I tried to talk to him later, he gave me this look—"

"I know the look," I interrupted. "Did he and Zachary ever connect?"

"I think Zachary intended to, in a casual way. Alex always maneuvered away from him. But he also watched Zachary, especially when Zachary was with Alicia."

"Who left first?"

"Alex and his grandmother. They said goodbye to me together, so I couldn't really talk to him. I tried to convey how bad I felt, but he looked at me like I was a stranger."

"On the plus side, you got what you wanted. I'm sure Zachary is history."

"But will Alex ever believe I didn't enjoy rubbing his face in it? Especially after all the stuff I've said."

When she stared at me with a hopeful expression, I said, "Oh, I get it. Against my advice, you interfered. Now you want me to fix things."

"Uh-huh," she said, nodding without the slightest trace of shame on her face. "If he's not at home, he's probably out at the bars—"

"Oh, for God's sake, Miranda, I'm not going to stalk Alex the way you do. Have you learned nothing from any of this? Stay out of it!"

"I am. But why should you? You haven't been bugging him about

Zachary, so he probably doesn't hate you."

"He doesn't hate you either," I said. "Go home. Let him brood for a few days. Can you do that?"

"I guess. But can't you—"

"No," I said rudely and pushed her from the sofa toward the door. Then, because I knew she really was upset, I hugged her. "Promise me you won't leap in that Mustang and go looking for him."

"All right," she muttered, then left. I went back upstairs, determined to follow my own advice.

Ten minutes later I pulled into Alex's landlord's driveway. Mr. Bryant's house was dark, as was the garage apartment. And Alex's truck was gone. I sat in my car for a few minutes, trying to decide if I really wanted to look for Alex at the bars. If he was out drinking and dancing, it was probably best to let him blow off steam.

Any other time, I'd have been the first to take him out partying after listening to his tale of woe. But this time seemed different. Even though I'd kept my opinions and comments about Zachary to the bare minimum, Alex knew I was just as skeptical of their relationship as Miranda was. It had already caused strain between us.

I glanced in my rearview mirror when lights from another car shone on me. I was going to be really embarrassed if Alex was coming home with a trick, which seemed possible once I realized the car was a cab. After a minute, the back door opened. I was relieved to see one person get out. Then Alex was at my car, tapping on the passenger window. I rolled it down. He leaned in, and I could smell alcohol.

"What are you doing here? Did I stand you up or something?"

"No. I was in the neighborhood—"

"And you thought you'd check out the damage. You and Miranda are always lurking, like Matthew and Meg in that movie I can never remember the name of."

"*Addicted to Love,*" I said.

"Right. It sucked."

"It wasn't that bad," I disagreed, playing Siskel to his drunken Ebert.

"Just because I'm wasted doesn't mean I can't remember a bad movie. There were roaches. Any love story with roaches sucks. I should know."

"*Victor/Victoria,*" I said gamely.

He looked confused for a minute, then said, "The exception proves the rule."

"OK," I said with a laugh. "I surrender."

"That's better. I have to go inside now. I'm drunker than you think."

"I doubt that."

"Oh, my God, you would argue with a fucking fence post," he said.

I watched him stumble toward his apartment, then I got out and helped him up the stairs.

"Maybe you are," I conceded.

"At last. I get to be the one who's right."

When we were inside, I gave him a sympathetic look and said, "Do you want to talk about it?"

"Everybody was right. He called my cell phone. He wanted to know why I left Miranda's party without talking to him. Can anybody be that fucking clueless? He reminded me that I'm the one he loves. He's only with her because of the kids. Blah, blah, blah. So I said, fine, then he wouldn't mind the three of us sitting down to have a chat. Oh, no, we can't do that. She can't deal with the whole gay thing. So I told him he's the one who can't deal with the whole gay thing. Asshole." I caught him as he swayed, then he said, "I'm gonna be sick."

We almost made it to the toilet, but not quite. As I stood there, looking down at my clothes and trying not to heave, I couldn't tell if he was laughing or crying. "Are you done?"

"That's just the icing on the Love Sucks cake," he mumbled in lieu of an apology.

"No, no, I'll be fine," I said in a long-suffering tone. "Let's get you to bed. If you're done, that is."

He ignored me and struggled with a bottle of mouthwash. After he spit in the sink, he wandered out of the bathroom. I stayed behind, cleaning up his mess before getting out of my reeking clothes. What really sucked was that I knew it was going to be a long time before I could get any leverage out of this. At least until the next potential boyfriend came along and dissolved the significance of Zachary.

I followed him and crawled onto the futon next to him.

Before I opened my eyes, I was aware of three things. The first was that I was freezing and had no covers to pull around myself. The second was that my bladder seemed to be unusually insistent, even for morning. And the third was that I was rock-hard, which meant that I had to make a choice about which of my needs was the most pressing.

Only then did I remember where I was and what had happened the night before, which really woke me up. I could see mist swirling around the vent of the air conditioner in Alex's bedroom window, which I'd turned on because we were having an unusually humid December. Apparently, this '70s relic lived up to its industrial-like clangor. All Alex needed was a hook hanging from the ceiling to store a side of beef in his room.

He was curled into a fetal ball, his head and one shoulder resting on my abdomen, which explained the urgent signal my bladder was sending. I wondered if I could manage to slide out of bed without waking him. I saw no need to thrust proof of my libido in his face, figuratively or literally.

When I tried to inch out from under him, although his eyes remained closed, one sweep of his free arm covered us in several layers of sheets and quilts. Which was great, but it didn't take care of my other problems. Until Alex, possibly suffering some kind of hangover dementia, turned his face in the other direction, rubbed a hand up the inside of my thigh, and decided for me which of my needs would be met first. I wondered if he even knew who he was in bed with.

"Alex?"

His other hand snaked up my chest until his fingertips rested lightly on my lips, effectively muting me except for moans that built to a final gasp of release. After my ragged breathing subsided into silence, he crawled out from under the covers, gave me a chaste kiss on the cheek as if he hadn't just given me sensational head, and said, "Speak softly, if at all. I've got a screaming hangover."

"Can you explain what just happened?" I quietly demanded.

"You took care of me last night. I took care of you this morning. It seemed like you needed a hand."

"That was more than a hand," I said. "I thought you once said we couldn't fool around because I threw up on you in college?"

"I canceled that out last night. Let's not make too much of it, OK? Heath sucks; Zachary sucks; love sucks; we're friends. I need Tylenol. Or morphine."

We went to the bathroom together, and I finally got to relieve my bladder while he rooted around in a drawer as he brushed his teeth. He handed me an unwrapped toothbrush, then gave a whimper of relief when he pulled out a bottle of aspirin. He swallowed several and moved around me to the toilet while I brushed my teeth.

"It's a good thing neither of us is pee-shy," I said. "Do you want the shower, or should I—"

He cut me off by taking my arm and leading me back to bed. Instead of turning the air conditioner off, he piled quilts on us again before easing his head to my shoulder and saying, "Can we not talk everything to death? Can we just *be* for a while?"

I wrapped my arms around him and rested my chin on top of his head. I had to admit that it was comfortable to cuddle in bed with him without making a big deal out of it. "But will you still respect me?" I asked.

"I never respected you," he said, and I could hear the smile in his voice before he sighed. "Aaron, we've known each other ten years."

"Twelve."

"Even better. We've seen each other through about a thousand crises. Shared our bodies with strangers. Given our hearts to the undeserving. I think our friendship can survive a little carnal knowledge without disintegrating. I just want to remember what it's like to be touched and held by someone who likes me."

"I never liked you," I said, and he laughed. Since he seemed so much better than he had the night before, I decided he was right. After all these years, Alex was probably the one person with whom I could cross boundaries and throw caution to the wind. I definitely would never mangle his emotions the way Zachary had, and he was the man I trusted most in the world, even more than Patrick.

I thought back to the early days of our friendship, when an occasional Alexander fantasy had accompanied my self-gratification. Although we'd casually touched each other, seen each other naked, brushed each other's lips with friendly kisses, and shared sex stories countless times in the intervening years, I could admit that I was still curious about him.

I felt like my heart was pounding loud enough to drown out the clattering air conditioner, and I realized what was missing. It was rare to be in Alex's apartment without hearing music. When I pulled away to ask if he wanted me to play a CD, his eyes looked a little fragile. I smiled to let him know everything was OK. He moved in for a kiss, the first real one we'd ever shared, and it was amazing. Within seconds we were all hands and tongue and cock, until he finally managed to say, "Nightstand. Drawer."

It was spine-tingling, toe-curling, mind-blowing sex. I wanted to savor it, but whenever I tried to slow things down, our gazes locked and it only got more intense. I'd never known a man who could make love with his eyes the way Alex did, and I surrendered, trying to give him as much pleasure as he was giving me.

After we stopped shuddering and could breathe again, I began exploring him with my mouth and hands. We'd sacrificed foreplay, which left me with a need to taste, smell, and feel all of him. He lay still, but when I occasionally stopped to look up at him, he was always watching me through half-closed eyes, and his smile communicated enjoyment and encouragement. I felt like I could stay that way forever, but he finally pulled me up for another deep kiss that sent currents through my entire nervous system.

I didn't move when he got up to get rid of our used condoms. He came back to the bedroom, pausing at the stereo to flip through a stack of CDs.

"Come back," I begged, and I saw him smile, but he kept looking until he found what he wanted. Then I smiled too, when I heard Stevie Ray Vaughan.

"Remember this?" he asked as he lay down next to me.

My memories of Stevie Ray were bittersweet. Alex and I had been devout fans of the Texas legend. When he died at the beginning of our junior year, we'd made a road trip to Austin, sitting on the rocks at Hippie Hollow, drinking beer while Alex paid homage on his guitar.

"It's hard to believe he died nearly ten years ago," I said. I closed my eyes and listened a while, suspended somewhere between waking and sleeping, and between my memories of Alexander and the new experience we'd just shared.

When I finally turned to look at him, his eyes were closed, and I wondered if he'd dozed off. I reached over to cup his face, gently running my thumb over the stubble on his jaw. I moved a strand of his hair behind his ear so I could get a better look at him.

"What?" he asked softly, his eyes still shut.

"Maybe I should encourage you to fall in love with jerks more often," I said. "The fallout works for me."

His eyes flew open and he said, "I wasn't in love with Zach."

"You did a good job of faking it."

He stretched, yawned, and said, "I've only loved one man in my life, and he didn't notice."

I remembered our senior year, when we'd all thought Alex was going to have a nervous breakdown over a severely closeted cellist, and decided it was best not to let him dwell on another unhappy memory of love gone bad. "I'm kind of hungry," I said.

"Ugh," Alex grunted. "Let's clean up and eat out. Or you can eat. I'd rather go shopping."

"What?" I asked, laughing at him.

"I have about a thousand dollars in guilt certificates that I've been given over the last few months. I could burn them in a ritual shitty boyfriend cleansing ceremony, or we could be practical and enjoy them together."

"Hmm," I said. "To what stores?"

He laughed and said, "Spoken like a true gay man."

We were both quiet a while, then I said, "Your offer's tempting, but as an expert in dodging serious discussions, I know what you're up to. I'm going to find some sweat pants, and while you take a shower, I'll scrounge around in your kitchen for something to eat."

"I'm warning you, it's meager in there."

"I live with Patrick. I know how to improvise. You don't have to eat, but you do have to talk. Don't try sneaking out the bathroom window. You're without a vehicle, so you won't get far. I don't want to call Miranda to hunt you down."

"You mean she's not parked outside?"

"Possibly," I said and got out of bed.

"Middle drawer," he said. "The black ones. I don't want you stretching the waist of any of my favorites."

"Beast," I said.

I found eggs and sausage well within their expiration dates. I smiled when I heard the shower running. He was being uncharacteristically docile. By the time he joined me, I was washing the dishes. I handed him a bottle of water and sat across from him with an expectant expression.

"I don't know what you want from me," he said. "Do you want to talk about what just happened?"

"No. I'm fine with that. I mean, if you are."

"I am," he said, then took a drink of water.

"You spent almost an entire year with Zachary. For part of that time, you let him come between you and your friends."

"Don't talk in generalities," Alex said. "If you feel like I neglected you as a friend, speak for yourself. Not everybody else. I've already apologized to you. It went two ways, you know. You were busy with Heath."

"Fair enough," I conceded. "Except you said you weren't in love with Zachary. If it wasn't love, what were you doing?"

He stared at his water bottle a while, uncapping and recapping it, before he met my eyes and said, "I'll talk if you let me tell it my way, without throwing in a bunch of snotty remarks or looks."

"I want to hear it. I'm not judging you."

"At first, I didn't know about his life. His family. He didn't lie to me, because I didn't ask any questions. We had a good time together, but it's not like I wanted to move in with him or anything. There are things you and Heath take for granted with the men you date because you *are* those things. Stable. Smart. Settled into careers that you like. I'm used to shallow attachments that never lasted past a couple of dates. I didn't know if that was because of me or because of the men I picked. Zachary was like you and Heath, but he didn't treat me like I was a loser. If I got down on myself, comparing myself to you or to him, he always said the nicest things. He thought I was interesting. He saw me as an artist. He didn't try to change me; he liked the way I am." He broke off to look at me, then said, "Go ahead. I wouldn't want you to sever your tongue."

"I'm just surprised by your critical self-assessment," I said. "Alex, you're like a magnet. Everybody's drawn to you. There's no reason to compare yourself unfavorably to anyone. Hell, Heath is anal-retentive and afraid to fall in love. And I'm resistant to change and…"

"And?" he prompted.

"Afraid to fall in love," I admitted. "But we're talking about you and Zachary, not me."

"I wanted a low-maintenance relationship. I wanted to spend my energy making Tragic White Men happen. If Zachary was inaccessible sometimes, or even if he seemed distant when he was with me, that was fine. I wasn't looking for a husband. Or even a boyfriend. What we had was something that I thought was working for both of us."

"Until Miranda got in your face with the news that he had a wife."

"I know you all think I let that slide, but I didn't. I confronted him. All I wanted was honesty, and he swore he was giving it to me. I told him, Aaron, up front, that I didn't have a problem with his situation as long as we all knew the truth. I didn't even care if he was still a husband to her. But I wouldn't be part of deceiving her. He assured me that he and Alicia lived totally separate lives. The only reason they stayed together was because it was best for the kids. But she knew he was gay. She knew he dated men. They were like friends, he said. I believed him."

"You're not stupid. Are you lying to yourself or to me?"

"I did believe him at first," Alex insisted. "But after a while, things didn't add up. Like I could never call him at home. Like he had no problem being with me, even in public, but he didn't want to be part of anything gay in a larger context. No clubs. No hanging out with my friends or my band. We could go to movies, restaurants, hotels, but it had to be just us. His reason was that we didn't get enough time alone together; he wanted to make the most of what we had. I let it slide because…"

"It felt good to be spoiled," I finished for him.

"Really good. But there was something else too. The part I'm not proud of. I rationalized that I wanted to help Zachary emerge into living fully as a gay man. But the truth was, I started feeling like I was competing with his wife. I wanted to win. Even if I didn't think I was in love with him. Even though I never saw us as a couple that was going to last forever. I wanted him to choose me over her. I think he used that to his advantage. Because it kept me from making demands or complaining. I wanted to be Super Boyfriend, so she'd look like Evil Wife. But I started playing with his mind. As in, *It's OK if you don't have time for me; I'm going to Southern Decadence.* Or, *Of course you don't have to go to my friend's party; I'm going with that guy whose number you found in my back pocket.* It was just a stupid game to me." His blue eyes were brilliant with tears. "Then last night, I saw her and realized that she has no idea. She never did. When I looked at him, he smiled at me, and I finally figured him out. He knows I won't expose him. Not because he deserves my silence, but because she doesn't deserve for me to blow her world apart. You asked what I was doing all these months. I don't know. But I never felt so small and mean."

"Don't be too hard on yourself. You're the only one who ended up getting hurt."

"And I'm so lucky that Miranda had a front-row seat to the bitter end of a colossal mistake."

"Trust me, Miranda isn't happy about that. None of your friends will take any pleasure in how things turned out."

"You're the only one I can face right now," Alex said.

When he started crying, I wished I could find a way to put it all in perspective for him, like he had for me after my disappointments with Heath and Colt. His tears seemed out of proportion to what he'd admitted feeling for Zachary, making me sure he hadn't told me everything that was bothering him. I pulled him up and held him, determined to stop badgering him. He aroused all my protective instincts, and I resolved to tell Miranda and our other friends to give him the time and space he needed to work things out for himself.

Ultimately, Alex outsmarted us, doing an about-face and agreeing to go with his family and Grandma Casey on a cruise. I missed him; I'd seen him every Christmas since we became friends. But it was easier to accept his absence when I knew he was getting over Zachary instead of getting more entangled with him.

I listened to a lot of Stevie Ray Vaughan and thought of our day together. I wondered if he worried about how things would be with me now. It wasn't every day that you had really hot sex with your best friend. I didn't feel awkward about it. In fact, I enjoyed thinking about how incredible it had been. Once again, Alexander had surprised me.

Christmas Eve morning, while I made rum balls with my sisters for the open house my parents were having that night, I was remembering the day I'd found out about Al Camino. Alex had said he was multidimensional, and I'd corrected him, telling him he meant multifaceted. It amazed me how much crap he tolerated from me.

"What are you thinking about?" Kelly asked, and I looked up to see that she and Stasi were both staring at me.

"What? Why?" I asked.

"You have an idiotic smile on your face," Stasi said. "The rum was supposed to go in the recipe, Aaron."

"I could never drink rum before noon," I said. "Vodka, maybe."

When I went back to work, Kelly said, "You didn't answer my question."

Normally I wouldn't have considered confiding in my sisters, but it had been taxing to keep quiet with my friends. I wanted to talk about it. I looked around to make sure no parents were lurking before I said, "I was thinking about something that happened with Alex."

"You had sex with your best friend!" Stasi practically shrieked, while Kelly popped a rum ball in her mouth and started chewing furiously.

"You wanna scream that again just in case one of the neighbors missed it?" I asked. She and Kelly exchanged a look of suppressed excitement, and I said, "It wasn't that earthshaking."

"That's too bad," Kelly said.

"No, the sex was earthshaking. Just unexpected. I'm hoping it doesn't make things uncomfortable for us. We haven't seen each other since it happened. Did you ever have sex with one of your best friends?" I asked Kelly.

"All my best friends are women," Kelly said.

"But if Alex was my best friend, I'd definitely give him a tumble," Stasi said. "I mean, you know, if I was single and he was straight."

"We didn't discover a sudden mutual lust for each other," I said. "I was consoling him after a bad breakup and…it just happened."

"Do *you* feel uncomfortable about it?" Kelly asked.

"I'm fine with it as long as Alex is." They shared another look, and I asked, "What?"

"Nothing," Kelly said. "Without knowing all the details—"

"That's all the details you're getting," I said firmly.

"You'll have to wait until you see him again, I guess," Stasi said. "But if things feel weird, talk it out with him. You've been friends so long that I'm sure it'll be fine."

I couldn't put her wisdom to the test, however, since the next time I saw Alex, he was already onstage with his band. The Dinks expansion was finished, and it provided the perfect locale for Tragic White Men's New Year's Eve show. The bar was packed with people ready to party, even if they didn't know they were celebrating the real beginning of the new millennium.

I got there late, as usual, because I'd been preoccupied with my new laptop, a post-Christmas purchase I'd splurged on after receiving one of my presents from Heath. He'd started our joint writing venture, and I'd lost track of time as I began adding to the story.

I pushed my way through the crowd until I saw Heath, who was leaning against Logan, both of them smiling while they listened to Tragic White Men. Heath still hadn't officially told me that Logan was The One, but I knew. I tried to conjure up a wraith of jealousy from our late romance, but nothing happened. After more than eight years, it was laid to rest. Heath hadn't been part of the deal made the year before, yet he'd managed to find a new love. Then again, on that fateful night, Miranda had predicted that Heath could find a husband in a day if that's what he wanted. He was definitely marriage material.

I turned my gaze from them to look at Alexander, smiling when I realized he was squinting through the lights and grinning at me. He looked as messily beautiful as ever—although his new winter tan made his blue eyes and white teeth even more striking. I was glad he was stuck on stage. Otherwise, he'd probably manage to find an instant boyfriend, which would be bad news for me because of the deal. I already had the coming year planned. Teaching, writing with Heath, and staying single. My life was good.

When Alex broke eye contact, I looked around until I saw our other friends. While I watched them, I thought of how things had changed over the past year.

Vivian and Patrick had survived their near breakup and the Supreme Court appointment of a Republican to the White House. They slapped REELECT GORE '04 bumper stickers on their cars and focused on the future. Patrick was still determined to restart his business career after the first of the year. Vivian had been discussing her options with Brett. Whatever they did professionally, I was sure she and Patrick would stay together. Even though she would argue every step of the way, including down the aisle, I knew if Patrick asked Vivian to marry him she'd say yes. In fact, it was probably time for me to start looking for a place of my own, since I was sure I'd be minus a roommate before too long.

I kind of liked the idea. Teaching hadn't made me rich, but several years of living like I was still a college student had helped me build a decent savings account. I could make a down payment on one of the more affordable bungalows in Montrose; one that hadn't already been renovated. My father would love to work on a project like that with me. Or possibly with Vivian. She was much handier at that kind of thing than I was.

As for Miranda's love life, she'd always ignored Heath's insistence that the deal wasn't a contest. I wasn't sure if she thought her conquest of Joey was a victory over Alex or over Joey. I tended to believe it was a victory over herself. She'd finally managed to commit to someone, and I was sure lesbians everywhere had heaved a collective sigh of relief. What I'd started to appreciate was that they brought out the best in each other. It was amazing to see Miranda flourish with the love of the right woman. My only hope was that Joey wouldn't feel compelled to write bad poetry about it.

Joey's drums faded into silence, and Alexander wiped the sweat from his face and held the microphone stand. The crowd quieted while everyone waited to hear what he had to say.

"Before we take a break, I want to slow things down and do a new song I wrote. I borrowed the title from Stevie Ray Vaughan. Of course," he continued humbly, "I can't play the blues like Stevie Ray. But I hope you guys like it anyway. It's called 'Lovestruck.'"

He played a little blues riff, and the audience responded with claps and whistles. I felt a warmth radiate outward from somewhere deep inside me. Apparently, I wasn't the only one who'd been thinking about our time together, and I was flattered that he'd made a song out of it. I felt like a starstruck teenager as I listened to him sing.

I loved you when you were with somebody else
I loved you when you were all by yourself
I loved you when you were down on your luck
I loved you baby 'cause I'm lovestruck

I used to watch you with those other guys
I used to wonder when you'd realize
I was the one that you were looking for
Take all I got and I'll still give you more

I'm lovestruck and I got my eye on you
I'm lovestruck, baby, nothing I can do

I loved you but you never gave me a chance
I couldn't even get a second glance
It's time for you to come and try your luck
'Cause I'm still a little lovestruck

I might as well have been alone in the bar when I watched the band leave the stage after the song ended. In my head, I was watching what looked like a montage of great movie moments, only they were memories of Alex and me. Over the years, we'd partied fiercely, cried for each other's heartbreaks, gotten sloppy drunk together, and thrown up on each other. We'd supported each other through bad classes, bad career moments, bad boyfriends, and bad haircuts. We'd misbehaved like kids when we needed to blow off steam. We'd cleaned up and endured the exacting scrutiny of his grandmother. We'd cruised men together and shared the most intimate details of our successes and failures in the bedroom. We'd played, fought, and fucked, and until the day I died, I knew he was the best friend I'd ever have. Heath was right. There was nobody like Alexander.

I realized that Patrick was standing in front of me, saying something.

"What?" I asked, trying to orient myself to the here and now.

"I said," Patrick repeated, "that if you've got a fucking brain left in that head of yours, you'll follow him outside and start making up for lost time."

"Huh?" I asked, but Patrick just shrugged at me as if I was hopeless.

I shifted my gaze to Heath when he said, "It's never too late to help a friend make a deal."

"What are you talking about?"

"God, you're dense," Miranda said. "He's so in love with you. Are you gonna make him wait forever?"

"You're all crazy," I said. "Alex isn't the kind of man who'd wait for—"

"You and Heath to lay your history to rest?" Patrick interrupted. "That's exactly the kind of man he is."

"No way," I said, unable to get my mind around what they were telling me.

"Do I have to lay out the evidence for you?" Vivian asked.

"You don't know the half of it," Miranda told her. "It's been going on since we were eighteen. They used to hang out in each other's rooms for hours. Alex was teaching himself to play guitar while Aaron read. It didn't matter what they were doing, as long as they were together."

"Tell me about it," Patrick said. "I felt like I had two roommates until our senior year, when Aaron ditched us for Heath and I had to put up with Alex by myself. I can't tell you what a joy *that* was. Especially when he distracted himself with that weird fiddle player."

"Cellist," I corrected him.

"Nothing's changed," Miranda spoke over me. "Whenever one stays away from the other too long, they either get frantic or morose. Alex nearly flunked out of college over it."

"He must have hated me," Heath said.

"It was worse because Alex was the one who introduced you and Aaron," Miranda said.

"I never knew that," Vivian said.

"Heath was one of Alex's roommates for a while. He moved out, and a few months later he and Aaron were dating and making Alex miserable. Not that Aaron noticed."

"You can stop talking about me like I'm not here," I said. "You're rewriting ancient history. Besides, Alex had no trouble staying away from me for months because of Zachary."

"Do the math," Patrick said. "Alex kept his distance after the night we were all at Dinks and I made your reunion with Heath public."

"And he didn't come back until he found out it was over," Vivian added.

"When anybody hurts one of them, the other is always there to pick up the pieces," Miranda said.

"That's the way best friends are," I insisted.

"It's also the way two people are when they love each other fearlessly," Heath said. "Alex loves you unconditionally and without reservation, Aaron. You're probably the only one who doesn't know that."

"Yeah," Vivian said, "especially since he just put it in a song for everybody in Dinks to hear."

"But he..." I trailed off, remembering something Alex had said: *I've only loved one man in my life, and he didn't notice.*

"Go!" Miranda yelled, pushing me.

I stumbled a little, then I realized what it must have been like for Alex. If they were right, he'd just shared his biggest secret, and now he was standing outside, probably alone, wondering if I'd ever figure it out and what I'd do about it.

My heart started pounding, and I couldn't get to him fast enough. When I walked out the back door of the bar, I saw him leaning against the wooden fence, his face in shadows.

"Alex?"

"Hey, Aaron." His voice sounded small.

"Alexander, come here. I can't see you."

He stepped into the light but wouldn't come any closer, as if he thought I might run away. I was afraid to move, so we stared at each other for what seemed like another millennium.

"Me?" I finally asked. He nodded tentatively. "How long?"

"I don't know," he said. "Always."

"That's a long time to wait for somebody as stupid as I've been," I said.

"You're not *that* stupid," he assured me. "What could I do? You don't feel the way I do."

"Come *here*," I said again. When he didn't move, I went to him. His body, rigid when I started kissing him, finally stopped resisting, and I realized that my memory of how good his kisses were had been inaccurate. They were better.

"Stop," he gasped, pulling back. "Just because we had good sex—"

"I've been trying to convince myself that you picked up techniques from those porn videos you score, but I'm wrong."

He frowned and said, "You didn't think it was good?"

"I know it sounds like a line, but it was the best sex I've ever had," I assured him. "Not because we did anything exceptional, Alex. Because it was us. You and me. You've always been the one that I—" I broke off and stared at him a few seconds, hearing my words as a confession. "You've always been The One. The man I know best and love most. The man who knows me. How could I have been in love with you for so long without knowing it? I wasted all that time."

"You didn't waste time," Alex argued. "You had to work out your stuff with Heath. Anyway, it wasn't just you. Two people can keep themselves busy when they're afraid to be in love. How's your schedule look now?"

"Funny you should ask," I said. "Other than this deal I made with some friends, I seem to be free for the rest of my life. Are you still afraid?"

"Not at all. I can help you keep up your end of the deal. But 'free' is not the right word," Alex said, gripping my shoulders. "You'd better mean this. I won't be able to let you go, Aaron. I love you too much."

"I'm not going anywhere without you, Alexander," I promised. "In fact, I need to hear you say you'll help me find a house that we can both live in, considering our opposite lifestyles."

"You and me? Together?" he asked. "Like a commitment?"

"That's usually the way it works. And don't say this is so sudden. It took me twelve years to get here. I want the whole thing. Your shit mingling with mine in the medicine cabinet and closets. Real food in the refrigerator and cupboards."

"Your porn mixed with my porn?" he asked, sliding his hands behind my waist and nuzzling my ear.

"Exactly. And not a futon in sight."

"It *would* make honest men of us with our YMCA family membership," he said.

"That's not an answer."

"Yes, Aaron," he said. "My answer is yes."

As we kissed, I heard Joey's drums explode, accompanied by shouts and whistles from inside Dinks. It was 2001, and I was with the man I loved. My life was *great*.